Charlesgate

"Here you go, Zyll." Jabe handed her a beer and watched as her upper lip sank into the head, branding her skin with ale.

He reached out and slowly wiped the trace of froth from her lip with his thumb. After the initial jolt at his touch, Zylla struggled to keep her composure and not melt under the stroke of his work-roughened skin. Transfixed, she stared as he studied her with hooded eyes and brought his thumb to his mouth to lick the foam.

His eyes sparkled. "So, you still think it's not your family ghost?" he asked.

Her attention floated merrily in her awakened senses and she ignored him. He flashed a crooked smile and she sighed.

"Zyll."

"Yes?" She smiled and leaned forward a bit.

"The lavender. At the Charlesgate. You still think it's not your ghost?"

She immediately straightened.

"Oh, well, no," she stammered. "I mean, I don't know. If it is a ghost, and that's a very big if, that is, I want to believe it's a ghost, that'd be pretty cool, but..."

"Yeah, yeah, I know. Assume that it is," he interrupted. "I talk to the damn thing all the time—I'd much rather be talking to something than nothing. It helps me to convince myself that I'm not insane."

Charlesgate

by

Dina Keratsis

A Wings ePress, Inc.

Contemporary Paranormal Romance Novel

Wings ePress, Inc.

Edited by: Leslie Hodges
Copy Edited by: Elizabeth Struble
Senior Editor: Elizabeth Struble
Managing Editor: Leslie Hodges
Executive Editor: Lorraine Stephens
Cover Artist: Keith Harris

Wings ePress Books
http://www.wings-press.com

ISBN 1-59088-978-1

Published In the United States Of America

January 2005

Wings ePress Inc.
403 Wallace Court
Richmond, KY 40475

Dedication

For my parents,

who prove that romance novels aren't fiction after all.

Prologue

Boston 1895
Lydia Berry's Journal
October 25

Papa liked to tell the story of our family curse on winter evenings when the wind threatened to shatter the windows of our Dorchester home.

I remember one such evening, so many years ago, when I was a small child.

After stoking the fire, Papa settled into his wing-backed chair to wait for Mama to light the lamp near her own smaller chair. She began to darn socks, and Papa leaned forward in his chair to rest his forearms upon his thighs, his gray eyes sparkling. In turn, Lily and I crawled closer to him and sat huddled under an afghan on the floor at his feet. Our eyes wide, I reached for Lily's hand and waited for Papa to begin his long tale about our ancestor, the infamous pirate, Charlotte de Berry.

Lily and I never tired of hearing how Charlotte disguised herself as a lad to join the crew of The Asp and how she soon lost respect for the lily-livered captain.

"Why, our Charlotte," Papa said, eyes bright, "although a mere girl, knew that she could run an entire fleet, not just a tiny ship!

"So, one night, she led a mutiny and slashed the captain's throat."

Here, Papa drew a finger across his neck and made a gurgling noise. Lily and I cringed.

"The remaining crew elected her as its new captain, then she finally revealed that she was female. Captain de Berry named the schooner Charnwood, and looted and murdered to rival ole Blackbeard himself!

"And she was a cruel mistress, our Charlotte de Berry was," he growled. "She liked to keelhaul her enemies. Do you know what that is?"

"I do!" Lily said with her head held high and a smirk on her lips. "It's when a man was tied under the keel of the ship and dragged over the barnacles until he bled."

"Very painful," Papa agreed. "You know how salt water feels on a cut, yes? Well, this is a thousand times more painful. Her favorite punishment, though, was stitching the lips of disobedient crew members."

I clapped a hand over my mouth.

"Yes, our Charlotte was cruel, but perhaps her greatest crime was that she ignored her bastard so..."

"Jeremy!" I chirped, and Papa nodded once. I was in love with Jeremy.

"And the lad loved his mother, even though she pretended he wasn't there.

"But one cold winter, everything changed. Our Charlotte docked the Charnwood in Boston—she lived on Salem Street, you recall. She stashed her stolen gold in the basement of the house, and donned the guise of the highborn widow, Lady Charlotte Berry. And in Boston, she met the honorable and handsome Admiral

Jabez Thayer of Her Majesty's Royal Navy. Can you guess what happened?"

"They fell in love," Mama spoke, her cheeks rosy from the fire.

Papa paused to look at Mama and smile, and his gray eyes crinkled at the corners.

"For the first time," he whispered, "her restless soul felt peace and she accepted Jabez's marriage proposal, privately resolving to end her life of piracy after just one more excursion. And so she told the admiral that she needed to sail to England for her trousseau.

"The admiral, of course, offered to take her on his ship, but Charlotte charmingly refused and said that her son could serve as chaperone. The admiral's suspicions were confirmed. He watched his Charlotte carefully, and when the Charnwood set sail, his crew followed. Charlotte engaged in battle, realizing too late that the leader of the H.M.S. Ferret was her beloved Jabez."

At this point, Papa shook his head slowly. With a sigh, he leaned back in his chair and lit his pipe. He puffed once, twice, before continuing.

"Our Charlotte was captured, and although he was grief-stricken, Admiral Thayer chose duty over love. He arrested her and at her trial, she was found guilty of treason. And do you know how treason was punished?"

Lily would always answer, while I would imitate the punishment by clutching my neck.

"Nix's Mate!"

Papa nodded his head, eyes agleam.

"Yes, sirree. Boston citizens gathered at the docks on the day of her hanging to jeer at 'Lady Berry' as she passed. Her lover and son rowed the criminal to the isle called Nix's Mate, which no longer exists, as you know, to be hanged.

"She refused a minister and did not show remorse for her crimes. Instead, she glared at Admiral Thayer with cold, dead eyes, and spoke her curse in a terrible voice."

Papa stood to loom over us and spoke in a crackling tone: "May ye and your descendants be damned to misery for all yer long lives, even as ye are made fat by my gold."

"Papa, how did they find the gold?" Lily interrupted.

"Ahhh. My practical Lily." Papa puffed on his pipe before he answered. "The Navy searched her house and found the gold hidden under what is now called Cheever's Arch, and King William gave the hoard to Admiral Thayer as a reward for his service."

"But the curse!" I whined impatiently.

Papa fixed his eyes so that I wanted to shrink beneath the floorboards. His Charlotte imitation always scared me so.

"And thee, my wretched son. Ye will lose your heart's love, and your daughters and their daughters will nae suffer at the hands of men. I will return from the depths of the sea to slaughter any that dare sell themselves in marriage."

"Papa," I whispered. "Is that why all Berry females die young?"

"Oh, Lyddie." Lily rolled her eyes. "It's just a tale. Mama's not dead, after all."

Mama snorted and said, "I should hope not."

But Lily had forgotten.

"Mama is not a Berry," I said. "Papa is."

And Lily laughed.

But we are adults now, and Lily and I are still as different as the dark and light sides of the moon. She is practical whilst I am dreamy. She is a fighter, and I am content to remain in my world of books.

Even now, she is downstairs with Sarah Putnam, in the Charlesgate auditorium, arguing for women's rights and for benefits for Boston's poor, while I sit here and wait for my child to be born, while I wait for death.

For unlike Lily, I know the curse of Charlotte to be true.

All my life, I've dreamed of pirate ships rolling in bloody seas, and when the headaches strike, she comes with her wretched stink of the decaying sea and her stitched lips, her eternal punishment, to moan her threats.

Since marrying my beloved Caval, my blue-eyed gypsy, she has been uneasy, following me with her red eyes. My headaches worsen, and even the lavender I carry with me cannot ease the pain. She grows stronger, and soon I will be dead.

I only desire to remain in the peaceful splendor of the Charlesgate and raise my family, but Charlotte wants my destruction, and she shall have it. I cannot fight fate.

But when Charlotte visits to wail her story of murder and revenge, she leaves unsaid one small part of the tale.

The curse can end.

One

Boston, Present Day

Zylla blinked at the computer screen as she felt the blood in her face pool into her toes. She pushed back her office chair, stood and turned toward the window. Below her, the sun glinted off bumper-to-bumper cars, transforming Storrow Drive into a river of colored jewels, but all Zylla saw were shades of gray.

"Hey, Zyll, the dean wants you to respond to these letters as soon as you can. I'll leave them on your desk, okay?"

"Okay," she said woodenly, without turning to face her work study student.

"Hey, you all right?"

"Sure." Zylla glanced over her shoulder, forcing a smile at Nicole.

Nicole shrugged. "Okay. Well, call if you need anything," she offered before shutting the door behind her.

Zylla sank into her chair and reread the email: "I got married this weekend, Zyllie. Kind of sudden, I know, but..."

No, she was not all right. Michael Sullivan was married. Mike, best friend and love of her life for the past thirteen years, was married. All hope that he would someday turn to her with eyes full of longing and lips full of passion was over. And now that the initial shock passed, she felt strangely empty and, she noted as she glared at the bright blue sky outside, slightly cranky.

She would have expected mind-numbing grief at such a disaster, would have welcomed it. Then, at least, she could sob into a pint of pistachio ice cream or entertain a Bukowski moment at Crossroads, the local pub down the street.

Zylla pushed the escape key and watched as the window disappeared from the screen, erasing the news just as easily as it had appeared. She spent the morning answering Dean Pendergast's letters, then grabbed a sandwich and raspberry smoothie at the Food Court for lunch. As she ate, she kept her nose deep in a Dickens novel, refusing to allow her mind to dwell on her increasingly angry mood.

By the time the clock blinked five o'clock, she had walked halfway toward her home in Cambridge. The April day seemed too hot, and as she headed over the Massachusetts Avenue bridge toward home, she tried to peel off her black cardigan, which stubbornly clung to her left arm, trapped underneath the strap of her shoulder bag. To increase her frustration, a young man in fatigues, who had been walking quietly in front of her, spun around and began to yell at an imaginary cow that followed him and caused all sorts of evil events to occur in his life.

With a grunt, Zylla yanked the cardigan so that the sleeve was finally freed from her arm—unfortunately, she used too much force and managed to hit herself on the nose with the back of her hand and the sweater sailed neatly over the rail of the bridge and into the Charles River.

Zylla vaguely wondered if the evil cow was in fact following her. She sighed loudly and the young man next to her jumped in her path. Zylla frowned and moved to the left, but the man scrambled in that direction also. She passed the cow man nearly every day and he always chose a random person at which to bellow. Of course, today of all days, it had to be her. She sighed again and let her shoulders slump. "Yes?"

The man's eyes widened. He opened his mouth and leaned toward her as he raised a trembling finger, pointing at her. Zylla rolled her eyes. "Moo," she said.

At home, she slammed a steak on the back porch grill and went into the kitchen to make a salad. Her roommate's bottle of red wine beckoned from the counter. Zylla wasn't supposed to drink wine. One sip would cause a migraine so painful that she would be forced to stay in bed, head pillowed in a bag of ice. But, dammit, she was twenty-nine years old and having a crisis. She wasn't quite sure what exactly the crisis consisted of, but when she figured it out, a bottle of wine might come in handy.

She uncorked the bottle and sat at the kitchen table. She would drink it straight from the bottle, a sure sign of love lost. Zylla tried to summon a few tears. "Bloody hell," she muttered and tried harder, without success.

"What is the matter with me? I just lost the love of my life. Haven't I?" The bottle of wine did not answer her and she re-corked it. Even Mike wasn't worth a migraine.

She had seen Mike for the first time in high school art class. He had walked into Mr. Callet's room for some supplies and Zylla had stopped breathing. He was Lancelot with black hair and blue eyes in which a girl could swim. All other boys paled beside him. Zylla had followed him relentlessly, but to Mike she was a skinny little wren in comparison to his gorgeous, raven-haired girlfriend.

No doubt his new wife was a super model. She snorted.

Zylla munched on her salad while waiting for the steak to cook, and thought about her friendship with Mike. She was grateful that he had been able to tolerate her mooning stares long enough to get to know her because she couldn't imagine a world without Mike's friendship, even if she could never win his love.

But she hadn't stopped hoping. And waiting.

Zylla ate her steak on the back porch—the hot spring day cooling into a purple evening was the perfect accompaniment to her mood. Twilight always disturbed her, but she never understood why. The sky seemed to change minutely, while Zylla never changed. Always, she was loyal to Mike.

While she dated a few men, her thoughts remained with Mike. She never let herself become emotionally involved with other men, no matter how much she liked them. Zylla frowned and stabbed the last piece of steak with her fork.

She never got emotionally involved in anything, really, except the Charlesgate. She had held the same job and had lived in the same apartment since college while she waited for Mike to come for her. Except now he wouldn't. The crease between her brows deepened.

There was only one thing for it, then—*Sixteen Candles* and pistachio ice cream. When her roommate, Anne, came home, they would figure out what to do about Zylla. Anne always knew what to do. She went inside, grabbed a spoon and a pint of ice cream, and put the movie into the DVD player. She plopped onto the couch and was about to press the remote when her finger froze in mid-action.

Something niggled in her brain, something that wouldn't wait for Anne. She put the ice cream onto the coffee table—she wouldn't truly enjoy the scrumptious roll of velvet cream on her tongue until she figured it out for herself.

Zylla chewed her bottom lip as the action helped her to think. She had become adept at waiting. All this time, she thought that she was content. Days passed and she was neither happy nor sad, until now. Now, she definitely knew that she was not happy. Mike's marriage didn't devastate her, as she would have thought. Instead, his message forced her to realize that she was discontent.

And suddenly, Zylla knew why.

She had waited for fate to give her a life instead of going after happiness on her own.

"I guess I don't love him after all. Not in that Cathy-loves-Heathcliff sort of way," she said.

Zylla felt her face drain of color. She wasn't in love with Mike and hadn't been for a long time, and she shook her head as she counted all the years wasted while she waited for him.

Well, it's time to change all that, she decided. Zylla took the pint and scooped a spoonful of ice cream into her mouth, letting the delicate coolness baptize her insides. She was almost thirty years old. It was time to start living her life.

Two

A sunbeam shot across Zylla's blanket when Anne opened the door to her room and chirped, "The sun's up. The bird is on the wing. Wake up, wake up, you lazy thing."

Zylla buried her head under the sheets and groaned. "It's Saturday, Anne. Go away."

"It's eight. Get up! We're going running."

"It's Saturday," Zylla repeated. "Besides, I have plans today."

Anne rested her leg atop Zylla's desk chair and stretched. "And those would consist of...?"

"Well..." Zylla pushed back the covers, stumbled out of bed, opened a dresser drawer and removed a tee shirt and sports bra. A run might make her sore enough so that she wouldn't feel the needle later on.

"I'm getting a tattoo today." She stuck out her chin in determination as she pulled her hair into a ponytail.

Anne froze in the middle of a deep knee bend.

"Of what? Why? When...?"

The phone trilled.

Anne finished her stretch as she reached for the receiver.

"Oh, I don't know. A new moon, maybe."

Anne's brow creased. "Hello?"

After a moment, Anne burst out laughing. "So that explains her sudden desire to get a tattoo. Wait a sec—she's right here."

Zylla stuck her tongue out at her roommate as she took the receiver.

At eight o'clock on a Saturday morning, only one person would be calling.

"Hey, Aunt Maddie. What's up?"

"Zylla Berry, if you get a tattoo, I'll disown you. Get over it. The boy wouldn't know what to do with you if he had you. Besides, I never liked his handshake."

"But..." Zylla sputtered.

"I'm getting old. I may die soon, and I want to hold a baby again before I die. And you had the prettiest bassinet when you were a baby. It's a shame for it to go to waste. Now stop mooning over that idiot and find a real boyfriend."

Zylla tapped her heel, but her aunt's tirade seemed to be done. "I am over it, Auntie M."

Maddie ignored the statement and Anne arched her brow.

"You know, some guy isn't going to make you happy."

"But you just said you wanted a grandkid."

"Only if that makes you happy, dear. Wait, you aren't upset?"

"Nope."

"Oh. Then why do you want to commit scarification on the body God gave you?"

"It's not scarification, Aunt Maddie. It's a tattoo. And I'm getting it to remind me to live."

"That's what breathing is for," Anne muttered under her breath, garnering a scowl from Zylla.

"How did you know about Mike anyway?"

"I saw his mother at church this morning. How are your headaches, dear?"

"Better. Haven't had one in a month or so."

"No strange nightmares?"

"Nope. Just your common, run-of-the-mill migraine."

"Good. About this tattoo..."

"Auntie M." Zylla gritted her teeth.

"Let me talk to Anne."

Zylla handed the phone to Anne. "She wants to talk to you."

Anne and her aunt could conspire all they wanted, but nothing would make her change her mind about getting a tattoo. Never again would she waste time waiting, and every time she saw that tattoo, she would remember that. Zylla grabbed her running clothes and sneakers and entered the bathroom, firmly closing the door behind her.

~ * ~

Five miles and four pancakes later, Anne and Zylla walked across the Massachusetts Avenue bridge to Boston and headed toward the Purple Pumpkin Tattoo Parlor.

Zylla inhaled the river air and smiled at Anne. "Ah, who needs a man when I have a roommate who can cook like you?"

"Because, my little mushroom cloud, although the way to your heart is through your stomach, which makes me wonder about your true gender, I certainly don't want to spend the rest of my life with you, let alone sleep with you."

"Hrrumph." Zylla stuck her nose in the air.

"Here's your street." Anne paused at the corner of Beacon Street. "I suppose you want to take a detour and visit the Charlesgate?"

"Of course," Zylla replied, already turning the corner and striding toward the end of the block. Anne jogged to keep up.

And there, on the corner of Charlesgate East and Beacon Streets, *she* waited—the majestic and marred brick and sandstone mansion that Zylla loved.

The corner of the building rounded into a turret, and Zylla followed its ascent to a green copper cone topped by a weathervane that soared into the bright blue sky above, twirling in the river breeze. Then her view dropped down to the Beacon Street entrance.

The name *Charlesgate*, entwined with stone vines and flowers, was carved above a Romanesque archway and beckoned Zylla to climb the steps and enter the green and gold tiled archway.

She looked at Anne and shrugged. "I have to try."

"I know." Anne smiled as she rested a hand on the rusty iron gate. "I'll wait for you on the steps."

Zylla trotted up the steps into the cool darkness of the alcove and lovingly gazed at the gold-green ceramic tiled walls. Along the ceiling, the glossy tiles sported figures of knights, cherubs, flowers and heraldic crests. Zylla ignored the chunks where tile was missing, just as she overlooked the broken lantern that hung from the ceiling on a rusted chain.

Instead, she turned to the iron and glass double doors, barely glancing at the yellow and black “No Trespassing” sign taped across them, or the thick chain and padlock wrapped around the door handles.

As always, Zylla wrapped her fingers around the grubby brass handle, closed her eyes, and pulled. And as always the padlock didn’t magically fall off to allow her entrance into the Charlesgate’s realm. She wiped the grease from her palm onto her jeans and rested her forehead against the glass, closing her eyes.

Instantly, the brief dizziness that sometimes overcame her when she visited the Charlesgate returned.

The first time it had happened, Zylla had barely swallowed her panic from the melting sensation in her body and the buzzing in her ears. Now, she was used to the random bouts of dizziness and glimpses of the past that occasionally visited her mind when she came here, pulling her into the Charlesgate. She simply put it down to too much caffeine and a vivid imagination, yet still couldn’t bring herself to tell Anne or Aunt Maddie about the episodes.

Each dizzy spell and its accompanying vision offered a glimpse into the Charlesgate. This time, in her mind’s eye, she entered the building with two women dressed in Victorian garb. She heard the clatter of horses’ hooves on the cobblestones before the door closed behind her, then she heard only the noises of the busy dining room down the hall—the harmonies from a piano, the clinks of silver on dinnerware, and the chatter of people. As she walked toward the sounds, her blue muslin skirt swished around her legs and the scent of lavender, sweet and calming, drifted to her nose.

Just as quickly, the sensory experience passed, replaced by the sounds of modern day traffic, and Zylla still stood outside the padlocked doors of the Charlesgate.

She sighed and looked up at the ceiling with its great flakes of paint hanging precariously by mere fibers and stared at the golden green tiles of the alcove's walls. They were so shiny that they looked wet. If she touched one, would she melt into that other world?

With hope, she reached out and pressed her index finger against the tile. Cold and dry, it did not pull her into her vision world, but Zylla felt a joyous tingle shoot through her finger, up her arm and into her blood. *As if the building were made especially for me*, she thought, and blushed at her own fancy.

But there was no denying that she had a strange tie to the building, imagined or not. Whenever she looked at the Charlesgate, a bittersweet longing rushed through her, and she had a desperate feeling that the fairy tale was eluding her by mere centimeters and that perhaps Heathcliff wasn't, after all, rotting in some bog on an English moor.

"It's a shame to let this building rot," Anne said, jarring Zylla from her reverie, and she turned to her friend, who had quietly entered the alcove to stand next to her.

"But," she continued, "better a ruin than a university dorm. At least it got some of its integrity back."

Zylla plopped down onto the top step and squinted into the midday sun. "You're right about that."

"Still," Anne added as she sank down next to Zylla. "It would be cool to meet the ghost."

Zylla opened her mouth to say that according to her research, there was no ghost, only stories concocted by college students under the influence of illegal substances.

"I know, I know." Anne cut her off. "But don't you wish there was?"

"Yeah." She grinned, and Anne laughed.

"You sure you want to go through with this tattoo thing, Zyll?"

Zylla extended her legs and crossed her feet at the ankles, to lean her body weight on her hands. She watched her feet while she answered Anne.

"Sometime last night," she began, "I realized that I wasn't in love with Mike, that I hadn't been for a good number of years."

She met Anne's eyes. "I wasted a lot of time waiting for Mike and I have nothing to show for it. I don't even know who I am! It's pretty damn scary, actually, and I've made up my mind to never waste time again."

Zylla inhaled and slowly exhaled before continuing. "But I know myself, and it's even scarier that I might just forget my new resolution and sink comfortably into another rut, letting another twenty years pass before the next crisis wakes me up.

"So I'm getting a tattoo, a permanent reminder to never forget."

Anne was silent beside her and Zylla shifted uncomfortably.

"So what are you going to do now?" Anne finally asked.

She drew up her legs and slumped forward, letting her elbows rest on her knees. "That's the problem. The trouble is, I really don't know what to do with what I know. And love."

"Your research obsessions, you mean. *Hmmmm.*" Anne twirled her gold hair in thought. "You have a degree. You could teach history."

Zylla wrinkled her nose.

"Well, what about writing, then? You're disciplined, and with your overactive imagination and all those weird nightmares you have, you'd be great."

Zylla looked over her shoulder at the broken Charlesgate with its gaping holes where windows used to be. Disconsolation settled in her belly. Here was a case where reality mauled the fairytale and turned happily ever after into a lonely pile of rocks.

If people only knew the grand history of the building!

"You could do something about it, you know," Anne said quietly, as if divining Zylla's thoughts. "Write an article. Write a book."

"I guess," Zylla shrugged. "But writing doesn't pay the rent. Besides, who really cares about this place anyway?"

Anne stared at her with a cool blue gaze. "You do."

She remained silent and after a few seconds, Anne stood. "Well, c'mon. If you're determined to go through with this tattoo thing, I'll hold your hand."

The two women trotted down the stairs and walked to the end of the block. As they turned the corner onto Charlesgate East, a white swish flashed in the corner of Zylla's eye, and she looked up at the Charlesgate's sandstone exterior. There, above the Moorish columns of the Charlesgate East Street entrance, a banner flapped in the breeze.

The words *Caval Construction and Management* marked the white cloth in big red letters.

Speechless, Zylla jumped up and down, clutching Anne's arm with one hand and pointing at the banner with the index finger of her other hand.

Anne barely noticed. Her eyes widened and she grabbed Zylla to stop her frenzied movement.

"Look," she whispered, "There's someone at the front door!"

Three

Jabe noticed the two women staring in his direction just as he straightened from retrieving his dropped keys. Given their shocked expressions, he immediately glanced over his left shoulder. Satisfied that no axe murderer followed him out of the Charlesgate, he focused his attention on the approaching women and surprise jerked his heart.

He had seen the dark haired woman once before, at the Cramps show about a year ago, and that one moment was enough to shift his reality. For a fraction of a second, his surroundings had dissipated and all he had realized was her existence as she glided past him in a swirl of lavender scented air. Just as suddenly, she had melded into the crowd in the Middle East Nightclub, and he had panicked at the thought of her disappearing.

Then some fragment of primal knowledge had erupted in his brain and he'd realized, in that second, that she was his. The thought had shot a strange calmness through his entire body, and, no longer concerned she had melted away, he had smiled to himself, certain that she would appear again.

Boston was a small city, but he hadn't seen her since, and he had nearly forgotten about her. Until now.

Now, his gypsy cut a very different figure than she did that night. Dressed in black from head to toe at the Middle East, she had been a punk vixen. Now, she wore jean cutoffs and a black tank top, her dark hair pulled back, and she seemed like just another young college student.

Yet, again, for a second, the world faded away and the same feeling of belonging washed over him, and he could swear he smelled lavender in the air.

He frowned and scratched the scruff of growth under his chin with his left hand, and the keys, held loosely in that hand, jangled him from his reverie. He lowered his arm and put the keys in the front pocket of his jeans as he jogged down the steps to meet the two women waiting on the sidewalk. He nodded to them, squinting his eyes against the bright sunlight.

"Excuse me," the blonde said. "We were hoping that you could tell us what's going on here. Last we knew, this building was condemned."

Jabe appraised the blonde standing in front of him. She was sexy. Damn sexy. She possessed the lethal combination of an ethereal yet straightforward manner. Her dark gold shoulder-length hair and navy-flecked blue eyes complimented her athletic build. If the woman next to her did not exist, he would already be half in lust with the blonde.

Yet his enchantress did exist and gazed at him with an expression somewhere between anticipation and adoration. His heart lurched. *She feels it too*, he thought. At once he wanted to snatch her into his arms, pull her into an alcove and greedily kiss her. He scratched the back of his neck where a trickle of sweat ran between his shoulder blades and forced his attention back to the blonde.

"Well, it *was* condemned, but Caval Construction was able to purchase it and now we're renovating the building."

His eyes darted back to Zylla, and he noted that her expression quickly changed from glee to despair, reminding him of those Greek theatre masks. He almost chuckled at her inability to be subtle until he realized that her interest was not for him, but for his answer to the blonde's question. Her beautiful eyes, too, focused not on him, but on the structure behind him.

"You seem disappointed," he gruffly commented.

Zylla felt Anne nudge her and she reluctantly dragged her gaze away from the copper framed bay window behind the man's head. She could have sworn that she saw a face in the window, but now only a black void stared back at her.

"I'm sorry." She smiled, then finally saw the man in front of her. He stood with his jean-clad legs slightly spread and his arms folded across a broad chest. Dark brows furrowed over stern green eyes that glared at her and the breeze, which lifted his long, wavy blond hair, revealed a silver hoop in one ear, reminding her of a Viking. She took a step back and licked her suddenly dry lips.

"Wh-what did you say?"

"You seem disappointed."

His voice was like bourbon, rough and smooth at the same time, and she felt less afraid of him. She tilted her head to the side in question.

"About the renovations."

"Oh," Zylla said. "Well."

She glanced at her beloved mansion and swallowed her shyness.

"Not really," she started. "I'm glad that the building is being saved. There's too much historical significance to let it rot..."

"I sense a 'but,'" he said.

Zylla paused, concerned that her next words might offend the construction worker, who lifted a dark brow at her.

She felt herself blush and blurted, "I just think that the Charlesgate may be better off as an obscure memory than turned into another cheaply reconstructed apartment building."

"Zylla's a bit idealistic," Anne amended, "and doesn't realize that construction companies would go broke if they renovated for integrity alone."

Zylla tossed a grateful grin at Anne before looking down at her feet and didn't notice the tug of a smile at the corners of his lips.

"Not many people know that this was once a famous hotel, let alone that it has a name," he stated.

Zylla raised her face to his, and he uncrossed his arms to extend a right hand. She took it and felt a pleasant tingle pass through his firm grasp into her.

"My name is Jabe Thayer. I'm overseeing this project."

"It's nice to meet you, Jabe?"

"Jabe. Like Gabe, only with a 'J.'"

She grinned. "I'm Zylla. Zylla Berry, and this is Anne Stevens."

He seemed reluctant to release her to take Anne's hand, and after a perfunctory shake, turned back to Zylla.

"Like Anne said, it's far too expensive to accurately restore such a building. The hand-carved Grueby tiles are irreplaceable, and the ceilings and marble work need specialists. Most of the original wood is ripped out or rotten.

"The time and expense of restoration will never make a profit," he continued. "And people don't really care, unfortunately. They'd rather have state-of-the-art amenities. Only an eccentric multimillionaire or someone who really loves the building would take on a full restoration. With the Charlesgate, even that eccentric someone would find it near impossible."

He sighed. "This poor monstrosity has seen too many renovations and transients. Nobody has a clue what the inside originally looked like." Jabe shrugged. "Maybe if we had the original floor plans..."

"I have them!" Zylla shouted.

She heard Anne laugh at his comical expression and say, "Zylla's been researching this building for the past three years and has collected a whole drawer of information."

Zylla chuckled as Anne shook her head slowly back and forth and drawled in her best Texas accent, "Man, if this isn't fate, then I'm a puppy with two peters."

Jabe's attention darted quickly back and forth as he glanced at each woman as if he were a small boy in a toy store.

"What? *How?* I looked through the city's records... What do you have?" His voice was brisk with excitement and disbelief and when he finally focused on Zylla, she grinned at his apparent self-restraint. He looked as if he wanted to grab her, turn her upside down and shake the information out of her.

His agitation was contagious, and Zylla's answer rushed out, assisted by her hands as they fluttered in impatience. "Oh, photos, articles, floor plans, architecture books, notes from the diary of the architect's sister... It's actually not much, just clues. There isn't much out there, but do you think the owners of the building would be willing to try to restore it if they had more info?"

He gazed at her, then suddenly grinned. "I'm sure that the owners would be interested in your assets. Can you come by Monday after construction stops?" He glanced at his watch. "Say five-thirty? I'll give you a tour."

"Really?" Zylla almost clapped her hands in glee.

"Really. See you then." He grinned at the two women, then turned and strode toward Kenmore Square, back straight and head high. He reminded Zylla of a warrior set out to sack the city.

~ * ~

"It seems that the temple of Michael Sullivan is completely demolished," Anne said, amusement in her voice.

"Huh?" Zylla's attention wavered back to Anne.

"He was smokin'," Anne exclaimed.

"Who?" Zylla again looked at the window and thought that it would look pretty with an Irish lace curtain, or rich damask.

"Jabe."

Now Zylla's attention was completely focused on Anne, who preferred pretty boys clad in Armani. Unfortunately, this propensity combined with Anne's strange luck only attracted pretty boys clad in Armani who were confused about their sexuality. As a result, Anne had a collection of fine crystal, great dancing partners, and some very odd tales.

Zylla was consequently surprised by her interest in the very masculine Jabe and wondered at the attraction. She shrugged mentally. Maybe he was gay. He did have long hair. And an earring. Yep, that was it. Poor Anne. She must have tortured gay men in a past life, thus cursing her to a Tantalus-like existence in this one.

"I thought you didn't like guys with long hair," Zylla commented.

"Guys no, but a man with long hair is an entirely different matter. Jabe is hotter than a prairie dog in a Texas desert."

A sparkle lit Zylla's brown eyes and she teased, "Maybe this one wears boxer shorts instead of pink silk panties and you'll live happily ever after."

Anne hit her arm. "Are you kidding me? I was talking about you. He's perfect for you, Zylla. He looks like one of those rogues from those silly books you read. You looked so smitten after he left. What were you thinking about?" She grimaced. "Please don't say Michael Sullivan."

Zylla rubbed her arm where Anne hit her. "Ow. No, of course not. I told you, I'm over him. I was thinking about how beautiful the Charlesgate will look when it's renovated properly."

Anne rolled her eyes. "You're the only person I know who could fall in love with an inanimate object. C'mon, we need to get going if you still want to pay someone to stick needles in you."

Zylla glanced at the wrought iron doors, which would soon open just for her, and the spring day suddenly burst in her heart. She was filled with hope.

The bewilderment and love she had felt when she first saw the Charlesgate, her yearning to devour all of the building's secrets, and the hours she had spent researching its history slumbered in one little file in her desk drawer, completely useless. She alone had seemed to feel the tragedy of a forgotten history and rotting building, but she had been powerless to do anything about it.

Until now. She had the power to fight for the dignity of this building, a champion in combat boots and L'Oreal's Real Raisin lipstick. She belonged to the world and the world belonged to her.

She laughed, and Anne raised a brow.

"Nope. I changed my mind. I don't need a tattoo."

"And this is because?"

Zylla smiled inside. She sensed that she had finally begun her life. "Not in the mood anymore." She pointed to the sun. "It's a happy yellow day, and a happy yellow day needs happy yellow underwear. Let's go to Victoria's Secret."

Four

Monday was an old man hobbling backwards. The Chronic Whistler one office over composed a duet with his neighbor, the Throat Clearer, and eight hours and five eons later, Zylla shut down her computer convinced that her nerves were permanently damaged. She spent the day processing graduation forms and calming seniors panicked about credit requirements. Last year, she had left work at this time feeling satisfied with the neat stack of forms on the corner of her desk and the smiling faces of relieved students as they left her office.

This year, her thoughts danced in anticipation of finally entering the realm of the Charlesgate. Even when the WFNX deejay played her favorite song, *Charlotte Sometimes*, during hits from the eighties hour, Zylla didn't calm down. When four fifty-nine blinked to five o'clock on her monitor's screen, she nearly skipped out of the office.

Fifteen minutes later, she crossed the threshold of Four Charlesgate East and her entire body tingled. A dizzy spell instantly shook her, and she closed her eyes to let the images pass.

This time, the lavender scent was overwhelming and the vision unusually clear. In it, a trim woman in a blue gown, her pale blonde hair in a smooth chignon, walked in front of Zylla. The woman turned to Zylla and held out her hand, a slight smile on her lips and gray eyes sparkling.

Zylla shook her head and the apparition disappeared.

Am I going crazy? Zylla thought, but at the same time, she felt accepted, as if she were part of the Charlesgate. If she was heading toward insanity, like her maternal grandmother, then she wished it would hurry up and take her completely. If going crazy meant visions like this, then she would be a happy woman, after all.

She shrugged, continued walking, and promptly slammed into something large and hard.

"Hey there, sweetheart." A man with bulging arms and reeking of cigarette smoke growled down at her.

"Ya can't come in here without a helmet," he said, as he pointed to the orange plastic hat on his head. "Ain't safe. Whaddya need?"

"It's okay, Frank." A man with graying temples and gentle brown eyes appeared behind him. "Mr. Thayer is expecting her."

Frank waved his hand in dismissal. "All right. I'm gone. See ya tomorra, Dennis." He placed a cigarette between his lips and winked at Zylla. "Have a good night, sweetheart."

Zylla smiled at Frank then turned to the man beside her and shook his outstretched hand.

"I'm Dennis." He smiled.

"Zylla."

"What a pretty name. C'mon, Miss Zylla—Mr. Thayer's office is that-a-way."

Zylla followed him down a hall cluttered with rigging, plywood and drop cloths, and finally entered a sun-filled white room overrun with metal folding chairs, tables and Styrofoam coffee cups. Through the windows, Zylla could see Charlesgate East and the greenery of the Fens where a homeless couple had already settled under an elm for the evening.

"There ya go." Dennis nodded his head in Jabe's direction. "He'll be done in a minute. Have a good night, now."

"Thanks," she replied. "You, too."

Jabe stood on the far side of the room talking to another construction worker. Still in conversation, he glanced toward her and nodded briefly. She sat in one of the chairs and pretended to peruse *The Globe* on the table in front of her, but the sensation of finally being in the clutch of the Charlesgate and the splendor of her recent vision was too thrilling to permit any concentration.

Pushing aside the newspaper, Zylla stood up and wandered to the doorway to peer down the dark hall, but the pretty woman in her vision did not reappear.

~ * ~

As he discussed tomorrow's plans with his employee, Jabe's glance slid to Zylla. She was dressed in black from her hooded pullover to her Levi's to a pair of steel-toed Doc Martin's. The outfit was entirely masculine, but at that moment he would swear he had never seen anything so feminine.

With a small jolt, he realized that he had looked forward to her arrival all day. He even had imagined whiffs of lavender as he worked in his office, puzzling over how to reconstruct the oddly designed ceiling structure without bringing the whole building down upon them.

Now, he caught her lavender scent from across the room and became impatient to finish his instructions for the morning. Finally done, he crossed the room to Zylla and felt his heart twitch when she smiled at him.

"Thanks for taking the time to see me."

"Thank *you*," he returned, indicating the files sticking out of her bag. "I'm curious to see what you've gathered on the Charlesgate."

He paused as he raised his thumb to his lips and gnawed on it slightly as he turned to the table beside him. "And," he added, "I have something for you." Jabe frowned as he rummaged through the small mountain of receipts covering the surface.

"Ah, here it is." He looked pleased with himself as he held out a small gold square of heavy paper to her.

"Oh!" Zylla reverently stroked the flower and vine embossed on the gilded paper. "This is the original wallpaper, isn't it?"

A broad grin spread over his face, revealing white teeth, one just slightly crooked.

"Yup. I found it when we tore down a wall, and the original wall was still intact beneath it." He glanced around the room. "Lots of little surprises like that around here."

"Can I keep it?" she shyly ventured.

"Of course. So, tell me..." He pulled up a chair beside her and straddled it, arms crossed over the back of the chair. "Sit down. Why are you so interested in the Charlesgate?"

She shrugged.

"I don't really know. Love at first sight, I guess, and when I saw the name carved above the door, I just had to find out about it."

He looked at her in complete understanding. "Almost like giving an amazing building back an identity in a world that forgot it."

Zylla stared at him. "Exactly." She laughed, breaking the quiet bond that had formed between them. "Who knows? Maybe I lived here in a past life. I even dream about the place.

"There isn't much out there. History, I mean." She pulled a roll of paper from her bag and unrolled it on the table.

"This is the layout for the first and second floors," she said. "I don't have much more than this, but I assume the upper levels would follow the same pattern as the second floor?"

Jabe was so enthralled with the treasure that she brought that he barely heard her. The building had been a great puzzle to him, the result of many renovations and hackwork that distorted the original form of the Charlesgate's interior.

Now, he could clearly see the U-shaped design of the structure. Within the U, the architect had designed a garden, which was currently a garbage-strewn asphalt lot.

Off the garden had been a huge dining room and another smaller dining area adjacent to it. He assumed the laundry, kitchen, and wine keep were in the basement, as with most turn-of-the-century hotels.

The remainder of the first floor was intended for mixed use. There were clearly marked spaces for various offices, a library, a mailroom, and a few parlors.

"This is amazing."

Zylla beamed.

"C'mon, I'll show you around a bit and you can give me a history lesson," he said, and they exited the office, turning left to walk down the hall.

"I don't know much about this architect, I'm afraid," he continued. "I recall Putnam from my studies at Harvard, but he wasn't my focus."

"From what I've read," Zylla commented. "Putnam was influenced by a vision of Utopia... *Oooooo*, look at this."

Now that they were past the scaffolding, Zylla could see that hall walls were made of white ceramic tiles decorated with green-gold ceramic molded arches, half-columns, and hand-carved tiles of the same hue that bordered the ceiling. Worn mosaic patterns covered the floor.

She could imagine the potted palms that once lined the hallways, perhaps in front of each faux archway. In contrast, the wall across from the Beacon Street entrance was made of deep mahogany. An arched door with stained glass of lavender and mauve inlaid with chunks of moonstones and rose quartz stood slightly ajar.

Zylla reverently touched a rose quartz. "Stunning," she murmured.

"It certainly is," he drawled from behind her, his eyes lingering on the lines of her body and the cool silk of her hair, his hands itching to rest on her hips and pull her against him.

Zylla, intent on the lines and patterns in the wood, did not notice his sultry tone. She passed through the doorway to a small cubicle.

"The mailroom," she stated. Beyond the mailroom was another arched doorway, sans door, and a larger room beyond that which she guessed used to be the doctor's quarters. She inhaled the scent of old wood and something sweeter beneath that. Lavender.

She turned to Jabe just as his eyes snapped from their perusal of her backside.

"This place just crackles with mystery, doesn't it?" she asked, and he became entranced with her smile and sparkling, grateful eyes. "Thank you so much for letting me visit."

"Well, there's plenty more to see, so let's get a move on, darlin'," he replied, touched by her simple joy. She was so childlike in her happiness that he felt like a deviant for his unwholesome thoughts.

They turned to walk back in the direction of Jabe's office. Just opposite his door, he pulled back a drop cloth and led her under an arch to a small alcove that housed a decrepit cage elevator. Once gilded and full of light, the elevator grilles were now grimy and black. A rotten, swampy odor wafted from the black interior.

"Creepy, isn't it?" he asked.

Zylla felt a little nauseous from the stench. It reminded her of beach hollows filled with trapped, decaying fish and seaweed leftover from the tide's retreat.

She swallowed. "Seen any ghosts yet?"

"Nope, nothing," he replied. "One of the guys swears he hears the little girl who fell down the elevator shaft, but he's quite superstitious." A smile tugged at his lips.

"As far as I can tell, there are no Mafia tunnels to the sea, either." He cocked his head to the side. "I suppose you've heard those rumors as well."

She nodded. "Who knows? There may be some truth to them. I have a friend who lived here while it was a dorm. Very practical, logical sort of guy. He suffered from horrible dreams while he lived here and woke to a cold invisible presence in the room."

She wagged her eyebrows at him. "Supposedly, this was a bordello in the nineteen-seventies as well. It became pretty scummy property. The story about the girl isn't true, though. No one ever died in the elevator shaft.

"It did break while three ladies were in it, shortly after the Charlesgate was built, but they were fine and emerged from the fallen cab all set for their bridge game."

Jabe chuckled. "That's the Boston Brahmin for you."

"I think the little girl rumor got started because there's a tile of Putnam's daughter, Elsa, near the elevator shaft. Some college student probably smoked a bit too much one night and made up the story. The tile should be..." Zylla scanned along the wall where it met the ceiling.

"Ah! There she is." She pointed to a ceramic tile of a little girl's head. She had long hair with a bow on top.

Jabe was astonished. "Wow. You knew right where it was just by reading about it? Impressive. So, she didn't meet an early demise, I take it?"

"Nope. She lived to a ripe old age." Zylla pointed to another tile. "That one is her father, the architect, John Pickering Putnam."

They were silent for a moment as they contemplated the visage of the bearded Putnam. In Zylla's mind, he was the epitome of the perfect grandfather.

"A stately old gentleman," he commented.

They continued along the corridor to the stairs. Before ascending, Jabe motioned with his arm to indicate the unexplored first-floor corridor.

"According to the plans you gave me, that area was the larger dining room."

Zylla was equally impressed with Jabe. Back in his office, it seemed that he had merely glanced at the floor plans, but he obviously carried a snapshot of the plans in his mind.

She couldn't fathom how the huge dining room had become a narrow darkened corridor. The few photographs she possessed of the original Charlesgate revealed an airy, light-filled chamber, not a narrow, dark passage.

In the photos, a smaller room, separated from the large dining room by Moorish arches, overlooked gardens. Zylla imagined that in the summer, white sheer curtains would dance in the wind and in the winter, thick glass doors would bar the cold, but allow plenty of light.

As if reading her mind, Jabe gently said, "The garden is a paved lot now."

They ascended six stories of stairs in silence, and Zylla silently thanked Anne for their five o'clock runs around Cambridge streets.

On the sixth floor, Jabe led her through neglected, lonely rooms, each with a fireplace. Some were brick, others mosaic or ceramic tile and some were solid wood, but no two were the same. The only consistency was that the fireplaces were missing great chunks of building material and the mantels were torn off. Zylla sank deeper into mourning for the demise of such artwork.

"Most of the mantel pieces were stolen or ripped from the wall and used as firewood. We removed the rest along with original doors and stained glass fixtures. They're safely stored away."

Zylla brightened. "Then the owner plans to restore them?"

Jabe stared blankly at her. The building was so far decayed that a full restoration would be highly expensive and time-consuming.

To save the building and make a profit, an owner was required only to ensure that the building was structurally sound and up to code. In a couple of months, the building would pay for itself. A full restoration would take three times as long and cost a small fortune.

Jabe, however, could not bear to butcher the smile on Zylla's face and manipulated the conversation back to her.

"Why do you care so much that this building be restored as it was?" he questioned as they walked through room after room.

She hesitated. "You can tell it was once beautiful and now it just seems to be struggling for breath." A sideways grin appeared on her face. "Plus, I'm a diehard romantic."

Jabe slowly nodded. He was once a diehard romantic, as she put it, always searching for Camelot and ready to slay dragons. Then he grew up.

"Like I said, there's not much research on the Charlesgate beyond sordid stories found on the Internet." Zylla drew a long breath. "But the information that is available proves that the building is well worth restoring. Emerson Library's archives kept a file on the history of the building. That's were I found the floor plans, old photographs, articles, and a tip that the diary of Putnam's sister is in the archives of the Massachusetts Historical Society."

Zylla glanced at Jabe to gauge his boredom level. "I can babble for hours about this if you let me," she warned.

"And I'll listen for hours," he said, folding his arms across his chest and leaning against the wall.

She smiled. "Well, once I read about Putnam's ideas of an architectural Utopia and the history of this building, I became more and more convinced that it was sheer evil to destroy this building, whether it be by tearing it down or converting it to generic condominiums for wealthy people."

At Jabe's questioning expression, Zylla explained about John Pickering Putnam's ideas to build a self-contained housing unit that allowed luxurious yet affordable housing for all social classes.

The building had been designed to allow fresh air, plenty of natural light, and modern sanitary systems, something which poor city dwellers lacked in crowded, filthy tenement housing of the 1890s.

"He created it to be a place of great beauty, but also a useful, healthy place, for all social classes."

Jabe was amused by her transformation into an authoritative scholar and had to struggle to keep his lips straight.

"The first floor was devoted to shops and utilities for residents' needs. Tenants could have a kitchen if they chose or could simply dine in the communal dining room. Rooms could expand and contract to make apartments smaller or larger, depending on a family's needs or income."

At this, Jabe's eyes lit. "Ah, that explains the odd architectural glitches we keep coming across."

"What do you mean?"

"Well," Jabe searched the room. "Ah, here's one. Come here."

Jabe pointed to a doorjamb in which was embedded another wall that pulled out.

"Once we started ripping down Sheetrock to expose the original horsehair plaster," he explained, "we found walls within walls. We just weren't sure what the purpose was."

They walked further along the corridor until Jabe entered a door on the right. She followed him through two rooms until he paused outside a doorway.

"This is what I wanted to show you," Jabe said, indicating the doorway. "After you."

Zylla entered the room and gasped. It was a corner turret room, filled with beams of bright sunshine. The room was in excellent condition. The floorboards gleamed golden and shiny and the walls, although dirty, appeared solid. A pretty pale green marble fireplace, completely intact, sat against the wall to the right of the door.

The ceiling was edged with tiny plaster rosettes and vines and the medallion in the center of the ceiling mirrored the edging. The chandelier, pieces of crystal missing, hung precariously by its wires.

Diagonally across from the door was a slit of a doorway that opened into the turret, which protruded onto the corner of Charlesgate East and Beacon Street. Zylla turned to Jabe.

"Go ahead." He laughed at her eager expression. "It's safe."

Zylla bounded across the room and easily fit through the tiny precipice into the three-sided copper and glass turret. The space allowed enough room for one person to stand—its only purpose seemed to be for viewing the Charles River and Kenmore Square. Now the neighboring building across Beacon Street blocked the river view and Zylla watched the passing cars below her. It was as if she were standing on the edge of a pirate's plank but instead of the ocean, she saw asphalt. She became lightheaded and stepped back into the room, but the dizziness remained.

For a second, she heard harpsichord music and inhaled lavender. She saw the warm glow of a fire in the hearth, the blonde woman curled in a chair before it. The woman looked up at her with soft gray eyes. Zylla blinked and the image was gone.

"Whew."

"Yea, it packs quite a punch, doesn't it?"

Zylla looked at Jabe but didn't hear him. She knew this room. She knew the blonde woman. She had dreamed about them. Zylla pressed her fingers against her temples. Insanity bound for sure. Her Aunt Maddie never spoke of family scandals, but Zylla once had heard Maddie's brother, John, tell stories about their mother, Zylla's grandmother. She had gone insane and committed suicide.

Zylla tried to shake the melting feeling and concentrate on Jabe, his sea-green eyes an anchor to her confusion.

"This room and the one directly above it are the most well-preserved rooms in the hotel," he said as they descended to the ground floor.

"The old walls were covered in Sheetrock, perfectly preserving the original features. Amazing, isn't it?"

Zylla nodded.

"We're heading over to the addition next."

They carefully picked their path over rotting floors and debris. "With the exception of the music room, most of it is in better condition than this section."

"That would be the old Barnes mansion, right?" Zylla remembered from her reading that Putnam had incorporated the adjacent building into the Charlesgate a few years after the hotel was completed.

"Yep," Jabe smiled, visibly pleased by her knowledge. "He did a good job of merging it into the main building, too. When we go back outside, you can see the difference because the Barnes mansion has no brick, but he brought the copper and medieval roofline right over it for cohesiveness."

They emerged from a dark hall into a bright, Italian villa-influenced stairwell.

Jabe affirmed her questioning glance. "Yep. Now we're in the addition. And this," he said as he struggled to pull open double iron doors, "is a mess."

With a low groan, the doors opened and Jabe and Zylla stepped into a large auditorium. The room was filthy and the once pretty teal of the walls and stunning carved ceiling were murky. The skylight in the center of the high ceiling surely supported an inch of dirt because no light penetrated to the floor where great holes gaped.

Zylla and Jabe each clapped a hand over their mouths and noses simultaneously. The same odor that hovered near the elevator shaft assaulted their senses.

"Phew! Is there water in the basement?"

"Naw, just rats." His nostrils quivered nonetheless. *What the hell is in that basement? A rotting whale?* Jabe thought as he looked at the black chasm a few feet from them. The room felt sinister, and Jabe shivered. He took a step closer to Zylla, repressing an urge to put an arm around her. He caught a whiff of her lavender and inhaled deeply, erasing the stench from below.

"This is where the great lecturers of the eighteen-nineties spoke," Zylla said, mostly to herself, but Jabe heard and looked at the stage where Zylla gazed.

"What were the lectures about?"

"Oh," she replied. "Women's suffrage, education, the plight of Boston's immigrant poor, and other political topics. Mark Twain visited here," she added reverently.

The rank odor interrupted her thoughts as it crept into her nostrils and permeated her nerves. When she had a migraine, the pain was often accompanied by a heightened sense of smell, and the odor in the Barnes mansion was sickeningly like the one that attended her rare migraine nightmares of bloody oceans and an insane pirate woman.

Despite the literary aura, she didn't want to remain in this hallowed hall much longer. She nervously looked around her and nearly panicked when she glimpsed Jabe's expression.

"What is *that*?" he exploded.

Zylla jumped and frantically swatted at her chest, convinced that he had spotted a centipede or similar crawly evil.

"What? Where?"

Jabe cautiously lifted the pendant that hung from a silver chain around Zylla's neck and bent his head to closely study the blue eye in its clear globe.

"Huh," he said.

Zylla, meanwhile, felt a different sort of unease that had to do with the close proximity of his face to her breasts. Her nerves were suddenly wavy and swimming, her mouth dry.

"It's not real," he said as he straightened his body and dropped the pendant.

"Of course not." She felt her face flush hot.

He blushed slightly and scratched his neck. "It's just that I've never seen anything like that before. What is it?"

Zylla laughed as her mortification quickly evaporated.

"I guess it is rather odd. It's called *to mati*. Superstition, really. It's supposed to ward off the evil eye. My *Yia-Yia*—that means grandmother in Greek—was born on Corfu, and although she scoffed at all other superstitions, she really insisted that this one had merit. I never take it off."

His eyebrow went up at that, envisioning her in nothing but creamy skin and that necklace.

"Berry... so, you're mom is Greek?"

She shook her head. He frowned and she continued, guessing his thought process. "My dad was. My parents died when I was little, and my mom's sister adopted me. That's why my last name is Berry and not Lyros."

"Sorry about your parents," he said softly. "I lost my dad when I was fourteen. I know how it feels. Are you close with your grandmother, your *Yia-Yia*?"

"No," she gazed up at him. "Unfortunately, she died soon after my parents. Stroke."

Zylla grinned, erasing the somber mood. "From the stories I heard, she was a real cool lady. Her name was Sophie, and by all accounts she was a tomboy with a penchant for ostentatious diamonds. Once, some neighborhood bullies beat up her little brother. He ran home crying and screaming and told my then thirteen-year-old grandmother what had happened. Well, I guess their younger sister immediately dropped to her knees and prayed, but Sophie grabbed a butcher knife and chased the bullies through the cemetery."

Jabe laughed as he imagined the scene.

"Supposedly, she could see ghosts, too," Zylla continued. "At least that's what the Berrys say. They're Scottish and one superstition claims that anyone born on December twenty-fifth can see ghosts, and..."

"And Sophie was born on Christmas Day?" Jabe finished for her.

Zylla nodded. "Yep."

"Could she really see them?"

"I guess. I only see the Berry family once every few years for the reunions and they swap all sorts of tales. *Yia-Yia* went to one cookout when my parents were first married, and she told Uncle John that a Victorian lady followed my mother everywhere she went, wringing her hands and frantically pleading."

Jabe rolled his eyes. "Of course she was Victorian," he mocked. "All proper ghosts are wailing Victorian widows that wear lemon verbena or lavender."

"Exactly," Zylla chortled, then paused. "Lavender. Mom's ghost wore lavender."

They both fell silent, surrounded by the eerie blue quiet of the music room and the rank sea smell pervading the air.

Jabe sighed and looked away from Zylla, his eyes scanning the increasing shadows in the great hall.

"Let's go," he said. "It's getting dark and there's no electricity in this part of the building. It can get treacherous at night with all the weak spots in the floor."

They exited from the Barnes mansion door, which spilled onto the Charlesgate East sidewalk, overgrown with weeds erupting from cracks in the cement. Around the corner, the brick sidewalk of Marlborough Street began and Zylla noticed more thriving weeds and smashed gas lanterns alongside the Charlesgate Hotel. She smiled inwardly. *All this neglect will be remedied soon*, she thought.

"How about you?" she asked softly. "I realize that it's your job, but you seem to love this place as much as I do."

Jabe scratched the underside of his chin before answering her. "I fall in love with buildings on a daily basis, but you're right, I do have a certain fascination for this one. I walked by it one day, just like I've done a million times before, and it suddenly grabbed me. The thought of a bulldozer getting it made me sick.

"I mean, I knew that an ancestor of some sort lived here in its heyday and maybe that's why I paid special attention to her."

"What?" Zylla felt that she might burst with the excitement that bubbled within her. "Who? Why didn't you tell me before?"

Jabe grinned and shrugged. "Slipped my mind. All I know is that he was the brother to my great-great..." He paused as he counted. "Great aunt, Cathy. His name was Caval, and he and his sister were orphans from Wales. He was murdered outside the Charlesgate sometime after it was built."

Zylla closed her open mouth.

"I'm jealous," she said.

He chuckled and started to walk down the street.

"I'm going to grab a bite before heading home. You wanna come?"

There was no answer.

"Zylla?"

He turned around to find that she hadn't moved from the doorway. Despite the dark, he could see that her face was pale and that her eyes glowed strangely.

Concerned, he rushed forward and took her arm. "What's wrong?"

"Wait a minute," she muttered, then glared at him. "That's Caval as in *Caval* Construction?"

He slowly nodded.

"*You* own the Charlesgate?"

"I'm afraid so."

Zylla stared.

"Couldn't resist it," he continued. "Although now I don't know how I can begin to tackle this monster. It's a mess and just about ready to fall down around my head. I don't know where to start."

He watched as the side of Zylla's mouth quirked and humor sparked her eyes. She indicated her bag, now devoid of floor plans.

"Well, now you do," she said.

"Now I do," he admitted.

"So it better be done right."

He raised one dark blond eyebrow. "Or else?"

"Or else I'll cut all that long blond hair off, Samson."

Five

Jabe chuckled to himself as he walked back to the Charlesgate for his motorcycle, remembering the wonder on Zylla's face when she realized that he owned the building. She had declined his offer to treat her to a burger and fries at the Underground in favor of a tedious evening researching his ancestor at the library, and he ate by himself.

He shook his head, frowning. Perhaps that was a good thing. He liked her too much already and was far too attracted to her for his own peace of mind. Besides, he needed to think.

"Mr. Jabe."

"Emmett. You're playing late today, eh?"

Emmett laughed and strummed his steel guitar. "Gotta earn my keep."

Jabe smiled at his friend, admiring his suit, replete with pocket watch and Harris Tweed cap.

"My good friend," Emmett sang. "What has you smiling one minute and frowning the next, *hmmm*? Have you abandoned your 'no women' rule, then? Tell 'ole Emmett all about it."

"Make much today?" Jabe evaded.

Emmett grinned slowly. "I did. A good day. The sun's out, and there are plenty of pretty women parading these streets just waitin' for a big strong man like yourself to scoop them up."

"No way. I've got enough trouble with that building of mine. Don't know what to do with the damn thing."

"Uh-huh. You got woman trouble then."

Emmett played a blues riff and continued talking.

"A building like that is like a fine woman. Treat her shabbily, take her for granted, and she'll be as bitter as a gouty ole' man. Accept her for the gift that she is, stroke her like a fine guitar, well..."

He grinned again.

"You enhance her natural magic. A good woman is a rare thing. You don't go turning your back on her. You accept her love with gratitude."

He looked at Jabe pointedly.

"Remember that, my friend."

Jabe laughed and shook his head. "All right, Emmett, my man. I'll catch up with you later."

Ignoring Emmett's mutters about stubborn young men, he walked on.

~ * ~

The doorbell rang just as he stepped out of the shower.

"Shit," he swore as he skidded on the bath rug. He wrapped a towel around his waist and ran to the front door, leaving wet footprints on the floorboards in his wake.

He threw back the door to find his best friend brandishing a bottle of bourbon and a banjo.

"Viking, you're all wet."

Jabe scowled at the obvious and stepped back to allow Rye entry. A cold drip from his hair trickled down his back and he rolled his shoulder in annoyance.

"What are you doing here, Billy Goat? I thought you had a gig tonight."

"Canceled it. Nolan's sick and we couldn't find a replacement bassist this late." Rye shifted the banjo on his shoulder. "Go get dressed and I'll meet you downstairs."

A few minutes later, Jabe trotted down the hidden staircase to his underground den, the main reason he'd bought the run-down Queen Anne.

The large, hidden room had been a speakeasy during Prohibition and Jabe had converted it into a huge, comfortable recreation room complete with pool table and bar.

Rye was lighting a fire in the fieldstone fireplace, so Jabe headed to the bar for a couple of tumblers. He returned to the sitting area and plopped down on the worn velvet sofa as he reached for the bourbon.

"So... what's up?" Jabe glanced at Rye's back quickly, then looked down at the liquor as it streamed into the glass. "Must be serious if you brought the Knob Creek."

The fire happily cavorting, Rye stood up and faced Jabe. "I ran into Emmett a little while ago. He said you were thinking too much and you needed some whiskey and banjo picking." A flash of white parted Rye's whiskers as he grinned and sat in the chair opposite Jabe.

"So here I am." He reached behind the chair. "Here's your baby."

Jabe accepted the banjo, a hand-carved creation of Rye's, and strapped it over his shoulder. Rye did the same and the two picked one bluegrass song after another, Jabe struggling to keep up as he mirrored Rye, watching his fingers fly over the strings.

After half an hour, he started laughing, shaking his golden mane. "I give up. I can't keep up with you."

Rye grinned back, his blue eyes laughing. "Solved your problem, didn't it?"

"Well," Jabe sipped his whiskey. "Not really. But it did clear my head a bit." He sat back, his smile fading. "It's the Charlesgate." Jabe scratched the underside of his chin, something he always did when perplexed.

"I bought it against my better judgment. Bought it on emotion." He folded his hands and leaned forward, resting his elbows on his knees. "It's the worst business decision I could make, a complete money pit. But it is possible to bring it up to code and rent apartments. Caval can make the money back."

"So what's the issue?"

Jabe held his breath for a second then let it out in a whoosh. "I met a girl."

Rye whooped. "Well, it's about time. I was beginning to worry about you with your banishment of the female sex. It's been, what? Four months?"

Jabe raised a brow. "Five. But who's counting?" He glanced down at his glass.

"No, no relationships." He jerked his head at Rye. "You know why. It's always the same. It starts out great and within three months, she's moved in and we're spouting 'I love yous' and 'forever,' then one or both of us realizes that we don't know each other. Or even like each other."

Jabe shrugged. "I'm sick of chain-smoking one woman after another."

"So it has nothing to do with the curse."

Rye's remark was more of a statement than a question, yet Jabe was silent for a moment as he thought about his reply, thought about his promise to his mother.

The Thayer curse. When he was sixteen, Jabe had fallen in love with Trisha Healy, a winsome brunette with green eyes and a crystalline laugh. He had met her at the Killington ski resort, where he had worked during winters. Trisha would visit the resort every weekend to ski with her friends.

For two consecutive winters, Trisha and Jabe had been inseparable and during the in-between seasons, they had phoned each other constantly, spilling deep secrets or giggling over nothing.

Jabe had lost his virginity to her in her room at the lodge and had told her that he loved her.

Trisha had laughed. She had a boyfriend whom she loved back home in Massachusetts. Devastated, Jabe had dressed quickly and left her room, his stomach nauseous and his heart heavy.

He walked home through the woods, leaving his mother's car at the lodge, letting the cold air fill his lungs until it felt like they would burst.

So that was love, he thought, and like his father before him, had drowned his bitterness in a half bottle of vodka. His mother found him in the morning, passed out at the kitchen table. Jenny put him to bed and nursed his hangover.

By nightfall, he felt much better and had gone downstairs where a hot dinner and his mother's displeasure waited. She said nothing, but her disappointment was palpable, and Jabe had eaten with lowered eyes.

"I'm sorry, Mom," he whispered.

Jenny sat next to him, and in her firm but gentle voice, replied, "You will not use the Thayer curse, real or not, and I think not, to excuse your actions.

"You have Cameron blood in those veins, as well, and I'll thank you to remember that the next time you seek to escape your misfortunes."

Jabe had been surprised that she brought up the rumored curse. His father believed that the unhappy lives of Thayer men were the result of a seventeenth-century hex that a woman put on old Admiral Thayer for his betrayal.

Yet Jenny never believed in the curse, and that night, so long ago, he had seen his mother's strength for the first time. Slim and fragile with her wheat-blond hair and cornflower eyes, Jenny Thayer had a spirit of steel.

She raised the two boys by herself, both before and after his father had died, and she didn't deserve a wreck for a son.

At that moment, he resolved to make something of himself, to grow into a happy, confident man. He had looked up into his mother's pained eyes and said, "Yes, ma'am. It won't happen again."

And it hadn't. At thirty-two, Jabe possessed good looks, wealth, individuality, great friends, and an ability to master anything with which he set his mind.

His only failing point was women. He was just bad at women.

Jabe sighed and stared into the fire before answering Rye. "No, not the curse." Jabe looked Rye in the eyes. "I wish I could blame it on that. I've just finally accepted the fact that I'm bad at relationships, and I'm not going to waste my time anymore."

He grunted and ran a hand through his hair. "No more switching my brand of woman every three months."

Rye's brow furrowed. "I'm confused. More bourbon?"

Jabe shook his head.

"If you are dead set against a relationship, then what's the problem with this girl?"

"Oh," Jabe waved his hand. "She knows about the Charlesgate. She's been researching its history for years and even tracked down the original floor plans."

"That's great. I remember you complaining that you couldn't find them."

"Yeah, well, there's a price. She believes that the Charlesgate shouldn't be restituted at all unless it's a full restoration, and I tell you, she nearly has me convinced."

Jabe closed his eyes and rubbed them with his fingers.

"But it would be a fortune, and I just don't know if it's possible, even if I'm convinced it's the right thing to do."

Jabe briefly explained the history of the Charlesgate and the architect's dreams for the structure.

Rye picked a few strings on his banjo then played a couple of rolls. "Of course, it's possible," he said over the twang of the strings. "That's why you became the architect and I became the musician."

Jabe chuckled and stood, stretched his arms behind his head, then wandered to the hearth.

He had met Rye at Harvard University's School of Architecture where they became instant friends, both sharing a love of music and Kentucky bourbon. Rye, however, had discovered that he had a greater passion for music than architecture and dropped out to start his own bluegrass band.

"You're worried about using old Jabez's money though, aren't you?" Rye nodded his head toward the large piece of parchment paper that was nailed to the wall with Jabe's family tree sprawled on it.

Jabe stoked the fire and watched as the sparks danced and landed on the hearth, finally disintegrating into the black floor.

When he had turned twenty-seven, Jenny had signed his portion of the Thayer inheritance over to Jabe to help him start Caval Construction. Jabe had used a small portion of the vast amount for that purpose and invested the rest, somewhat wary of the hoard.

Jabe had not been overwhelmed by his sudden status as a wealthy man—rather, he felt the money was tainted, curse or no curse. It had brought unhappiness to countless Thayers before him, and Jabe was superstitious enough to believe that ill-gotten money brought ill luck.

As he had told Rye before, the Thayer wealth had begun with Admiral Thayer's reward from King William for hanging a treasonous woman—his lover. The fortune had belonged to the hanged woman, and Jabe felt that it was somehow wrong to profit from another's misery, even if that someone was a criminal.

And profit the Admiral had done. The wealth had accumulated through the years by means of advantageous marriages and wise investments, but gambling, robbery, and murder had also assisted its growth.

Despite the warmth of the fire, Jabe felt an icy finger swivel down his spine. He shuddered.

"I guess I am a little afraid of it. It's blood money, in a way. Using it for personal gain doesn't feel right to me. It's all going to charity, anyway, if I don't have kids."

He shrugged. "Even then, I'd set up a small trust for them and donate the majority." But even as he spoke, he thought otherwise. In the case of the Charlesgate, the money would not be used for mercenary reasons, would it? Instead, it would aid in fulfilling Putnam's promise to the city, a residence of splendor that all individuals and families could afford. His ancestors' ill-gotten means would well serve humanity in this one structure.

Jabe thought about Zylla's wistful expression when she had seen the mangled fireplaces and how that sadness would be whisked away when the Charlesgate was restored to its former glory. He wanted to make her smile again, like she had when he handed her that section of gold wallpaper, as if it were a diamond ring and not a crumbling piece of the past.

He frowned. *Best not think along those lines.*

"... if you were going to use it for the greater good, that is."

"She is different than the others, though," Jabe stated suddenly, having not even heard Rye's words. He began to pace in front of the fire, hands clasped behind his back.

"I mean, I've been attracted to plenty of girls in the past few months, and Zylla's no exception, but there's something about her."

"Who?"

"Zylla."

"Who's Zylla?"

Jabe stopped pacing and stared at Rye for a second before realizing that he had missed Rye's advice.

"I'm sorry, I wasn't listening."

Rye snorted. "That's obvious. I said that I don't think it would be a mistake to use the money on the Charlesgate. It seems like you'd be using it for the greater good."

Jabe nodded. "I think you're right."

"Now, who's Zylla?"

"The Charlesgate girl." Jabe suddenly gasped and slapped a hand to his forehead. "Oh my God. I forgot to tell you. You won't believe who she is."

Rye's head tilted to the side.

"Do you remember the Cramps show about a year ago?"

"Yeah, it was at the Mid East. Great show."

"And do you remember that woman I fell halfway in love with? The one that I said would be my soul mate, if such creatures existed?"

"Damn." Illumination dawned on Rye's face. "It's her?"

Jabe nodded needlessly.

Rye rubbed his lip and murmured, "And you'll be seeing her quite a bit, what with the Charlesgate, right? Well," he grinned maliciously. "You can't stop fate, after all. It's only a matter of time."

Jabe shot a glare at his friend. "Not if I have something to say about it."

Rye shook his head slowly, amusement in his eyes.

"And what do you say about the Charlesgate, then, Viking?"

Jabe grinned broadly. "Pour me some whiskey, Billy Goat, and let's have a toast. I'm going to bring her back from the dead."

Six

Upon leaving the Charlesgate, Zylla ignored her stomach's supplications for sustenance and raced to the Boston Public Library. Disbelief throbbed in her head. Not only did Jabe own her beloved Charlesgate—he was related to it, so to speak.

She entered the library and paused at the bottom of the steps as she tried to focus on where to begin. Since the Charlesgate was the premier residence of Boston at the turn of the century, Zylla knew that Caval's name would be listed in *The Social Register* of one of those years. Satisfied, she trotted up the stairs and headed to Social Sciences.

Within ten minutes, she found Caval's name in both the eighteen ninety-four and eighteen ninety-five *Social Registers*, and made photocopies of the pages. His name was not listed in the eighteen ninety-six register.

He was murdered. Zylla shivered at the memory of Jabe's words as she inserted the photocopies into her knapsack.

Zylla stopped short at the exit when she realized that if Caval had been murdered, then his death was most likely recorded in the newspaper, and since he was not listed in the eighteen ninety-six register, she could assume that his death occurred in late eighteen ninety-five.

Narrowing down the exact day would take quite a bit longer, and the library's lights were already dimming. Zylla raised a brow as she mentally listed her tasks for the next work day. Nothing that couldn't wait until Wednesday. Actually, there was nothing that couldn't wait until next year. She sighed. Unless graduation or finals were imminent, her job was boring. Since she felt guilty receiving a salary for indulging in Internet research, she reasoned that she might as well feel guilty for calling in sick. And somehow, Caval's murder seemed much more important.

~ * ~

Tuesday morning, she awoke at six o'clock, stretched her arms, and hopped out of bed. She whistled tunelessly while donning her running clothes and nearly scared Anne into shock with a wide smile.

"Hey there, my favorite roommate," Zylla trilled. "It's beautiful out. You wanna run to Boston this morning instead of Harvard? Then maybe we can grab a coffee and bagel. Hey, how was your date the other night?"

Anne's eyes widened. "Whoa, whoa, whoa. What the hell happened to the don't-speak-to-me-before-I-eat-Zylla that I know and love?"

Zylla simply shrugged.

"Uh-huh." Anne bent to tie her sneaker. "Well, it's raining, in case you didn't realize that in your fog of happiness, but sure, we can run to Boston." She paused to yawn.

"No breakfast, though. I have to go to work early today, and my date was horrible. He likes to wear women's underwear."

"Another one?" Zylla wondered at the possibility of meeting two such men in a month's span.

"You know," Anne sighed as she straightened. "I did everything right. He's the president of a huge corporation, for godsake! We've dated for two months and haven't done anything but kiss. Sunday night after dinner and a movie, I figured it was time to move it along a bit. So, in the middle of a healthy little make-out session, I unzipped his pants, and..."

"Women's underwear?" Zylla supplied.

"Black lacy bikinis."

Zylla cringed.

"Aaagghhh!" Anne grabbed Zylla's arms and shook her, a desperate gleam in her eyes. "What's wrong with me, Zylla?"

~ * ~

"Anne." Zylla panted as they ran along the wet pavement of the bridge, the conversation about Anne's love life in tow. "We've been over this before. You said it yourself. You don't want to fall in love with some man because you'll become dependent on him, so you intrinsically hone in to men who are, ahem, unavailable. They're safe. Only they're not safe because you get hurt anyway."

Zylla slowed to a fast walk. "Can't speak and run at the same time. Smoked too much in college."

"But Zyll," Anne persisted, as she wiped sweat and rain from her brow. "I do want to fall in love. Really."

"Well, if you know what you want, then that's half the battle. Now all you need is to realize that you can be independent and still maintain a healthy relationship. It's not so hard."

"Oh sure," Anne drawled, sarcastically. "And you, the virgin huntress, know so much about relationships."

Zylla's eyes flashed a warning at Anne before she calmed herself.

"Well, according to Aunt Maddie, both my parents were hopeless, mooning romantics, so as an inbred romantic, I suppose I know what I'm talking about."

Zylla's face brightened in inspiration. "Read *Middlemarch*. Poor Dorothea wants to maintain her independence and goes and marries an impotent old fart in a misguided attempt to—"

"I read *Middlemarch*," Anne interrupted. "And that doesn't count because she had to get married. It was the culture."

"Yes, but my point is the same. She chose to marry the old man, thinking she'd be able to be independent and useful, but he imprisoned her. Only when she dropped her fears and married for love was she completely free to be herself."

"That's not a very feminist message of independence," Anne argued.

Zylla brushed away Anne's statement with her hand. "Feminism-scheminism. What do they know? You keep your independence by letting go of it."

"What in Sam's Hill does that mean?" Anne slipped into a deep drawl.

Zylla shrugged off her annoyance. "All I'm saying is you'll never find your hero if you don't lose your fear."

"But if you don't find the right hero," Anne countered, "you're doomed. Dorothea is a case in point."

"True, but that's because she didn't know herself. Once she accepted herself, she found Will."

"Damn lit majors." Anne scowled.

The two argued the philosophy of George Eliot most of the morning, causing Anne to be late for work and Zylla to truly sound hoarse when she phoned into work to tell her assistant, Nicole, that she was ill.

~ * ~

Zylla always tiptoed across the floor of the library's entrance. Built during the Gilded Age, a few years after the Charlesgate, the library's entrance never ceased to amaze her with its golden glow and the two giant granite lions. She felt like Cinderella in the palace, and was grateful that such a show of wealth and power belonged to the general public.

By three o'clock, however, all animation had departed from Zylla's body. Her lower back and leg muscles ached from sitting in the same chair for countless hours. Her eyes were gritty from searching microfiche files, but she stubbornly ignored her aches.

She had skimmed both *The Boston Globe* and *The Boston Herald* daily newspapers in the years eighteen ninety-five and eighteen ninety-six and despite the urge to pull her hair out, she persevered. She found the small blurb, a few lines really, in *The Boston Traveler* dated October twenty-seven, eighteen ninety-five: "Couple Murdered Outside Prestigious Back Bay Residence."

Zylla yelped and the man next to her glared.

"Sorry," she whispered.

> *Two residents of the prestigious Charlesgate Hotel were brutally stabbed outside the 535 Beacon Street address late last night. The identities of the man and woman are given as Caval and Lydia Berry, husband and wife. Assailants remain at large. There is no known*

cause for the murder, but police speculate that it may be related to the increasing violence in the city due to labor workers' unrest. Mr. and Mrs. Berry leave behind an infant son, Jemmy. Mr. Berry leaves a sister, Mrs. Catherine Thayer, and Mrs. Berry leaves her parents, Mr. & Mrs. Jedediah Berry, and a twin sister, Miss Lily Berry.

Zylla could hear nothing except the thud of her irregular heartbeat and the violent waterfall of blood rushing to her feet as she slowly stood. Dizzy, she clutched the table edge for support.

The man next to her glanced over, sent his chair flying as he lunged to catch her before she fell. As the stranger's hand grabbed her elbow, Zylla shook her head to regain her composure.

"I'm okay." She smiled at him. "Thanks."

His expression wary, he asked, "You sure?"

She nodded. "I just stood up too quickly. Thank you."

He frowned and hurriedly retreated to the safe haven of his studies. Zylla turned back to the screen and copied the article into her notebook, then wandered into the stately Abbey Room to think. The dark oak and murals of King Arthur's tales in that room soothed her, and she was able to examine her swirling emotions.

Fate. It's all fate, she thought. First the Charlesgate, then Jabe, and now the possibility of a joined past. If she tried to reason that it was all coincidence, then she'd certainly go mad. There was free will, of that she had no doubt, but free will tangled with fate somehow. The entire concept was bigger than Zylla, and she wouldn't waste brain cells worrying over it. Some things were better left to the Maker. Besides, this sort of stuff happened all the time, at least in the books she read. So she simply welcomed the joy of not only finding Caval, but also the possibility of discovering an ancestor.

Alarms jolted her brain, however, when she later called Aunt Maddie to tell her of the great discovery. Aunt Maddie, usually calm and teasing, greeted Zylla's announcement and subsequent questions with cold disdain.

When Zylla pushed to discover the cause of Madeleine's strange attitude, Maddie clipped, "I don't want to discuss this any further," and disconnected the call.

Stunned, Zylla replaced the receiver in its cradle, and tried to ignore the hurt Maddie's tone had caused. Curiosity about Lydia Berry soon overcame her, and she thought of her Uncle John, Maddie's brother.

Zylla only saw him once every few years at family cookouts, but she had a deep fondness for her uncle. With his bald head, crossed-armed stance, and anchor tattoo on his forearm, Uncle John was a formidable man, but the twinkle in his blue eyes and easy Berry grin gave him away. Best of all, he told Zylla disturbing bits of family lore that other adults refused to mention. He told her about his mother, who had gone raving mad and spent her days carving jack-o'-lanterns before turning the knife on herself, and about a great-aunt who lived in the Ozarks, shot possum, and practiced voodoo. He talked about ancestors who were long dead, and Zylla shivered as she remembered one tale of a woman who had sewn people's lips together.

Zylla also remembered the time Maddie overheard Uncle John whispering such stories to her. Maddie's eyes had turned to ice and her mouth became a grim line.

"Aw, c'mon, Maddie, lighten up," he had chortled.

Maddie had said, "She doesn't need to hear such things. She's too young."

"Pshaw."

Maddie clenched her fists and ordered Zylla into the kitchen to dry dishes. Later, when Zylla asked Maddie if any of Uncle John's stories were true, her aunt deftly changed the subject. Zylla had assumed that Aunt Maddie knew nothing of the family history. Now Zylla believed that Aunt Maddie knew much more than she had thought.

How else was she to account for her aunt's behavior on the phone? Maddie wasn't the type of person who believed in stuffing unpleasant subjects under the rug—she always encouraged Zylla to discuss whatever was on her mind.

Zylla shrugged. Uncle John would know. She left a message on his answering machine, then headed for the Charlesgate to tell Jabe about Caval.

On impulse, she swung by the Underground for a couple of roast beef sandwiches. It was almost five, after all, and Jabe might be hungry.

Dennis greeted her at the entrance with a wink and a bright smile.

"Going home?"

His grin widened. "Yes, I am. To my little woman and a great big steak. Jabe's in his office, honey. Go on in."

"Thanks, Dennis. Take care."

Zylla whistled as she entered the building and was halfway to Jabe's office when she stopped, mid-step and mid-note, then backed up slowly and sniffed. No, she wasn't imagining it. The peppery sweetness of lavender floated in the air.

Zylla closed her eyes, but her brain didn't tilt in dizziness, nor did she experience her usual foray into the past.

She opened her eyes slowly.

"Huh," she said, and walked to Jabe's office.

~ * ~

Jabe's reaction to seeing Zylla, her cheeks rosy from exercise and eyes glittering russet, was immediate, and he strained from throwing her down across his desk and ravaging her.

Instead, he took a deep breath and forced himself to think of banjo tablature.

"So," he said, "you want another tour?"

She smiled and held out the bag from the Underground. "Just wanted to thank you for yesterday. Roast beef."

His stomach growled in answer, and they both laughed. Jabe took the bag and opened it to peer inside.

"And to show you this."

"What is it?" he asked, as she handed him her notebook.

"I found him." Her voice was proud. "In a newspaper from eighteen ninety-five. It's about Caval."

He skimmed the words.

"He took her surname," he commented. Realization dawned on his face, and she read the question in his green eyes when he looked up from the notebook.

"I don't know for sure." She shrugged. "Berry is such a common name, but at the same time, it sort of..."

"Makes sense?" he asked.

"Exactly."

"Can you find out for sure?" He stepped closer to her and placed his hand on her lower back. The scent of lavender tickled his nostrils, and he stifled the urge to pull her closer.

Ushering her into the hall, he said, "C'mon we'll eat on the roof. You haven't seen that yet."

Zylla explained her interaction with Maddie as she they climbed seven flights of stairs, walked a passage to the Barnes addition and up one more flight of stairs. Jabe pushed open the black wood door, and Zylla followed him onto the uneven floor of the roof.

It was heaven.

The gentle wind and afternoon sun wrapped around the two as they scanned the city through the parapets of the Charlesgate's roofline.

From here, Zylla could see the river winding alongside Storrow Drive and the giant Citgo sign above Kenmore Square. She closed her eyes imagined what J.P. Putnam must have seen on his first visit to the roof. With the rest of Back Bay behind him, he would have found peace in the lush greens of the Fens and the muted teals of the Charles River.

She opened her eyes, wishing that the signs and traffic would disappear, just for an instant, so that she could experience that same peace. Instead, when she opened her eyes and turned to Jabe, the feeling she experienced was far from peaceful.

Zylla inhaled sharply.

His loose hair streamed back from his face whenever the wind blew in a certain direction. With stormy eyes, he drank in the city beneath him, his noble profile and expression indicating pride of ownership. One booted foot rested on the low wall of the roofline, his arms crossed in front of him, sunlight turning the hair on his arms to gold.

He was the Summerlord of Welsh fairytales: the mythical King Arthur descended from both human and faerie races.

My God, Zylla thought, *Lancelot was nothing compared to Jabe.*

He happened to glance at her during that moment and his breath blocked his throat at the open desire on her face. She gazed at him as if he just slew an invading army on her behalf, and the pride that settled in his chest nearly drowned him.

Five months of freedom nearly down the drain for the promise in her eyes, and he mentally shook his head.

No way, he informed his stirring loins. He knew what would happen. He would have pursued Zylla relentlessly until she fell in love with him, they'd be happy for about three months, and he'd move on to the next woman, the cycle never-ending. He had fought too hard to break that habit.

He arched a brow. Still, Zylla sprawled on his bed would be an apt spoil of war.

He scratched under his chin as he blissfully pondered that image, then exhaled loudly and grabbed the sandwich bag from the roof ledge.

"Let's eat," he said, too loudly. "I'm starved."

Zylla gave him a warm smile in agreement, and his heart lurched in response.

Nope. This was it. After today, he wouldn't see Zylla again. He tore a chunk of roast beef with his teeth as if to solidify that decision.

Seven

The phone trilled just as Zylla stepped from the bathroom. She hastily shook out her hair and wrapped a towel around herself. Ghostly tendrils of steam followed her as she scurried into the kitchen to grab the phone.

"Hello?"

She inwardly grinned at the familiar voice on the other end, and a little thrill jolted down her spine.

"It's the first of May, and I plan to celebrate this fine pagan day at the pub down the street from me. Wanna come out?"

"Sure. What time?"

"How about eight at the Brendan Behan. You know where it is?"

"I think so. Anne goes there once in a while. Centre Street, right?"

"Yep. See you soon."

Zylla hung up the phone and stood in the middle of the kitchen, water trickling down her skin to the linoleum floor. A flash of panic fluttered across her belly.

A date. What was she going to wear? She cursed her youth and wished that she had spent more time playing with dolls instead of acting out X-Men with the neighborhood boys.

By seven-thirty, clothes and shoes were strewn across her bed and floor. Why was everything she owned black? Aunt Maddie had warned her about this. "A splash of color would do you good, dear," she heard in her head. Well, at least she had the new yellow bra.

Zylla entered the Behan promptly at eight in her usual outfit of jeans, boots and tank top, all black, her yellow undergarments a secret smile to herself.

As her gaze skimmed across the small room, she appreciated the dark wood and cozy atmosphere. Already, all six tables and most of the barstools were filled with people, and Zylla could hear their cheerful voices beneath the Irish music that drifted from the speakers perched on corner shelves close to the ceiling. Gaelic road signs spotted the walls and leather bound books rested atop the mantel of the tiny, bricked-in fireplace.

Zylla was certain that Dorothy's twister had dropped a bit of Ireland in Jamaica Plain in the form of the Brendan Behan Pub. She nearly expected James Joyce to be smoking a pipe in the corner. An empty bench waited near the hearth, and Zylla claimed that as her own while she waited for Jabe.

Her leg bobbed up and down in anticipation.

"Relax, Zylla," she muttered to herself. "He's just a friend." The image of his strong jaw-line popped into her mind and she imagined that same jaw descending to hers as he took her lips in a kiss. Her leg bobbed harder.

"Aye, Jabe," the bartender called, and Zylla's glance darted toward the door. Jabe raised a hand to the bartender while his gaze searched the room. A lazy grin appeared on his face when he spotted her, and his eyes sparkled as if he and Zylla shared a private joke, before he turned his attention to the bar.

"Guinness?" the bartender asked in a booming Irish lilt.

Jabe turned to Zylla, brows raised in question. She nodded.

"Two, Dan. Thanks."

Zylla fidgeted under Jabe's stare and averted her eyes to look anywhere but at him. Instead she noticed the gawks he received from some of the women in the room.

She swallowed and looked at Jabe again. With a glint in his eyes and a knowing smile, he drove through the growing crowd, never taking his eyes off her. She returned his smile, suddenly proud that he should choose her above everyone else. In one second, he made her feel like a celebrity.

"Hello," he said as he sat next to her.

"Hello," she returned quietly.

His mouth opened, but whatever he was about to say was deafened by a deep roar.

"Thor!"

Jabe cringed.

"Thor?" she questioned, and he nodded reluctantly.

A man wearing a yellow Sex Pistols t-shirt, purple Liberty-spiked Mohawk and a crazy grin hopped over to them, leaned down, and heartily thumped Jabe on the back.

"Hey, hey, hey, Thayer. Many moons have passed, my friend."

Jabe rose, laughing, and hugged his friend, a purple spike narrowly avoiding impaling his eye. "My brother. How goes the road? Still riding?"

"Rain, snow, sleet, and Newbury Street babes, yes." His lopsided grin disappeared. "Steve was hit the other day. Broke both legs. No insurance, couldn't afford it, and his wife's just out of the hospital with a new baby girl."

Jabe nodded, his jaw clenched. The story was all too common and he clasped his friend's shoulder in commiseration. "I'll buy you a beer. Still drinking Tremont?"

"Great, thanks."

Jabe pulled Zylla to his side. "Zylla, this is Pete," he said and turned to Pete. "Pete, meet Zylla."

Jabe started toward the bar, then looked over his shoulder at Pete with a quick wink. "Don't scare her off while I'm gone."

Pete took Zylla's hand and lifted it to his lips for a kiss.

"*Mon dieu, cheri,*" he said, affecting a bad French accent. "Such beauty."

Zylla burst out laughing, and Pete grinned back.

"May I?" she asked as she removed her hand from Pete's and reached up to touch one of his Liberty spikes, so called for the fact that the wearer bore a striking resemblance to Lady Liberty, especially when the hair was dyed green.

"Of course, milady."

Zylla squished the stiff hair between her fingers and murmured, "I've always wanted onc of these."

"It takes a couple of bottles of Elmer's Wood Glue," he stated. "Come over some time and be my Barbie. We can play dress up, too."

"Ahem," a gruff voice said.

Jabe handed them their drinks and raised a brow at Pete.

"Ah, I'm just going to run to the little boys' room," Pete said. "Be right back."

Zylla, oblivious to all but the frothy brew in her hand, sipped her beer.

"Ahhhh," she sighed. "Nothing better than a pint of Guinness."

"Except for a woman who knows it," Jabe returned and raised his glass to her, earning a slow smile in return.

Damn. Her lips were entirely too chewable. Perfectly sinful. Hunger shot through his body as he looked at her.

Zylla caught the heat in his expression and dropped her eyes and, suddenly nervous, began to tap her feet to the Pogues CD playing in the background. She gained composure in listening to the salty jig and dared to glance at Jabe again.

It was a mistake.

His head lowered, he stared up at her with an expression dark with desire, and her insides dropped into her belly. His eyes smoldered, and he took a step toward her. Her soul slammed to her feet.

Too soon, too soon, her mind warned, and she took a step backward only to collide with the wall. Jabe parted his lips and she nearly dropped her pint. She had to do something to stop him before she fell under his spell. He was Svengali, and she just wasn't ready for him.

He took a step closer, and his breath warmed her face, melting her insides. Suddenly, inspiration struck.

"Thor!" she shouted.

Jabe clenched his fists, and his smolder turned to a scowl.

She laughed, somewhat relieved that the spell had shattered.

"What is this Thor business all about, anyway?"

Jabe's scowl fled and he sighed long and hard. "When I first came to Boston for grad school, I needed a part-time job, so I temped. That lasted about two days. Couldn't bear being cooped up." He sipped his beer. "So I became a bike messenger."

"Oooo, I love when those guys deliver packages," Zylla interrupted. "All sweaty and gorgeous. And they all have that Byron thing going on."

"Ahhh, are we telling the Thor story?" Pete asked, having just returned from the bathroom to hear Zylla's comment.

Jabe snarled.

"The hot young receptionists are a perk to our job as well," Pete added, with a meaningful leer.

"Yeah, well, I said as much to *The Boston Clip*'s reporter when he interviewed me about the job."

She looked at him questioningly, and he added, "He just picked me randomly off the street. Cursed by fate." Jabe rolled his eyes.

"Anyway, among listing the many hazards of the job, I jokingly added that I had become a bike messenger to ogle those hot young receptionists."

Zylla narrowed her eyes at him.

He shrugged. "Well, it *is* a perk. Anyway, *The Clip* isn't what's called a quality paper, and the reporter didn't include any of the serious discussion about the hazards of being a messenger. Instead, he described my long blond hair, stressed my receptionist comment, and dubbed me Thor, the rogue messenger hell-bent on wheelies and women."

"The Mass. Ave. Fabio," Pete said with a wide flourish of his hand.

Zylla grimaced. "Eew. Well," she considered. "At least you didn't get stuck with Fabio for a nickname. Thor is a much more respectable appellation."

Jabe groaned.

"Change of subject," Pete said as he stepped between Zylla and Jabe. "Tango?"

"Huh?"

"Would you like to tango?"

"To the Pogues?"

Pete nodded.

Zylla shrugged, gave her beer to Jabe, and held out her hand to Pete. The two stalked the floor for several seconds until mutually deciding that they had no clue how to tango.

Jabe, amused, returned Zylla's beer and jerked his head toward the bar. "I'm going to get another. You want one?"

She shook her head, indicating her half-filled glass, and Jabe went to the bar.

"How about a poem?" Pete asked her, distracting her gaze from Jabe's backside. "I composed it just for you a few seconds ago." He cleared his throat, leaned closer to her, and began to speak in a measured cadence:

"Zylla
of my heart
drifts
before me in light
and the gold in her eyes
gleams
as she slays
all the fiends
in my dreams."

He drew back and beamed.

"Wow." She smiled. "No one's ever composed a poem on the spot for me before. Thanks."

"Hmmm," he said. "You didn't fall to your knees with desire. Why is that?" Instead of waiting for her answer, he said, "Are you tired, baby? 'Cuz you've been running through my dreams all night.'

"You don't give up, do you?" she asked.

"Never."

"Well I'm going to the ladies' room. When I come back you may resume your conquest."

"Might I escort you to the facilities?"

Zylla glanced at the sign for the women's room door not five feet away.

"Certainly," she ceded, and took his arm. After three steps he bid her *adieu*.

~ * ~

"Where's Zylla?" Jabe sipped his beer as he scanned the room for her.

"Temporarily inconvenienced," Pete said. "I really like her."

Jabe grinned. "That's because she doesn't run away once you open your mouth."

"Yeah, well, so." He glanced sideways at Jabe. "You two an item?"

"No."

"Excellent. Because I think..."

Jabe clamped a hand on Pete's shoulder and, surprised by the fierce jealousy that suddenly shot through him, slowly shook his head.

"No," he said as he crossed his arms. "Forget about it."

"Aw c'mon," Pete complained. "You stole my last three prospects."

Jabe glowered. *No*, he mouthed.

She was his.

"She's mine," he clarified to a protesting Pete.

~ * ~

"Milady," Pete said to Zylla when she returned from the bathroom. "I do beg your pardon, but there seems to be a lovely blonde damsel in distress all alone by the bar."

"By all means..." She curtsied. "Do attend her."

Zylla watched his purple Mohawk as he sliced his way through the crowd.

"He's great," she said to Jabe who nodded absently.

She looked up at him, wondering at his silence.

"Listen," he said. "It's almost last call, and I live just around the corner. If you're not tired, why don't you come back to my place?"

She was tired, but she was too wound up from the beer, music, Pete's effervescence and Jabe's proximity. Her brain warned her to go home where it was safe, but her heart told her that there was no safer place than with Jabe. Every nerve within her strained to be with him.

"C'mon," he urged. "A city bar closing at one a.m. is uncivilized. Come back to my place, we'll shoot some pool and talk."

"You have a pool table?" she asked.

Jabe laughed in response.

"Whaddya say?" He raised his right hand and said with a thick burr, "On the graves of my Scottish forefathers, I won't touch you. If you get tired, lassie, you can sleep in my tartan and I'll take the thistles."

She should refuse, but she couldn't help but think that thistles wouldn't be so bad if he was in them.

"I'm up for a few games of pool," she said.

At the bartender's signal for last call, they watched as Pete scampered to the bar in exaggerated frenzy. The blonde in distress took the opportunity to escape to the ladies' room. From across the room, Zylla and Jabe laughed.

"So," Jabe asked. "How'd you like Pete's poetry?"

"It was entertaining." She grinned. "Is that a game both of you play?"

Jabe sipped from his pint. "Naw. I take the easy road and quote John Donne. He's the master of wooing women."

"Ahhh," she smiled conspiratorially. "You're confiding your seduction secrets. I guess I really am safe from your advances."

His eyelids half-closed and he gazed down at her with a strange light in his eyes. He took a step closer. "I didn't say that," he whispered in a husky voice.

Panic rose in her throat as desire swarmed through her. She put her hand on his chest in protest, but that motion only caused him to rest his hand on her hip and slowly pull her toward him.

"You promised," Zylla exclaimed, but her voice sounded weak.

"True," he admitted with a lopsided grin and inwardly cursed his honor. He raised his pint to her and downed the rest in one gulp. "I may not be a saint, but I do have my morals."

Eight

The sprawling Queen Anne set atop a low hill would have been, in Zylla's opinion, the perfect haunted house. Painted in dark grays and plums with blood red accent, Jabe's Jamaica Plain home was a veritable Addams Family mansion.

He unhitched the wrought iron gate, and they walked up the winding, cobblestone path to the front steps. Continuing around the porch, they entered through the side door that opened into a state-of-the-art stainless steel kitchen.

To the right, a flight of stairs led upstairs. Jabe reached above him and twisted the switch on an antique wall sconce so that light flooded the stairwell. On the second floor, Jabe led Zylla into the dark greens and reds of his bedroom, then strode across the room to open the door to what seemed to be a large walk-in closet.

Zylla shot him a questioning glance, but he was already in the closet, his back to her. She watched as the back panel of the closet slid into the wall. Yawning darkness beckoned.

Jabe turned to her with a mischievous grin before he stepped into the darkness. Seconds later, soft light revealed a smaller chamber made out of barnboard.

"C'mon," he said. "This is the best part."

She hesitantly stepped through the first closet and took his outstretched hand. The second room was actually a landing for a twisting staircase. At the bottom, Jabe let go of her hand and groped in the darkness until he found a lamp.

Zylla's mouth dropped open as light permeated the darkness. They had emerged into a huge rectangular chamber. The barnboard walls and thick floor-to-ceiling posts were covered with antique-framed sepia-tone photographs, posters from nineteen twenties France, ancient swords, Civil War rifles, wagon wheels and other antique store paraphernalia. Worn rugs sprinkled the widely planked floors and overstuffed chairs and sofas welcomed a visitor to sink into their velvet haven.

"I'll get the chill out of here in a second," he commented as he walked toward the giant fieldstone fireplace.

"Great," she said. "Do you need a couple of roommates, by any chance?" she jested. "Anne cooks up a storm, and I have a thing for cleaning."

He laughed and rested a hand on the stone mantel. "This room is the whole reason I bought this place. The house was falling apart, but there's a lot of land here, for a city, and the house is meant for Halloween." A sheepish grin spread across his face. "My favorite holiday," he added.

Jabe paused as he lit the kindling and shook the match to extinguish the flame. "But then I saw this room, and it was all over."

"What was it originally? A wine cellar?" she guessed as she sat on the green velvet sofa in front of the hearth and ran a finger along the smooth wood of a sea chest that served as a coffee table.

Jabe stood with a sigh. "I'm not sure," he puzzled. "It was purposely built with the house—the wall with the fireplace is the side of the main house. This room is adjacent to the basement but juts out much farther than the main house. There is only land above us," he explained.

"The previous owners said that it was a speakeasy in the twenties, but it was just a dirt cellar when I bought the place." He looked around him. "It's my haven."

He paused, lost in thought, and asked, "You want a drink?"

"Sure," she replied and twisted her head to watch him stride to the far end of the room, which was still shrouded in darkness. He flipped a switch and a calming blue light highlighted a black-topped, fieldstone bar. A red felt pool table waited in front of the bar.

Zylla gasped and bolted from the couch to the back of the room. "I'll rack up."

His eyebrows shot up in surprise. He didn't think she was serious about wanting to play pool. He used the excuse merely as a pretense to spend more time with her. Usually, women he brought here didn't know how to play, didn't want to know how to play, and only used the game as a chance to slink around the table in micro mini skirts, which was fine with him, but a woman who could actually shoot was something else altogether.

"Great," he said. "Do you want another Guinness? I have it on tap."

"You have Guinness on tap?" she asked then ran around the bar to ascertain that for herself.

"Jabe," she stated. "You are a god."

He looked down at her with eyes so darkly green and burning that she unconsciously swayed toward him.

"And you," he murmured, "are a goddess." He bent his head and leaned in to claim her lips. Jabe felt her sweet breath on his mouth and reality smacked him. He jolted back and returned to building the Guinness. If she didn't quit looking at him with those liquid eyes, he was going to forget his promise to her.

Zylla, on the other hand, was confused. All of the sudden the atmosphere suddenly changed from one of mirth to one of tension and she couldn't clear her head to think because her blood was riled from his almost-kiss.

Jabe handed her the pint and stalked to the pool table. He grabbed a hunk of blue chalk and scrubbed at the tip of his cue, lips a grim line. They played three games without speaking a word and Zylla soundly beat him each time. Jabe won the fourth game, but he suspected that she had purposely missed a couple of shots. He stared at her with hooded eyes.

"I couldn't let your ego be destroyed by a mere girl," she confessed, biting her lip in mock remorse.

He smiled and the tension in the room fled.

"Do you play?" she asked, indicating banjo suspended on the wall.

She followed Jabe to the sitting area near the fire and sat while he took his banjo from the wall then sank down next to her on the sofa. The fire blazing, Zylla sipped her drink, whiskey now, as Jabe played an old mountain tune.

He stopped mid-song, cursed, and stood. "I can't believe I forgot to show you..." he muttered, walking briskly to the back of the room and lifting a large framed document from the wall.

"I meant to point this out first thing."

Zylla cleared the coffee table as he returned, and he placed the item down. Jabe's family tree.

"I figured you would want to see this," he said, pointing to the name *Catherine [Unknown Surname]*. "Caval's sister," he added.

"So, Caval took Lydia's surname because he didn't have one of his own. How romantic." she said.

Zylla looked at the names and lines in front of her, the intricate design they made. A complete picture, a map, a piece of art.

"This is beautiful," she said with a catch in her voice. "You are so lucky to have this, to know your history."

Jabe had forgotten about their lunch on the Charlesgate roof when Zylla related the tense conversation with her aunt. "You don't know your family tree at all?" he prodded.

Zylla shook her head, then amended, "Well, I know my paternal side, all the way back to the Byzantine Empire, in fact. My father had it all computerized. But it's my maternal line that is a mystery. All the crazy stories..."

Jabe thought for a moment. "You could have it traced, or do it yourself for that matter, since you're so good with research."

He stood and walked backwards to the bar. "Want another?"

At Zylla's nod, he spun around to walk forward. "I guess you'd start with your mother's records and track from there," he called from the bar.

"Yes," Zylla replied absentmindedly as she perused the names on Jabe's family tree. With her finger, she traced the names of his parents, Jenny and Scott, and older brother, Kent. A sister, Maggie, died at five months. Further back, next to Catherine's name, Jabe had written Caval in blue ink. Her eyes followed the Thayer line to the top where it began with Admiral Jabez W. Thayer, Scotland, b. sixteen hundred and sixty-eight. She smiled. So this was where Jabe's name hailed.

"What's the 'W' for?" she called.

Jabe smiled as he walked back to the couch and sank onto it.

"Here you go." He handed her the beer. "It stands for 'Wayland'. It's my middle name as well. Welsh," he explained. "It means 'from the forest' or something like that."

"It suits you." She smiled.

"There's a bit of a story around Old Captain Jabez."

A lock of wheat colored hair fell forward from behind his ear, and Zylla's fingers itched to push it back for him.

"He had a lover, a noblewoman of some sort, I think. She was found guilty of treason, and my ancestor sentenced her to death." Jabe snorted. "Some love, huh?"

He rubbed the growth under his chin, his brow furrowed in concentration. "The lady was very wealthy and as a reward for his loyalty, the English king turned the fortune over to the admiral. So the lady, on her scaffold, cursed the money and swore that all Thayer men would be unhappy in love."

Zylla's eyes snapped merriment at his tale, and Jabe grinned, revealing one perfect dimple.

"I knew you'd appreciate that story."

"Any truth to the curse?"

"I don't believe in curses," he stated. "But I will admit that there's been more than a fair share of misery in the Thayer family, most of it self-inflicted."

Hesitating, he studied her for a moment. "There's a lot of wealth in the Thayer family," he confided and studied her reaction.

She nodded once, urging him to continue, and he let out a quiet sigh of relief.

Upon finding out about his wealth, most women immediately acted differently around him. Some draped themselves all over him, willing slaves, while others that had ignored him before suddenly treated him like a king. Still other women turned away coldly, as if he were a speck of dog shit on the bottom of their expensive heels. All had one trait in common: a strange light, jealous greed, glinted in their eyes.

Zylla, he was pleased to discover, was not like most women. He sensed that the sparkle in her eyes was for the romance of the story, and he wished that he had buckets of such tales to spill for her.

"To a believer in hexes, the money does seem cursed." He shrugged. "Others would say it was abused. It all depends on how you look at it."

Smiling, he added, "You, I suspect, would say cursed."

She laughed in agreement. "And you?"

"Abused. There's so much drinking, divorce, gambling, and violence down the whole Thayer history. Instead of being selfless with money, they learned to be selfish."

He took a deep breath. "That's why I've decide to use my share of the money to restore the Charlesgate and run it like Putnam planned."

Zylla tackled him, and Jabe toppled backwards into the pillows.

"Oh, you are the absolute best!" she exclaimed and blessed his cheek with kisses.

Jabe went stock-still and his features became granite. Zylla drew back, blushing.

"Sorry," she said, "I didn't mean to jump you."

Jabe let his breath out in a slow exhale. "Honey, you can jump me any time you want."

His voice was a ragged growl, and Zylla swallowed hard before scrambling off of him.

"You can stay there, you know," he said, amused. "I don't mind."

"What..." She cleared her throat and looked down, frowning at her hands. "What about you? What Thayer vice do you own?"

"Well, I like to drink, but not excessively. And lord knows I wouldn't mind being Mad Max, so maybe violence is a problem, but I guess my misery is women."

He gazed at the dying embers of the fire and murmured, "If I ever find a woman who truly understands me, I'll never let her go."

~ * ~

Using her finger as best she could, Zylla brushed her teeth with toothpaste, then swished water around the inside of her mouth. Now it tasted like Guinness and toothpaste, an unsettling combination, but better, she thought, than orange juice and toothpaste and at least the grit was gone from her teeth.

She switched off the bathroom light and walked into Jabe's room to undress in the gray gloom of predawn. She pulled on the worn Ramones t-shirt that Jabe had loaned her, and inhaled the clean scent of laundry detergent and something that was entirely Jabe.

Zylla sighed. She really liked him. He was smart, capable, fun, and it didn't hurt that he looked like a walking romance novel. And, she admitted ruefully, she was a tad bit jealous of that woman he had not yet found.

She crawled between his sheets and snuggled into his warm scent, easily falling into a sleep and a dream of Jabe standing proud on a hilltop, wind rushing through his hair, a green plaid kilt rustling against his bare legs, and a claymore in his hands.

Pain woke her, and she groaned as she prepared to get up to go to Jabe's kitchen for an icepack to ease the migraine. She struggled to open her eyes, to sit up, but she couldn't, and she knew it was happening again, even before the stench of the rotting sea hit her nostrils.

Behind her eyes, black and red waves heaved and boiled, tossing a ship from one swell to another, the cold wind whipping the ship's frayed Jolly Roger. She heard the tortured cries of the crew and above that, the low cackle of a woman.

Terror gripped Zylla and although she was partially awake, she fought to come to full consciousness. She managed to open her eyes, the blinding pain piercing her brain.

The walls moved. They undulated and wavered, revealing faces, distorted and cruel, as they pushed from the walls. Moans and hisses surrounded her in a tornado of threats, and Zylla screamed, but no sound burst from her lips.

The only answer her soundless plea received was the snicker of the mad pirate woman who appeared with these episodes. Zylla squished her eyes shut to no avail. The snarled black hair and violet-red eyes loomed over her, and a screech stabbed her eardrums. She blocked her ears with both hands and waited. It was almost over now. The vision, nightmare, whatever it was, always dissipated after this point. Just one more trial to go through.

Slowly, she opened her eyes, and the woman pushed back her web of hair to reveal her mouth, which was stapled with black stitches, caked with dried blood.

Then something happened that had never occurred before.

Two bloody hands reached forward and clutched Zylla's arms while fear curdled in her stomach. The stench of rotting fish was unbearable as the creature leaned closer, the ends of her hair brushing Zylla's face.

She whimpered, and the pirate moaned, as if in pain. Her mouth moved, and Zylla watched, in wide-eyed repulsion, as the stitches ripped through the cracked flesh of her lips and the mouth started to open.

She gasped and sat up straight in bed. It was over. The soft pink light of full morning revealed no monsters hiding in the corners, no blood smudges on her arms where the pirate clutched her. Her frantic breaths slowed, and she hugged herself and rubbed her arms to chase away the lingering remnants of the nightmare.

Her eye still pounding, she stepped out of bed and silently crept down the stairs to the kitchen.

~ * ~

He just plain liked her.

Jabe pulled his grandmother's soft afghan to his chin and stretched out on the velvet sofa, watched the last sparks of the fire die, and thought of Zylla asleep in his bed.

He liked her reserve and quiet beauty, her sudden bursts of passion, her humor and intelligence, and that she could drink whiskey without cringing. He liked the fact that she wore combat boots and still walked like a woman should walk, all curves and silent invitation.

But the woman screamed sex and two minutes in her presence sent blood roaring to his ears and screaming to his loins. He had to have her.

Dammit. He punched the back of the sofa. No way was he going to pursue this. Attraction faded. Just a couple of months, maybe a little longer in this case, then they could safely be friends.

But damn her lips, he thought as he punched the sofa one more time, rolled onto his side, and went to sleep.

A crash startled him from sleep, and he bolted from the couch and stumbled into his discarded boxers before racing up the stairs to his empty bedroom and down another flight into the kitchen.

~ * ~

"Wanna make me a cup, too?"

Zylla spun around.

"I'm sorry," she lamented. "I dropped the kettle. Didn't mean to wake you."

He waved a hand. "Don't worry about it. The sun's up. It's officially morning and I make a mean bacon and egg platter."

"With buttered toast?"

He nodded. "Lots of butter."

"In that case," she said, turning off the gas, "we need coffee. Tea is far too civilized for a breakfast like that."

As he approached, Jabe noticed her taut, pale face and haunted eyes.

"Hey," he said gently, lifting her chin with his hand. "Is something wrong?"

"I woke up with a migraine. Still hurts a little bit, but it's going away. If you have any ibuprofen, that'd be great."

Jabe stretched over her to open the cabinet above her head, and she saw only the broad expanse of his chest with its smooth, golden skin and crisp hairs. She closed her eyes and seemed to inhale the morning sun, the warm heat of his body enveloping her, causing her to sway on her feet. If she could just touch that heat, she knew the pain would go away.

Without thinking, she leaned forward and rested her forehead on Jabe's chest. One strong arm encircled her as he dropped the tablets on the counter behind Zylla to hold her in both arms. His lips brushed the top of her hair, and she snuggled into him.

"You're shaking," he whispered, then pushed her hair behind her ear to look at her face.

Jabe frowned. He could see the pain in her eyes—her usual spark was gone, but what worried him more was the speck of fear that crouched in the russet depths.

"What's wrong?" he asked, more gruffly than he intended. "It's something more than the migraine."

Zylla bit her lower lip. Only Anne and her Aunt Maddie knew about her strange fits. She had been seven when the first episode occurred. Startled awake by a nasty odor, Zylla watched in horror as the pink and white striped wallpaper of her bedroom had undulated and groaned. A long, bony hand slipped around the edge of the closet door and Zylla looked up to see a deranged face peering at her.

She screamed and screamed for Aunt Maddie, who had been in the next room. Zylla could hear the rustling of student papers as Maddie corrected them.

Within minutes, the episode ended and Zylla had run to Maddie, sobbing. Her aunt had convinced her that it was a dream and that she had not heard Zylla's screams, but when similar episodes periodically occurred, along with the onset of migraines, Maddie had ushered Zylla to a neurologist.

"I'm fine, really," Zylla answered and studied the terra cotta floor tiles.

Jabe was silent.

Sighing, Zylla said, "I've had what my doctor calls sleep paralysis narcolepsy. I haven't had an episode in a while, and this one was worse than usual."

She kept her eyelids lowered in apprehension of his reaction. When he didn't speak, she dared a peek. She saw nothing but concern and comfort in his eyes, and Zylla drew courage from his patient expression.

"It's very mild," she continued. "Not like the kind where you fall asleep suddenly. The doctor says that these episodes sometime occur with migraine disorder. It sometimes happens when I haven't slept well for a few days. It's pretty scary. I'm dreaming but awake at the same time."

"What do you mean?" he asked.

She shook her head slowly. "I don't know how to explain it. It's like being trapped between sleeping and waking. I guess it's a hallucination of sorts, like you're stuck in a haunted house for a few seconds."

One corner of her mouth turned up. “Sometimes I think I’m going crazy, but Aunt Maddie assures me that I was born crazy so I have nothing to worry about.”

Jabe chuckled and ran a thumb along a dark circle under her eye. “You sure you’re okay?”

“Yeah, really.” She shrugged. “They’re kind of inspiring, the nightmares. They’re always about pirate ships and a crazy pirate woman. I have no clue why, must have been something from my childhood, but pirate lore is now a hobby of mine.”

She gave him a sweet, brave smile, and he pulled her tight against him as if the action could chase away her demons. A low grumbling from her stomach rewarded him.

“Jabe?”

“Yeah?”

“Can I get that breakfast now?” she mumbled against his shoulder.

“Darlin’, you can have whatever you want,” he said as he stepped away from her. “I’ll get you some water first so you can take your medicine.”

Jabe rubbed his arms, trying to erase how empty they suddenly felt. He tried to ignore the longing to carry her into his bedroom and wear away her pain with his body and instead concentrated on other ways to help her.

“Why don’t you put on some of your lavender?” he asked as he poured coffee beans into the grinder. “I heard that’s supposed to help headaches.”

The grinding of the coffee filled the kitchen, drowning Zylla’s reply.

“You know,” Jabe continued. “A few girlfriends ago, I bought one of those scented candles to, uh, set a romantic mood. I think it was lavender. I’ll go look for it after I get the coffee going.”

Zylla gave a startled laugh. “You measure time by ex-girlfriends? Remind me to never date you.”

He flicked the switch on the coffeepot and turned to her, his eyes hot and serious.

"Why not?" he murmured. "I'll treat you like gold and I'll never cheat on you."

Zylla's eyes widened and she swallowed the sweetness of his words as he trotted up the stairs.

~ * ~

"Ah, so the prodigal roommate returns." Anne glanced up from *The New York Times* crossword as Zylla entered into the kitchen.

Zylla beamed.

"So, my little Artemis, did you show off your new yellow lingerie?" she asked as she waggled her brows.

"No," she emphasized. "Nothing happened. Not really, anyway. He slept on the couch."

"With all that hair there is the possibility that he's gay," Anne pondered. "Although that's my department." She studied Zylla's tired but glowing face. "You are all sparkly and happy though."

Zylla sighed as she sank into the chair opposite Anne. "I have a wee crush."

"And is it reciprocal? Or are you on another Mike Sullivan adventure?"

"I don't know." Zylla pouted. "He seems like he wants to kiss me, but he hasn't tried. He did cook breakfast, though, and he took care of me when I had one of those episodes."

Anne grimaced. "You okay?"

Zylla nodded. "Uh-huh. All gone. What did you do this weekend?"

Anne sipped her coffee and made a face. "Blech. I'll make a fresh pot. Um, I hung out with my sister in Concord. We watched horror flicks and tried to figure out what's wrong with the new guy I'm dating."

"Billy?"

Zylla grabbed Anne's crossword and studied it absentmindedly.

"Yeah. He's gorgeous, kind, smart, stable, and he plays drums in a garage band for fun." She sighed. "I'm just waiting for him to tell me he's been in love with his male bass player for the past ten years."

She handed Zylla a cup of coffee. "Oh, I almost forgot. Your Uncle John called. Something about some family research you're doing. You gonna call in sick again tomorrow to work in the library?"

Zylla muttered, "I wish." She tapped a pencil against her lip and frowned at the crossword.

"If you quit your job, you can do it full time," Anne sang, then scowled at Zylla. "Hey, give me back my crossword."

Zylla returned the crossword then picked up her coffee. The memory of Jabe playing his banjo popped into her mind. *Jabe.* She smiled. He even had a romantic name. She thought of how his right hand, large and strong, had deftly picked the strings of the instrument and how he had looked at her with hot eyes. Zylla jumped up from the table, upsetting the coffees and causing Anne's pen to skip across the page. Anne tossed her a reproving look.

"Sorry," Zylla said as she wiped the mess with a paper towel. "I'll just go in the other room and call my uncle."

Uncle John picked up after two rings.

"Zylla Berry. How's my little witch?" He chuckled, merriment in his voice.

"Great. And how's my favorite uncle?"

"Oh, pretty well, pretty well. What's this you want to know about the family tree?"

Zylla explained her library research and Aunt Maddie's odd behavior.

"Yep, Mad tends to be a mite over-protective of you. She doesn't want to lose you like we lost our sister, that's all. But I admit, she does get odd when the family ghost and the hex is mentioned."

"What hex?" Zylla asked, suddenly excited.

"Oh, you know, something about Berry women and violent deaths. Just old stories. Nobody really knows. I never believed in any ghost. I think it's something our mother made up. She was crazy, you know."

He coughed. "Gotta quit these cancer sticks, dammit."

Zylla waited for him to catch his breath.

"Now, Mad doesn't believe in curses, or didn't anyways, but when Cindy and your pap died, and your grandmother right after, I think Madeleine got scared. Our family does seem to have a lot of untimely deaths and, from what I recollect from the family tree, they were all female.

"That's childbirth for you," Zylla said.

"Mebbe so. Mebbe so. But your Aunt Maddie got scared, like I said, and got her temper up whenever anyone mentioned the curse. She even tore up the only copy of the family tree. It was old and faded anyway, but she angered a lot of the Berrys when she did that."

Great blotches of red popped in Zylla's head and her ears buzzed. How dare Maddie destroy her past? All she had of her parents and ancestors?

Silence crackled until Uncle John swore. "Dammit, Zylla. You're just like your mother—I can feel that temper right over the wire. Now cut it out. Maddie was wrong, but she thinks she did what was best for you."

"But..." Zylla sputtered.

"But nothing. Calm down or I won't tell you what I do recollect from the tree."

Zylla quieted instantly.

"Now it ain't much. But that name you mentioned, that Caval, well, I recollect it because it was a weird name. Poor kid must have been beat up awful good with a name like that. Anyways, he did marry a Berry girl. Lydia was her name, and they died on the same day."

Zylla barely heard the remainder of the conversation and couldn't remember hanging up the phone. Zombie-like, she walked into the kitchen and slumped into a chair to stare blankly at the clock.

"What's up?" Anne looked up from her crossword and reached for an orange from the blue fruit bowl to gently toss it between her hands before settling down to the task of peeling it.

An orange tang filled the yellow and white kitchen and as they shared the fruit, Zylla related her library discoveries, Aunt Maddie's strange behavior, the conversation with Uncle John, and the confirmation that her ancestor, Lydia, was married to Jabe's ancestor Caval.

"Did you tell Jabe about the connection?" Anne questioned.

Zylla shrugged. "He sort of guessed as much. He thought that it would be weird if Lydia Berry wasn't one of my Berrys."

She bit into another slice of orange.

"Fate," Anne stated.

"Hmmmmm," Zylla said. "Let me see some of that crossword and tell me more about this Billy."

Nine

"Monday, Monday," Zylla sang, mourning the start of yet another workweek and mentally counting the years to retirement.

It wasn't that she hated her job. Not really. It passed the time from nine to one. By then, her work was complete and more often than not, she would spend the rest of the day browsing the Internet.

Last week, inspired by Jabe's family tree, she had spent her afternoons emailing genealogical societies and drafting her own family tree. She still had a lot of digging to do, but she felt pleased with the few twigs that had already sprouted.

Last night, she had dreamed about pirates, stormy seas, and foreign ports—thankfully, it had been just a dream and no pirate with sewn lips and bloody hands harassed her. The dream had been so real that Zylla actually felt seasick upon waking, and for a moment, she longed to live in another time. She planned to spend today reading about seventeenth-century pirates on the Internet.

Now, Zylla turned on the computer and while it booted, she stared at the rain splashing her office window and didn't feel much like doing anything. Dean Pendergast was out of town, and the students were gone for the summer. Zylla had absolutely nothing to do except pick lint off the floor.

She was so unenthused that a whole day to spend researching pirates and her ancestral history seemed like a chore. The day yawned before her, and the gloom of outside seemed to seep into her office. Discontent slithered down her spine and guilt at having nothing to do welled in her belly.

She reminded herself that she had completed all of her assignments and even prepared for the next semester. The dean had just given her a yearly review and was more than pleased. She was paid well, had great benefits, and truly enjoyed her coworkers.

Zylla ignored her discomfort and suppressed her jealousy of the recently matriculated students, each one certain of their place in the world. If only what she was meant to do would scream out at her, then she would have a good start, but her heart's content barely murmured from deep in her body. What could she do with what she knew?

Each time the answer seemed to bubble to the surface, Zylla hastily busied herself with some unimportant task like cleaning her computer screen or watering the office plants. Distracted, she convinced herself that for now, it was enough to be free of the Mike obsession. The rest would come later, she was certain. And if the guilt-laced panic then crawled from its home in the tips of her toes, she would conquer a slightly more difficult task, like reorganizing Dean Pendergast's already color-coded files and blame the little ripples of nervousness on caffeine.

~ * ~

"Whatcha doin'?"

Zylla looked up and blinked at Anne, then glanced back to the notebook in front of her.

"Writing. I keep having dreams about pirates—I think from all the research I've been doing, and since I can't stop thinking about the dreams, I've started a dream journal. It's kind of fun, actually."

"Huh. Well, I'm going to bed. Got an early meeting tomorrow."

"G'night."

Zylla stayed up late to record all her dreams, and although tired, was happier the next morning. She spent the day on the Internet, reading about the female pirate Grace O'Malley.

Grace's life was so appealing that Zylla worked all day Saturday writing a character sketch about a beautiful, powerful female pirate who owned a fleet of ships, but only sailed on her favorite vessel. Zylla named it *Charnwood*.

She worked on her tale so late into the night without a break that she woke up at three o'clock in the morning with severe nausea and stabbing pain around her left eye. She stumbled into the kitchen for an ice pack and migraine medication and returned to bed for a sleep troubled by another narcoleptic episode.

This time, she dealt with her fear of the nightmare by sketching the woman with sewn lips into her dream journal. Finished, she held the sketch out in front of her, pleased that her unpracticed drawing skills were still intact.

She gave a little laugh as she saw that she had romanticized her nightmare demon on paper and made her a formidable Amazon.

"There's my pirate queen," Zylla whispered to herself.

Tall and shaped like an hourglass, the pirate held the cross-armed, leg-spread stance of a strong man. Her long black hair formed errant tendrils around her sharply lined face, and her eyes spit fire and madness. Her mouth was the only feminine feature about her, but the upper lip was curled in such a snarl that no man would dare approach her.

She placed the picture on the kitchen table and went to her room to get her notebook with the pirate tale. When she returned, Anne was leaning over the table, studying the sketch.

"What's her name?"

Zylla's brow creased in thought. "You know, I can't figure that out. I even looked at one of those name-your-baby sites on the Web."

Anne smiled sweetly. "You could name her Anne."

Zylla stuck out her tongue.

"Whatcha going to do with all your scribbling?"

Zylla shrugged. "You know me. Just my current obsession. I'll get tired of it after a while and shove it in my desk. Besides, it keeps my mind off Jabe."

"He hasn't called in a while, huh?"

"Nope," Zylla sighed. "He called me at work a couple of times to ask questions about my Charlesgate research, but that's it. That's okay," she added quickly, although her heart sank just a couple of inches. "We're friends. There may have been some attraction there, but friendship is better anyway."

"Liar," Anne called as she headed out the door.

Zylla nodded then returned to her notes, letting herself become lost in the world of violence and treasure. When Monday came once again, she barely noticed.

~ * ~

"Oh, God." Jabe's head collapsed on top of his folded arms that rested on the table.

The maelstrom of reconstruction had descended upon him and swept him into complete chaos. His temporary office in the Charlesgate, littered with blueprints and coffee cups, served as a tollbooth for construction workers, heating and air system consultants, plasterers, stonemasons, and reporters interested in the activity surrounding the long abandoned building.

The impossibility of his path wore at him until Jabe ultimately doubted his decision to restore the grand dame of Boston's Back Bay.

And the money! When he thought about the money that poured through his fingers for renovations, he shuddered. Millions of dollars from his dissolved trust were feeding the project. His workers thought he was slightly crazy, risking all for one dump of a building. Even Dennis referred to the building as the Bride of Frankenstein.

Of course, the men had no idea of the amount of money in Jabe's trust fund, and that it was no risk to Jabe to use that money. But Jabe's conscience twinged nonetheless. That money could support many future generations of Thayers and establish a few charities for the city. *Was it right to use it for one building?*

Jabe raised his head and peered through the door at the dark hall, quiet now that the men had gone home for the day. It was worth it, he resolved, only if he achieved his goal of continuing Putnam's plans. He squared his shoulders against the cold fear of failure that stalked him.

He would not lose his home or his business, but he sensed that a large part of himself was now intertwined with the fate of the Charlesgate. If the end result was just a solidly restored apartment building, quickly completed and just as quickly filled with tenants, a business deal, like all the other housing complex jobs he'd completed, then he would be a failure.

Alternatively, if every nook and cranny was restored to their original state, but exorbitant rents were charged to compensate for the monetary loss, therefore housing only wealthy clients, again, he would fail.

Only a complete restoration and the fulfillment of Putnam's ideas of a communal micro-society—rich, middle class, and poor living in healthy, luxurious conditions, would bring Jabe a sense of fulfillment. In a way, Jabe felt as if he owed this to the souls of the architect and his ancestor's brother, Caval. The process, he thought with a wry grin, might shorten the fate line of his own soul, however.

With a long sigh, he rubbed the back of his neck with one hand and pressed his eyes with the fingers of the other. He had not taken a break in two weeks. He worked alongside his crews during the day, but long after the men left at five o'clock, Jabe could be found in his office, studying floor plans and amending his own project management outlines. He subsisted on pizza, coffee, and antacids, but raced to and from his home in Jamaica Plain on his bicycle, instead of his Indian, in hopes of countering the effects of a less-than-wholesome diet with exercise.

Alone in the Charlesgate during the long nights and weekends, Jabe labored to create on paper the visions he held in his mind. He foresaw what the building could be, what she *deserved* to be. Underneath the cheap drywall, rotted wood, and chunks of fallen plaster, he envisioned shiny wood, potted ferns, and the gilded sparkle of the cage elevator. He heard music sprinkled with the laughter of patrons who would visit the Charlesgate's newly opened restaurant. He felt the warm breeze that would toss the white gossamer draperies separating the dining room and English garden.

During the workdays, however, Jabe was plagued with doubts and disorder. Dust, pandemonium, and an overwhelming feeling accompanied historical renovation—hell, any renovation. But the Charlesgate had been raped and beaten repeatedly over the years, and her core was reduced to insanity. Although Jabe had all the money to bring her back, he didn't have the time to neglect his other properties and construction business. He was practically living with the building now, and he still couldn't wade through her armor of problems to coax even a glimpse of a smile from her facade.

Jabe had hired teams of workers to solve her issues. City inspectors visited him daily, and pulling permits from them was like digging out one's own abscessed wisdom tooth without anesthesia. Heating and air consultants, fire safety engineers, electricians, and Jabe himself infiltrated her walls to determine the best approach to install state-of-the-art systems, only to encounter mazes of faulty wires and other fire hazards. In their investigations, the fire safety consultant discovered a narrow passageway surrounding the entire basement. Apparently, the tunnel served no purpose in the construction of the building and both Jabe and the engineer were perplexed to its existence.

"Perhaps there was some truth to smuggling tunnels that ran to the sea after all," Jabe mentioned to the engineer, remembering his conversation with Zylla.

Occasionally, he ripped down drywall to reveal thick, double-brick walls and sometimes, in these walls, he found whole rooms with mahogany pocket doors, nearly untouched by time. Occasionally, he glanced up to see gorgeous plaster ceilings, intricately molded and carved with whimsical designs. Boston's best plasterers were already bidding for the painstaking but highly profitable job of ceiling restoration.

Yet much of the building had been gutted and hacked when the building had been converted to a dorm. The wide skylight that allowed an arrow of sunlight to pierce the very center of the building had been torn out long ago and covered with a crude tar roof. The beauty of the open-air first floor dining rooms had been walled to construct industrial kitchens and cafeterias for college students.

Kitchens and bathrooms in each apartment no longer existed, and now dorm lavatories, dingy and dark, needed to be torn out. He still shivered in revulsion when he remembered the swarm of cockroaches that had sped away when he had switched on the light of a second-floor bathroom. Exterminators arrived every single day to decimate the rodent and cockroach infestation of the building. It was a full-fledged war, which the exterminators would eventually win, but in the meantime, Jabe flinched every time the tip of a rat's tail whipped or cockroach scurried out of view.

The building herself seemed to thwart him. Tools went missing, men came to blows over nothing, and the general atmosphere of the building with its gloom, creaks, faded hues, and shifting shadows lent an air of depression, which his men had acquired.

All construction jobs had their fair share of accidents, but the Charlesgate seemed to have a freakish amount. Broken bones, concussions, and severe headaches plagued his men, and more than one worker had voiced complaints that the dead fish smell from the empty basement made them ill. More than once, Jabe witnessed Frank jerk his head to the side in alarm and quickly make the sign of the cross.

"What was that all about?" Jabe had asked at one such time.

Frank had laughed nervously and shrugged. "Just thought I saw somethin', boss. Been inhalin' too much plaster dust."

The hair on Jabe's arms rose, despite Frank's dismissal, and he reluctantly searched the shadows. He had found nothing, of course, but it had unnerved him just the same.

Yet at precisely these moments, when he felt like leaving his damaged lady to the rats, he would feel a cool breeze on the back of his neck and he would imagine that he could smell Zylla's lavender. Only for a second. But just enough to remind him of Zylla and her brilliant smile when he told her of his decision to restore the Charlesgate.

He felt the breeze now although no windows were open in the office, and Jabe inhaled the lavender that scented the gentle wind.

"Thanks, Casper," he whispered to the still room and thought of Zylla.

He couldn't wait to see her again, to feel the electric currents that passed between them, and to hear her easy laughter. He would take a break from this Byzantine mess this weekend, he thought, then cursed as he remembered his 'date' on Friday night. An ex-girlfriend was coming to town, the one that reminded him of an Irish Setter, and he promised her weeks ago that he would take her to see the Cosmic Psychos at the Middle East.

Saturday, then, he'd see Zylla on Saturday.

Ten

"Hey," Anne called as she strolled into the living room where Zylla stared at the television. "It's Friday night and we're sitting here like two pathetic high school girls waiting for our crushes to call us. We're going out."

Zylla had stared blankly at Anne during her outburst, then returned to watching television. The History Channel had just started a program about female pirates and Zylla was quite content to sprawl on the couch and munch popcorn.

"I'm not going out."

Anne whimpered. "Oh pul-lease come out with me. One of those *grrrrr* bands that you like are playing at the Middle East," she cajoled.

Zylla held out the bowl of popcorn to Anne, a speck of curiosity on her face. "Oh yeah? Who?"

Anne chomped on a kernel, forehead furrowed as she tried to remember.

"The Cosmic Psychos," she exclaimed triumphantly. "Please, will you come?"

"Okay. Only for you."

"Yay! I'll go get dressed."

Anne scampered to her room, and Zylla continued to watch the show. Thirty minutes later, Anne yelled for Zylla and wearily, she rose and ambled into Anne's room.

"Wow. You look great."

Anne wore a brown leather miniskirt, suede thigh-high boots and a red silk blouse. She looked like a model. Zylla nodded.

"Yup. Perfect. Ready to go?"

"Are you going like that?" Anne's face was a mask of horror.

Zylla glanced down at her black pullover and jeans.

"Well, yeah. What's wrong with what I'm wearing?"

"Zyll, we are going to a nightclub," Anne flatly stated.

"Yes, and it's the Middle East, not Lansdowne Street," Zylla retorted sarcastically. "Besides, with the band we're seeing, it's safer in combat boots than in those flimsy things you're wearing."

Anne shrugged and patted her shoulder affectionately.

"My little Zylla. I know there's a girl in there somewhere. Let's go," she finished with a sigh.

"Oh, wait." She stopped short and spun on her heel, nearly causing Anne to slam into her. "I forgot to turn off the TV."

Anne waved her back. "I'll do it. Do you want me to stick a tape in?"

"Naw, don't bother. I missed most of it anyway. It's cable. It'll be on again."

In the living room, Anne grabbed the remote and started to push the power button when she heard the narrator finish, "*and that was the end of the exploits of the pirate Charlotte de Berry.*"

Oh, cool, Anne thought. *I have to remember to tell Zylla about that.*

After turning off the living room light, however, the entire apartment was bathed in darkness, and Anne stubbed her toe on a kitchen chair. The pain shot up her leg and she swore loudly, hopping on one booted foot. By the time she met Zylla on the front porch, Anne had entirely forgotten about the program.

~ * ~

"And there he is," Anne crooned, her gaze focused on a spot across the smoky downstairs room at the Middle East. Zylla followed Anne's gaze and spotted Jabe leaning against the bar in blue jeans, white t-shirt, and inky motorcycle boots. "Wow," she said.

"Now aren't you glad we came out?" Anne beamed as she turned to her friend, only to witness Zylla's eyes narrow and her upper lip curl. Anne looked behind her and this time saw a red-haired vixen smeared all over a smiling Jabe.

Zylla opened her mouth to speak to Anne, but found that her throat had locked. She inwardly flinched in surprise. The jealousy strangling her insides was uncalled for, she reminded herself. Jabe was nothing to her. Or rather, she amended, she was nothing to Jabe. Besides, jealousy was a ridiculous emotion, completely useless. She let out a breath and felt immediately saner.

"Uh-oh," Anne warned. "We've been spotted."

Reason abandoned Zylla and her stomach began to munch on itself.

"Easy, Zyll," Anne hissed out of the side of her mouth then turned to grin at Jabe. "Hey there, how's your building growing?" she asked cheerily.

"Well enough."

He reached for Anne's outstretched hand and shook it warmly, but his gaze was on Zylla who raised her eyes to his glance. For a second, the heat in his eyes disarmed her jealousy, heat that she innately knew was for her. Then just as quickly, a flash of anger returned as he introduced the willowy redhead.

Her name was Elayne, and Zylla felt like a weevil in her presence. With long, silky red-gold hair, Elayne possessed huge green eyes and pouty lips. She wore no bra under her black tank top and a gauzy skirt in different hues of green.

Intimidated, Zylla couldn't seem to speak, and Anne broke the awkward silence by complimenting Elayne's gorgeous hair, which caused Elayne to twirl one long tress around her finger and gaze fondly at it. For the next ten minutes, she chattered endlessly about shampoos, conditioners, and the trials of fending off split ends.

Anne gritted her teeth while Jabe watched Zylla, who ignored them all and stared at the opening band as they left the stage.

Finally bored by her own conversation, Elayne clutched Jabe's arm and whined, "Jabey, let's go. The band's about to start and I need another drink."

"Zylla," Anne bit out after the couple left. "What is your problem? He was staring at you the entire time."

“I know,” Zylla stammered. “I just, I just couldn’t talk.”

Anne sighed in annoyance. “Well, thanks to you, I know now about every hair molecule contained on that vapid girl’s head.”

Zylla watched Anne storm toward the bar, then turned to the solace of the Cosmic Psychos.

Quivers of awareness shot through her body, and she didn’t have to look to know that Jabe stood beside her once again. He was so close that she could barely breathe and when she inhaled, his clean scent intoxicated her.

Zylla caught a quick movement out of the corner of her eye, and realized that Elayne hung on Jabe’s right arm. A surge of red lightning raced through her brain. *Who did he think he was? The arrogant bastard, standing, smirking no doubt, between the two of them, as if they played tug-o’-war with him. He, no doubt, would gallantly go home with the winner.* Well, she wasn’t going to play and to confirm that thought, she crossed her arms over her chest.

Zylla forced herself to stare stonily at the stage, but her mind was obsessed with Jabe. Her feelings bounced between anger and desire. Jabe stood at her side as if he belonged there. Too close, but not touching her, he breached her space and created a tension that pulled at her from a coil deep inside her body and soon, Zylla believed that he did belong there. Her lack of power suddenly frightened her, mixing precariously with jealousy. Her lack of control was infuriating and her mind screamed in rebellion.

Anne appeared at her left side and broke the spell.

“I hate long red hair. I hate scummy men with stupid lines. I hate couples who are in love and pretend not to be. And most of all,” Anne yelled, “I hate this band!”

“You’re the one who wanted to come,” Zylla hollered back.

“A moment of insanity on my part.” She pointed toward the ceiling and mouthed, “I’ll be upstairs at the bar.”

Zylla nodded, common sense telling her follow Anne, but she was too determined to show Jabe that she wasn’t affected by his nearness. Lifting her chin, she focused on the stage until the band finished then turned abruptly on her heel and walked up the stairs without a passing glance at Jabe.

At the bar, Anne handed her a whiskey.

"Thanks."

Away from Jabe, anger and jealousy fled, and Zylla felt ashamed by her behavior. How stupid she was! She didn't own him. She had no right to jealousy or anger. He had done nothing wrong, made no promises, made no overtures. She'd created the attraction in her mind just as she created Jabe's motives for simply standing next to her. Of course he would stand next to her. They were friends! She felt foolish, and the censure on Anne's face confirmed her foolishness.

Zylla sighed, long and slow, and Anne managed a smile.

"Better now?"

"Yup," she answered. "Sorry you didn't have a good time."

Anne shrugged, tossing her gold hair over her shoulder. "Stars weren't aligned tonight, I guess. Let's go home. Maybe Billy called."

Zylla swallowed the remainder of her whiskey, swirled it around in her mouth then plunked the glass onto the bar. As she turned to follow Anne through the crowd to the door, Elayne suddenly hopped past, leading Jabe by the hand. He trailed behind her, grinning broadly and when he spotted Zylla, the grin grew wider.

"Later," he leered, winking at her.

Zylla's knuckles turned white as her nails bit into her palms.

~ * ~

A knock on the door cracked the still morning, startling Zylla from her genealogy work. Tightening the sash of her robe, she stood and walked to the open front door. Sunlight filtered around a large form and through the screen.

Jabe.

Jabe was standing on her porch at nine o'clock on a Saturday morning. Straight from the arms of Elayne, she surmised, and the rage from the previous night soared in her veins.

"Hello," she said coolly, through the screen.

"Hello yourself," Jabe replied with a perplexed frown at the angry crease between her eyes. He grinned suddenly and held up a bag from the corner bakery.

"Hungry?"

They sat on the porch swing in silence, sipping coffee and eating muffins, the warm early summer day stretched taut between them.

Zylla loathed herself for the devilish churning inside her, and despised Jabe all the more for the amused smirk on his face. *Jerk.* She bit into the moist chocolate chip muffin.

"Nice day, isn't it?" Jabe asked, but Zylla only stared at the potted pink geranium that hung from the porch roof.

Jabe choked back a laugh. Damn, he liked her. She was almost worth breaking his six-and-a-half month female-free sojourn. He had never met anyone like her. Even her bad moods intrigued him.

He had been watching her closely this morning. He knew she had been jealous last night, and he sensed that jealousy also sparked her surliness this morning. He also knew that Zylla was sensible and jealousy alone could not sustain her ire. Until he could figure out what caused her extended anger, there wasn't much he could do except wait.

His patience was proving to be fruitful.

It seemed with each bite, the furrow between her eyes smoothed out just a little bit more and the black glare in her eyes melted to a warm brown. With a silent chuckle, he realized that Zylla with an empty stomach was a volcano on the verge of eruption. Highly diverted by this fact, he popped a chunk of blueberry muffin into his mouth and chewed heartily.

She swallowed the last bit of muffin and forced herself to face Jabe. Stealing a quick glance, she saw that his features were calm and that he appeared to be enjoying the breakfast despite her moodiness. Slowly, she turned toward him and raised her eyes to his meet his tranquil gaze.

"Feel better now?" he asked.

"I was fine before," she snapped and was immediately contrite.

"I'm sorry. I guess—I guess I was just hungry."

Jabe laughed. "I'll say. You have my friend Rye beat when it comes to bear-like behavior. I'll be sure to carry trail mix at all times that I'm with you."

Spirits restored, Zylla smiled brightly. "You're very patient," she said.

"My mother taught me well." He grinned at her. "Oh, I almost forgot. I brought you something."

Jabe reached inside his leather jacket and pulled out a rumpled brown paper bag.

"Here you go."

"What is it?" she asked when her hand encountered a beanbag of soft silk. She removed her hand from the bag, and a pleasant lump that smelled strongly of lavender rested in her palm.

"What is it?" she repeated.

"It's an eye pillow. For your headaches. Store it in the fridge and it'll feel real nice when you put it on your head."

She beamed at him. "Thank you. This is really sweet."

On impulse, she leaned forward and kissed his cheek and grinned when Jabe blushed.

"It's nothing, really. You probably have enough lavender already, but I figured you might like it."

The crease between Zylla's eyes returned.

"You know, you've mentioned that before, but I don't wear lavender. I don't wear any scent at all, actually."

"Yes you do," Jabe insisted. "I always smell it when you're around. It's one of the first things I noticed when I first saw you last year."

Zylla tilted her head. "Last year? When? How?"

Jabe's blush deepened.

"At the Cramps show. You walked by, and I smelled lavender." Jabe reached forward and stroked her cheek with a finger.

"You took my breath away."

Zylla held her breath as Jabe leaned forward. Jabe parted his lips, and she closed her eyes, bending forward to meet him. His hair tickled her skin, and she shivered.

He sniffed.

Zylla's eyes popped open.

"I don't smell it now, though."

"I told you. I'm not wearing any," she replied, somewhat crossly.

Jabe studied the sky as he thought. “You know,” he began. “Come to think of it, except for that one time at the Middle East, I only notice it at the Charlesgate.”

He frowned. “And sometimes when you’re not even there.”

Zylla’s eyes widened and when she spoke, her voice cracked with excitement. “Now that you mention it... huh... that’s really odd...” She stared into space.

“What?”

“I was just thinking. When I first started going to the Charlesgate, I would smell lavender, too. Sometimes it was very strong, but I just kind of assumed it was part of the wood, like that horrible smell that’s in the music room. Anyway, I don’t smell it too much anymore.”

“That stench of rotten fish? Yeah, we can’t get rid of that. It’s actually from the basement, closed up for too many years. You don’t smell the lavender anymore?”

Zylla shook her head. “A waft here and there. But not like I used to.” *And no more neat visions either*, she mourned. “You do?”

“All the time.”

Jabe leaned forward to rest his forearms on his thighs.

“Maybe it’s a ghost.” He looked back at her and tossed her a sheepish grin. His eyes widened. “Hey, maybe it’s *your* ghost, the Victorian lavender lady.”

Zylla grinned. “Or maybe it’s yet another family ghost. Maybe it’s Lydia.” She shrugged, her smile fading. “It makes sense, in a way. She was murdered there, and she has a connection to both of us. It’s Lydia,” she stated, her skin prickling. “I’m certain.”

“Well, then, maybe Lydia *is* your family ghost.”

Zylla considered that for a minute, then said, “Naw, can’t be.” She fingered the glass eye that hung on a silver chain around her neck. “I’ve got this, remember?”

Jabe laughed. “C’mon, you really think that thing works?”

A blush fanned Zylla’s cheeks. “Well, yeah, sort of. I mean, I’ve never seen the ghost or anything—” She broke off, suddenly pale. But she had seen something, in the beginning, when she first started to visit the Charlesgate, hadn’t she? The dizzy spells, the past era, the gentle-eyed blonde woman...

"What's wrong?" Jabe asked, straightening in his chair.

"Nothing."

"You just look white all the sudden."

"The sun." She pointed to the fiery orb. "It's getting hot out, that's all. I'm fine."

It was nothing. Nothing but her caffeine-induced imagination. She sipped her coffee.

Maybe the Charlesgate had a ghost, after all, and maybe it *was* Lydia, but certainly not the family ghost. Aunt Maddie wouldn't fret about her wearing her evil eye if the ghost was the sweet blonde lady. The lavender was just a coincidence, a popular enough scent in the olden days, like lemon verbena.

Zylla smiled at Jabe, but his lips were tight and caution flickered in his eyes. She tilted her head in question.

"Good show last night, huh?" he asked.

Elayne's specter rolled through Zylla's blood, and the coffee suddenly tasted stale.

"The band was great, although poor Anne wasn't too fond of them. Too loud and angry."

Jabe was silent, and Zylla glanced over. He held her gaze.

"That woman I was with. Elayne. She's an old girlfriend who was in town to see the band. She asked me to go with her." He paused to gauge her reaction but none came. "Nothing happened."

Zylla's eyes betrayed her happiness, though she schooled her tone to remain diplomatic. "You don't owe me an explanation, Jabe. It's not my business."

Jabe leaned toward her. "It is when I'm about to ask you out. My house, seven o'clock." He grinned impishly. "There will be plenty of food."

Eleven

As Jabe promised, there was plenty of food. He had grilled swordfish, served bruschetta and white wine.

Finished with her second helping, Zylla declared, "*Mmm*. That was positively rapturous."

Jabe barked in mirth. "You talk about food like other people talk about sex." His tone dropped an octave and he said, "I can't imagine what you'd say after an extraordinary bout of fornication."

Zylla shrugged and reached for another bruschetta. Jabe watched as her face turned as red as the tomato on the toast.

"Zylla? Are you blushing?"

She felt Jabe's gaze bore into her and she self-consciously nibbled on the bruschetta as she acted her best to pretend she hadn't heard him.

"Zyll?"

She brushed the crumbs from her hands and sighed. "I wouldn't know," she muttered.

Jabe's musical choice for the evening was opera and at that moment the climax of an aria penetrated the reply that stuck in Jabe's throat.

"What?" Jabe choked, already guessing her answer. "What do you mean 'you wouldn't know'?"

"Well..." She swallowed and sipped her wine. "I'm a virgin." All embarrassment fled at Jabe's incredulous expression and she giggled.

"We do exist you know. At least for the purpose of luring unicorns."

Jabe regained his composure and arched a brow. "Unicorns are extinct. Especially in the city." He poured a glass of wine then leaned back in his chair.

"How is it possible that you are still a virgin at..."

"Twenty-nine," Zylla finished for him.

"Let me guess," Jabe drawled. "You're waiting for marriage."

Zylla bristled at his sarcasm. "And if I am? What's wrong with that?" she challenged.

"Marriage," Jabe scoffed, "is a ridiculous notion created by religion and civic law. I don't need a priest or public servant involved in my personal life to tell me God, or the law, acknowledges the validity of my actions."

"Sounds like a practiced speech, Jabe. I take it you've had a few offers." She quirked a brow and smirked, but after a few seconds of silence, she replied. "I see what you mean, though. I even agree to some extent. But a true marriage sees beyond the laws of man and creates its own laws. It exists in a higher realm. If the world needs a priest or laws to verify that union, so what?"

Jabe didn't respond.

"Besides, I'm not waiting for marriage. I was waiting for Michael Sullivan, and I waited a bit too long."

Jabe froze with his glass midway to his mouth and forced himself to swallow the twinge of envy that iced in his mouth. He cleared his throat.

"*Was* waiting?"

"My best friend, Mike. He was my first love." She sighed. "Unrequited. He didn't feel the same way." Her eyes darted around the room and she blushed.

"When we first met he thought I was 'repulsive'," she admitted. "At least that's what a mutual friend told me. But after a while, Mike got used to me hanging around and we became really good friends. And I guess I always hoped that he'd love me back," Zylla whispered.

She glanced quickly at Jabe and her fears were confirmed. She had been ashamed to admit Mike's initial reaction to her crush, afraid that it would somehow taint Jabe's opinion of her and all the admiration that shone in his eyes when he looked at her would disappear, that he would think her repulsive as well. By Jabe's stony features, she guessed that she was correct.

"So I waited," she continued as she twisted her napkin under the table. "It's not like I'm totally inexperienced. I have dated, but I just haven't taken the final step, if you know what I mean.

"Since I was sixteen, I lived this sort of suspended dream, waiting for Mike to love me. But he didn't, and now I don't really mind. I'm just ashamed for wasting so much time. I'm babbling." She laughed quietly and shrugged one shoulder then looked down at the mangled napkin in her palm. "Anyway, that's why I'm still a virgin."

Jabe drained his glass and stood abruptly. He *was* repulsed, but not with Zylla. He was amazed at her tenacity, although it had been wasted on some twit who didn't deserve more than passing notice from her.

High school crushes rarely worked out and it was no shock that Zylla's was unrequited. But to rebuff a lovelorn girl by calling her repulsive was intolerable. He was appalled by the idiot's callous treatment of her and couldn't fathom how she forgave him enough to become his best friend.

"What an asshole," he finally said. "I can't believe he said that."

Zylla only saw the green fire in his eyes and the white knuckles of his clenched fists and felt herself turn redder. He was upset about Mike's comment, but he hadn't denied Mike's opinion. She chewed the inside of her lip and inwardly scolded herself for baring her wound. She had never even told Anne about her hurt pride, but now she wished she had confessed to her roommate instead of Jabe. She pushed back her chair and bent over the table to pick up Jabe's plate.

"What are you doing?" he snarled, still dwelling on Mike's insensitivity to another human.

Zylla's head snapped up, and she bit her lip. "Just clearing the table," she whispered.

Jabe's features softened as he crossed the room and took the plate out of her hands. "Nope. Tonight's on me. Let's go to the Behan for a couple of pints."

At her hesitation, he sighed dramatically and leaned forward, pulling her hand into the crook of his arm.

"C'mon, let's get out of here."

~ * ~

As he waited for Dan to pour the Guinness, Jabe stood with his back against the bar, thumbs hooked in the front pockets of his jeans. He watched as nearly every guy in the place glanced at Zylla, some gazes lingering longer than others. Other women would have returned the appreciative looks or turned away in pointed disdain, but Zylla was oblivious. If by chance she did catch a guy staring, she quickly looked down or nervously fingered her hair.

Jabe's frown deepened.

"Here ye go, Jaber."

"Thanks, Dan."

Jabe generously tipped the bartender and picked up the pints. As he crossed the room to her, he suddenly understood that she still believed that asshole Michael. She thought of herself as a freak, a blemish, undesirable.

He stopped in his steps and smiled, a wide roguish grin that caused more than a few of the Behan's female denizens to squirm on their benches. Jabe strutted to the table and straddled the bench across the table from Zylla. He had no problems showing her just how desirable she really was.

"Here you go, Zyll." He handed her a beer and, before beginning his assault, watched as her upper lip sank into the frothy head, branding her skin with ale.

Jabe reached out and slowly wiped the trace of froth from her lip with his thumb. After the initial jolt at his touch, Zylla struggled to keep her composure and not melt under the sensual stroke of his work-roughened skin. Transfixed, she watched as he studied her with hooded eyes and brought his thumb to his mouth to lick the foam.

His eyes sparkled.

"So, you still think it's not your family ghost?" he asked.

Zylla's attention floated merrily in her awakened senses and she ignored him. Jabe flashed a crooked smile.

"Zyll."

"Yes?" She smiled dreamily.

Jabe affixed a sober expression on his face. "The lavender. At the Charlesgate. You still think it's not your ghost?"

Zylla immediately straightened.

"Oh, well, no," she stammered. "I mean, I don't know. If it is a ghost, and that's a very big if, that is, I want to believe it's a ghost, that'd be pretty cool, but..."

"Yeah, yeah, I know. Assume that it is," he interrupted. "I talk to the damn thing all the time—I'd much rather be talking to something than nothing. It helps me to convince myself that I'm not insane."

She laughed. "Okay, okay. Then yes, I think it's Lydia. So, yes, it's a family ghost, but not *the* family ghost, the thing that scared Yia-Yia. It can't be. I think it would have tried to hurt me, despite the evil eye."

"You could take it off." He jerked his chin at her throat. "The eye. See what happens." At the doubt in Zylla's expression, he said, "C'mon, you don't really think that your necklace does anything anyway, do you? It's a piece of glass!"

"I don't know," she replied, nervously fingering the necklace. "I'm scared to take it off, to be honest."

"Zylla, it's superstition, nothing more. I promise."

She sipped her beer then cradled the glass between her two hands as she looked away from Jabe's challenging stare. People were trickling into the Behan at a steady rate now, and the air was thick with heat and laughter. She took a deep breath and leaned across the table, closer to Jabe.

"I never told you how my parents died," she stated.

"No, you haven't."

"I don't remember them. I was real little when they drowned. We had a lake house, and my mom was wading in waist-high water."

Zylla blew out a breath, ignoring the sting of tears in her eyes. Jabe took her hand, rested his thumb against her palm, and she felt stronger.

"The police thought she must have stepped in a hole, she just disappeared. My father went in after her and never came out. Aunt

Maddie saw the whole thing. She watched her sister and brother-in-law die. By the time she reached them, it was too late."

"I'm sorry," he whispered, squeezing her hand.

Zylla smiled wanly. "Sometimes I get so sad it hurts, but that's only once in a while. I'm lucky—I have Aunt Maddie. She adopted me and raised me as her own."

He shook his head slowly. "I can't imagine what she went through."

"Maddie is a strong woman," Zylla replied. "She's very practical as well."

Jabe looked at her, suspicion growing in his eyes. "Which makes it pretty weird that she is so adamant about you wearing that thing, doesn't it?"

She was nodding before he finished his sentence.

"I was hurt when Aunt Maddie blew off my questions about my genealogy and was pretty furious when Uncle John told me that Aunt Maddie destroyed the family tree. Once I started researching on my own, I felt more in control and somehow realized how out of control Maddie must have been feeling when I brought up the family history."

"It's just a genealogy though, Zyll." Jabe scratched under his jaw, frustration etched in the movement of his hand. "It's natural to want to know your history, and it's bloody abnormal to hide it like some family skeleton. What neurosis does she have that she needs to 'control' a piece of paper?"

He sighed, let go of her hand, and pushed his fingers through his hair.

"I'm sorry. I don't mean to put down your aunt. I just don't get her."

"No offense taken. I mean, that's exactly how I felt when I got off the phone with Uncle John. After a few days, though, I started to remember things."

Jabe frowned and tilted his head in question.

"Just little things, stories actually. Aunt Maddie never insisted that I wear the evil eye, you see. She's not superstitious, right?"

Jabe nodded slowly.

"But she always told me that it was my Yia-Yia's deathbed wish that I never take it off."

"Because she saw the Victorian Lavender Lady at your cradle."

"Right. But Yia-Yia lived with us, Aunt Maddie and me, and Maddie treated her as if Yia-Yia was her own mother instead of my father's.

"Aunt Maddie had been brushing Yia-Yia's hair, the same day she had banished the Victorian ghost, when my grandmother had a massive stroke. She never spoke again and died an hour later."

"So she couldn't have had a deathbed request," Jabe muttered. "Why would Maddie lie about the necklace?"

Zylla took another sip of the beer and licked her lips. "I think she was too proud to admit that she was scared. She never talks about her family. Ever. Her own mother went mad and killed herself, and there are lots of creepy stories about murdered women in the family, my mother included."

Jabe shook his head, not understanding.

Zylla continued. "Uncle John gathers all the Berry cousins together for reunions every so often, and of course, they get to talking about those skeletons you mentioned.

"One summer, Maddie had put me to bed. She had this seven o'clock bedtime thing." Zylla rolled her eyes. "It was such a bummer. Anyway, I sneaked out of bed and hid under one of the picnic tables to listen to the adults talk about those old bones in the closet."

Zylla grinned, and Jabe laughed, eyes glinting, remembering. He and his brother, Kent, had pulled similar antics when they were young.

"Someone mentioned my parents, and since Aunt Maddie was inside washing dishes, no one worried about hurting her with the stories. One of my cousins said the police found bruises in the shape of fingers on my parents' ankles, that someone, or something, murdered them.

"I didn't believe it and almost gave myself away by exploding from under the table, kicking and screaming, but then Uncle John said—I'll never forget it—I remember his exact words."

Zylla cleared her throat, and did her best imitation of her uncle's western Massachusetts accent, which caused a burst of mirth from Jabe despite the serious topic. "He said, 'Tis the truth. My sister was there. She said that on that day, a horrible stench came off the lake, not t'all like freshwater smells. It smelled like low tide, she said, and when they pulled the bodies of our sister and John from the water, there was seaweed wrapped around their necks. Now you tell me, how does seaweed come to be in a freshwater lake?'"

Jabe visibly shivered. "God."

"I know." Zylla nodded. "It gets worse. Right after..."

"Hey, you two!" Laughing, Anne plopped onto the bench next to Jabe. "I figured you'd turn up here."

"A couple of bad pennies, the both of us," Jabe joked as he stood to greet Anne.

"What are you doing here tonight?" Zylla asked.

Anne waved her hand as if the answer were obvious. "Oh, we had dinner over at Doyle's and figured we'd pop in here in case you and Jabe stopped in after your dinner." She looked from Zylla to Jabe and back again. "How was that, anyway?"

"Yummy. Who's 'we'?"

"Ahhh, this is much better than that awful din from last night," Anne crooned, indicating the bartender's choice of Enya for the evening. All three were silent as their ears picked out the plaintive melody beneath the chorus of Irish and American accents.

"Who's 'we'?" Zylla repeated.

"Well, you're about to..." A firm hand attached to a muscular bare arm placed a bottle in front of Anne. "And here he is." Anne beamed at the tall figure that loomed next to her, her bright blue eyes almost cobalt in joy.

"Zyll, Jabe, this is Billy."

Billy slid onto the bench next to Zylla. His lean athletic build and chiseled features reminded her of a young Paul Newman.

At Zylla's scrutiny, Billy held out his arms and looked down at his own body before smiling at her. "Well, do I pass muster?"

Startled by his blunt question, Zylla blurted, "You look like Paul Newman."

Billy looked at Anne and they both laughed.

"You get that a lot, huh?"

Billy nodded. "I do. But it's a compliment. *Cool Hand Luke* is my favorite movie."

"Mine too, man," Jabe chimed. "The egg scene..."

The hours passed quickly, and Zylla barely noticed the pint glasses and beer bottles that bred on the table, the consistently dimming lights, and the three men beginning a traditional music session in the corner. She unconsciously kept time with the bodhran and swayed quietly to the fiddle while conversing with Billy. She liked him immensely and easily discerned that he regarded Anne with warmth and respect. She noticed that Jabe liked him as well and that further bolstered her good opinion.

"So, Jabe." Anne leaned her elbow on the table and rested her sharp chin in her palm.

"Anne." Jabe mimicked her gesture, causing her to giggle.

"Has Zylla told you about the book she's going to write?" She gave Zylla a sideways glance.

"I am not writing a book." She ground the words between her teeth. "They are just notes."

"What are just notes?" Billy asked.

Zylla sighed dramatically and told the group about her pirate research and the character that she had created.

"From your nightmares," Jabe guessed. "That's cool. You *should* write a book."

"It may never get published," Zylla said weakly.

He shrugged, then leaned back in his chair, lifting his right booted foot up to rest on his left knee. "So what?"

His question trembled on the smoky air of the pub and three faces dared her to reply.

She didn't.

A crack of applause snapped their attention to the corner where the musicians, sweat running down their faces, finished a reel.

"My turn to buy," Anne stated.

"I'll help you," Zylla said, rising from the bench, grateful for the escape from Jabe's question.

~ * ~

"So you like him?" Anne asked.

Zylla contemplated her friend then looked at the table where Jabe and Billy chatted. "Well, since you never let me meet any of your past boyfriends, I take this as a good sign."

"That's the real reason we're here. I was kinda hoping that you guys would end up at the Behan so you could check Billy out." Anne hesitated, rested her forehead on Zylla's shoulder and cried, "Zyll, I'm in love. Truly, madly, bone-crushingly in love. So I can't trust my own judgment. But I trust yours. Do you like him? Really?"

Mirth bubbled inside Zylla. Never, ever had she witnessed Anne lose her composure, especially over a man. Normally, she swaggered with the spirit of a Texas longhorn. Never again would she let Anne berate her for being a maladjusted romantic. Then she saw the plea in Anne's expression, and she wiped away the smirk that settled on her face.

"Yes. I really like him."

Relief flooded Anne's face, and Zylla kissed her cheek.

"And I hope he loves you as much as I do."

Anne's usual sarcastic grin appeared and she drawled, "Oh, for God's sake, Zylla, you are a decrepit romantic."

She turned to the bar to pay for the beer and handed two pints to Zylla before picking up the others. "One sandwich short of a picnic," she added.

Zylla stuck out her tongue at Anne's back and followed her back to the table where Billy took a beer from Anne and led her to the edge of the crowd that watched the musicians. Jabe remained seated, watching Zylla under hooded eyes.

Before she could sit, Jabe's arm whipped around her waist and yanked her sideways into his lap, causing the liquid in the pint glasses to splash over the sides.

"Uggghhh." She scowled, slamming the glasses on the dark wood table and shaking her hands. Drops of water and Guinness sprinkled the air. Zylla wiped her hands on her jeans and struggled to rise, but Jabe clamped his other arm onto her thighs. She peered into his face.

"You're drunk." She sniffed.

"Aye, lassie, tha' I am," he growled in a deep brogue.

Lulled into the concept that an intoxicated Jabe, especially a humorous one, was less dangerous, Zylla tentatively lifted her hand to stroke the dark gold of his sideburn. His cheek scorched her palm, and the smile fled her face as his gaze locked with hers. Slowly, deliberately, he lowered his gaze to her lips then raised his eyes to look into hers once more.

Her heart spindled, and she gulped back a nervous laugh.

"Kiss me," he murmured. "I haven't felt soft lips in a long time."

Zylla swallowed her panic and pretended to be as flippant as Anne. "What? Have you been kissing frogs?"

He barked a sharp laugh, and Zylla released her breath at the reprieve. Again she attempted to rise and again the vise on her lap tightened.

"Kiss me."

"No."

"No?" An eyebrow rose.

"No," she insisted with a shake of the head.

"Why?"

"Because." She bit her lip then rushed on, "Because I'm afraid you'll break my heart."

"Ahhhh."

Jabe glanced at his hand that claimed her jean-clad thigh then back at her face. "It's just a kiss."

Not to her. Jabe tugged at her subconscious already, haunting her dreams. If she kissed him, she thought she'd be lost. But her blood sang with his admission of desire and she couldn't stop herself from touching her lips to his cheek.

Jabe sat absolutely still while she tattooed his face with kisses. Her lips melted holes in his cheeks, forehead, chin, nose, and when he closed them, his eyelids. She shied away from his lips. They were naïve, tender kisses, but they jarred every nerve in his body until he couldn't see anything but a naked and writhing Zylla underneath him.

"You're driving me insane," he moaned, and Zylla dragged her face from his, torture in her eyes. "I'm not going to lie to you," he murmured. "I'm not looking for a relationship. I've had too many, and they all end the same."

"Maybe you pick the wrong women."

Jabe's gaze fell on her lips again and he leaned forward, his mouth a rustle away from hers. "And maybe I've found the right one," he whispered into her breath, all jest in his eyes dark now.

Tingles sparkled through Zylla's body as his lips brushed hers, branding them with a rose-hued flame. He pulled back to regard her briefly. Then the color of his eyes swirled into hers as his mouth again dipped down. Her eyelids sank and her lips parted.

The intimacy was shattered when a drunken man stumbled into them and spilled his cold beer down Jabe's back. Jabe grimaced—arching forward as Zylla leapt off his lap, already running toward the bar for a towel.

"Shit!"

Jabe reached around to pull his wet tee shirt from his skin and did his best to squeeze out some of the liquid. Then he pulled his hair forward and repeated the procedure.

"Shit," he said again, remembering their near-kiss and its power to divorce him from reality. He had only meant to show her that she was desirable, and steal some pleasure from her as well. It couldn't hurt. Just a couple of make-out sessions. He liked her and wanted her, and he had fooled himself into thinking it was safe to fall off his wagon. He knew now that kissing her would wipe away his self, utterly and completely.

He and Zylla could only be friends. He could do it, he assured himself, clenching his self-control in his fists. No problem. He shook his head clear, silently thanking heaven for floundering sots in crowded bars.

Twelve

Her downfall had been the baklava, Zylla thought as she raced through the ivy-framed brownstone archway into her office building on Bay State Road. Jabe had treated her to lunch at the Middle East Restaurant, and the syrupy dessert had been certainly to blame for her affirmative response to Jabe's question of whether or not she wanted to accompany him to New York City this weekend.

She had sipped her coffee, fascinated by Jabe's discourse on the history of the Chelsea Hotel and its theoretical similarity to the Charlesgate when the waitress had placed the baklava in front of her. One bite and she had been lost. The nuts and flakes had melted down her throat in a river of honey.

She had closed her eyes, so encompassed in the taste of the dark, molten gold delectable, that she had barely heard Jabe speak.

"I have an appointment with the owner of the Chelsea this Sunday and thought that you might want to see it as well. You wanna come?"

Zylla had heard a voice say "yes" and opened her eyes wide, shocked to realize the declaration had originated from her own mouth.

Now she quaked with the anticipation and apprehension. On the one hand, she was finally going to see the city Anne spoke of ceaselessly.

With Jabe.

On the other hand, she was going to sleep in the hallowed halls of the Chelsea Hotel.

With Jabe.

He cared about her. She knew that. And he wanted her. When his lips brushed hers at the Behan the other night, she felt the voltage between them. Besides, no man would pay for an entire trip to New York without the expectation of sex, right?

The problem was, Zylla was more than a little in love with Jabe, and he made it quite clear that he didn't want a relationship. But, oh, how she wanted him! Sometimes she ached with longing to melt into his arms, lose herself in his mouth. Wouldn't it be enough just to be friends with Jabe, and also have a sexual relationship with him?

"I waited for true love, and look where that got me," she whispered to herself, but a twinge in her heart nagged her. What was the point if there was no love?

Zylla moaned and turned down the corridor to her office. She needed her comrade in arms. She needed Anne.

"Hey, Nicole." Zylla waved as she rushed past the reception desk.

"Hi, Zyll. Hold up."

Zylla retraced her steps and at Nicole's warning glance asked, "What is it?"

"There's a student here to see you." Nicole raised a brow meaningfully. "Tammy Fisch."

Zylla rolled her eyes in response.

Last semester, Tammy Fisch had been caught plagiarizing a history paper and now faced expulsion pending the results of her summer trial. Before her initial questioning, Dean Pendergast had entered Zylla's office and asked her to sit in the room with him to act as a witness.

"I don't trust her," he had murmured and during the interview, Zylla had concurred with his opinion. Tammy had blamed everyone except herself for her actions and when she realized that the Dean's business-like composure would not melt into pity, she had promptly burst into tears. The dean had refused to capitulate and Tammy's tears had turned to fury as she accused him of trying to ruin her life.

Zylla had nearly tasted blood from biting her tongue so hard to keep from making a caustic remark. She was impatient with people who didn't take responsibility for their own actions and blamed others for their self-caused misery.

Zylla sighed, then threw her shoulders back to face the inevitable confrontation. Then, remembering the events during her last experience with Ms. Fisch, Zylla thought it wise to avoid meeting the girl alone. Turning to Nicole, she whispered, "Why don't you join me?"

After the tearful accusations at an impervious Zylla and appalled Nicole ceased, and Nicole ushered Tammy out of the conference room, she returned to her office and picked up the receiver to dial Anne's number.

Anne's smooth, low voice answered after two rings.

"Ibis Marketing. This is Anne Stevens."

"Anne," Zylla whispered urgently.

"Zyll," Anne echoed, mocking Zylla's theatrical tone.

"Jabe just asked me to go to New York with him this weekend. What should I do?"

"Do you want to go?" Anne replied nonchalantly.

"Well, yes, but..." Zylla paused. "What does it mean?"

"Zylla, dearest. It means that he wants you to go to New York with him."

Zylla heard the smirk in Anne's reply and spat, "Anne Stevens, you know exactly what I mean!"

Anne chuckled, unwillingly to relent just yet. "Well, according to what you keep telling me, you're just friends, right?"

"*Righhhhtt*." Zylla's voice wavered.

"Well, you and I are just friends and when we go away together we usually share a room."

A short pause filled the air and Zylla could hear the clicking of Anne's computer keys.

"But Anne, we get a double."

"Yes?" Anne teased.

"Well, what if there's only one bed? What am I supposed to do?"

"Why, Zyll, you just have to do what you think is right." With an impertinent click, Anne disconnected the call.

~ * ~

Jabe folded his arms and leaned his head against the window and muttered, "I hate small planes," before drifting into sleep. Zylla smiled at his grumpiness and opened the book about female pirates that she had purchased at the University Bookstore. She felt some trepidation when the shuttle lurched to life. The plane shuddered and groaned in rebellion at being woken, but it quickly climbed into the descending sunlight and sped cheerily along until they landed in New York.

Even the rush hour traffic that still gripped Manhattan didn't irk Zylla as much as the five o'clock Boston subway. Her mind swallowed all it could of Manhattan as the cab crawled to its destination of 222 West Twenty-third Street.

Jabe paid the driver while Zylla stepped onto the sidewalk in front of the impressive wrought iron and red brick structure rising at least ten stories. The building intrigued her and she tentatively, almost worshipfully, walked toward the entrance.

Two plaques stood sentinel on the columns framing the front door. Zylla scanned the list of names on one plaque, then the other. Arthur Miller, Dylan Thomas, Brendan Behan, and Thomas Wolfe. Zylla was humbled just standing beneath the red and white awning.

"Impressive, isn't it?" Jabe asked quietly.

Zylla nodded. They stood in silence until Jabe placed his hand on the small of her back and ushered her into the hotel's lobby with its magnificent mahogany fireplace and original artwork created by Hotel Chelsea tenants.

A young couple in business attire laughed with the turbaned desk clerk. The woman held the hand of a small child who, in turn, tugged on the leash of a Golden Retriever. Zylla giggled as the tot lifted the leather to his mouth and gnawed on it until his mother finally noticed.

Zylla guessed that the family lived at the Chelsea and immediately hoped that the Charlesgate would someday emanate such a welcoming atmosphere to all walks of life.

"Yes, sir." The desk clerk nodded to Jabe after the family had headed toward the elevators. "May I be of assistance?"

"Please. I have a reservation under the name Thayer."

The clerk scanned his reservation book. "One room, correct?"

Jabe glanced at Zylla, who suddenly appeared fascinated by a potted fern, then inhaled sharply before holding up two fingers.

"That'll be two rooms. Thanks."

Zylla felt herself blush, chagrined that he obviously did not want to sleep with her. At the same time, she let out the breath she hadn't realized she was holding, momentarily thankful that he had declined. She fingered the little blue eye around her neck as Jabe received their room keys. Fate had decided for her and that was fine, she thought, biting her lip. Now she could relax and enjoy New York.

With Jabe.

~ * ~

The weekend was far from relaxing. The city heightened Zylla's senses until she felt that she might spontaneously combust.

Saturday morning she woke to sunlight plowing through the shuttered doors to the balcony. She climbed out of bed, stretched, opened the doors and stepped out onto the wrought iron balcony of the third floor. To her right, the elongated neon "Hotel Chelsea" sign proudly jutted from the building and below, yellow taxis sped by as a few people wandered the street.

It was very early, but Zylla was full awake. Since she doubted that Jabe, a self-proclaimed night bird, had awakened yet, she opened the laptop Jabe had forgotten when he had brought her bags into her room. All night she had dreamed of turbulent seas and foreign ports and now she positively itched to record it, and hoped that a little of Dylan Thomas's spirit would inspire her.

By nine o'clock, she was beaming with pride. Her pirate queen remained unnamed, but a story was forming nonetheless. Zylla was so excited about her fledgling novel that she left her room and walked down the parquet hallway to knock on Jabe's door. When he didn't open it, she knocked a little louder and was rewarded with a flurry of mumbled curses from beyond the door.

"What?" Jabe demanded as he flung open the door, squinting through sleep-filled eyes. He slowly grinned when he saw Zylla, who had taken a few steps back into the hallway to avoid his temper.

Unfortunately, this gave her a better view of his boxer-clad, golden body. Jabe's long blond hair was tousled and his work-hardened form emanated warmth from a night's sleep. His smile clearly said 'I adore you', and begged her to fall forward and melt in his arms.

But she didn't.

Instead, Zylla froze and finally stammered, "Um, let me know when you want to grab some breakfast," and rushed back to her room before he could reply.

They walked to the Village and ate breakfast in a small French restaurant where Jabe read Zylla's writing on his laptop and said simply, "You amaze me." Zylla didn't really believe him, but she blushed inwardly at his response. That compliment made all the difference to her.

They spent the rest of the morning and early afternoon wandering around shops in the Village, pausing to hear street musicians, and to purchase sausages from a vendor.

Zylla absorbed the smells, sights, and sounds of the city with calm acceptance, and after she matter-of-factly bargained with a street vendor for a used suede jacket that brought out the orange-gold flecks in her eyes, Jabe again remarked, "You amaze me."

"Why, whatever did I do now?" Zylla chimed.

Jabe shrugged, shaking his head and gazing at her with proud eyes. "Most people who come to New York for the first time are either over-awed or over-intimidated. You just seem completely at ease here." He paused for a moment. "You are a wonderful companion."

"Thank you." Zylla smirked. "You may take me to Florence next weekend."

Jabe barked out a laugh and tossed an arm around her shoulder to pull her close and kiss the top of her head.

~ * ~

Despite the blisters on her heels, Zylla dragged Jabe out that night to the Knitting Factory to hear a couple of bands. The evening was a whirlwind of dancing and drinking, and she barely kept up with Jabe as he twirled and dipped her through tune after tune.

She felt the shock waves that jolted them every time he pulled her to him. After each dance ended, they were both rendered incapable of speech. His green gaze locked onto hers and Zylla knew she couldn't be imagining the longing she saw there. But he never made a move toward her.

Her dismay increased when they returned to the Chelsea that night with piles of Chinese takeout. Both starving, they greedily ate pork-fried rice and chicken fingers dipped in sweet honey until their eyes glazed over.

Jabe grabbed two waters from the room's refrigerator and motioned for Zylla to follow him out to the balcony. The warmth of the summer day had disappeared, but Zylla didn't mind. She sighed and sat cross-legged on the concrete. Jabe leaned over the wrought-iron rail for a moment before turning his head to look at Zylla.

"You okay?" he asked.

"*Mmm-hmm.*"

"I meant to ask you," he ventured. "You never finished telling me about why you won't take that off." With a quick nod, he indicated her necklace, an eerie blue globe in the night lit sky.

"Oh, yeah." Zylla frowned. "Where did I leave off?"

"Your uncle had told about finding the seaweed in the lake, ah, around your parents."

Zylla watched as a yellow cab sped down the now empty street below the Chelsea.

"Yes," she murmured and continued in a louder voice. "Aunt Maddie had gone into the hospital for some minor surgery. I was fourteen, but she didn't want to leave me alone, so she sent me to her brother's house.

"Uncle John and Aunt June had a dinner guest one night and after we ate, I went into the other room to read a book while Uncle John went outside to smoke. I heard the lady say something like, 'Isn't that the girl whose parents were murdered by,' then she whispered, and I couldn't hear anymore."

Zylla paused to swallow a long drink. "Whew! The food was salty, huh?" she commented and gulped some more water. "Anyway, then I heard Aunt June say something about how it was the same thing that killed my grandmothers and that she didn't really believe the stories about the mad woman that followed the Berrys around.

"Then they started talking about other things and I was too stunned, and curious, to read anymore. Luckily," Zylla added with a smile, "Aunt June's friend was a terrible gossip, just like Aunt June, and she brought up the subject again."

She cleared her throat and mimicked: 'Well, I was told that your sister-in-law saw the ghost, too.'"

"What did your aunt say? " Jabe asked.

"She said that Aunt Maddie broke down during Yia-Yia's funeral. Uncle John took her into the funeral director's office and sat with her while she sobbed and ranted about Yia-Yia's stroke. Maybe Aunt June was exaggerating, I don't know, but she told her friend that a nasty odor was in the room right before Yia-Yia's stroke, the same smell that was near the lake. Yia-Yia started to shake in fear and said something in Greek, and Maddie saw a face in the mirror."

"The Victorian lady?"

Zylla shrugged and avoided Jabe's eyes. "I guess so. I don't even know what's true, and it doesn't matter. All I know for sure is that Yia-Yia died the same night she took off her evil eye to put on me, and I guess I'm a little scared to take it off."

Jabe was silent, and Zylla looked up at him.

"I guess I would be, too," he said quietly, then faced the railing and leaned his arms on it to stare at the New York night.

The aspect of him at that moment, leaning over the rail with that noble profile, reminded Zylla of a dream she'd had the previous night. In it, she watched Jabe from a long way off. She was desperate to get to him, to tell him something, but couldn't move or speak. He couldn't see her.

He was dressed in tight tan breeches, black boots and a loose cream-colored shirt. Head held high, hair streaming out behind, he appeared the picture of cold power. But his sea green eyes revealed a deep sadness.

In the dream, she longed to wrap her arms around him and rest her cheek against his hair-matted chest in comfort, and she had woken pining for the same thing. As she remembered the feeling of that dream, Zylla's expression became one of quiet yearning.

"What is it?" he asked softly as he glanced down at her.

She stood. They were so close that she could feel the hair on his arm tickle the skin of her own arm.

"Nothing," she said, then dared, "I dreamt about you last night."

"Thank you."

"Thank you? I didn't do it on purpose!"

Jabe cocked an eyebrow at her. "Didn't you know that it's a compliment to dream about someone?"

"Then you should be feeling pretty fine about now," she joked. "Because I dream about you all the time."

The mirth in his eyes diminished and Zylla felt certain that he saw through her façade of humor and was revolted. Her eyes downcast, she felt the heat rise to her face.

The bellow from a cab's horn disturbed the silence between them. Zylla heard Jabe inhale sharply and found herself facing him, his hands on her hips. The air between them grew charged with shimmering heat.

Jabe gazed intently at her lips and growled, "I dream about you, too."

His mouth lowered until it was an inch away from hers, and she parted her lips in response to the low moan that rose in her throat. Her hand lifted to stroke his cheek, rough from the weekend's growth, and her finger toyed with the short hairs of his sideburn. Her other hand stole into the hair at the nape of his neck. At her touch, his grip tightened and she instinctively swayed toward him, brushing her lips against the corner of his mouth.

A choked groan broke from Jabe's throat and his entire body stiffened. Zylla froze and saw that Jabe's jaw was clenched, his eyes raised heavenwards.

"I've got to go to bed," he muttered. "'Night, Zyllie."

He let her go and flashed a crooked grin before leaving her on the balcony.

She felt rejected and ugly, and wrapped her arms around herself at the sudden chill. Zylla swallowed a rise of tears and forced up her chin. Then she went to bed.

~ * ~

She woke a few hours later with the need to write. She ordered bagels and lox with coffee from a deli nearby and nibbled as she wrote.

Jabe knocked and entered her room shortly after noon.

"Your door was open," he said.

"I know," Zylla twisted in her chair to face him and blushed as she thought of last night. Then she noticed his bloodshot eyes and said, "You look awful."

"And you look..." His eyes wandered to the table where the bagels and coffee decanter beckoned. "Absolutely scrumptious."

"Anything left?" he asked, but was already peering into the bag and pulling out a bagel. He made a sandwich, poured a cup of coffee and straddled the chair nearest Zylla.

"Did you get anything done?" he asked after swallowing a barely chewed chunk of bagel and cream cheese.

"A few more pages," Zylla replied. "It's more time-consuming than I thought and while my mind can completely imagine a scene, putting words on the page is somewhat daunting. It's torture," she smiled, eyes mischievous. "But I love it!"

Jabe laughed. "Go on and get dressed," he said, rising from chair. "The manager is giving us a tour of the hotel today then, I'm afraid, it's back to reality."

Zylla pouted at that, and Jabe cupped her chin with his palm.

"We'll come back. I promise." He dropped his hand abruptly. "Meet me in the lobby in about ten minutes."

Jabe's explanation for the Chelsea Hotel trip had been that he needed to examine the hotel's restoration to compare it with that of the Charlesgate given the similarity of the two buildings.

Built in the eighteen eighties as an apartment hotel, the Victorian Gothic Chelsea had boasted a skylight from lobby to ceiling—roof gardens, and spacious, luxurious apartments with expanding rooms and high ceilings. She had been Queen of the City.

Now, the skylight was covered over, two of the three dining rooms converted into living quarters or office space, and most of the mahogany and stained glass was gone.

The Chelsea certainly wasn't what she originally aspired to be, but she still produced a sort of magic and, in turn, she helped to create magic, given her illustrious tenants. Just standing in the lobby caused Zylla's mind to brim with creativity. The hotel reminded Zylla of a damaged Auntie Mame, happily ready to nurture her nieces and nephews.

Still, the Chelsea's loss saddened her, and Zylla wanted better for the Charlesgate. She sensed that Jabe did, too, and this opinion was sustained when she saw Jabe's eyes glaze over in polite boredom during the architectural tour of the Chelsea. Yet whenever their tour guide recalled histories of visitors such as Mark Twain and William S. Burroughs, Jabe's attention snapped to Zylla and his eyes gleamed as he watched her. After the tour, Jabe whispered, "Are you inspired yet?" and Zylla nodded dreamily.

It wasn't until they were settled on the plane, high above New York City, when Zylla realized that Jabe's motive for the trip wasn't to compare and contrast the two hotels, nor was it to seduce her as she had initially guessed.

'*Are you inspired yet?*' he had asked. He'd insisted on reading her writing and took time to critique her pages. She even suspected that he had left his laptop in her room on purpose. Zylla suddenly understood that Jabe's true purpose for bringing her to the Chelsea was to encourage her writing, to turn her pirate scribbling into a work of art.

She turned to Jabe, napping with his head against the plane's window. She admired his form, seemingly carved from the wilderness, raw virility seeping from every pore. And at his core was a steadfast heart that cared about her.

I love you, I love you, her mind cried, surprising her with the truth. She accepted it without the lacing of angst that surrounded her love for Mike, and she was grateful for the knowledge, grateful that such a man was on her side. She slipped her hand into his and quietly murmured, "Thank you for inspiring me."

Jabe, without opening his eyes, raised her hand to his lips and kissed the back of it before placing their joined hands his lap. The security of her hand in his almost made up for the fact that he didn't return the type of love she felt for him. *Really it did*, she thought, ignoring the lump in her chest.

The strength of his hand over hers promised lasting friendship. It was enough. Almost.

Thirteen

Zylla spent the better part of Saturday scouring the clothing stores that graced Newbury Street. She costumed herself in garb after garb, searching in vain for the outfit that would transform her into the sex goddess she wasn't quite sure existed within her.

At two o'clock, she left the dressing room of Betsey Johnson and swore off shopping forever. Entering a sidewalk café, she sat by the window. To passersby, she appeared the vision of cool relaxation as she sipped her iced coffee. But her stomach growled angrily in anticipation of the tuna melt on its way, and her eyes promised violence to anyone who might dare approach her.

She tore into her sandwich seconds after the waitress placed it in front of her and for five minutes, her mind went blank, happily swirling in the sensation of tuna and melted cheese between two pieces of wheat toast. Her body nourished, she could approach her problem with a clear mind.

She belonged to Jabe. The knowledge gnawed at her until she could think of nothing else and her mind kept returning to the same fact: they had been dancing the same reel since she had met him in April. July was nearly over, and Zylla felt as if she might spontaneously combust. *At least that,* she thought as she wiped her fingers and took another sip of her coffee, *would end the turmoil.*

They saw each other nearly every day, talked and laughed for hours, desire suspended in the air between them. But he never touched her, not really.

At the end of each 'date', Jabe never failed to wrap his arms around her for a goodbye hug. It was not the quick, friendly hug of acquaintances or the sincere clutch between good friends. No, Jabe pulled her to him as if he simply could not get close enough, face burrowed in her hair and hands at once everywhere and nowhere, lingering too long at the sides of her breasts, pulling her a little too near.

After what seemed to be a century, Zylla would draw away, but Jabe's hands tarried at her waist, his breath hot near her ear. If she would turn her head just a bit, he would have to kiss her. But she never did, more afraid of rejection than of the churning unreality that claimed her when he held her.

Zylla curled her napkin into a tight ball and tossed it on her empty plate. With all the time they spent together, Jabe and Zylla might as well be married. *Without the consummation,* she thought glumly. She was having a summer fling, well, without the fling.

The time had come for Zylla to act. She had to know. If he rejected her, so be it. She would learn to live with her feelings. And if he wanted her, then maybe, just maybe, their lovemaking would lead to something wonderful.

Except that she'd already spent five hours on Newbury Street and her inner sex kitten was still asleep on the windowsill. She groaned and folded a ten-dollar bill under her plate to cover the meal and tip and pushed open the glass door to exit onto the street.

"Oh, I'm sorry!" Zylla said as she promptly bumped into a woman just entering the coffee shop and her face quickly registered shock as she recognized Anne.

"Hey, you." Anne smiled. "I saw you in the window there and swore I was seeing the look of a lonely little rosebud. Whatcha doin' down on Newbury Street?"

Zylla opened her mouth to speak then narrowed her eyes at Anne, nodding slowly. She bit her lip.

Anne was the embodiment of fashion. In a fitted sundress of plum silk, her gold hair back in a loose chignon, Anne was the vision of effortless sophistication, but when she dressed for a night out clubbing, she easily slid into the role of urban chic, sexy and cool.

"What? What?" Anne demanded, unnerved by Zylla's scrutiny.

Zylla straightened and exhaled through her teeth, resolved. "Anne," she stated. "Make me a woman."

Anne flashed a wide grin and flung an arm around Zylla's shoulders. "Baby, I never thought you'd ask."

~ * ~

"I can't wear these!"

Zylla stared at her reflection in horror. Her lower half looked as if it had been dipped in leather, and she was sure that if she bent over the pants would split.

"You have to break them in a bit," Anne said. "Once they're worn in, you'll never want them off."

Zylla tugged at the leather that seemed to shrink by the second and doubted she'd ever wear them again. They looked great in the store with its pulsing music and eager salesgirls, but in the warm glow of everyday life, Zylla's courage faltered.

Anne had brushed Zylla's hair until it fell like silk against her bare back. She had made up Zylla's face until her eyes were smoky and her lips a seductive vermilion that matched her tube top. Black snakeskin boots and the blue eye talisman were her only accessories.

"Nope, it's not me," she repeated. Zylla glanced desperately at her combat boots, abandoned and resentful in the corner of her room. Her trusty black Levi's lay in a crumpled heap on her bed. She unzipped the leather pants.

"Are you crazy?" Anne gawked. "You look incredible! You should be on a runway!" Then Zylla tried walking in the three-inch high black snakeskin boots. Anne suppressed a giggle.

"Well, maybe you should just stand on the runway. But at least you look like a model."

"I look like a slut." Zylla cupped her breasts and lifted them a bit. "You sure I don't sag?"

Anne rolled her eyes and sprayed the air with a burst of scent.

"Walk through."

Zylla obeyed and was enveloped in a bergamot cloud. "*Mmmhnn.* That smells so good I want to eat it."

"That's the point, my naïve goddess." Anne paused. "So, are you unlocking the chastity belt tonight?"

Zylla looked aghast. "Hell, no!"

She tried to sit on the edge of the bed, felt the leather threaten to split, and immediately straightened again.

"I aim to conquer, not be conquered. I just need to know if he wants me or not. I need to know where I stand with him."

"And you think if you dress for sex, you'll know for sure?" Anne mocked.

Zylla frowned then said, "Well, yeah. I mean, if he rejects me when I'm at my absolute hottest, then I'll know he's not into me."

"Zyll," Anne stated flatly. "Let me remind you a little something about men. They're dogs, plain and simple. No," she amended. "Dogs are nobler. If you go into that club, dressed like that, you'll have every man in the club panting after you, including Jabe."

Zylla chewed her bottom lip.

"Look, my point is, you didn't have to go buy a whole new outfit just to figure out if Jabe wants to make a move on you. One, he's male and you're an attractive female. Right there you have a green light. Two, if you want to know if Jabe specifically wants you, hell, I could tell you that. I've seen him Zylla-watching, and if something's holding him back from the feast, it sure as hell isn't a lack of attraction."

"Well, I'm sick of waiting," Zylla snapped. "I swear if he doesn't kiss me tonight, I might implode."

"And all this for a kiss." Anne indicated Zylla's outfit with her hand.

The fire in Zylla's eyes was replaced by a sparkle. "Well, maybe a little grope or two."

Anne laughed and drawled, "Honey, you'd better make sure you hide the key to that chastity belt. Jabe doesn't look the type of driver who slows down for dangerous curves, if you know what I mean, and you've got more than enough for him to handle."

Zylla waved her hand in dismissal. "I'm calling a cab before I completely lose my nerve." She turned and headed to the kitchen with shaky steps.

Behind her, Anne chuckled at Zylla's wobble.

"Remember, put your weight on your toes, keep your shoulders back and go forth in sin, my child, go forth in sin."

~ * ~

The red walls and black velvet drapes of the Lizard Lounge eased the flutters in her belly. Now if she could only make it to the bar without stumbling over the damn stilts Anne called shoes.

She ordered a Knob Creek and while waiting for the bartender to return, she scanned the room for Jabe. She didn't spot him through the dense crowd, but noted that the band, Jabe's friends, were climbing onto the low stage to tune their instruments under the red lights.

Zylla sipped her drink and watched the sound check procedure, oblivious to the attention her new image invited. Once the band played in earnest, she was lost to the surrounding world entirely. Her emotions swam with the lonesome melody and she only knew that she needed to be closer to the music. Somehow, that desire glided her along to the front of the room, despite the snakeskin heels.

That five men on no more than a banjo, mandolin, guitar, standing bass, and fiddle could produce such magic awed her. This was whiskey-drinking, moon-howling, boot-stomping, heart-smashing mountain music and her blood sang right along with it.

The forward driving banjo rolls capitulated her spirits into the ether while at the same time, the lonely wail of the fiddle nearly made her weep, as did the lead singer's voice. Scabbed and honey-tinged, his voice melted into her bloodstream, forcing her eyes to close and her torso to sway to his bittersweet despair.

~ * ~

Jabe inhaled sharply when he spotted the sylph that leaned against the bar. Now *that* was some eye candy. He lifted the bottle of Sam Adams to his lips while he watched the dark haired goddess out of the corner of his eye. He swallowed the beer and promptly choked when he realized that it was Zylla who stood, long and curvy at the bar, wearing nothing but a second skin.

My God, he thought, then couldn't think at all. By the time he had recovered from shock, the Amblers were playing and Zylla stood at the base of the stage. He started toward her, but although her attire promised sultry evenings and unfurling blossoms, she seemed unreal, untouchable.

An aura surrounded her and outside that space, men gawked and a few women narrowed their eyes, but Zylla didn't notice. She was nothing short of stunning in those clothes that hugged every curve and inlet of her body, her hair streaming down her bare shoulders and back.

He watched expressions of awe, happiness, lust, and longing travel over her face. He frowned, disturbed. Her expression was the manifestation of undiluted love. He folded his arms and glared at Rye. He would have to kill his best friend.

"Shit," Jabe swore and swallowed a great swig, drowning the jealousy he despised. A useless emotion—jealousy. Besides, if he intended to keep Zylla at arm's length, then he didn't need the green ogre egging him on. He shot a quelling glance at Rye again, for good measure, and headed toward Zylla to penetrate her magic circle.

From the stage, the lead singer announced a short break and Zylla descended into a swirl of movement, voices, and insecurity as she remembered where she was and what she wore. As the Lounge's stereo system blared on, Zylla searched the crowd for Jabe.

In seconds, her gaze locked with his, and she felt heat flame her as his glance slowly raked her body up and down. When his eyes met hers again, she squirmed at the smoldering gaze leveled on her.

He stalked toward her. She fingered her necklace and looked for an escape. He smiled. Her mouth went dry.

"Hello, darlin'," he rumbled.

Speechless, she raised the corners of her lips in reply and was saved from responding by the arrival of Rye and two of his band mates. Rye laughed and embraced his friend, patting him hard on the back.

"Great sound," Jabe said as he broke the embrace and turned to greet the rest of the band. Meanwhile, Rye's dancing blue eyes, tinged with the slightest regret, swallowed Zylla whole.

"Ah, Viking," he said to Jabe without turning from Zylla. "I should have known that you'd swipe the prettiest girl here."

Enchanted, Zylla laughed.

She spent the next thirty minutes surrounded by three of the band members while Jabe chatted with the other two. She felt drunk and high and ecstatic. By some miracle of creation, the entire band was good-looking, and three of them encircled her, vying for her favors as if she were a maiden and they were her knights. She was half in love with them all—Rye and his eyes that lit flame blue when he laughed, Alex with his silent, dark looks, and Mitch, the pretty boy in suede pants and a poet shirt.

She flirted and smiled, and laughed at her surprise that she was capable of flirting. Once again, she felt like she belonged to the world. She felt alive. For the first time, she noticed the stares of men and the glares of women.

And she loved it.

Her conscience reminded her that it was all fleeting—the emotion, the attention, the airbrushed veneer she sported, but she let her pride smash that little voice and reveled in glory.

A few feet away, Jabe basked in that glory. He stole glances at her while he talked with Shaun and Max, enjoying her contagious laughter and obvious happiness. He felt a twinge of jealousy when Rye's arm encircled her waist, but Jabe banished it when he raised his eyes to hers and was nearly scorched by the heat. That combustion was for him. He inhaled the fire and stored it deep down in his belly. She was his.

For the second time that night, Jabe frowned. He shouldn't be staking claims. He wasn't being vigilant enough. He needed to abide by his decision to keep Zylla as a friend. He would not cross that line. *Dammit.*

But at the end of the band's break, Mitch clasped Jabe's shoulder and said, "Your girlfriend is just beautiful, really beautiful." He shook his head and groaned, "You are so lucky, man."

Alex punched his shoulder, winked and slurred, "If you get sick of her, pass her along to me."

And Rye just nodded his head, that old gleam in his eye that told Jabe he was both proud and reproachful, his 'you've got a good one here so don't screw it up' look.

Pride and desire swelled in Jabe's body and his mind shrugged off all reason. He wanted Zylla and she wanted him. When the band ascended the few steps to the stage for their second set, Jabe went to her side to stake his claim.

Fourteen

The touch of Jabe's hand, firm at her waist, erased Zylla's mind. His thumb snaked under her tube top and tattooed her skin in small circles, causing her breasts to tighten and rise against the thin fabric. She was grateful that the band had returned to the stage because she was no longer capable of speech. Zylla wasn't all that sure she could walk anymore.

She felt the intense heat from Jabe's eyes and turned into his arms, lightly touching his cheek with her fingertips, stroking his eyebrow with her forefinger. Still, his predatory gaze did not waver. He rested his other hand on her waist and brushed his lips against hers, his hair a blond waterfall around them.

Jabe kissed her with relaxed ease, a sort of playful banter. He ran his hands down her forearms and twirled his fingers through hers, dancing, teasing, bodies still inches apart. Just lips and fingers. His tongue cajoled and hers made witty reply.

When he slanted his head to deepen the kiss, Zylla's senses careened. She twined her fingers through his hair and grabbed the back of his head for balance, as well as to bring him closer to the heat spreading through her limbs.

Jabe heard her silent plea and pulled her tight against him before suddenly remembering where they were. The throb of the music and the chatter of people cleared some of the lust from his mind, enough to feel ashamed for mauling her in public, yet not enough to ease the ache in his loins. His erection pulsed to the thrum of the bass as it begged to be released from its denim prison. He had to break the heat between them or he'd take her right against the wall.

"Do you want to dance?" His voice was rougher than he intended.

Zylla stared at him blankly for a minute then laughed. "Are you kidding me? I can't even walk in these things."

She lifted one well-heeled leg and nearly toppled over, but Jabe caught her fall as he barked out a laugh and rested his forehead against hers.

"You look stunning tonight."

She shrugged, eyes downcast. "It's not me, not really."

Jabe's eyebrow arched. "Apparently, it is."

Zylla shyly raised her eyes to his and he nearly groaned at the desire he saw spinning there. He rested his hands on her hips as she raised her palm to cradle his neck. Jabe inclined his mouth over her full lips, open to receive him, and again felt thunder deep in his belly. He was surprised to find that he enjoyed this lazy communication, this slow-building fire that nevertheless burned hotter than any he had ever built. He cradled her head in his hands and she gripped him tight in return. Jabe broke their kiss and gave her a lopsided grin.

"It's natural kissing you," he said.

"And dangerous," she whispered.

He looked at her quizzically and she teased, "You make me forget my otherwise virtuous nature."

At once his eyes smoldered and when he spoke again, his tone was husky. "I'll take it."

"What?"

"Your virtue," he growled.

This time when he kissed her, he clutched her to him and tore at her lips as if he were rabid.

"Jabe," she breathed into his mouth.

"I want you," he muttered between kisses. She nodded.

He inhaled heavily. "Are you sure?"

"Yes please," she said quickly, lifting her face to be kissed again.

~ * ~

Zylla didn't remember the cab ride to Jamaica Plain, nor did she remember getting from his front door to his bedroom, although she vaguely recalled devouring an apple and Jabe sucking the stickiness from her fingers.

She became conscious again in the candlelit cavern that was his room, where the hot breath of him ignited her own passion, and his rough, wild hands peeled her like a sweet nectarine until she stood naked and raw in his arms.

He wore only his jeans, and the golden, fiery skin of his chest and arms warmed her skin so that she yearned to cleave to his very essence. Zylla couldn't think anymore, could barely breathe, as his lips and tongue welded her to him. His hands on her were at once fierce and protective as they roamed her skin, consumed her heavy breasts, and stroked her thigh. She sighed into his mouth and he scooped her into his arms and placed her on the bed.

"Zyll," he moaned against the crook of her neck, and his mouth meandered over her body, causing her to mutter senseless words that only he could fathom. His fingers delved inside her and Jabe groaned, kissing her again, hot and rough, on her mouth.

"Jabe," she whispered in urgent, quiet tones that caused him to groan again, and she embraced empty space as he left her arms and the bed.

Zylla's eyes opened. He stood by the bed, chest heaving, mouth parted, passion-darkened eyes asking a question she wasn't sure she understood.

She was sure that she'd done something wrong, that she was suddenly repulsive to him, but the fear of losing him was momentarily greater than her pride.

"Jabe?" she questioned softly and reached out to take his hand to pull him down to her. Her fingers threaded through his hair as she lifted her face to take his mouth with her own. His kiss was insistent and wild and she felt his fingers work at his button and zipper.

In an instant, his naked, beloved weight sank onto her. His hairy thighs meshed against her silky ones, his hard stomach muscles quivering against her skin, and the powerful length of his organ pressing against her swollen center.

"Jabe," she whispered achingly.

He froze, the tip of him barely touching her, and cradled her head in his hands, forcing her to look into his eyes.

"Are you sure?"

"Yes," she whispered.

His mouth swept downwards and took her parted lips, and his tongue dipped and swirled within her mouth until she sank boneless into his pillows. Jabe ran his fingers along her arms in search of her hands and when he found them, he laced his fingers with hers as he nudged her knees apart with his legs. He took a deep breath then captured Zylla's eyes with his gaze.

The phone trilled.

Zylla's head snapped to the side and her body shifted toward the offending sound.

"Jabe..." she trailed off as the ring shrilled again.

"Relax, darlin'," he gritted through clenched teeth. "The machine will get it." He dragged kisses across her cheek, capturing her mouth once again.

"But," she said into his mouth, "it's late. Maybe..."

"*Shhhh*, baby, it's nothing," he whispered between kisses, and Zylla willingly submersed herself to his insistent lips when she heard the click of the machine. "It's nothing," he muttered, and he shifted his weight atop her as he again poised himself to enter her heat.

"Viking, Jabe, if you're there, man, pick up."

Jabe's head shot up and his hand tensed on Zylla's breast at the frantic quiver in Rye's voice.

"Um, okay, I hate to, well... it's about two-thirty. Jabe, man, if you get this, get down to your building. The Charlesgate's on fire."

Fifteen

"Stay here, get some sleep," Jabe said as he pulled a tee shirt over his head, but Zylla was already out of bed, groping the floor for her leather pants.

"No way. I'm coming with you," she replied and grunted as she tugged on the stubborn leather.

"Okay," Jabe said tersely, but Zylla saw the relief in his eyes. He was frightened, she realized, of what he might find, and she guessed he didn't want to face it alone.

Downstairs, he stopped at the hall closet and fished out a shiny red helmet, which he tossed to her. She caught it with both hands and fastened it on her head as she followed him to the front door.

Outside, he climbed on his Indian and the engine roared. He gripped the handlebars and looked over his left shoulder.

"Climb on."

Zylla settled onto the seat behind him and put her arms around his waist. The hot summer evening had subsided into a cool night, and she shivered into Jabe's heat.

"You ever ridden one of these before?"

"No," Zylla shouted over the engine's din.

"Just hold on and relax," he suggested then kicked the bike into gear.

No traffic clogged Jamaicaway due to the late hour, and in minutes, they glimpsed the red and blue lights of fire engines and the thick black smoke curling into the city lit sky.

Rye leaned against his battered white van, which was parked on Beacon Street opposite the Charlesgate, and Jabe rolled behind it to park.

Rye jogged over to them. "Thank God you're here, Viking." He clapped Jabe on the shoulder and shook his head. "I'm sorry."

"Thanks for calling, man," Jabe said, but his eyes were adhered to the sight of orange flames lapping out of a first floor window. "I've gotta go over there," he muttered and ran across the street to speak to the police.

"What happened, Rye?" Zylla asked, smoke and grief stinging her throat.

Rye lifted his hand and let it drop as he stared while a firefighter smashed another window to reach the flames that just danced out of the hose's reach.

Finally, he said, "Beats me. I was just heading back home after dropping Nolan off when I saw the smoke and trucks. Had a feeling it was Viking's building, so I stopped." He turned sorrowful blue eyes on Zylla.

"I'm sorry," he said and put an arm around her.

A tear swiveled down her cheek and she brushed it away. With no lights on, the Charlesgate looked lonely and abandoned again and, as if to reinforce Zylla's thought, the building groaned.

"Phew," Rye said, fanning the air. "Smell that? I thought the breeze was carrying the stink of low tide into the city, but it's worse than that, and it's coming from the Charlesgate. Something in the fire, I suppose, but it makes me want to puke—it's like a rotting corpse or something."

Despite her sadness, Zylla half-groaned, half-laughed. "Thank you for that image, Rye. But you're right, it does smell like dead fish." The stench reminded her of her nightmares and apprehension gripped her. She crossed her arms, shivering again, and Rye pulled her closer against his suede jacket.

"We've smelled it before, actually," she added. "Jabe seems to think it comes from the basement." Zylla shrugged. "Maybe whatever it was caught on fire."

"Hey." Jabe jogged toward them, a grim smile on his face. "It's not that bad apparently. Captain Turri says it's contained to one room, my office."

Her face fell. "Oh no, Jabe. All your blueprints and notes."

He smiled tiredly. "Copies. I keep the originals at home." He brushed the wetness from under Zylla's eye and stroked her cheek for a second before dropping his hand and continuing. "They think it's arson, although they're not sure how the perpetrator got in the building in the first place. It was sealed tight when they arrived. A neighbor saw the flames and called it in.

"The captain said that the only reason for arson might be revenge, profit, or fun." He scratched under his chin then raised a brow. "It's gotta be the latter 'cuz I just can't believe... Anyway, they'll get the dogs in here later to sniff for accelerants."

"It's almost out?" she asked.

"Yep." He smiled then frowned as he saw her shaking beneath Rye's arm.

"Hey, you're freezing, darlin'." He held out his arms and she walked into them. He smelled like smoke and his natural scent, and she melted into the heat and safety of his embrace, all foreboding now vanquished in Jabe's arms. He kissed the top of her head.

"Why don't you go on home? It's going to be a long night of waiting, and I'd rather you be curled up in your bed. C'mon, I'll get you a cab."

"I can take her home, Jabe," Rye said. "Where d'ya live?"

"In Central," she replied as she reluctantly pulled away from Jabe's arms and faced Rye.

"Right near me," he said cheerily. "I'm over on Bigelow. Let's go, I'll have you home in a jiffy."

Jabe leaned forward and kissed Zylla's lips briskly. "I'll call you," he said, but he had already started walking back to the Charlesgate.

~ * ~

Instead of walking as usual, Zylla rode the CT1 into Boston on Monday morning. The commute was slow and the grizzled man beside her smelled like a hangover, but she didn't care. The sky was bright blue, the Charlesgate was still standing proud, and the sun's rays pricked over skin that Jabe had blessed with his hands only two days ago.

"I liked having you in my bed last night," he had said when he called her on Sunday to tell her about the Charlesgate's condition. His voice had been gruff with sleeplessness and lust and had jarred memories of his hands on her skin. Jabe wanted her, and she felt grateful and happy. Maybe tonight they would continue what they had begun. She would give herself to him, he would declare his love, and she would feel like this forever.

She sang tunelessly as she entered the office, causing Dean Pendergast to poke his head out of his office and Nicole to quirk a puzzled grin.

"Good morning," Zylla called then continued to sing her path to her cubicle.

"What's wrong with her?" Nicole mouthed to the dean.

"She's happy, apparently." Then he frowned, his long bearded face suddenly made even longer.

"It's *Monday*."

"Yes," Dean Pendergast replied thoughtfully. "You think...?" He lewdly waggled his brows.

"No doubt." Nicole laughed.

In her cube, Zylla blithely scheduled conferences, arranged travel plans, updated files, and began to plan the August faculty off-site meeting in Gloucester while images of Jabe flit through her day. His mouth on her breasts. His eyes when he lost control. His voice, hot and low, in her ear. Her body curled into his.

She traveled the day on autopilot, walking through her tasks with the aura of Jabe surrounding her. She could taste him in her mouth and smell him through the wafting air. She saw swirls of bright colors in the space around her head. Prince's *Dirty Mind* album spun in her head. Certainly, Saturday had been the best almost-sex she'd ever had.

When five o'clock announced its presence, she assessed her workspace and finalized her appraisal with a nod. She felt useful. Purposeful. Reconciled with herself. And she owed it all to Jabe. She'd always possessed too much angst. *That's the trouble with being a virgin. Too much angst. Too much wallowing about in the mud crying for Heathcliff.*

Soon, she thought with a wicked grin, she wouldn't be crying for anything but Jabe as he rid her of her virginity forever.

~ * ~

Jabe stared at the blueprint spread out on the table but couldn't see anything except the bliss in Zylla's eyes after he'd kissed her.

The light of Monday morning poured into the memories of the weekend, destroying all magic and leaving him with the metallic taste of failure.

"Ah shit," he drawled and slammed a palm onto the blueprint-frosted table. The thick reek of smoke and that fetid low tide odor pervaded the entire first floor of the Charlesgate. Even when he shut the door to his temporary office, the charred memory of his old office seeped into the room.

"Where are you with your lavender when I need you, Lydia?" he said to the air.

Nothing happened.

Damn women. His well-ordered world had spun off its axis as a result of vexing females. The peace he had achieved was gone. Vanished in a weekend.

Jabe buried his face in his hands and drew his fingers down, causing a wake of white streaks to follow the path of his fingertips. If only Zylla hadn't... what?

If she hadn't walked into the Lizard Lounge looking like a rock 'n' roll goddess? If she hadn't brimmed with infectious joy? If she hadn't looked at him with starving eyes? If, if, if...

It was easy to place blame on her at night, but daylight refused to let him lie to himself. The truth was he was proud that she wanted him when she could have anyone in that bar. His ego had been ripped from his jeans and stroked until it waved disdainfully at his brain. He sighed and left his office.

"Dennis, I'm going out for some air," he called to his foreman. Jabe stuffed his fists into his jean pockets, slumped down the steps of the Charlesgate and stalked toward Massachusetts Avenue and Newbury Street. He didn't notice the bright greens of the Fens or the scantily clad women that passed him. He only knew that it was too hot, too sunny, and there were too many damn people on the street for a workday.

"Shit," he muttered. In the time between two rolls on a banjo he had managed to resume his habit. Only this time he had really screwed up because it was Zylla, a person who would have been a second Rye to him, and now she would just be another woman on the Jabe wheel.

The cycle would start again. He'd blink and Zylla would be at his house every night, demanding his time, sucking meaningless words of love from his mouth. Three months and it would be over. Except Zylla had no experience with bitterness and breakups. That was the trouble with virgins. Thank God she still was.

"Hello, my friend."

The musical baritone lured Jabe back to the traffic and bustle of Massachusetts Avenue and Emmett's round face.

"You seem to have some trouble in your head. Again." Emmett struck an E minor to accentuate Jabe's mood, bringing a distant smile to Jabe's face.

"She must be very beautiful, eh? To cause such a miserable face."

"Yeah, she's something, all right." Jabe heaved a sigh and stared blankly at the giant Citgo sign, remembering Zylla writhing underneath him, wonder and lust racing alternatively across her face. Damn virgins and their trouble. He wanted to bury himself in her again and again to claim that trouble. He shook his head as if the motion could erase the image.

"But you care about this one, hmmm? Like that building of yours?" Emmett rested his left foot on the rung of his stool, adjusted his guitar, and began the opening chords of "In the Pines."

Jabe considered the pavement while reflections of Zylla played in his head. Loving her caused his entire body to weep in bliss, and he admitted to himself that he'd never before experienced a sexual encounter like that. No, he didn't want to admit, couldn't admit, just how much he did care.

A passerby threw a few coins in Emmett's guitar case.

"Thank you, sir," he said with a tilt of the head and turned to Jabe, waiting for his answer.

Jabe grinned. "You know, Emmett, sometimes I think you are my Jedi master."

Emmett returned a slow smile. "Yoda I am not, young Jabe. But sometimes I feel that old." He removed his hat and pointed to his white, curly hair.

"I'll see you later, Em." Jabe raised a hand in farewell, dropped a buck in the case, and walked on aimlessly.

Yes, he cared. His heart told him that his life needed Zylla in it, but his mind was smarter. Because he cared, he would zip in his ego and keep her at a distance until he could be the friend she deserved.

Behind him, Emmett began a song that lamented men who lose their good women. He directed his voice at Jabe's back, the latter having squared his shoulders in determination to face a war that Emmett was sure he would lose.

~ * ~

On Tuesday, she dialed Jabe's office phone. It was after six, but he was no doubt still wandering around the Charlesgate, planning and jotting down ideas.

"H'lo," he answered.

"Hey there. I was just wondering if you wanted to grab a drink after you're done there?"

"Uhhh." He paused. "Tonight's not good. I'm planning to hook up with Rye."

"Okay," she chirped. "Maybe some other night this week, then?"

Jabe hesitated. "Probably not, Zyll. I really need to get some stuff done. You know, this building..."

"No problem," she said, a smile in her voice. "I should work on my writing anyway. Just call when you have some time."

"Will do."

She hung up, humming *Charlotte Sometimes* and abruptly stopped, puzzled.

Huh, she thought.

The room's colors seemed to fade, and Zylla fell a couple of levels on the fluffy, gold-tinged white cloud she'd floated on for the past three days.

"Huh," she said out loud.

Jabe was often too busy to talk or meet with her after work, but she understood and knew they would inevitably hook up sooner rather than later. So the words of their brief phone conversation did not faze her. But this time, something was different.

His tone was wrong. It was kind. Too kind. Like a stranger. *Will do*, he had said. She hated the politeness in his voice. It hurt her chest.

Maybe he was just in a bad mood. But her heart still drooped in her chest, and the fluffy white cloud ripped itself from under her feet, tossing her into the air. Zylla managed to clutch the uneven edge of the cloud before it floated away completely, and she hung on, waiting for a phone call that never came.

Sixteen

Zylla walked home from work on Friday. The sky was overcast and the wind wild, and the combination cheered her immensely, momentarily easing the ache from Jabe's silence. Nearly a block from home, she spotted Rye.

"Hello, beautiful." He grinned, his dancing eyes igniting her own smile. "I'm just heading home. Come for a drink?"

Zylla started to nod but Rye added, "Jabe'll be there in a half hour or so." At her hesitation, Rye grabbed her hand and crooned, "Let's go. I cook a mean burger."

His eyes were filled with a strange understanding and, with a shaky smile, Zylla walked alongside him to his two-level condo on Bigelow Street.

All of her trepidation was forgotten when she walked through the door to Rye's home. A fire in the wood-burning stove cast a cheery glow on the unseasonably cool summer day and dispelled the gray air that filtered through the sliding glass doors.

"What a great home!" she exclaimed.

The olive walls were offset with one brick wall where an antique salmon brocade sofa with big, soft pillows beckoned. Bookshelves, greenery, and a small calico cat welcomed her, and she longed to pull a book down and curl into the huge slate blue leather chair nestled in the far corner.

A spiral staircase, which divided the living room and kitchen, led to the second floor and a skylight. The small kitchen on the other side of the staircase was of brick and tile and the outside wall was entirely of sliding glass, lending a wonderful view of the Victorians across the street.

"Thanks. It's comfy enough for me and Moose." He scooped up the cat stretched on the sofa, gave him a quick buss on his furry little head and put him back. The cat meowed, arched, and curled up on a pillow to doze. Rye looked over his shoulder at her on his way to the refrigerator.

"Why don't you put some music in, eh? Beer okay?"

"That'd be great."

She chose Johnny Cash and sat on the couch to admire the oil paintings and stringed instruments hanging from the walls. The buzzer jarred the lazy tones of *I Still Miss Someone* and Zylla jumped, a flight of nerves suddenly diving into her belly.

"That'll be Jabe," Rye stated unnecessarily and pushed the lock release. A few seconds later, the door opened.

"My brother," Rye said as he clutched Jabe in an embrace. Jabe smiled and reached for one of the two bottles Rye held.

"That for me?"

Rye shook his head slowly, and Jabe's head swiveled to where Zylla waited on the sofa. She nearly flinched at his blank stare and curt hello, and her fingers slipped a little from the edge of her cloud.

Jabe's eyes leveled on Rye, and the latter moved cautiously past him to sit by Zylla on the sofa. Jabe ripped open the refrigerator door and clanked out a beer. He popped the cap and swallowed half the bottle before taking a seat on the leather chair and propping one booted foot on the matching ottoman.

Zylla kept her eyes downcast for the most part, but was confused by what she saw in Jabe's face when she did manage to brave a glance. One minute his face seemed gripped in agony and longing, and in the next second changed his expression changed to disdain. Both casts made her insides drop and her blood stir, and she hated herself for wanting him.

After a few minutes of awkward conversation, Rye rose and headed to the kitchen. He pulled lighter fluid from under the sink and a box of matches from a drawer then crossed the living room to the deck door.

"I'm gonna go start the grill." He opened the door and a gust of wind poured into the room. "If this damn wind will let me."

"Can I help?" Zylla pleaded.

Rye threw a look at the stony Jabe, sighed, and said, "It'd be great if you'd set the table. Just poke around for whatever you need."

Taking her beer, she hastily got up and disappeared around the staircase into the kitchen. Rye shot Jabe another glare then disappeared onto the porch. After what seemed like days to him, Jabe took a breath and followed Zylla.

"So, have you been writing at all?"

She felt so nervous that her ears buzzed. "What?"

"Have you been working on your book?" he asked tersely.

She reached behind her hair and massaged her neck muscles as she answered in a small voice. Jabe studied that hand enviously, but she didn't notice.

"How about you? How's my, I mean, the Charlesgate?"

It is *your building, Zyll,* his treacherous mind thought. *It's always been for you.*

"Good. Great. You'd be amazed at the change." For a brief moment, his eyes sparkled. "You should stop by..." He broke off and covered the awkward silence by rapping his knuckles on the counter.

She opened a cabinet, by some miracle the right one, and took down three blue and white dishes.

"Let me," Jabe interjected, taking the plates from her. Their hands brushed, and Zylla nearly cried because she missed his touch and his friendship. He put the plates onto the wobbly antique dining table.

"Zyll," he began as he turned to her, intending to say something to take the hurt from her eyes. But then she was in his arms, his mouth gobbling hers, her hands in his hair, grasping and hungry.

He clutched her hips tight to him and thrust one thigh between her legs. She moaned into his mouth and he couldn't hear anything except red desire. He shoved his hands under her tee shirt so that his fevered skin could heal itself on her smooth back while his mouth sucked and dragged at hers.

"Hey, the grill is... well, alrighty then." Rye spun on one heel and re-entered the living room.

Mortified, Zylla broke away, pushing at Jabe while he struggled to bring her back. "Stop, stop," she whispered, pushing frantically against his chest. *Don't stop, don't stop*, her heart cried. Hope swelled in her veins and her mind was giddy. She had one leg back up onto that cloud.

"I'm just going to use the bathroom," she said, smiling, and Jabe watched her with half-lidded eyes, his lips ragged from her kisses. She turned away and peered into the living room where Rye was flipping through CDs.

"Rye, where's your bathroom?"

"Upstairs." He grinned at her, wide and conspiratorial, and she beamed back.

In the upstairs bathroom, painted ox-blood red and illuminated by a huge round skylight, Zylla looked in the mirror at her flushed cheeks and wild hair and was elated. Jabe still wanted her. He wasn't ignoring her! He *was* just busy. It was all in her head. Hadn't Anne told her that she was crazy?

Zylla reached into her pocket and pulled out her tube of L'Oreal Real Raisin as she hummed along with the last few bars of *Ring of Fire*. The music ended and pieces of conversation spiraled up the stairs. Zylla listened absentmindedly until she heard Rye say, "What *is* that girl doing in there?"

"Probably reapplying makeup."

Zylla looked at the tube in her hand and smiled as Rye scoffed, "Why? She doesn't need it."

"She is beautiful," Jabe agreed.

"You going to stick with this one?"

There was silence and she paused, lipstick resting on her bottom lip, as she awaited Jabe's answer.

"Probably not."

The smile in her body plummeted to the floor and lay still.

"Why not?" Rye's tone was incredulous and almost made her weep with gratitude. Her stomach, in the meantime, had begun to digest her heart.

She could hear the shrug and self-disgust in Jabe's voice. "Because I'm stupid. Or smart. Take your pick."

Zylla watched her reflection pale and freeze. Then her bottom lip trembled and embarrassment crept to her face, melting her frozen pose. She felt confused and angry and hurt and insulted, then she didn't know what she felt. A blanket of mortification smothered her emotions. The world suddenly seemed shabby and she felt like its cheapest commodity.

Her leg slid from the cloud, followed by her fingers, which slipped slowly from the thinning edge. She silently fell until she lay, miles below, crumpled on the ground. When she could breathe again, she squared her shoulders, lifted her chin and headed down the stairs to make her apologies to Rye.

"I completely spaced, Rye. I'm so sorry." She managed a tremulous smile. "I was supposed to meet Anne for dinner tonight. Girls night out."

"Just call her up and invite her over," Rye suggested, then caught the brightness behind her eyes and the strange pallor of her skin. He nodded and kissed her cheek, silently cursing Jabe and his stupidity.

~ * ~

Zylla stood on tiptoe to reach into the cabinet for another package of coffee filters.

"No guy is worth this, Zyll. You look like hell."

She turned to stare blankly at Anne.

"Hello in there? Where's the girl who tells me to get over it every time some dork tramples on my heart?"

Zylla blinked in response.

"I even bought you pistachio ice cream to make up for all those times you bought me flowers to cheer me up. Hon, he's not worth it, I promise you."

Zylla shrugged and looked at the linoleum. "I'm fine, Anne. I've just been caught up in my book, you know, not enough air. I'm really making progress, though." She poured the grinds into the filter and switched the machine on. Coffee began to dribble into the pot.

"Zyllie," Anne pleaded. "All you do is come home from work and drink way too much coffee. My God, your hands are shaking! And you sit in that hot, stinky room with the blinds shut and stare at your computer for God knows how long. You've lost way too much weight and the circles under your eyes are so black that you look like a raccoon."

Anne took a deep breath. "Honey, you're bound to be two pickles short of a sandwich in less than a month, and I'll have to call the authorities to take you away and you'll eventually turn into one of those women with fifty cats and blue hair."

"I don't like cats," she replied. "Blue hair is a possibility, however." She hugged Anne. "I'm fine. I'm a little depressed, but I'll be okay, really."

She poured a cup of coffee and headed back to her room.

"I gotta write. Big scene coming up."

Anne let out an exasperated sigh and made the motion of strangling someone's throat with her hands. Zylla shut her door with a click.

The truth was, if she stopped writing, her throat would close up, her body would begin to tremble, and she'd race to the bathroom every ten minutes to dry heave. As it was, every morning she woke up with an empty hollow in her belly and a sharp sting of pain, all because Jabe had cut her out of his life. She couldn't cry anymore, but her eyes burned and ached, and phantom tears rolled down her cheeks.

She found her solace through the cruelty of her pirate queen's rule aboard her ship, *Charnwood*. Lady Charn, as Zylla finally had named her, took her revenge on a cheating husband by torturing men. She reveled in mutinies, practiced keelhauling on a daily basis, and when a crewmember tried to rape her, she'd cut out his tongue with a rusted knife, and stitched his lips together. When he died of starvation, she tossed his body to the sharks.

Lady Charn wasn't afraid to speak her mind. When she wanted a man's body for a night of pleasure, she simply took him, then discarded him the next day, smacking her lips, sated until her need rose again.

Zylla didn't particularly like her pirate creation, but when she wrote, she became Lady Charn, reveling in her pirate queen's breeches, and never felt the pain of being cast overboard herself.

After writing the scene, Zylla had another cup of coffee, the caffeine keeping her too jittery to feel, and took a shower. While she washed, she noticed that her hipbones were too sharp, and when she looked up too quickly, she felt dizzy.

Anne's right. I look like hell. I feel *like hell.* Anger surged through her and chased the coffee jitters from her body.

"This is ridiculous," she muttered as she traced her hollow cheek with a finger and pushed a dark circle under her eye. No man was worth bony hips. God, she looked like a crow.

It had been three weeks since she'd seen Jabe at Rye's house, since he had kissed her so hotly, since he'd spoken to her. Her pirate queen would have castrated him a long time ago. Her pirate queen would have eaten.

Zylla dressed in something other than sweatpants or work attire for the first time in three weeks, then went to the kitchen and ate the chicken breast and salad that Anne had prepared for her in hopes that she'd eat.

After, as she shoveled pistachio ice cream in her mouth, her anger sharpened. She still wanted Jabe. She laughed aloud, and the weight on her heart lifted as she acknowledged the truth she had been trying to forget. He may not want her anymore, but by God, he couldn't just call all the shots. He couldn't end things before they began, not even giving her a chance.

Zylla remembered the tattoo she didn't get. Yes, she deserved a say in the matter. She wasn't going to wait for Jabe to decide her life.

She washed her dishes, dabbed on some lipstick, called a cab, and headed out into the warm night.

~ * ~

Now that she was here at his door, she again felt gauche and jittery. She squeezed her eyes shut, took a deep breath, opened her lids, and knocked. Both eyebrows shot up when the door opened immediately, and they remained raised when a stunning woman with chiseled cheekbones and short, spiky hair flashed a smile at her.

Zylla felt her cheeks burn and she stammered, "Oh, um, I'm sorry. Wrong house."

She turned quickly, but the woman grabbed her arm.

"No, no!" she said frantically, laughing. "You're here for Rye's birthday, right? The party's upstairs, no, downstairs. I forget!"

The woman threw her hands into the air, rolled her eyes, and laughed. Zylla thought her voice sounded like wind chimes.

"Wherever Jabe's hidden lair is! I'm Lynn."

For the first time in weeks, Zylla really smiled. "I'm Zylla. It's nice to meet you."

She followed Lynn to the upstairs closet in Jabe's bedroom and felt her stomach roll sickly as his scent assaulted her, reminding her at once of his burning body on hers. Knots formed in her belly and her legs trembled as she descended the stairs to the speakeasy.

With a roaring fire, dance music, and low lighting, the room was warm and welcoming, but Zylla was certain that her lips were blue with fright. Then she saw Rye and his eyes twinkled at her.

She started to walk toward him when a flash of purple zipped toward her and she found herself bent back until her hair brushed the floor.

"Finally, we tango."

Pete's face loomed above her with an expression that wanted only a rose between his teeth. Zylla wanted to laugh, but she was too conscious of being a spectacle to respond to Pete's flirtation. Her throat closed, and the back of her eyes began to burn.

"Hey, don't I get a kiss for my birthday?" Rye said, and gently lifted Zylla to her feet and out of Pete's embrace.

"*Mon dieu,*" Pete swore in his fake French accent. "Always stealing zee women."

"Thank you," Zylla whispered as she hugged Rye to her. "You're always coming to my rescue."

He gave her a quick squeeze and murmured, "Mmmm, you're too good to be true."

Rye pushed her away from him to hold her at arm's length while he peered into her eyes. "How are you, really?"

"Good. Really." Zylla paused. "Except, I didn't know that there was a party tonight." She chewed her lip.

"Awwww, don't worry about it. All you need is a drink," he said, propelling her to the bar.

"I love my friend," he continued, "but he's an idiot."

The idiot approached the bar as Rye poured whiskey for Zylla, and Rye kicked her foot in warning.

"Hi," she said simply.

"I'm glad you came," Jabe returned, the side of his mouth curled in a smile. Zylla's insides calmed at the warmth in his voice. "This is Clay."

The man who accompanied Jabe to the bar flashed a perfectly straight, white-toothed smile and tossed his head so that his blond bangs shivered, casting a mysterious slant to his face. His body was perfect and tanned, and his clothes seemed tailored to fit him. He looked like a Calvin Klein model, gorgeous and sexy. But fake. Zylla instinctively didn't like him. Beside her, she could swear that she'd heard Rye growl.

"Hey." Clay smirked, appraising her with a nod, and she cringed. He was too cocky, used to getting any woman he wanted but as she easily saw through that type of guy, she wasn't impressed. She imagined that a thin layer of slime coated him.

"Zylla," Jabe said, "I think that you and Clay might get along real well."

She had to bite her tongue to keep her mouth from dropping open while Rye just shook his head.

"Oh?" She turned to Clay. "Well, perhaps we'll talk later." With a cool smile, she dismissed them and turned to Rye. After a stunned silence, she felt the two leave.

Rye let out a tired sigh at the anger flashing on her face. "No," he said to her. "He's trying, in his own delusional way, to make amends. Sometimes, Zyll, we guys are pretty clueless."

Seventeen

Jabe swore under his breath. He belatedly realized that Zylla thought he was passing her off to the next guy. Which, he shrugged, he was.

When he saw her descend the staircase, he had felt his mouth go dry and his body instantly harden, and he had known that he was lost. He had mentally cursed Rye. Damn Billy Goat had invited her, knowing that Jabe couldn't say anything since it was Rye's party in the first place.

He had missed Zylla tremendously—her conversation, her laughter, her frowns, and her mouth moving against his. He had tried to ignore that last thought and concentrated on how to mend his friendship with her, to return to their easy camaraderie before that glorious night she had spent in his bed.

Then Clay had walked by with the stares of forty women following him and inspiration struck. If she were with someone else, he wouldn't consider touching her. He conveniently forgot that Clay used women like a hay fever victim used tissue, but at that moment, he only knew that women thought Clay was hot and Zylla was a woman. Now here he was, shamed by her rebuff and finding solace in a crabmeat canapé.

He stopped chewing and froze. There was that sweet little blond that he had chased a couple of years ago in between relationships. What was her name? Lisa? Leslie? Leslie, that was it.

She stood with a few other women over by the fireplace, wearing a tight red dress, three-inch heels, and a look on her face that promised hot, sticky passion. She licked her upper lip with the tip of her tongue. Jabe groaned.

~ * ~

Zylla participated in conversations in a state of anxious grace and fought her desire to search the room for Jabe, but then she caught Rye staring over her shoulder, anger brimming on his face. Before Rye could stop her, Zylla turned to see Jabe with a beautiful blonde, the kind of girl who kept up with the latest fashion, not one who preferred combat boots to heels. The blonde sat curled up on the sofa and Jabe stood behind her, his fingers playing with her long hair.

Zylla tried to turn away, but she was compelled to look even as grief strangled her. Her insides ripped to shreds, she simply watched as Jabe slowly pulled a red ribbon out of the woman's hair and brushed her tresses with his fingers. He curled her hair around his fist, baring her neck then bent his head with parted lips to...

Zylla spun around, and Rye steadied her.

"Be brave," he said.

She nodded and tried to think. *Be brave.* Yes. What would Lady Charn have done? Chopped off the blonde's tits and tossed them to the rats, Zylla thought wryly then reminded herself that it was not the woman's fault. What would Lady Charn do if she were not hellbent on violence?

Zylla looked back at the sofa but although the blonde was still there, Jabe wasn't. Her eyes roved the room and rested on him. He stood at the bar, watching her, and all the loneliness that had speared her over the past three weeks surged and spun into an anger so keen that she could taste it on her tongue.

"You okay, Zyll?" Rye said.

"I will be." She squeezed Rye's arm, never taking her eyes off Jabe, and walked to the bar.

Jabe stifled an admiring grin as he watched Zylla approach with her head held high and cool fury in her eyes. He had lasted all but five minutes with Leslie, who wore too much perfume, unlike Zylla, who revived a room with her own clean scent. Leslie's eyes were dead and pale, not russet and glowing, and her hair, well, her hair was straw, not ripples of chestnut silk.

"We need to talk," she said.

He nodded and went to stand by a stool at the quiet end of the bar. He waited for Zylla to sit, then followed her lead, and waited for her to speak.

"I know what you're doing."

Her voice was steely, and he cringed at the hurt she hid behind that metal.

"You made a mistake." She rolled her eyes. "Or nearly made a mistake, and now you're afraid that our night of almost-sex means that I want you to be with me always, maybe even get married and have a dog or a kid or three." Her gaze leveled him. "And you'd be right."

Jabe stiffened and his face became unreadable.

"So you've been pushing me away, maybe thinking that I'll start to hate you, fall out of love with you, move on. But love doesn't work that way, Jabe, and I love you." Her voice quavered, and she paused, swallowing hard as she stared at the bar. Then her head shot up and sparks lit her eyes.

"And I want you to love me, too, but here's where you're wrong. I don't *expect* you to."

Jabe arched a brow but said nothing.

"All I expect is honesty. If you don't want me in your life, then do me the courtesy of telling me to my face."

Jabe felt heat rise to his cheeks, and he leaned closer to her, the ends of his hair tickling her bare arm. He raised his hand and lifted her chin, forcing her to keep eye contact.

"I do not," he said slowly, "ever want you out of my life."

Tears trembled in Zylla's eyes, and he cursed himself for the hurt he had caused her. *Stupid, stupid.*

"I thought I was saving you pain in the end," he said, putting a finger to her lips when she parted them to retort, anger drowning the tears. "And I thought I was saving myself pain. I can't be near you without wanting to throw you down on the floor and take you until you can't think, and I won't do it, Zyll, I won't. I can't. Not to you."

He brushed a thumb across her lips then let his hand fall into his lap. Her knee bumped his, and he inhaled sharply, gripping his thigh to stop himself from pulling her against him.

"I care about you more than you know, Zyll," he said, his voice cracking. "And I want you. But I can't give you what you want, what you deserve. Relationships and me are bad news, I don't know why, but I don't want to risk finding out with you.

"You're part of me, don't you know that? You've given me the Charlesgate, shown me that what I do matters. I can't lose you, and until I can stop thinking about you in my bed every minute of every day, it's better if we stay apart. That's why I've been avoiding you."

He pitched her a lopsided grin. "Lust fades. Eventually."

Sadness was etched on every part of her, and he grabbed her hand.

"Zylla, I'm sorry. I was stupid. I meant well, but I see now what it did to you. I haven't been a very good friend, have I?"

She slowly shook her head.

"It won't happen again. You have my complete honesty from this point on, if you'll take it?"

A smile quivered on Zylla's lips.

"Thank you," she whispered. A hot sheen burned in her eyes, and her lips parted.

"Oh!" she exclaimed and propelled herself into Jabe's arms, kneading his back with her palms.

"God, I missed you, Zyll!" He kissed the side of her neck and buried his face in her hair.

"I missed you, too, you jerk," she sobbed.

After a minute, she broke from him, and hastily wiped her eyes. "I'm going to go. I'm not really in a partying mood," she said with a slight smile.

"I thought Rye had invited you. To torture me," he added with a snort.

"Nope. Came of my own volition. Call me tomorrow," she said shyly as she climbed down from the stool. "You owe me a beer."

He grinned at her retreating back.

Suddenly, she stopped and tossed over her shoulder, "I still think you're wrong."

His brows knitted in confusion.

"About this, what's between us," she said. "Isn't it better to make a mistake on love than to regret what might have been?"

For a few seconds, their gazes held before she walked across the room and up the stairs.

Suddenly feeling tired and old, Jabe rose and headed to the pool table where Rye studied him with sad eyes. "You let her go, huh?"

"For now," he said.

Eighteen

She simply could not handle another Monday. Zylla dragged herself from between the sheets and stumbled to the bathroom for a shower. Now she was awake, but a feeling of unbalance persisted, and as she passed the mirror, she caught herself scowling. If this had been last Saturday morning, she would have blamed the discontent in her bones on Jabe's silence, but everything had changed since Saturday night.

She may not have won true love, but she did not sacrifice herself in the battle. She was proud that she had acted like an Aries and stood up for herself rather than try to win him back by twisting herself into the woman she thought he wanted, or suffer in silence. Her decision to confront him at least earned her truth, and she had to respect his decision.

Zylla ignored the edginess that bounced through her body and tightened the fluffy yellow towel around her before she opened the door, steam billowing out behind her.

"What's wrong, my little ornery filly?" Anne asked from her roost on the kitchen counter, where she liked to sip her morning coffee.

"PMS, I think," Zylla replied as she walked into her bedroom. "But I'm not really sure. I just feel off, like I forgot to do something really important."

Anne placed her coffee cup beside her and hopped off the counter to follow Zylla.

"Rent's not due yet. Did you forget to pay the electric bill?" she suggested, leaning against the doorframe to Zylla's bedroom.

"Nope." Zylla stopped combing her hair as she pondered her emotions. Her eyes widened. "I guess... *hmmnn...* I guess I feel kinda guilty."

"Guilty?" Anne questioned, surprise in her voice.

"Yeah, like I'm doing something I shouldn't be doing."

The concern on Anne's face morphed into enlightenment.

"Well, there you go! It's Monday, silly. Reality. Demons. All that."

Huh? Zylla mouthed then fished a semi-ironed sundress from the closet.

"You said it yourself. You are not doing what you are supposed to be doing. How many times do we have to have this conversation?" Anne asked, suddenly frustrated.

"Stop blaming PMS, or Jabe, or the weather for your unhappiness, Zylla, and have the balls to do what you want to do. You want to write, then just write!"

She paled at Anne's spurt of anger and quietly replied, "I am writing, Anne."

"No, no, no, my dear!" Anne's face sprouted red splotches. "That's a hobby. Quit your job and write. You'll feel a hell of a lot better."

Zylla's temper snapped. "And are you going to pay my rent while I eat Ramen noodles and stare at my computer until they turn off the electricity because I couldn't pay the bill?" she mocked.

Anne's eyes flashed blue fire. "Don't give me that crap! If you really wanted it, you'd find a way to make it happen. If it doesn't work out, so what? You can always get another office job. You're just too damn scared to try. It's pathetic, Zylla, it really is."

"Why the hell are you so angry, anyway? It doesn't affect you." Zylla yanked the sundress over her head and pulled it down over her body, letting the towel fall to the floor.

"Because," Anne shouted, "I love you, you idiot! You're my best friend and I hate seeing you unhappy." She drew a long breath and slowly exhaled, then spoke again, her voice a calm drawl. "You're supposed to be living life, remember? Consider me your own personal tattoo."

Zylla, eyes downcast, stood rigid, droplets of water trickling down her back, soaking the sundress. She refused to scratch the skin where it itched beneath the wet fabric. When she didn't respond, Anne sighed.

"C'mon, Zyll. You're halfway there. Don't let your pirate queen down. Don't let *yourself* down."

Anne left the room, quietly shutting the door behind her.

~ * ~

By the time she reached work, the anger and hurt that Anne's sudden attack produced had been replaced by that same sense of unbalance that had started the day.

She tried to ignore the sinking sensation and avoided being alone by chatting with Nicole for thirty minutes before settling in her cube. Zylla pressed the start button on her computer, dropped her bag on the desk, and sat down as she turned on the monitor.

I hate my job, something in her mind whispered and the unsettled feeling dissipated.

"No," Zylla said to her computer. "I love my job. Well, maybe I don't love it, but it's important. The dean depends on me. Students depend on me. And I'm talking to my computer."

"So?" the voice asked. *"You excel at your job. But you are bored here. Every second you spend here you die—a lot."*

Zylla shifted, uncomfortable in her skin, as she tried to stifle the truth of her mind's words. Once again, Dean Pendergast was out of town. The August rush was over, and the faculty only needed scheduling done and fall semester course work prepared. Nine o'clock and she had nothing to do except work on her genealogy.

She was bored.

"But what'll I do?" she demanded of the computer.

No answer was given, and Zylla sighed, resigning herself to another day of Berry searching on the Internet. She opened the browser window and froze. A great heaviness soared up her legs, into her chest, and her ears roared. Her feet felt bolted to the floor and she could no longer lift her arms. She felt as though she teetered on the edge of madness and wanted to run or cry, but quite simply could not.

Zylla had been seven when she last experienced a panic attack. She and Aunt Maddie had lived in the old Berry House, the brown birthmark of Quinapoxet Street. The house held so many memories that it breathed.

Gray-brown and dilapidated, there had been no electricity on the second floor where thirteen creaky bedrooms and a rattling attic door waited for Zylla. Yet in the kitchen, where it was safe and warm, Zylla ignored her bedtime dread while she munched on sugar cookies and listened to Aunt Maddie read *The Hobbit* until she forgot about the ghosts upstairs. But there had been other mysteries in that house.

In the mud room off the kitchen there had been three doors. One led to the backyard and one opened to wooden stairs that ran down to the dirt floor of the basement. The other, painted light green, always remained locked.

"What's behind there, Aunt Madeleine?" a young Zylla asked.

Aunt Maddie's gentle eyes sparkled with mischief and her rosebud cheeks had glowed. "The sea," she whispered, laughing softly.

Zylla had never questioned it. To this very day she wondered if the sea, wild and green, would have roared into the kitchen to carry them both to a magic land if that door had opened. But she had never really feared that, either.

It was the basement that had cast her into her first panic attack on her seventh birthday. Before that day, she and Smudge, her black and white pointer, would visit the basement on rainy days. Together, they would explore the darkness for adventure and would later emerge into the kitchen covered in dirt and cobwebs, Smudge's tongue happily lolling from her mouth.

On the day of her seventh birthday, Uncle John and Aunt June had visited with Zylla's cousins and a birthday cake and presents, and Aunt Maddie asked Zylla to fetch a gallon of ice cream from the big freezer in the basement. She started down the dark stairs when Uncle John cheerily called, "Don't let the bogeyman get you!"

"John! Don't scare her like that!" Aunt June scolded. "Go on, Zylla dear. There's no such thing."

It had been too late. Zylla stared at the long, rickety stairs before her and peered into the dark corners below them. Was that a growl she heard?

She took one step down, then another, heavy panic festering in her bones with each step. Then she froze and stood still and staring on the third step until Aunt Maddie found her. Her aunt had taken Zylla's hand and together they had completed the journey to and from the freezer.

By the time they returned to the kitchen, Zylla had completely recovered, as if the incident never occurred, but she would never play in the basement again and if she had to run an errand for her aunt, she would run as fast as she could, taking Smudge with her.

"Hey, Zyll, I need to get your signature for my timesheet." Nicole's voice trailed off. Tossing pen and form onto the desk, she grabbed Zylla's wrist to feel her racing pulse.

"Zylla! What's wrong? You're as pale as a ghost!"

She turned wide, scared eyes to Nicole's face but couldn't speak. Fear had gripped her mind in its strong jaws and begun to chew.

I'm losing my mind. Right here in this horrible office, I'm going stark raving mad. My God, I wish it would hurry up and finish. I can't breathe.

"I think I'm having a nervous breakdown," she managed to whisper.

"Okaaay. Why don't we get you some air?" Nicole said as she helped Zylla to her feet and led her out of the office, down the stairs, and onto Commonwealth Avenue. They walked in silence until Nicole led her down Beacon Street to the Fens and Charlesgate East where the Charlesgate Hotel waited.

No, Zylla's mind registered. *Jabe's there. I can't go there. He'll think I'm a nut. I am a nut.*

But the hotel beckoned, and Zylla found herself walking up the steps to the Charlesgate East alcove, the quiet side, away from construction. She gratefully sank onto the cool concrete and instantly felt comforted in the arms of the old hotel. The awful fear began to melt and tears of relief sprang to her eyes.

"Oh boy," Nicole said as she plopped down next to Zylla and threw an arm around her shoulders.

~ * ~

Jabe shook his head to clear his vision.

The blue lines of the floor plans were getting to him. The constant banging, sawing, pounding, and swearing was getting to him. The disappearance of Lydia and her lavender was getting to him. The suddenly cold, suddenly hot September weather was getting to him.

Zylla was getting to him.

He removed his hands from the table he leaned on, straightened and stretched, a long groan emitting from his throat. A growl from his belly echoed. Maybe he should call her for lunch later, start being that friend he promised he'd be. If only he could get the thought of her naked and writhing under him out of his head.

"I need some coffee," he muttered.

Taking a left out of his office, the din of hammers banging and men cursing assaulted him, and he swerved on his heel to reverse direction toward the Charlesgate East exit, inhaling peace as he walked.

He should have slept with Leslie Saturday night. As he didn't, he was fairly sure that a night with his ex-girlfriend Samantha would end this sexual obsession with Zylla.

Samantha worked as a stripper in Providence. She had a sharp tongue, pretty face, and gorgeous body. She slithered like a snake and growled like a tigress and by morning he'd be nothing more than a shell. Then he could be a good friend to Zyll, no distractions.

Except, he realized as he emerged from the entrance and witnessed Zylla crying on the steps, she needed a good friend now.

Concern flooded his face as he hurried to her and put his hand on her shoulder.

"What's happened?" he asked the girl next to Zylla.

"I think she's having a crisis of sorts."

"I gathered that," he said wryly as he sat next to Zylla and pulled her head against his chest.

"I've got it from here," he said to the girl, barely looking at her. *Thank you, but you can go*, he meant.

Nicole studied him suspiciously. "Who are you?" she bluntly asked, hands on her hips.

"It's okay, Nic." Zylla sniffed into Jabe's shirt. "I know him." She lifted her head and turned grateful eyes on Nicole. "Thanks for helping me out."

"Okay. Get better. I'll see you tomorrow?"

Zylla nodded.

As Nicole crossed the street, Jabe lifted Zylla's chin with his hand and searched her eyes.

"What's the matter, darlin'?" he asked, wincing as he realized that her tears might be a result of their discussion of Saturday night, then quickly dismissed that assumption when he saw traces of real fear in her brown eyes.

"It was just a panic attack," she said, "but for a while, I thought that I was finally going insane like Grandma Anna. It was horrible." She sighed. "I really want a cigarette."

He looked at her, surprised. "You don't smoke." He furrowed his brow as he tried to recall a time when she had indulged in that habit. "Do you?"

"Not anymore. I used to. And I really want one right now."

"No, you don't," he said and she glared at him with eyes that were not her own. They were dark and cold and demanding.

"Okay, okay, hold on."

Jabe went into the Charlesgate and returned with a Marlboro Red and a lighter.

"Compliments of Dennis."

Her mouth almost watered. This was just what she needed to relax her and put her thinking back on track.

"You're not going to want it," he warned.

"Yes, I will," she muttered as he brought the flame to the tip of the cigarette. She inhaled and grimaced. It tasted like the bottom of an astray.

She waved the cigarette at him and sputtered, "I don't want this."

He flicked an amused glance at her, took the cigarette, and crushed it on the step. When she smiled wanly, Jabe put his arm around her, drawing her into him.

She sighed and relaxed into him.

"Okay now?" he asked and she nodded, pulling away from his chest. "Want to talk about it?"

She shook her head.

"All right. Stay here, then. I'm going to run around the corner for a coffee. Do you want anything?"

"Hmmm. Coffee would be great. Cream and sugar, please."

He hesitated, and she forced a full smile to ease his concern about leaving her alone.

But it really wasn't okay, and she knew she had to solve this nagging in her brain as she sensed that ignoring it would only bring on that horrible panic again. She could already feel it creeping up her legs and overcame the sensation by taking a deep breath and recalling how she felt a few moments ago, curled up against Jabe. He had stroked her back and kissed her forehead, and a lock of his hair had tickled her cheek.

Zylla closed her eyes, smiling at this recent memory and was able to relax completely, letting fear and thoughts sift through her. Suddenly, she smiled, and the panic fell from her completely.

"I hate my job," she said to no one in particular and grinned broadly, which is how Jabe found her when he returned with the coffee.

"What is it?" He smiled and handed her a coffee.

Zylla pushed the plastic tab back and took a sip. Bottom of the pot again, but that was okay.

"I'm going to quit my job," she announced and gave a nervous laugh.

Jabe arched a dark brow.

"I'm going to be a writer," she said and this time, her laughter rippled through the late summer air.

Nineteen

Anne slid into the chair opposite Zylla and removed her sunglasses. Her expression wary, she smiled briefly in greeting.

"I'm glad you came," Zylla said and drew a long breath, inhaling the tension between them.

They were seated in the window alcove of the Middle East Restaurant, on a raised dais, surrounded by potted ferns and filtered sunlight and miles away from the clinks of silverware and chatter of other patrons.

"I gave my two-weeks notice today," Zylla said and searched for approbation in Anne's face. When she didn't find it, she ventured, a little shakily, "I'm going to give my writing a chance to flourish."

Anne grinned, broad and proud. "Good for you, Zyll. This is great. It'll be hard, but I know you can do it." She frowned. "All because of what I said this morning?"

After the waitress took their order, Zylla answered Anne. "Yes, well, no, not really. Sort of." She smiled slightly. "You helped propel me in the right direction. A panic attack did the rest. So dinner's on me. Thanks for being my tattoo."

"No problem, babe. I'm a lot cheaper than a tattoo, and with me, there's no risk of infection." Anne paused and fingered her spoon. "So, uh, how are you going to support this newfound happiness?"

Zylla winced. "Well, I figure I can waitress at nights."

The drinks and appetizers arrived and an earthy aroma rose to their noses.

"You're a horrible waitress."

The waitress stepped back, aghast.

"Not you," Zylla explained. "She meant me."

"Ahhh. Good," the waitress said, shooting them a dubious glance as she left the table.

"Good one, Anne. Now she'll spit in our dessert." She dipped a piece of pita into the hummus. "Or I could temp a couple days a week. It's boring, but it's enough to live on if I stick to those Ramen noodles for a while."

"Blech. I'll feed you, babe. Actually..." Anne said between bites, "we need someone at the firm to handle administrative stuff a couple times a week. Interested?"

~ * ~

On the days that she didn't temp at Ibis Marketing, Zylla developed a routine of waking at dawn, running, and writing until noon. After a quick shower, she would walk to the Charlesgate for lunch with Jabe, all awkwardness between them gone.

Today, her usual pattern just wasn't clicking. She had woken late to a muggy and hazy autumn morning and by eleven o'clock she had written exactly one sentence. And it wasn't a very good one at that.

It was just too hot. This was a day for the mall, but she didn't have money for temptations that lurked within all that air conditioning. The only other possible relief was the cool interior of the Charlesgate with its river breezes.

Thirty minutes later, Zylla donned a hardhat, grateful that the ugly orange encumbrance smothered her hair, frizzy from the moist day. Dennis escorted her through the minefield of workers.

"We're almost at the homestretch now," he said. "Just the second floor and this one left to finish."

His wizened face broke into a grin, and she was reminded of her Uncle John.

"I never thought we'd bring her back, but Thayer saw it through."

Zylla could hear the pride reflected in his voice.

"Only the basement after that, but we can tend to that after she's open for business. No-one's really looking forward to that work anyhow."

"How come?" she asked as they turned the corner onto the Charlesgate East hallway.

"Well, it's odd. The men are sort of scared of the basement. Gives them the creeps." One shoulder shrugged. "Some places are like that. One fella swears he saw—"

"You're early!" Jabe called from the end of the hall.

A fresh spurt of longing assaulted Zylla at Jabe's approach. He looked as if he just left the Viking wars. Loneliness for what she could not have surged through her.

Dennis gestured goodbye.

"Thanks, Den," she said and stopped in front of the old gilded elevator, where men worked diligently to fix it, to wait for Jabe.

As the two embraced, a great groan and snap penetrated the air, punctuated by a scream and final deafening crack. A worker teetered on the edge of a gaping hole.

Zylla froze, watching in slow motion, then she and Jabe rushed to pull him to safety.

"Frank's down there, in the elevator," the man uttered, wide-eyed and pasty, but Jabe was already lowering himself into the elevator shaft. Dennis whirled around to race back and follow him. Other workers scrambled toward them with shouts of "What happened?" and "Call nine-one-one!"

The elevator had crashed into the dank basement, broken on its side, a frayed cable coiled around it. Inside, Frank was silent.

"Frank. Frank!" Jabe yelled as he and Dennis searched the sides of the car for the opening. The elevator was decrepit enough so that Jabe and Dennis managed to pry the metal side away.

Frank was sprawled at the opposite end, pale and quiet. A bone protruding from his right leg ripped through his blood-soaked jeans. Jabe forced his mind to turn elsewhere to prevent the gorge from rising in his throat, as he jumped into the car.

"He's breathing!" Jabe called as he removed his fingers from the still man's throat. Frank's eyes fluttered open.

Ambulance and police sirens squealed closer and closer, then grew silent as the vehicles came to a quick stop. Snatches of red and blue lights flickered above them. In the darkness below, Jabe felt Dennis shiver beside him.

"It reeks down here, boss," he said, gagging. "I didn't notice it before, but it sure is strong now."

"I know," Jabe replied. "It's almost as if the river has taken up residence down here. We'll be out soon, I promise."

Out of the corner of his eye, he saw something large darting across the floor. He blinked into the darkness.

"Hello?" he bellowed.

"What is it?" Dennis whispered.

"I don't know. I thought I saw someone." He turned his attention back to Frank and tried to ignore the hair that stood straight up on his arms.

"The men are right," Jabe said. "It is pretty spooky down here, huh?"

Frank, eyes half-open, began to keen in low scared tones. Jabe comforted him until the medics and police arrived, and finally he and Dennis were pulled from the dank chasm so that the EMTs could reach Frank.

"He'll be okay," Jabe announced to the tight faces of his men and Zylla. "It looks like he has a bad break, and he's a little dazed, but he's okay."

Sighs of relief and nervous laughter bounced through the hall and Jabe said, "Why don't you all take the afternoon off? The sun's coming out. Go to the beach and get some fried clams on me."

Laughter erupted into cheers, which became louder as a conscious Frank was brought from the basement and placed on a gurney.

As the medics started to wheel him away, Frank spotted Zylla from the bed he was strapped upon and howled in an unearthly voice. The cheering stopped abruptly and everyone froze in place, eyes locked on Frank.

"Ye scurvy sea witch!" he screamed, followed by a pitiful whine.

Everyone's attention swiveled to Zylla and she edged close to Jabe's side. He put his arm around her and she felt tension quivering in his muscles, just as she felt his protection melting through her.

She stole a sideways glance at Jabe. His lips were set in a grim line and his eyes glittered. He looked as though he would readily throttle Frank if it were not for the fact that the man was broken, strapped to a stretcher and obviously out of his mind.

"It's yer fault that this happened, ye bitch!" Frank continued.

"What?" Zylla, confused and horrified, sidled even closer to Jabe. Frank looked like he wanted to kill her. His expression was contorted and terrible, and he snarled and gnashed his teeth. His irises were a crazed red-violet and she broke into a clammy sweat at the promised violence she saw there.

"That's enough, Frank!" Jabe thundered.

Frank's head twisted toward Jabe and he cackled, low and gravely. "Ye whipped cur. 'Tis yer fault as well. How dare ye break the code? Women on ships is bad luck, ye bastard.

"Beware, Jabez," Frank warned. "She'll sew yer lips shut afore the next tide. Mark me words."

Before the orderlies could attend their raving patient, Frank began to keen again. His eyes rolled back into his head, and he passed out.

A few moments later, he was taken away in the ambulance and the shaken crew began to wander from the hallway, some glancing at Zylla curiously and others muttering about the necessity of psychiatric evaluations before being permitted to wield a hammer.

Zylla, legs still shaking, turned to Jabe.

"You okay?"

"Uh-huh." She nodded. "More than a little weirded out, though. I mean, I tend to be a freak magnet, always attracting the crazy ones on the T, but this..." It was too much for her brain to handle.

"I think I'll go home now." She reached up to remove the hard hat and handed it to Jabe. "Sorry for disrupting your work."

"It's not your fault, Zyll." He laughed. But it was, sort of. Jabe frowned suddenly. In the three weeks that he and Zylla were apart, work had flowed smoothly at the Charlesgate.

True, he missed the lavender that had seemingly disappeared and hated the gloom that hung over the Charlesgate in its absence, but there were no mishaps, missing tools or near accidents that had occurred until Zylla started showing up again, bringing Lydia back with her.

And now Frank with his broken leg and schizophrenic moment.

Jabe pressed his eyes shut and rubbed the back of his neck. A breeze from the open window tickled his skin, and he caught the spicy aroma of lavender riding in with it.

And then he remembered that Frank had called him Jabez. Nobody called him Jabez, not even his own mother. And what was all that about stitching his lips together? Hadn't he heard that before? For the second time that day, a waft of lavender reached his nose.

"Oh, Lydia," he whispered. "What is going on here?"

~ * ~

Zylla peeled off her clothes as she walked into the apartment and headed right for the shower, a scalding rejuvenation to erase the morning's humidity, Frank's weirdness, and that funk from the basement.

She dressed, popped Tom Waits into the CD player, and went outside on the porch to comb her hair, inhaling the clean breeze and sunshine that flushed out the moist air. It was peaceful here, with kids rollerblading down the sidewalk and Anne's pink geraniums surrounding her.

Her head now clear, she wandered back inside, leaving the heavy wooden door open, and gathered her makeshift genealogy chart and her dream journal. Frank had said something about sewn lips, reminding her of her nightmares and subsequently, Lady Charn, almost as if Frank had read her fledgling novel. *Yet he hadn't, so how had he known?*

There was a message here, buried somewhere in her family's past, Maddie's cold fear, and in her vivid dreams and migraine hallucinations of her crazy pirate woman. All she had to do, Zylla sensed, was dig out the answers in this Byzantine maze.

She had begun to read entries in her dream journal when a knock at the screen door sounded and Jabe entered with Rye right behind him. Roused from her concentration, Zylla's heart hopped, for the second time that day, at the sight of Jabe. Even the sunshine seemed to fill the room because of his presence and when he smiled, she felt its warmth from her toes to the ends of her hair.

"Great album," Rye commented and sang along to *Chocolate Jesus*, but Jabe didn't seem to notice and crossed over to Zylla to stroke her cheek and look into her eyes.

"You sure you're okay?" he asked her.

"Of course," she replied with a shrug. "I mean, it was a little odd. Frank's behavior. Like we were in a time warp or something."

"Not a time warp," Rye interjected. "A possession. Frank's an asshole, so he's prime target for possession. Your family ghost, maybe?"

Zylla turned to Rye. "Jabe told you what happened?"

"He told me everything," Rye replied meaningfully, holding Zylla's glance.

Jabe shot him a quelling look. Rye ignored him and sat at the table.

"You two belong in an Edgar Allen Poe story. I might have to write a song about it." He laughed, but his dancing eyes flirted with seriousness. "Jabe tells me you don't know too much about your family."

"No," she sighed. "I don't. But I've been working on it, and you're on to something with that family connection possession thingy. I constantly dream about a woman with her lips sewn shut. Frank couldn't have known. Unless..."

"*That's* where I heard that before." Jabe snapped his fingers before registering Zylla's words. "Nope," he said. "Rye's the only one who knows, and he just found out himself."

"Then it is more than coincidence," Zylla muttered.

"Did you find anything more about Lydia?" Jabe asked as he pushed off from the counter. "Mind if I get a drink?"

"Of course! I'm sorry." She blushed, appalled by her lack of manners, and rose halfway before Jabe waved her down. "I'll get it. Rye, you want anything?"

"Just water."

Jabe raised an inquisitive eyebrow at her.

"Same," she said. "Thanks."

While he poured drinks, Zylla unrolled her family tree and placed it in front of Rye. They studied it, heads together, until Jabe stepped between them and put the glasses down.

"So, what do we have?" He bent over the table and leaned on his palms.

Zylla inhaled his nearness, soap and sweat and sunshine. His hair was pulled back in a ponytail and she sat on her hands to prevent herself from reaching up and tucking in a stray strand that escaped from the band. Every molecule in her squirmed with his proximity and she felt dizzy.

"Well..." Rye's voice snapped her focus back to the paper. "She's captured names and dates all the way back to before the American Revolution. This is pretty good, Zylla." Rye looked at her with renewed interest. "You did all this on the Internet?"

"Most of it. I sent some e-mails to genealogical societies and made a few phone calls. Most of my family stayed in Western Massachusetts. Lydia's father was the only one to move to Boston."

Her mouth twisted into a frown. "But I can't get any info before Samuel Berry."

"Zylla's great at researching," Jabe said with a proud smile.

She shook her head at the compliment. "I just like to do it, that's all."

"William Berry, died seventeen hundred and sixty-three, married Sarah," Rye read. "They had two children, Kent and Sarah Berry. Kent had one child, Samuel Berry, died in seventeen hundred and seventy-five."

"He must have been killed in the Revolution," Jabe interrupted.

"Probably. Luckily, he married before that and had two sons, Fred and Jedediah. Fred and Jed—poor kids. Rhyming names." Rye chuckled. "Fred married Zillah Whitney. There's where you got your name, Zylla."

Zylla beamed. "I know. Isn't it great? I wish Aunt Maddie would have at least told me that."

"Their kid, Nathaniel Berry married and also named his son Jedediah, who married Miss Caroline Bart at Boston's Holy Cross

Cathedral in eighteen hundred and sixty-one." Rye looked at her. "How'd you find that out?"

"It was in the city's marriage records."

"Cool." Rye was impressed. "Then Lydia and her twin sister, Lily, were born in seventy-two. Lydia was killed on October twenty-seventh, eighteen hundred and ninety-five, but she and Caval left a son, Jemmy, who eventually married Betsy Sheard. They had a daughter, Anna. Anna had Madeleine and Cynthia Berry. No father?"

Zylla shrugged. "I think they had different fathers. Family rumor is that my Grandma Anna was a little unstable and rebellious before she totally went off her rocker."

"Then there's you. And that's it."

"Yep. That's it," she replied.

"Well, it doesn't tell us much history, unfortunately. Nothing that sheds any light on a crazy ghost, anyway."

Jabe pointed at a few individuals on the list. "But it does tell us that a lot of people in your family died very young. Especially the women."

Rye shrugged. "That's not so unusual given the times."

"True." Jabe's lips were a grim line and Zylla sensed his unspoken thoughts.

"With the exception of my parents and Lydia, we don't know how the rest died, Jabe. Rye's right. We can't assume anyone else died violently."

The three silently studied the chart once more.

"Hmmm," Rye wondered. "Maybe it's best if we stick with what we do know."

"Well, we know that *we* started with the Charlesgate, our family histories, I mean," Jabe stated, but his eyes told her he meant more than just their related ancestry. "We know that your great-great-grandmother was married to the brother of the woman my blood-uncle married."

"Jabe's aunt, in other words," Rye stated, trying to puzzle out Jabe's tongue-twister.

"Well, yeah, but I'm trying to stick to blood relations here." He turned back to Zylla. "So that's our family connection. And Lydia and Caval were murdered."

"This is so cool. Proof that fate exists," Rye exclaimed and both Zylla and Jabe laughed at his enthusiasm.

Jabe pushed off the table edge and began to pace the room.

"So that brings us back to the Charlesgate and you, Zyll." He scratched under his chin. "And Lydia's lavender."

"A lavender ghost." Rye was grinning now, clearly thrilled.

"If it is a ghost," Jabe continued, "we're assuming it's Lydia since she was murdered and died there. Plus, Lydia is related to Zylla, and Zylla's family ghost lived during Victorian times and wore the scent."

"So if Lydia is Zylla's family ghost, then she is the one that supposedly murdered your parents." Rye shot an apprehensive glance at her. "Sorry, Zylla."

"It's okay," she said then chewed her bottom lip. "But my evil eye is supposed to keep the ghost away. I wouldn't smell the lavender at all if it's my ghost, if the thing exists."

"But, Zyll," Jabe said. "You're *assuming* that the pendant works. Who's to say it's not anything but a superstition?"

"Then take it off," Rye said. "See what happens. We're right here, and you can always put it back on if something goes wrong."

"No!" Jabe thundered.

Zylla jumped in her seat and Rye appeared dumbstruck but Jabe didn't care. He only knew that at Rye's words, he felt a hideous crawling down his spine and fear assaulted his every nerve.

"Absolutely not. It may be an old wives' tale, but her grandmother believed it protected her. It stays on."

Zylla almost tore it off right there. Ever fiber of her being rose in revolt against his orders. But she too felt a shiver of dread and remembered, even in the bright sunlight, her night fears and the evil pirate queen who was much more controllable on paper.

Rye broke the uneasy silence. "Again, it comes back to the Charlesgate. That's the connection. There, you have Lydia, Zylla's ancestor, who wears lavender just like the ghost that supposedly haunts the family."

"But..."

Rye held up his hand at Jabe's protest. "I don't want to hear it. Don't give me any crap about 'it may not be a ghost, you can't prove it.' Bullshit," he stated. "There are too many coincidences for it not to be real—there are too many coincidences for Lydia *not* to be the same ghost that's haunted your family. Besides, the Charlesgate has always been rumored to be haunted, and now we have proof, in a way."

Jabe closed his mouth, and a snort of amusement escaped Zylla at Rye's easy handling of Jabe, who reminded her of a stallion chomping at the bit.

"The eye, if it works at all, obviously doesn't work at the Charlesgate." Rye gulped the rest of his water. "Probably because it's Lydia's home turf. She's all-powerful there."

"But, Rye, you're discounting all the accidents. Well," Jabe amended, "all the accidents that exceed a normal construction site. None of them are directed at Zylla.

"Even Frank," Jabe continued. "He's the one that got hurt, not Zyll. I just don't think there's a connection between the 'murderous' Berry ghost and the spirit of Lydia Berry, if it is Lydia. Sure, she was murdered there, so it's logical that she's at unrest, but who's to say that the mischievous ghost isn't another poor fool who died at the Charlesgate?"

"And then," Jabe said, cocking his head to scratch under his chin. "Maybe this has nothing to do with Zylla at all. Maybe this ghost simply doesn't want the Charlesgate restored."

"No," Rye said, half to himself. He looked at Jabe. "That doesn't make sense. You told me about what happened to Liam."

"What happened?" Zylla asked. "Who's Liam?"

Jabe turned to her as he leaned back in the chair, folding his arms. "Liam is one of my workers. He fell off a ladder a few weeks back. Claims he was pushed."

"Yeah," Rye said. "And he said that he smelled some sort of flower around him before he fell. You said that right after he was pushed, a slab of plaster fell from the ceiling. If that slab had fallen on him, he might have been hurt. If he hadn't been pushed, he might have even been killed."

Rye's blue eyes studied Zylla and Rye. "I have a friend, an ex-girlfriend from high school, really. She and her family lived in one of those ranch houses in your typical suburban neighborhood. One year everything went to hell. Her parents started fighting, her sister was paralyzed in a car accident, her dog got leukemia."

"And I thought the Thayers had some bad luck," Jabe muttered.

Rye furrowed his brow. "It wasn't bad luck, according to Julie. She'd come home from school and every door, window, cupboard, drawer, whatever, would be open and Shadow, that's the dog, would be shivering under the table.

"Once when she was home alone with the dog, Shadow started growling and barking at nothing, and Julie watched as the front door opened and closed. On its own. There was no wind."

Zylla visibly shivered.

"After this, her entire family started noticing things. They had bad dreams, kept getting sick, and just plain didn't like the house anymore. They finally moved.

"My point is, did you ever stop to think that the Charlesgate itself might be the problem? That it's just an evil place? Maybe this spirit is trying to protect you all."

"And you did say that Lydia, or whatever the lavender smell is, made you feel safe," Zylla whispered, turning to Jabe.

Jabe nodded slowly, his thoughts stamped on his face.

Rye stood up. "I don't know, I really don't, but this is going in circle and I gotta go. I'm playing tonight and it's getting late."

"I'll walk you out." Zylla rose and followed Rye to the screen door.

"Where are you playing tonight?" Jabe called.

"Toad."

"Maybe we'll show up."

"I hope not," Rye replied emphatically. "I hope you find something better to do then stare at my scraggly face." He kissed her cheek. "Bye, Zyll. You're too good for our Viking."

She blinked at his retreating back. After a minute, she returned to the kitchen where Jabe had resumed pacing.

"I hear what Rye's saying," he spouted, "but I can't believe the Charlesgate is evil."

"Can't or don't want to?"

Jabe stopped moving and shrugged. "Both, I guess. But c'mon, it's ridiculous. Buildings aren't evil. I mean, look at the Amityville horror. A hoax."

"Really?" Zylla sounded mildly disappointed. "Still, it's no less ridiculous than a ghost, and we seem to be accepting that theory readily enough."

Jabe's brow furrowed and Zylla guessed that he was dwelling on every strange incident that had occurred at the Charlesgate. She, however, felt the afternoon's drifting light on her face as it beamed through the kitchen window, accompanied by the smell of approaching autumn. It was probably one of the last chances to enjoy the city at night before cold weather arrived.

The afternoon's conversation seemed far away and insignificant now. She was scared before, but it was the gripping, consuming fear of telling ghost stories around a campfire in the woods, or trying to call Bloody Mary from the bathroom mirror.

She could laugh at her fear now and she did.

"What?" Jabe looked up at her, a lopsided grin splitting his too-serious lips.

"Forget all this stuff, Jaber," she teased. "Let's go get some dinner then check out Rye."

"Somebody's feeling frisky this evening."

Jabe strolled over to her and placed his hands on her waist, trapping her against the counter. Sunlight danced between them and their gazes joined. Slowly, magically, he leaned in to brush his lips against hers.

Alarm pulsed in her head, even while her fingers ached to pull him close, but she managed to force a laugh and push him away.

"Why not?"

Why not? Why not? Was he daft? Didn't he pretty much tell her that there was no chance of a relationship between them? Did he think she was his plaything?

Aghast, she pitched him a scathing glare, but Jabe returned her look and his expression alone quelled the anger that popped at his question. He looked like a perplexed little boy and at his confused and hurt look, Zylla inhaled and said, "Because you'll break my heart."

She hoisted herself to sit on the counter in the hopes of appearing casual. Jabe took a step closer and placed a palm on each of her thighs and fingered the frayed spot of denim covering her right thigh.

A long, hot sigh slithered through Zylla's body, but she forced a look of mild reproach and said, "Friends, remember?"

Jabe poked a finger through the newly created hole in her jeans, his mere touch igniting her skin.

"I don't think I want to be just friends," he murmured.

Not missing a beat, Zylla swatted his hand from her leg and smiled sweetly. "And when you figure it out, let me know. Until then, I don't trust this side of you."

Jabe dropped his gaze and she dipped her head to study his reaction, but his face remained unreadable. After a long moment, he raised his eyes to hers and lifted his hand to cup her chin.

"Well," he said quietly. "I'm a patient man. I'll just have to make you trust me."

Twenty

Zylla woke to a trilling phone and an overcast sky. Well after nine o'clock, her intention of rising at dawn to run before settling in front of her computer with a cup of Earl Grey had been dashed.

Last night, she and Jabe ate dinner at a local tapas restaurant and gone to Toad for Rye's show. The bar had been packed with rowdy college students and between getting jostled and trying to remain impassive to Jabe's smoldering looks, Zylla had been so exhausted that the shrill of the phone had barely penetrated her consciousness.

"Hello?" she asked, pushing on her eyelids in an attempt to wipe the morning's blur aside.

"Yes, hello," said a female with a tinge of a Southern accent. "I'm trying to reach a, um, Ms. Zylla Berry."

"This is she." Suspicion laced her reply and she was ready to hang up at the first mention of a cellular phone sales pitch.

"Hello, Ms. Berry. My name is Judy McCabe. I just read your recent entry on the genealogy website and took the liberty of phoning. You did list your number at the site."

Zylla stared blankly at the bottle of purple dishwashing liquid near the sink for a second until her sleep fogged memory stirred.

"Oh! Do you have information about William Berry?"

"I believe I do. Your William was married to Sarah McCabe, and they had two children, Sarah and Kent, correct?"

"Yes, yes!"

"Well, Sarah was sister to Brian McCabe, my ancestor, and for some reason, my family has a copy of Sarah's marriage certificate. They were married in Amherst, Massachusetts with William's father as witness. His name is Ian Berry."

"Oh, you're a goddess, Judy."

"I'm glad I could help. Good luck on the rest of your search."

"You, too," she replied and hung up the phone, resting her hand on the receiver as she chewed her bottom lip. Then, with a little cry of joy, she snatched up the receiver again and dialed information.

After a few phone calls to Amherst, Zylla had traced her family tree to Ian's parents, Daniel Berry and Ciara Kelly. Here again, the wedding certificate proved crucial, and Zylla learned the name of Daniel's father, Jeremy T. Berry.

Another Jeremy, she thought and wondered if Lydia had named her son after this long-ago ancestor.

The town where the marriage had occurred was Charn, Massachusetts, and Zylla called information for the number of Charn's town hall.

"Ah, dear, you'll want the library," the clerk replied. "All of our town's records are there. We're a very small town, you see," she added with a chuckle.

Zylla hummed while she toasted a muffin and brewed some coffee. Minutes later, she sat at the kitchen table, one hand curled around a warm cup and the other hooked around the phone receiver.

The voice at the other end sounded ancient. "Charn Library. Henry Thomas speaking."

"Hello, Mr. Thomas. My—"

"Henry will do."

"Pardon me?"

"Henry will do."

"Oh. Yes, well, thank you. My name is Zylla Berry and I am trying to trace my ancestor who may have settled there in the mid-seventeen hundreds."

"You don't say!" The man's voice lifted with excitement. "Yer a Berry, are ya?"

She bristled with anticipation. "Yes, sir."

"Well, we have the whole of the Berry family history here, leastaways the American branch. But surely you know that, dear, all the Berrys do."

"No," she replied dully. "Actually, I don't know a thing about my family. Not really anyway."

"Well, now, ain't that peculiar. The Berry family is rooted here, started this here town. Wait, now. I recollect something of you. Zylla, you say? You're Cindy's girl, ain't ye? Yep, and yer Aunt Madeleine took on yer bringing up after little Cindy passed.

"Madeleine never was one for family lore," he muttered while she listened ardently. His voice brightened. "Now, which Berry do ye need to know about?"

"Well, sir, I've traced all the way back to the name Jeremy T. Berry, but I can't find anymore information."

Henry chuckled. "Well, ye come to the right place. Ole' Jeremy is famous around these parts."

"He is?"

"Heck, yeah. He founded the town!"

"What?"

"Yes, ma'am. Our Jeremy traveled all the way from Boston, dragging his poor step-daddy with him, to dig his home in the wilderness, so goes the Charn legend.

"Ole Admiral Thayer met with misfortune in Boston and was already a bit touched when they moved out here, always muttering and looking over his shoulder, but he was a kind man, and loved young Jeremy like his own.

"Why, Jeremy even took on the Admiral's name, built a farm out here, and he and the Admiral lived in solitude for a few years until settlers trickled in around him."

Zylla could hear Henry rasp as he caught his breath.

"The town, small as it was, and still is," he added, "looked to Jeremy as a natural leader. He was honest and God-fearing so the men respected him, and the ladies were taken with him. He had them looks—black hair, violet eyes or some such pretty boy nonsense."

He guffawed. "When the town decided they needed a name, they asked Jeremy to bless it. He called it Charn after the ship he was born on."

Zylla was rendered speechless, but Henry continued. "Not much to tell after that. The Admiral died youngish, insane at the end. He had been a very rich man, but his son from a previous marriage inherited everything, not poor Jeremy."

She could hear the shrug in his voice.

"Just as well. There was some legend that the money was cursed, caused the Admiral's insanity. It seems he killed his lover for the Crown or some such nonsense.

"Anyway, Jeremy caused many tears amongst the town's ladies when he married an Indian girl from a local tribe. They had five children. All females. All died as young'uns. Finally, Daniel was born, and the Indian girl passed on yonder during the birthin'."

"Do you..." Her voice was froggy and she cleared it. "Do you have the names of Jeremy's real parents?"

Henry's sigh was audible through the receiver. "'Fraid not, Miss Zylla. Jeremy changed his name back to Berry after Admiral Thayer died, said it was his family name."

"Oh," she said, disappointment heavy in her voice.

"But yer aunt knows. She has the family tree that Jeremy himself created. He never showed it to no one but the next in line to receive it. He wrote his real parents' names on it. Had his reasons for hiding it, I s'ppose. There's always been talk of a family bogie. All hogwash, if you ask me. Stories to make children behave.

"You just go ask Madeleine for Jeremy's tree. She probably has it in a box somewhere."

"I will," she replied sadly, hurt and angry that her aunt had destroyed such an artifact. "Thank you very much for your time, Henry."

"No trouble a'tall, dear, no trouble a'tall."

~ * ~

Zylla rose and hung up the phone.

It was fate. *As sure as Texas has cactus*, she could almost hear Anne echo. Excitement simmered and bubbled inside her as she realized that she was rooted to her ancestor, Jeremy, in a much more direct link than by some odd knot on the family oak.

And Jabe was mixed up in it as well. Their families had come together not once, but twice. Twice! First through Caval and Lydia, then through Jabez Thayer and his adopted son, Jeremy Berry.

She poured another cup of coffee and as the cream sank into the brown depths, she laughed aloud. No, not twice, then. Three times.

"Me and Jabe," she said aloud. *And three times is the charm.*

Her head swirled as another realization struck her. Jeremy had named the town Charn, and Zylla had named her fictional pirate ship, *Charnwood*, and her pirate, Captain Charn. Zylla reasoned that she could have picked up the name at a family barbecue, but something tugged at her thoughts, prickling her skin.

Maybe, just maybe, she had dreamed it. Maybe Jeremy was trying to tell her something through the mad visions of blood and violence on the boiling seas.

She bit her lip and frowned. Somehow, she knew, it all depended on discovering who Jeremy's mother had been. She closed her eyes and saw the mad woman of her migraine nightmares. Black hair and red-rimmed violet eyes—a deranged Liz Taylor.

And maybe, just maybe, Jeremy's mother.

Her skin burned and her mind itched just like the day she had first seen the Charlesgate. Determined, she picked up the phone and dialed.

Zylla's strategy for a light tactic failed as the first words left her lips.

"Hey, Auntie M." Her cheer sounded forced.

"What did you do now, Zyll?"

Better to just blurt it out then. "I traced our family history all the way back to before seventeen hundred and forty. We have Native American blood in us, did you know that?"

"Yes," Maddie replied cautiously. "I did know that."

"Well, I wish you told me," she snapped, instantly scolding herself for losing control of the conversation.

Maddie, as she had expected, said nothing.

"This woman's husband, Jeremy, was adopted by Admiral Thayer, my friend Jabe's ancestor. Weird, huh?"

Zylla swallowed. She could feel Maddie's chill through the receiver. "I know you had the family tree at one point. I need to know the names of his real parents."

Maddie replied in clipped tones. "*You* define who you are, Zylla, not your ancestors. Carve your own life."

She blinked. For a second, Maddie's words sliced into her and self-doubt paralyzed her. *No*, she then thought. *I am carving my own life. With a fruit knife perhaps, but at least I'm the one wielding it.*

At Zylla's silence, Maddie snapped, "I fail to see why you are so hell-bent on this little project, anyway. You should spend your time on something useful."

Zylla's temper erupted and rolled off her tongue in great molten waves. "This is useful! This explains who I am, where I came from! It's my history! You have no right to keep it from me!"

She couldn't express to her aunt the thoughts and feelings that were so clear inside her. She was too embarrassed to admit she needed her ancestry to feel rooted, to be a part of the greater human family. She couldn't tell her aunt how lonely she had been growing up, despite Maddie's unconditional love. She couldn't explain how she had felt at family reunions where cousins, who grew up together, away from Zylla, had studied her curiously, as if she were some insect specimen. And because she was shamed by her loneliness, she covered it with great blotches of red rage.

"You never talk about them! You never talk about Mom or Dad or even your own mother. There's something wrong with that! You can be the coldest woman sometimes, Aunt Maddie."

Instantly, the anger fell away and Zylla regretted her last words. "I just... I just don't understand. I'm only asking for a simple fact. If it's not important, then why can't you just tell me?"

"Zylla, you don't..."

Maddie's voice sounded strangled and wet, and Zylla felt guilty. *Aunt Maddie, crying?* She had never seen her aunt cry. Yet when she next spoke, her voice was frosty.

"I don't know who Jeremy's parents are. I need to get some work done. I'll talk to you later." Maddie hung up the phone with a cool click.

Madeleine wasn't superstitious, but she had enough Scottish blood pulsing in her veins to know that you didn't say the devil's name aloud for fear of calling it forth.

It was the second time Maddie deliberately had lied to her niece.

Twenty-one

Zylla caught snatches of conversation coming from the den as she entered her dimly lit kitchen after an after-hours stint at Ibis. Five-hundred and fifty sealed letters later, Zylla feared that the American flag postage stamp would be forever emblazoned across her mind.

"Anne?" she called.

"Hi there," Anne said as she bopped into the kitchen. "Thought I heard the door open. There's *someone* here to see you."

Zylla smiled. From the leer on Anne's face, she knew Jabe waited in the other room and her heart bounced in her chest.

"I'm heading out to meet Billy. I'll see you tomorrow."

"Yep. Say 'hi' for me," Zylla chimed as she walked into the living room, a wide smile plastered on her face. "Oh my God. Mike!" Zylla squealed and jumped into his open arms, wrapping her legs around his waist.

"*Mmm...* I've missed you, Zyllie."

He squeezed her and she buried her face into the warm crook of his neck to inhale that woodsy scent of his that had carried her through high school.

"Mike," she started, but her voice was muffled against his skin and she pushed away and dropped her feet to the floor. How could she forget how stunning he was? Perfect skin and haunted eyes teeming with dreams. Full lips that perpetually verged on a sudden smile. Sir Lancelot on her faux Oriental carpet. Her body sighed in forgotten desire and she clumsily broke away from him, unable to finish her words.

One eyebrow raised, he quipped in his low voice, "So... are there any good graveyards we can hang out in around here?"

Zylla regained her composure and smiled back at him, remembering the hours after school they had spent talking in Northampton's cemetery. "Not really. All the good ones will be locked up..." She glanced at the clock on the wall. "In about an hour."

Disappointment wavered in his eyes, and Zylla saw something else—a pain that she hadn't seen since his high school girlfriend had broken up with him so long ago. And she remembered.

"Where is she?" She asked, head flicking back and forth to look for another person. "Where's your wife?"

Mike rubbed the back of his neck. "New York City, I believe," he sighed heavily. "We're getting a divorce."

Zylla gave a startled laugh and she schooled her shock into sympathy as she melted into his blue stare. He had eyes that made a woman want to save him, and Zylla was no exception. She scooped up his worn leather jacket from the sofa and handed it to him. "Put this on," she said. "I know exactly where we'll go."

He tossed his jacket over his shoulder and followed a purposeful Zylla into the kitchen where she rummaged through the fridge.

"Aha!" She turned and grinned, brandishing a six-pack of Guinness. "My emergency stash."

~ * ~

As she placed the bottles into her backpack, Mike's eyes reflected appreciation of her figure and he unconsciously shook his head. Instead of chasing after real-life versions of the superwomen he drew for Enigma Comics, he should have snared *this* woman years ago. Except that he hadn't realized that Zylla was meant for him until a couple of weeks ago when the odd dreams began.

He watched as the lights from the oven hood and refrigerator shimmered in her hair, catching hints of red and gold in the brown. Had it always been so beautiful? In high school, the skinny, eager, brown-haired Zylla was an annoying little girl who seemed to appear everywhere he went. He had clenched his teeth in frustration every time he spotted her sitting in yet another one of his classes or hanging out near his locker. He had just wanted her to go away.

Then, after listening to her conversations with other students in art class and participating in a few himself, he had come to admire her intelligence and sense of humor. He had appreciated her goofy romanticism, so like his own, and enjoyed their talks during picnic lunches in the cemetery across from school. He had known that she loved him, but she had never tried to undermine his relationship with his girlfriend and honorably took the role of best friend when he had needed advice.

When had Zylla become as stunning as his comic book creations, as gorgeous as his soon-to-be ex-wife? The difference was, of course, that Zylla was three-dimensional whereas his characters and Allison were mere cardboard, he thought with a self-effacing smirk.

When Ally had left, Mike had been surprised to discover that his anger was directed only at himself. A second shock followed when he began to wake at various hours, drenched in sweat and desperately wanting Zylla. Finally, in an odd state of urgent calm, he jumped in his car and drove east to Boston.

Now, as he gazed at her shapely legs clad in black tights and army boots, body bent over her backpack so that her skirt crawled up the back of her thighs, her silky hair falling along her face, his body confirmed what his mind recently discovered: he loved her.

"Ready?" She straightened and faced him.

Mike simply raised one eyebrow and crooned a line from his favorite Cure song, *Charlotte Sometimes*, as he took Zylla's pack from her and headed toward the front door.

~ * ~

"Wow."

Standing on the sidewalk of Beacon Street, Mike tilted his head back and studied the intricate stone vines and flowers that interlaced with the word *Charlesgate* over the archway of the vestibule.

"Wow," he said again and turned to Zylla. "So this is the place you've been e-mailing me about all this time. Your dream home."

She beamed. "Almost as perfect as a renovated Gothic abbey, isn't it?"

"Almost," he agreed as he climbed the steps, turned, and sat on the top stair. Zylla trotted after him, sank onto the step, and remembered that in April, she and Anne had sat in this same place. She had entered the world of the Charlesgate that day. And the summer-like arms of Jabe.

She reached into her backpack and pulled out two bottles, snapped the caps off with her jackknife, and handed one to Mike. They clicked bottles in a mute toast and drank in silence, the swish and pull of the drinking and traffic from Massachusetts Avenue the only sounds heard on the quiet back street.

A breeze rustled through the few trees that lined the street and the many that stood sentry in the Fens. The edges of leaves were already starting to turn the yellows and reds of late September. Summer was over, Zylla realized, taking her Summerlord with it. But, she brightened, she had the Charlesgate as well as a new life as a writer. True, she hadn't written more than seven chapters, but they were solid and in her mind, she already thought herself a novelist.

Besides, Jabe was still a vital part of her life, she reminded herself, ignoring the quick rip of sorrow in her chest, and her lovely Lancelot was sitting right beside her. Mike was beautiful and for the first time, Zylla understood Guinevere's betrayal of her king. Then she remembered that Guinevere was condemned to burn at the stake. A chill brushed her skin and she shivered.

"You cold, Zyllie?" Mike asked, already shrugging out of his leather. "Want my jacket?"

"Nope." In high school, she would have said yes even if it were a hundred degrees just to be able to wear his jacket. She smiled at the thought. "Thanks, though. I'm not cold. Just got spooked for a second."

Mike glanced into the dark shadows in the alcove. "This place kind of has that creepy feeling. Like trying to go to sleep after a Hammer horror." He paused. "But I get why you love it."

He stared at the ground again and the mourning delineated in his profile reminded Zylla of high school and his defeated face after his girlfriend dumped him for Darrin Jacobs.

"It's not so bad," he started, sensing her intense worry. "Honestly. I'm really just ashamed of myself for falling so hard and completely ignoring her character. I fell out of love within a month after the wedding."

He reached inside his jacket pocket, pulled out a soft pack of Marlboros and shook a couple of cigarettes from their residence, offering one to Zylla.

Her stomach lurched at the thought of attempting another cigarette and she shook her head, waiting as he fed one between his lips and flicked his lighter. The quick flare illuminated a glowering stone face in a column and Zylla abruptly glanced away.

"She was absolutely the most gorgeous thing I ever saw," he continued, and jealousy twinged in Zylla.

"Long black hair, big dark eyes, perfect body, very goth. She always had this half-smile on her face, like she had the secret to all life. So of course I had to discover it." He gave a chuckle that ended with a sigh. "I asked her to marry me, just like that, certain that I'd found 'the one'. I was so damn afraid of losing her that marriage seemed the only alternative." He paused as he inhaled and exhaled smoke in one long breath.

"But, I think she was just enthralled with the novelty of marriage." He glanced at Zylla under heavy-lidded eyes and hesitated before he said, "I think I pleased her vanity somehow."

Zylla nodded. Mike was not a narcissist, but they both knew that women clamored around him with expressions reserved for superheroes or baby animals. He was flattered, of course, but he was mostly embarrassed, as though his skin was an ill-fitting outfit and the style all wrong for him.

"Once she realized I'm as dorky as the next guy, she started to resent the marriage and me. And to be honest, I started to dislike that she wasn't the deep, dark, intelligent, mysterious woman I had imagined her to be."

Zylla put her hand into Mike's and squeezed. He smiled sadly and brought her hand onto his lap, idly playing with her fingers and causing pleasant waves to squiggle up her arm.

"Of course, that's the image she has of herself. She thinks she's some sort of goddess." He laughed and shook his head. "Once I got over being angry with her for my own shallowness and realized that I should be angry at myself, I was able to resign myself to a miserable life. I knew I married the wrong woman, but being a good Catholic," he said, flashing a sudden grin, "I figured the marriage deserved some work." Mike opened her knapsack for a couple of more beers and handed one to Zylla.

"The fact that she slept with more guys than I can count on one hand in the five months we were married really aided in destroying my illusions, thank God." His eyes rolled heavenwards. "Otherwise, I may have remained in a state of flagellation for the rest of my life. The moral is," he said, eyes sparkling, "never sell your soul because you fear losing someone. It's just plain dumb."

Zylla rubbed her thumb along his palm and questioned, "So you're really okay?"

He glanced at her, seemingly startled, then laughed sharply.

Doubtful, Zylla worried that Mike's mind had been permanently damaged from the separation. He seemed a little too happy after such a crisis.

Mike laughed again, deep and throaty. "I didn't come here to talk about Allison, though, Zyllie. I came to see you." He swigged his beer before speaking again. "You remember all those conversations we had in the graveyard? About dreams and fate and the meaning of life?"

"Of course." Zylla chuckled. "Once you got used to the fact that I was your perma-stalker, we had some brilliant talks."

A grin sparked on his face. "Well," he began. "I've been having these dreams lately and have no clue what they mean. I was hoping you could help figure them out. They're the kind of dreams that cling on for days after you wake up, you know?" He stood up and ventured into the dark alcove where the ceramic faces gazed back at him, glistening unnaturally.

She rose and followed. "What do you mean? Give me an example."

"Just an image really. You and me. In it, we're on a city street, and I'm dressed in an old suit, like a Dickens's character, top hat and all.

But you, you are dressed like you do now, but you have blond hair and gray eyes.

"I have a bird's-eye view of us in the dream, and we're walking under gas-lighted street lamps. That's it. It just feels good. A great dream. I wake up feeling like I belong, you know?"

Zylla suddenly realized that he was closing the distance between them, that squiggles of electricity passed back and forth between their bodies. His eyes were filled with longing and dark lust and she thought *finally* and *too late.* Those potent lips that had kept her awake for so many years moved onto hers and she was transported deeper and deeper into the darkness of the alcove, images of stone and ceramic faces swirling behind her eyes.

She was in a sort of wild *déjà vu* full of strange currents and simmering tension. He kissed her slow and deep until her knees shook and as his mouth became impatient and rough, she clung tighter to his muscular body, fearing she would lose consciousness.

Kissing Mike was like listening to Rye play the banjo. She wanted to weep and weep until all the sorrow fled, and when he broke away and she gazed at his face, she saw that tears streamed down his cheeks, mirroring her own.

"That was weird," Mike said in a shaky voice, and he wiped the wetness on Zylla's cheeks with the end of his tee shirt.

"Uh-huh," Zylla replied and reciprocated by wiping his tears with her hands. "It was heartbreaking."

"Let's not do that again."

"Nuh-uh," she agreed.

His eyes gleamed. "You know I love you, Zyllie."

Her throat had a funny little catch in it. "Well, it certainly took you long enough to figure that out, didn't it?"

He grunted. "What can I say? Men are fools." He kissed her hand.

"Let's go," she said. "We'll go shoot some pool, huh?"

Mike nodded and pressed her hand, and they cantered down the steps to the sidewalk, turned onto Charlesgate East, and smacked right into Jabe.

~ * ~

"Zyll, what are you doing down here so late?" Jabe's insides lit with surprise and he was still smiling when he looked left to greet her companion. Then he noticed their clasped hands. The smile transformed into a scowl and his grip was tighter than usual when he shook Mike's hand after Zylla's introduction.

Recognition dawned in Jabe's mind as he processed who Mike was to Zylla. He was fairly certain his blood turned green and the realization that he was jealous, an emotion he had easily suppressed in the past, and worse, the milksop Zylla was in love with knew he was jealous and responded with a glint of the eye and a raised eyebrow.

Jabe couldn't speak—he feared he would sputter if he tried. So he clenched his fists and shook his head tersely when they invited him to shoot pool and ground his teeth as Mike threw an arm around her shoulders and grinned widely.

Jabe stalked past them, jolting Mike's shoulder as he went.

Zylla was dismayed by Jabe's rudeness and turned to a smiling Mike to apologize. "He's never acted like that before..." She broke off, her face red. "I don't get it. I mean, he even walks old ladies across the street."

Mike laughed and grasped her face between his two hands, peering into her worried eyes.

"Zyllie, now I know we aren't meant to be together. That man is crazy about you. Just as you are about him." He dropped his hands to rest on her shoulders.

"He is not in love with me," she said sadly. "He's not. He told me. If he's acting out now, then it's just a guy thing. You know. Territorial pissing."

Mike threw back his head and nearly howled.

"I don't think so, Zyll. He was stamping his hoof for sure, but he was mostly hurt. I think he thinks you've moved on." He lifted her chin with his hand, forcing her to look into the swirls of his blue eyes. "Trust me."

She looked so despondent that he drew her to him and squeezed her tight. She muttered against his skin, "Mike, why do guys always want a girl when it's too late?"

"I don't know, Zyllie." He rested his chin on the top of her head, which was nestled against his chest. "I suppose we realize we can't have her anymore. The impossible dream." She felt him shrug. "Or it could be that you've stopped loving us and we miss that pair of brown eyes mooning at us."

"Is that why you came to see me?" She moved away from him and studied his face.

The corners of his lips turned up and he said thoughtfully, "No, no... something pulled me to you. I thought you were it. Then when we kissed, well..." He shook his head.

"Was it..." She swallowed hard and cringed in anticipation. "Was it revolting for you?"

Mike looked at her as if she were crazy. "God no! It was incredible. But it broke my heart, like you said. Made me feel sad and lonely, like I'd lost you." He grinned again. "I think we must have been siblings in a past life or something. Twins probably. We're meant to be together, just not... together, you know?"

She nodded, smiling in relief. "That's how it felt for me, too." She slugged his shoulder. "If you just kissed me in high school, I wouldn't have wasted all that time on you!"

After the mirth faded, she added, "It's too bad, though. That it didn't work, you and me."

"Yes." Mike sighed. "It is."

They walked toward the Crossroads Pub, hand in hand, the shadow of the Charlesgate looming over them.

Twenty-two

Mocking jealousy latched onto Jabe and refused to let him breathe, so he went home to a bottle of Knob Creek and his banjo in hopes of chasing the green demon away. Yet after an hour of picking, sipping, and finally glaring into the fire, Jabe still couldn't dispel the image of Zylla and Mike wrapped around each other in naked splendor.

He had been a coward. He had wanted her for months but conveniently convinced himself that he was brave in denying the longing mirrored in her eyes. After all, he thought, sneering at the bottle of bourbon, constant torment was better than relieving himself in her for a couple of months before the whole thing went to hell, right? At least Zylla would be a friend forever, his comrade in arms for life, right?

The fire hissed in answer.

"The truth is," he muttered at the derisive flames, "Zylla is the brave one." He had run from her rather than confront his desires, and if it were not for her courage and honesty, they wouldn't be friends now.

He laughed bitterly. And he had already messed that up, easily slipping into complacency, secure in the fact that Zylla would always be there. He might marry someday, have a couple of kids, but Zylla would be right by his side, a sort of adopted family member, always making him laugh and steering him straight.

Never in his visions of the future had he considered the possibility that Zylla would marry. He had never imagined sharing her or watching as she devoted herself to some other man, someone like Mike. No, he had never counted on that.

Until tonight.

He tightened his grip on the glass as he lifted it to his mouth and swallowed golden fire, not even feeling the burn anymore. At the moment when the bourbon sloshed into his belly, he knew that she would always live inside of him. He had no control over it—she was in his DNA. He wanted Zylla, breathed Zylla, loved Zylla, and suddenly, he was very sure he always would.

He loved the crinkles at the corners of her eyes when she laughed. He loved the shadow of her lashes splayed on the rise of her cheek. He loved how she made him feel like a warrior. He loved her honesty and uncomplicated nature and all the nooks and crannies that went with it.

And with that acceptance came a happiness previously unknown to him, accompanied by relentless urgency and fear that it was all for nothing. That he was too late.

~ * ~

At the knock, Anne sauntered across the kitchen and into the small foyer, squinted through the peephole, then threw open the door with a smile. Sunlight flooded the entryway and she shielded her eyes from the morning rays.

"Jabe," she said warmly as she pushed the screen door and held it open for him to pass. "What brings you here so early on a Saturday?"

Jabe granted her a quick smile before his features turned to granite again. He pulled his dark sunglasses from his face as his gaze riveted to Zylla's closed bedroom door, a cold light in his eyes.

"She in there?"

Anne shook her head. "*She* went for a run."

"With him?" Jabe snarled.

"You mean Mike?" The corners of Anne's mouth lifted as she began to understand. She turned her back to him and took the teapot from its resting spot on the back burner of the gas stove. As she headed toward the sink, she smiled sweetly at Jabe. "I'm going to make some tea. Would you like a cup?"

"No." He folded his arms and leaned against the counter. "Thank you," he added gruffly.

Anne hummed, thoroughly enjoying his discomfort, knowing that he was at war with himself. She knew that he ached to ask if Zylla and Mike slept together last night, but his pride shackled him to silence. *One up for Zylla*, Anne thought.

Jabe felt ridiculous standing sentry in Zylla's kitchen, waiting for her to come home as if he was an angry father. Or a jealous lover. Which he was. Sort of. Steam rose from him in palpable waves and while he acknowledged that he had no right to seethe over Zylla's night of passion with Mike, he couldn't stop imagining Mike's hands roaming over her.

He realized that he was glowering at the door and immediately turned his head to glower at Anne. She merely smiled and reached for the teapot that whistled in a tone to match Jabe's mood.

The screen door slammed and Zylla stumbled into the room, panting, drenched in sweat, and frantically pulling her clingy tank top away from her overheated skin.

"Ugh, it's going to be miserably hot today," she announced as she walked into the room then stopped short at the sight of Jabe in his worn jeans, close-fitting white tee shirt, and stern, proud visage. She nearly swooned. How could anyone be so murderously gorgeous this early in the day?

She smiled, all of her feelings for him darting from her face in little prisms of bliss and Jabe's face softened. In that instant, all traces of anger and jealously, fear and dread, emptiness and loneliness retreated from the battlefield within him. Zylla sparkled and the light behind her smile was only for him. Confident and calm once more, he strolled to the cabinet, grabbed a tall glass from it and poured cold water into it. A knowing smile on his face, he held out the glass to her.

"Oh, I absolutely love you," she gushed flippantly as she grasped the cold glass then froze at the somber respect in his eyes.

"I know," he replied softly.

Zylla's heart ping-ponged inside her chest and she blinked slowly to erase her mind's conjuring, yet when she opened her eyes, the new light in Jabe's eyes was still there. And she knew.

He loved her.

With her eyes, she accepted that love and the warm glow of that entity flowed back and forth between them, binding them, making them oblivious to the world outside.

"I'm just going to go out and read on the front porch," Anne said, chuckling as she left the room.

Zylla broke the magic first, lifting her glass and gulping the last drops of water. She reached for the decanter and poured more water for herself. "I haven't seen you in a bit," she said.

He raised a brow. "You saw me last night."

She blushed and lowered her eyes, silently thanking fate that he hadn't witnessed the misbegotten kiss she and Mike had shared.

"Yes, well, I mean I haven't talked to you." She raised her eyes to his. "I found out a lot more information about my family tree Friday morning."

He gave her his full attention as Zylla recapped her conversation with Henry and the discovery that Admiral Thayer connected Jabe's family and her own once again, this time with the adoption of Jeremy Berry.

"Strange," he said. "There is a Jeremy Thayer on my family tree, but no record of his offspring are recorded." He shrugged. "But then, why would there be? He's not my direct ancestor."

He paused and gazed at her. "It just all gets weirder and weirder, doesn't it? It's either fate or..." He grinned and sang, "It's a small world after all."

Zylla groaned. "That's a horrible song and now it will be stuck in my head the rest of the day, thank you very much."

He laughed low in his throat and moved toward her to rest his hands on the counter edge, trapping her.

"Don't." She pushed him away, still uncertain about his change in emotions for her.

"Why not?"

"I'm all sweaty and I stink," she suggested lamely.

"I like your stink," he whispered, bending his head forward and nuzzling her neck. She closed her eyes and nearly gave into the tugging of his lips on her skin when inspiration struck.

"So what did you think of Mike?"

The question had the effect Zylla expected. Jabe pushed away from the counter and began pacing the kitchen floor. "Didn't like him," he growled. "Shakes hands like a little girl."

Zylla smiled. Mike was dead on about that jealousy thing.

"Aunt Maddie said the same thing about him. Oh..." Zylla's eyes widened and she stepped closer to Jabe. "I forgot to tell you about my chat with Auntie M."

After she explained her failure to obtain Jeremy's true parentage, Jabe's brows drew together and he stated, "I'm really starting to dislike your aunt."

She melted at the fury in his eyes. He had eyes that could snap between merriment and menace in one glance. Jabe carried a sword at his side, it seemed, and Zylla instinctively knew that he would always use it to defend her if she needed. He gave her courage to trust herself and a wave of gratitude swept over her.

"Don't," she pleaded. "You've only heard this one side of her behavior and it's not really her. Maddie is the best woman in the world. You'd be the first to love her."

Jabe sighed and gripped her hand. "I'm sorry," he said. "I just don't get her deal, that's all."

"Neither do I."

After a brief silence, Jabe let go of her hand and began to pace. "Listen," he said, his change in tone so abrupt that Zylla was momentarily taken aback. "How are you managing with temping?"

"What do you mean?"

"I mean, if I were to offer you a part-time job, great pay with benefits, would you be interested?"

Zylla furrowed her brow. "What's the job?"

"Once the Charlesgate is done, I'll need help managing it. It's a full-time job, but I don't want to give up Caval Construction. And you need the time to write. We could run the business together. Plus," he said, a slow smile dawning on his face. "One of the benefits is an apartment, rent-free."

"You're kidding me," she replied, shocked. Jabe nodded and she yelped. "Yes, yes, yes!" she yelped as she grabbed Jabe's hands and danced him around the room. Suddenly, she stopped and struggled to compose her features. "Sorry," she said. "Not very professional of me." She hollered again and danced in place.

"Whatever is going on in here?" Alight with laughter, Anne appeared in the doorway.

"You'll never believe it." Zylla laughed and began dancing again, leaving Jabe to explain. He offered Anne an apartment as well, but Anne told him of her plans to move to New York with Billy to open their own marketing firm. Jabe glanced at Zylla and caught the woeful expression on her face.

"Well," he said to Anne. "The city's just a short flight from Boston and you and Billy will always have a place to stay."

"Thanks, Jabe." Anne threw an arm around Zylla and gave a quick squeeze. "Take care of my girl."

"I intend to," he stated and faced Zylla. "You up for shooting some pool tonight?"

She nodded.

"Great. I'll pick you up at seven. We can grab some dinner first and talk about the job." He kissed Zylla briskly on the cheek and winked at Anne. "See you later."

Aware of the broad grin on his face, Jabe trotted down the steps and jaunted along the sidewalk. She had no idea what was coming. At the corner of Brookline and Massachusetts Avenues he laughed out loud and didn't mind the skeptical stares of passers-by.

Whistling, he crossed the bridge into Boston and walked the short length to turn onto Beacon where the Charlesgate waited at the end of the block. He breathed in relief when he noticed Rye's white van parked next to his motorcycle.

"'Bout time you got here," Rye grumbled and glared at Jabe from where he sat on the fifth step. "This had better be good. This morning light thing is a bit much for me."

"Trust me, Billy Goat," Jabe said, clapping his hand on Rye's shoulder. "You'll be well paid."

A half-hour later, Rye climbed into his van, singing merrily. In his pocket was the title deed to Jabe's Jamaica Plain house and soon the keys would belong to him as well. All he had to do was spend the morning at area antique stores to purchase a few key pieces of furniture and oriental rugs, something that he would happily do for free, especially since Jabe had disclosed his plans for the evening.

Jabe's grin faded as he watched Rye drive away, and he unlocked the iron-barred glass doors and entered the hallway.

In the bright sunlight, the marble and wood gleamed and the tesserae of the restored mosaic floor sparkled like jewels. He turned left and walked to the end of the hall where the mahogany door of his three-room office suite stood open, ready for him.

The walls of the reception area were painted terra cotta and blended nicely with the dark stained oak floors. Heavy, eighteenth-century cherry furniture decorated this room as well as the two offices connected to it. The natural light that flowed through the windows, despite the first floor location, gilded the room's colors.

These rooms were the only fully furnished ones in the hotel. That would all change by tonight. Jabe glanced at the old sea captain's clock on the mantel and hastily picked up the telephone receiver to begin making calls.

~ * ~

At seven, Jabe's black and chrome Indian roared to a stop in front of the duplex where Zylla waited in the old wicker rocker on the porch. She watched as Jabe removed his helmet, his long hair tied back with a piece of rawhide. She cocked her head to the side as he drew closer.

He seemed different tonight. It was the shirt, she decided. He wore his jeans that looked like worn velvet, but the shirt tucked into those jeans was crisp and forest green. Instead of work boots, he wore black motorcycle boots.

"You look great," she said as he approached, taking the steps two at a time. Jabe caught the arms of the rocker with his hands to halt its movement and leaned in so that his lips were a few inches from Zylla's.

"It's as dressy as I get for special occasions," he said in a low voice that stirred answering desire from deep within her.

"And tonight's a special occasion?" she managed to stammer.

He straightened and winked as he held out his arm to her. She rested her hand in the crook of his elbow and rose from the chair to walk toward the bike.

"Jabe?"

He handed her a helmet and after she eased it onto her head, he stepped closer to fasten the chinstrap.

"All set?" he asked, amusement on his face. She nodded and he climbed onto the bike and started the engine. "Hop on," he said over his shoulder.

As they drove over the bridge, Zylla couldn't think of a more perfect moment than sitting behind Jabe on his trusty steed while speeding into Boston and watching as the dusky sun sparkled on the Charles.

He turned onto Beacon Street.

"We're stopping at the Charlesgate?" she yelled.

He nodded once before turning onto Charlesgate East and gliding to a stop in front of the entrance.

A strangled yelp emanated from Zylla as she rather ungracefully hopped off the back of the bike. "It's all done, isn't it? That's the special occasion!"

Jabe's only answer was to take her hand and lead her through the glass door and into a dream.

~ * ~

Luminaries lined each side of the hall, sending waves of color over the mosaic floor and wall tiles. In a tri-cornered alcove near the entrance, the gilded elevator glimmered. As they neared the garish lady, Zylla's arm brushed against the soft fronds of one of the potted ferns standing sentry on either side of the cage door.

Jabe led her along the path of flickering light and around the corner. On her right, the carved mahogany woodwork of the reception office and mailroom gleamed and boasted the restored door of opaque mauve glass that Zylla loved when she had first seen the inside of the Charlesgate. Moonstones and rose quartz inlaid in the glass glowed in the candlelight.

"My offices are in that suite." Jabe pointed to his left. "But this," he said as he flung open the double doors at the end of the hall, "is what I want to show you." He reached along the wall and flipped the light.

In an instant, the cast iron chandelier sparked to life, casting shadows over the intricately carved ceiling. Table lamps warmly lit the room, revealing nooks that contained chairs and settees upholstered in gold-green. Walls not lined with floor-to-ceiling bookshelves were painted ox-blood red and matched velvet-draped windows. Next to one settee, a Georgian writing desk begged for a guest, an inspiring bust of Shakespeare perched atop it.

"There's another library on the Marlborough Street side. It's smaller, though. No pool table."

And there was the crux of it. Smack in the middle of the huge room, directly under the chandelier, a red felt pool table reigned.

Zylla closed her eyes and could almost smell the cheroots of Victorian men as they played billiards and argued politics in this room, and when she opened her eyes, his face reflected her happiness.

"You did it, Jabe," she whispered.

He poured them bourbons from the bar built discreetly in one corner of the room, and they played pool until Jabe noticed that Zylla had been silent for quite some time.

He positioned the white ball in a strategic point on the red felt then allowed his gaze to drift upwards to her face. She stared at the chalk cube as if she were about to slaughter it. He knew that look.

"Hungry?"

"A little," she replied. "Where do you want to go?"

"Can you wait until after you see your apartment?"

Zylla's face broke in a grin. "I was hoping to see it."

Twenty-three

They rode the elevator to the sixth floor, and Zylla followed Jabe down the dark hall to the where the corridor turned. He stopped and unlocked the corner apartment, pushed open the door slightly, and handed her the keys.

"All yours," he chimed, and Zylla felt a thrill shimmy up her spine as she prodded the door open.

They entered a cream-colored foyer trimmed in dark wood. The floor was tiled in a sable and cream Moroccan pattern and a great Moorish lantern descended from the high ceiling.

"There's the kitchen," Jabe said as he propelled her toward an arched wood door with a tiny quarter moon carved into it. "Some apartments won't have kitchens if the tenants don't want them," he continued. "A subdivision of the main restaurant will cater to those who prefer healthy, home-cooked meals, delivered. I figured you'd want a kitchen, though."

Zylla smiled absently, but had barely heard him. Her eyes greedily drank in the huge room with white tiled walls, granite countertops and black marble floor with inlays of white tiles. Jabe had already installed a heavy oak table and chairs to match the wood and glass cabinets, and state-of-the-art cookware hung from iron racks. She could practically smell aromas of food cooking and her stomach rumbled.

To the right of the massive stainless steel oven was a doorway that revealed a curving stairwell. Zylla looked at Jabe in question.

"That goes upstairs to another apartment. There's a great room up there that we just finished. C'mon, I'll show you."

As they entered the stairwell, he pointed to the locks on the heavy door. There was a catch in his voice when he next spoke. "You can keep this locked, of course."

He quickly turned and jogged up the stairs, but not before Zylla caught the odd light in his eye, a cautious, almost pleading glint that disappeared as quickly as it came.

The dining room at the top of the stairs was painted olive green offset by dark mahogany paneling that crawled halfway up the walls. Above the wood, on the outside wall, three stained-glass windows, evenly spaced, let in jeweled light. A medieval oblong table surrounded by twelve carved wood chairs and a matching sideboard adorned the room.

"This is stunning, Jabe. I feel like I'm in Camelot."

"Glad you like it," he said in hushed tones.

They retraced their steps downstairs through the kitchen and into the foyer where three more doors waited to be opened.

"That one's a closet." Jabe indicated the door to the left of the entrance. "And that's the bathroom."

A warm yellow glow flooded the room when Zylla switched on the light. The bathroom was done in the palest green Italian marble, and at one end was a glass-walled shower big enough for three people—directly opposite was a sunken tub. Alongside the wall was a two-sink vanity and giant Victorian mirror.

Zylla snorted. "How am I supposed to be a suffering artist in this place?"

Jabe laughed. "I can shut off the hot water, if you want," he said, and she shot him an evil glare.

The third door yielded an empty room painted creamy coral with white trim. A golden oak floor and a brightly colored mosaic fireplace added more cheer to the room and reminded Zylla of summer. Across the floor, sliding wood doors stood closed. As if he read her mind, Jabe said, "Go ahead." She strode across the room and carefully slid the doors into the walls.

And gasped.

Candlelight splattered airy shapes against the butter-trimmed maize walls and intricate plaster ceiling. A smiling woman dressed with pixy-punk hair stood at attention in the center of the room next to a linen-covered round table loaded with pretty china plates and silver dome-topped dishes.

"Hey there," the woman said.

Zylla smiled. So she hadn't imagined the smell of food after all.

Her gaze danced to the far corner where the glass-paned turret waited to give her vertigo again, but this time, she didn't need to be in the turret to feel the dizziness. This was Jabe's Spring Room, the spot she loved so much when she first toured the Charlesgate. Jabe was giving her the best suite in the mansion.

Her mind unable to process the sensory overload, she nervously fingered the blue eye talisman resting against her skin. "What is this, what are you doing?" she stammered. "This is too much, Jabe. You could rent this place for thousands. All I need is a broom closet, really."

He took her hand and led her to the table where he pulled out the chair for her. Numb, she automatically sat. He leaned down from where he stood behind her, his mouth tickling her ear.

"You deserve it." He stepped away and introduced the woman. "This is Krista Kranyak, by the way, owner of Ten Tables, my favorite spot in JP."

Krista uncovered platters of saffron and almond trout and grilled vegetables, then expertly poured the vintage wine for Jabe's perusal.

"Excellent, thank you," he said, eyes glittering.

"If there's nothing else, then I'll leave, sir," she replied, voice bubbling with mock deference.

Jabe's feigned expression of gravity crumbled and he laughed. "Krista, cut it out. Go home. Say hi to your girl for me."

Krista flicked a laughing glance at Zylla, inviting her to join in the joke, but Zylla was dumbstruck, her eyes darting everywhere and nowhere at once.

Krista squeezed Jabe's shoulder. "I think you did too well. The poor girl is in shock," she muttered, shoulders shaking in merriment.

"Dessert is in the freezer. Lavender ice cream." She quietly left the room, sliding the doors closed behind her.

Jabe sat back and watched Zylla's pale face as she ate mechanically, then perused the room, trying to see it as she did. Rye had chosen perfect furniture, as Jabe knew he would. An elegant Georgian table against one wall boasted the hottest new laptop, and a matching chair with a seat pad of pale green watered silk promised hours of comfort.

Scatter rugs in swirling gold, green, and butter yellow warmed golden oak floorboards, and Scottish lace panels dressed the three windows in the room, hiding window seats upholstered to match the rugs. The slim turret windows remained bare.

Next to the pale green marble fireplace, a cheery fire ablaze, Rye had created a cozy reading area. A chintz-covered easy chair with matching footstool placed next to a round marble-topped table invited a person to sip tea and surrender to a good book.

Pleased, Jabe turned to Zylla and her wide eyes, and a fresh surge of doubt washed over him. She hadn't said anything. Maybe she hated it. He swallowed.

"I can repaint it," he challenged, snapping Zylla out of her shock.

"Huh?"

"The room. If you don't like it, I can repaint it, get different furniture."

Zylla nearly choked on a piece of trout. "Are you kidding me? This room is like something out of Jane Austen." She rolled her eyes. "Now I have no excuse not to finish my book. I'd be ashamed otherwise."

The dimple appeared in Jabe's face just as Zylla's smile fell. "But it's too much, Jabe. I don't understand. It's just too much."

His confidence restored, he waved away her dismay. "Don't worry, darlin'." He laughed. "Once you start managing this place, you'll wonder why I didn't buy you a villa in France. Besides," he said, shrugging. "This place isn't that great. Look at that mantel over there, all chipped."

Zylla glanced at the mantel, with its lavender-filled vase and the huge gilded mirror that lorded over it, and looked back at Jabe as if he were crazy.

"Looks perfect to me."

"Nope." Jabe pressed his lips together and shook his head as he rose from his seat. "Go see for yourself."

Puzzled, Zylla got up and went to the fireplace. She first saw her own face and the bushel of lavender reflected in the mirror, then lowered her gaze to the smooth, green-veined mantel.

"But," she started, confused by the glittering object at the base of the vase. "Jabe, it's a diamond. Did you find it during restoration?"

Zylla felt addled. She was missing something here, but what? He must have found the ring and was giving it to her, but shouldn't it go to the historical society? Yet it didn't appear to be old. She looked up at his solemn face and suddenly she knew. Her voice squeaked. "Are you, are you...?"

"Zylla," Jabe whispered reverently. "Marry me."

She stared at him blankly for approximately three seconds. Then she pitched herself forward into his arms, laughing hysterically.

"You haven't answered, you know," he said.

She sprang out of his arms and bounded across the room then back again. "Yes, yes, yes and yes!"

Jabe reached onto the mantel for the ring and placed it on her finger.

"Is this real?" she murmured.

"Of course it's real!" he snapped.

Zylla belatedly realized his assumption and looked up at him with apologetic eyes. Her fingers toyed with the closures of his shirt and he eased her closer to him. "No, I mean, us. Did you really just ask me to marry you?"

"Oh. Well," he said, nodded slowly as his lips descended to hers, brushing back and forth across them until she leaned fully against him. "I sort of told you," he muttered, "but whatever works."

Zylla's smile dazzled, and he crushed her with ravenous kisses until her arms slid under his arms and around his back. Her fingers tore at the muscles there, urging him to devour her completely, to drive away the pressure that climbed inside her.

His mouth dragged across her cheek, chewed her slender neck, and threatened to tear great chunks out of her very flesh.

"Jabe," she cried.

He lifted her easily into his arms, green eyes revealing his intent. His upper lip curled up as he lowered her onto the floor and kneeled above her as he guided her arms over her head where he held her wrists with one hand. With his free hand he traced the contours of her face. The heat in his eyes hypnotized and her gaze locked to his as his mouth once again descended to hers.

"Beautiful," he whispered before his mouth claimed hers again, moving in a drugging rhythm. She suddenly knew how a blossom laden with pollen felt, her lips thick and her limbs useless as he continued to plunder with his tongue and stroke with his hand.

His fingers snaked behind the hair at her nape and rubbed before trailing down and up her side, and his hardness ridged against her thigh. Zylla could barely breathe with want of him and she arched to lodge him firmly between her thighs.

A guttural moan erupted from Jabe and his kisses grew fevered as he released her wrists and used both hands to tug at the shirt tucked into her jeans. His hands seared her bare skin as they pushed the jersey up over her breasts. Off now, he flung it across the room and slid one hand down her throat to the swell of her breasts while the other cupped the side of her head, fingers entangled in her hair.

Zylla happily sank into the soft rug, her body heavy and her brain deliciously light. She relished in his rough kisses, the scrape of stubble against her skin. Her delirium ended when she felt Jabe's hands fumble at the buttons of her jeans.

With all her will, she turned her head to the side, her shaking hands pushing at his broad chest. "W-wait," she muttered. "Wait. Stop. Jabe. Wait!"

Jabe lifted his head slowly and glanced at her with slumberous eyes then lowered his head to her breasts. Zylla clutched his ponytail and tugged.

"Ow!" Jabe sprung from her, anger stamped on his face. "If you wanted me to stop all you had to do was say so."

She rolled her eyes, and straightened her black lace bra and watched as confusion quickly replaced the anger on Jabe's face.

"Why are we stopping?"

"Because," Zylla said imperiously, "I've waited this long to have sex. I might as well wait until the wedding. Besides..." She walked over to her shirt, snapped it from the floor and shook it.

"The last time we did this, look what happened," she said before struggling into her jersey. "You stopped speaking to me for three weeks. Since we have a wedding to plan, we really can't afford a repeat of that. We are going to do it the right way." Zylla tucked the top into her jeans then looked at Jabe steadily. "We're waiting until we're married."

Jabe groaned. He lifted his hand, opened his mouth, then closed it and let his hand drop to his side. Finally, he said, "Okay, on one condition."

She raised both eyebrows.

"We get married very soon."

"When?"

"How about tomorrow?"

Zylla blew a strand of hair from her face in reply.

Jabe scratched under his chin. He paced to the fireplace and studied her through the mirror. "One month then, in November. We can have it here, at the Charlesgate."

A slow smile appeared on her face and she nodded. "Perfect."

Jabe took her face in his hands and slanted his mouth over hers. Neither was aware of the lavender scent that enveloped them in fierce warmth, nurturing their union.

~ * ~

On the short ride to her house, bubbles of panic tore through Zylla as the giddiness and lustful stupor disintegrated. *Why was he marrying her?* she thought. It was too sudden. Too unexpected.

Beneath the helmet, she chewed her bottom lip. Was he acting out of some misbegotten sense of jealousy, some testosterone-driven contest between he and Mike?

In front of the Cambridge duplex, the Indian sputtered as Jabe turned off the ignition and twisted to the side to see Zylla. He removed his helmet.

"What's wrong?" he asked tiredly. "You can't possibly be hungry again."

"Why are you suddenly wanting to marry me?" she demanded as she removed her own helmet.

Jabe studied the porch light for a second then looked at her. "Because, Zylla, I realized that life without you isn't any life at all, and I love you.

"And..." He smirked. "I realized that I just don't have the patience to wait for you to trust me. Marriage, you see, is my only alternative, one that I don't object to in the least."

"Wait," Zylla said, narrowing her eyes at him as they walked to her door. "That big ole dining room that's upstairs from my apartment. Who does that belong to?"

He grinned wickedly.

"You were pretty darn sure that I'd say 'yes', weren't you?"

He cocked an eyebrow, then waggled both of them. "Wait 'til you see the bedroom. There are two walk-in closets, a king-sized carved birchwood bed, compliments of Rye, and a fieldstone fireplace."

"Great." She laughed. "All we need now is a bearskin rug."

He gathered her into his arms. "Well," he said, "we'll get one. I plan to do a lot of hunting."

Zylla frowned. Jabe had told her that he and his brother used to hunt deer in Vermont, but they had used the animal for food. She had no idea that he hunted as a hobby and wasn't sure that she approved.

"What do you hunt?" she asked censoriously.

He bent his head and brushed his lips against hers, sending all sorts of frenetic chills down her spine.

"You," he replied.

~ * ~

Jabe returned to the Charlesgate to ensure that all the luminaries had been extinguished. After all that work, the last thing he needed was another fire.

The main hallway dark, he took the elevator to the sixth floor. The hair rose on his arms. Despite its new light and polished metal, the elevator continued to give him the creeps, and that smell of the docks on a summer day still crept up the shaft from the basement.

He opened the door to Zylla's apartment and was assaulted by a surge of lavender.

"'Bout time you showed up, Lydia. Do you approve?"

As usual, he received no answer, and he sighed loudly. "I wish you'd just show yourself, so I'd know for sure," he muttered as he walked through the apartment.

He checked each candle in the Spring Room, but all seemed to be snuffed. Before switching off the light and leaving, he scanned the room one last time.

He felt proud and humble, proud of the results of the labor of he and his crew, but thankful that it was accomplished. They didn't do it alone, he was certain. In his mind, moments like this justified a supreme being.

He turned off the light and just as he spun on his heel, he caught the dim flicker of a votive candle.

Jabe strode toward the fireplace where the candle smoldered.

"Ow, dammit," he swore as he thrust out a hand and grabbed the mantel to catch his fall. The toe of his boot had caught on something and caused him to trip.

He crouched down to feel the along the floor. One of the marble slabs of the fireplace rocked when he put pressure on it. His boot must have caught the edge where marble met floorboard.

"Damn." He had been certain that all the tiles were secure—he had checked them himself. His lip curled in consternation as he pulled up the marble and propped it against the wall so that Krista didn't trip on it when she arrived tomorrow to pick up her dishes. A wooden square was more noticeable than a slightly raised marble slab that matched all the tiles around it.

Except that there was no wood under the slab. A one-inch ledge of plywood rimmed the area, enough of a protrusion to support the tile. Dark, empty space seemed to fill the center, but from the dim light of the street lamps, Jabe discerned that the hollow was not deep and that something rested on its floor. He rose, a joint in his knee creaking, and went to turn on the light to better see what rested in this shallow grave.

Worn leather greeted his palm as he clutched the heavy weight. A book. He flipped through the yellowed pages, careful not to break the fragile paper, and the motion fanned a musty odor to his nose.

What a relic, he thought, thrilled with his find. *Wait until Zylla sees this*. He admired the even, slanted black writing that was consistent on every page. It seemed to be a journal or a log of some sort: every page or so was headed by a date over a hundred years old.

Awestruck, Jabe meandered toward the small table where he and Zylla had eaten dinner and snapped on the table lamp. He cleared the plate away and brushed aside the crumbs, carefully placed the book in front of him, sat down, and opened to the first entry.

> *15 April 1893. I am twenty-one years old today and am quite perturbed by the event. Father took Lily and I for a picnic lunch on the Common where all the Berry cousins joined us and although I was pleased to see them, I am not yet cheered. All I wish is to be let alone today with my books and tea so that I may mope properly, but Lily won't hear of it.*
>
> *"Lydia," she said. "You promised to attend the lecture and dinner tonight, so don't even bother with the excuse that your head aches. Honestly, Lyddie, I sometimes wonder that we are sisters. Perhaps you are right and some faerie changeling stole your soul at birth for I simply cannot account for your constant brooding."*
>
> *She is right, of course. I am unnatural.*
>
> *The women at the Charlesgate are of two sorts. There are wealthy socialites who gamble at bridge and sip tea while sending scathing looks toward other females, and there are those like Sarah Putnam and Lily who march the halls with fire in their eyes and suffragist language on their lips.*

I belong to neither group. Sometimes, I wonder if I even belong to this world.

Kate has arrived with my tea. Dear, sweet Kate with her lilting voice and tales of Ireland. "Ye have too much of the Celts in ye, darlin' and not enough of the English that curses yer poor sister," she tells me. Poor Kate. Her cough is getting worse and although I know Sarah's brother, John, pays excellent wages, I fear her tasks as a maidservant are too burdensome for her.

Oh, but how she is indispensable to me! She understands my loneliness and longing for some dark prince to spirit me away to his lair. Alas, such does not exist in this world, especially not in Boston. I am twenty-one today and cursed to be an old maid forever.

Yup, Jabe thought, still somewhat stoned by his discovery. *Fate again*. "Zylla is going to hop around the whole damn building over this one," he said aloud, and a strong burst of lavender answered him.

"I guess this is my proof that you're real, huh, Lyddie?" Jabe grinned at the air and returned to her journal.

Twenty-four

The tips of dawn's fingers had barely peeked over the horizon when Jabe silently closed the brittle pages. He stared at the swirls in the pale green marble until the first sounds of traffic crashed the silence.

Poor Lydia, he thought.

He clenched his teeth to steel himself against the fear that rose to his throat while his mind worked to convince itself that what he read was simply not true, that Lydia had simply possessed an overactive imagination.

He flipped to Lydia's last entry, dated October twenty-five, eighteen hundred and ninety-five, and re-read the tale of the Berry family curse and Lydia's last words:

> *All my life, I've dreamed of pirate ships rolling in bloody seas and with my headaches, she comes with her wretched stink of the decaying sea and stitched lips, to moan her threats.*
>
> *Since marrying my beloved Caval, my blue-eyed gypsy, she has been uneasy, following me with her red eyes. My headaches are worse, and even the lavender I carry with me cannot ease the pain. She grows stronger, and soon I will be dead.*
>
> *I only desire to remain in the peaceful splendor of the Charlesgate and raise my family, but Charlotte*

wants my destruction, and she shall have it. I cannot fight fate.

But when she visits to wail her story of murder and revenge, she leaves unsaid one small part of the tale.

The curse can end.

Yet there is hope. She will not kill me until my child is born, for she cannot kill an unborn Berry: because of her son Jeremy's vow, she is forbidden to extinguish the Berry or Thayer families. And if I have a boy, I will name him Jemmy, after Charlotte's son. My child will be a reminder of his namesake and the hope he had promised.

For Papa's winter tale isn't finished, and Charlotte's specter knows and fears it.

While Charlotte was dying in the noonday sun, young Jeremy, stricken by his mother's words, recovered enough to amend her curse. He clipped a tress of black hair from his mother and a blond tendril from Jabez. As he braided the two together, he vowed, "May a descendant of Thayer and a child of Berry meet again. If they have the courage to hold love above all else, then my mother's reign will end, and all the souls she intends to destroy will be at peace."

And to this, I add my own charge.

May I remain on this earth to ensure the success of Jeremy's promise. May I have the strength to fight Charlotte when the two lines meet again. Left alone, Charlotte will never allow this event to occur, and she must not prevail.

The Berrys are my own as well as hers. She will not destroy my family.

Jabe's head spun, and he rubbed his temple, trying to ease his mangled thoughts. Wafts of lavender suddenly made him sick and he opened a window to inhale the crisp fall air.

"So you are real, Lydia, but that doesn't mean the curse is real, that Charlotte is real. You were murdered, but there's no proof it was Charlotte. No proof at all."

He closed his eyes against the morning light. "It doesn't matter anyway," he murmured. Curse or no curse, the point was moot—Zylla was a Berry and he was a Thayer. The lines met again and fell in love. "We're getting married," he told Lydia. "Isn't that good enough?"

Yes, he thought, opening his eyes and breathing a sigh of relief as he shrugged off the sense of foreboding that gnawed at him. He clutched the journal close as his thoughts swirled again.

His ancestor, Jabez Thayer, had killed his lover, Charlotte de Berry, Zylla's ancestor, and Charlotte had cursed both families before hanging.

Jabe thought of all the money the Thayers possessed, the same money that had caused so much misery to Thayer males as far back as he could recall, money that had been won by the death of Charlotte de Berry, its rightful owner. Although, Jabe mused, she hadn't really deserved it either, given her profession.

Countless Berry women slaughtered for committing the sin of marriage, at least according to Lydia, and there was no longer any doubt in Jabe's mind that it was Lydia who walked about the Charlesgate expelling lavender. But maybe, just maybe, Jabe thought, Lydia was insane. Maybe she had heard that old Berry tale one too many times and had started to live for it.

"What if it is true, though?" Jabe asked the clear blue sky. Was the tale something all Berrys had believed in, something the women had caused to come true simply because they had believed? Or were all Berry women wired to know, able to see and hear Charlotte?

No, he thought. Lily hadn't believed. Did Maddie? Is that why she never married? He sighed loudly. Maybe only the special ones believed, like Zylla's Yia-Yia even though she hadn't been a Berry at all, or Lydia with her migraines and nightmares. Just like Zylla, he realized and chuckled. Genes were a strange phenomenon.

"God," he said. *Just like Zylla*. Jabe's belly lurched as fear tugged it. Zylla *was* wired for the Charlotte gene, and his mind listed all the symptoms—her migraines, the sleep narcolepsy, the crazy woman with sewn lips, her dreams of pirates and wild seas. She may not have heard the tale, but by God, she knew it. She was writing it!

But Maddie had heard the story and had kept it from her niece. All of his anger at Maddie's secrets melted into a surge of gratefulness. Maddie knew Zylla well and understood if Zylla had known the tale, given her nature, she would have lived her life in fear, somehow accommodating the curse.

And maybe Lydia had been protecting Zylla all along, in her own way, starting the fire, causing the accidents, possessing Frank—all to scare Zylla away from marriage.

Jabe's head snapped around, but nothing moved in the room except dust motes in the sunlight. Had he only imagined it, or did the lavender just give a derisive snort?

"Lydia?" he asked. No one answered and Jabe scratched at the underside of his jaw. *Maddie was right*, he thought. *Zylla should never know the truth.*

Resigned, he scooped the book from the floor and brought it to the fireplace. He closed his eyes for a moment, sighed, and placed it into the grate, fingers refusing to break contact with the history.

A memory of Zylla studying his family tree popped into his head. He opened his eyes again and swore under his breath. This was her history. He couldn't destroy it.

~ * ~

Over the next three weeks, Jabe saw Zylla infrequently. Both were often at the Charlesgate at the same time, but Jabe was working overtime moving his office to the new facilities in the Charlesgate, designing plans for the basement and attending to business that he had neglected for so long.

Zylla, on the other hand, barely found time to arrange her new two-floor apartment between wedding arrangements and managing the Charlesgate. When not tending to tenants, she could be found directing and hiring a full time staff of chefs, waiters, housekeepers, and reception clerks.

Although Jabe would glimpse a sweet pining in her eyes when their paths crossed briefly, he could see that Zylla was exhilarated and distracted by the upcoming nuptials and her part in reviving the grand dame of Boston.

Their chaotic schedules prevented Jabe from dwelling on the journal he had hidden in his desk drawer. In the moments when he stopped moving, or in those seconds when Zylla looked at him with eyes full of worship, his conscience cringed. But then one of his employees would bustle in or Zylla's expression would brighten and he would nearly forget all about that little book in the back of his drawer.

His guilt disappeared completely when his accomplice in secrecy came to town a week before the wedding. The thing was, Jabe liked Madeleine. He liked her cool gray eyes that shone like moonstones when she looked at her niece. He liked that she wore her pale blond hair in a loose chignon and that she dressed like a woman from the nineteen-forties, although she was too young to have emerged from that era. He liked her reserve and calm manner.

When they were introduced, Maddie appraised him and he sensed that she saw his very character in that one glance. When they shook hands, she had looked at her niece with a slim eyebrow raised, then back at him to say, 'Nice handshake'. He knew he had somehow passed Madeleine Berry's test and was now one of the family.

And when she turned to Zylla, taking her niece's small chin in her hand and saying with a catch in her throat, "I'm so proud of you," Jabe loved her. He finally understood why Maddie kept her knowledge away from Zylla. She kept it for the same reasons he did, despite the guilt. Madeleine remained quiet because she loved Zylla.

~ * ~

Maddie laid the clothing bag on her bed in Jabe and Zylla's pretty coral-colored guest room and unzipped it to reveal Cindy's wedding gown.

"We can still go dress shopping if you want," Maddie explained as she pulled a mass of ivory satin from the black bag. "But I just want to make sure... I want you to see your mother's first."

Zylla's eyes softened and she lovingly stroked the gown. A two-layered confection, the dress had a princess cut overcoat embroidered with seed pearls. The sleeves flared in medieval fashion and the skirt separated to reveal a silk underdress.

Zylla squealed. "It's exactly what I want."

"Your mother would have wanted you to wear it." Maddie smiled. "She would have loved to see you." Maddie's voice broke off at the last word and startled, Zylla glanced up from the shimmering material.

Maddie's eyes brimmed with tears, and she brushed at them furiously as she tried to speak, but found her words caught in a choke.

Zylla bit her lip, then reached out to hug her aunt. She had never seen Maddie unravel and it scared her. For the first time in thirty years, she felt like an adult.

"Sometimes," Maddie sobbed, collapsing onto the bed. "Sometimes I miss her so much. You were, were..."

Zylla grabbed a box of tissues from the bureau, plucked a handful, and shoved the box and the cushion of tissue into Maddie's waiting hands. She plopped down onto the bed beside her aunt and tentatively petted her back as Maddie fought another burst of tears. As usual, she succeeded.

"You were just like her when you were little. Both of you covered in mud, hunting dragons through the forest, scaring the neighborhood boys. When I was young, I read books and sipped tea with my dolls. Still do. Well, sans the dolls, of course." Maddie managed a tremulous smile.

"Cindy was always chasing some new passion or another, then suddenly giving up on it, just like you seemed to do, until recently," Maddie continued quietly. "She was scared, I think. And then she met your father and she wasn't scared anymore."

Bitterness scarred Maddie's voice. "And then she died." She seized Zylla's hand and squeezed it tight, her eyes imploring. "I hope I raised you right, Zyllie. I never wanted you to be scared like—" Her voice broke again and she paused. "I just wanted you to be brave enough to follow your own heart and not be led by romantic fancies."

Maddie closed her eyes and when she opened them, she faced her niece. "About the other, our family history," she said haltingly. "I couldn't tell you because—"

"No," Zylla interrupted. "It's okay. I understand. We don't have to talk about it."

Maddie smiled, her eyes searched Zylla's and found trust. Relieved, she rested her hand on Zylla's pale cheek in quiet gratitude.

"Let's go," Zylla said, smiling brightly. "Jabe promised you a tour of the building."

Maddie laughed, wiping the last of her tears, her nose still red from crying. "Well, dear, if it's anything like this apartment, I'm already impressed."

~ * ~

"I can't believe this is your home," Maddie exclaimed in hushed tones, squeezing Zylla's hand.

Zylla whispered in return, "I can barely believe it myself. I keep waiting for you to wake me up to go to school."

They emerged from the elevator into the bustling lobby to wait for Jabe, and Zylla shook her head, still astounded that she actually lived in the Charlesgate.

When she had moved into her new home, Zylla was amazed that Jabe had already installed a spiral staircase from the Spring Room to their seventh floor bedroom. She loved the wide fieldstone fireplace and giant birchwood bed, although she couldn't wait for him to move in to chase away the loneliness.

She had hoped to befriend Lydia, but so far she hadn't smelled a hint of lavender, and she often awoke in the middle of the night with a sense of menace surrounding her, something that was decidedly not her hygienically pleasing relative. Nor did she like riding the elevator at night. The murky odor from the basement sometimes drifted to her nose, reminding her of painful migraines and their horrific visions.

Zylla crossed her arms and shivered. At least the ocean death odor seemed to be nonexistent today.

"See you later, Den," Jabe called to the retreating back of his foreman as he joined Zylla and Maddie. "So, are you two ready for lunch? I'm starving."

They walked the length of the broad hallway until it emptied into the dining area, resplendent with its mosaic floors and carved black marble fireplace large enough to stand inside. Tables and chairs dotted throughout the room allowed space to move about, or, if one wished, to dance.

Near the fireplace, a grand piano on a raised dais waited to be played and with the additional effect of potted greenery dashed about the room, Maddie was reminded of "Casablanca." She glanced at Jabe and was grateful that he didn't resemble Humphrey Bogart.

As Jabe seated Maddie, Zylla realized that this was the first time she had relaxed in weeks. Wedding plans, moving, and the opening of the Charlesgate occupied her time from early morning until the time she went to bed.

She had only seen Jabe in passing or during quick daily consults when she would ask questions like, "What flavor cake do you want?"

Jabe's would consistently reply with a shrug and "Whatever you want, dear." Then he'd leer at her and waggle his brows.

In four weeks, she had written only one scene in her book and a particularly disturbing scene at that. On top of it all, she seemed to be allergic to her engagement ring.

Zylla absentmindedly rubbed her chapped ring finger while her eyes scouted the room. *Ah, but all the work was worth it,* she thought. Now that she could breathe, she saw that the teams of cleaning people, the interior decorators, the interviews, and the dozens of people she had supervised in order to bring the Charlesgate to its present state were worth all the hassle.

This room, like all the others, seemed to breathe a thankful sigh of life. To her right, she could see passersby on Charlesgate East peek into the arched windows of the restaurant—to her left white sheers billowed from the Corinthian arcade that opened onto an outside patio.

From the patio, three steps descended to what used to be the paved, garbage-strewn parking lot. Now green grass, flowering trees, and herb gardens edged winding brick paths and stone benches, creating an enchanted sanctuary bound on three sides by the U-shaped walls of the Charlesgate and by a pretty brick enclosure that led to the alley.

"There's a garden on the roof, too," Zylla said to her aunt, who turned to see what Zylla studied so intently.

"Well," said Maddie, snapping her napkin and spreading it on her lap, "I'll just have to borrow a book from your lovely library and visit up there."

Jabe smiled. "Aunt Maddie, if you ever decide to move to Boston, I will build a library into an apartment for you."

Maddie beamed. "Thank you, dear, but I prefer the quiet country life." She sipped her wine and finished the salmon and capers on her plate.

"However, I promise to visit often, especially when you sponsor those chamber music recitals that you spoke of. Will those be held in the dining room?" She frowned at the ceiling, wondering at the acoustics.

Jabe shook his head. "Nope, those will be in the Barnes Music Room. We'll see it after lunch. It's one of Zylla's favorites and where the ceremony will be." He winked at Zylla.

"You've done a beautiful job with this building, Jabe," Maddie praised. "My niece has always loved the Charlesgate and has kept me apprised of its resurrection.

"Thank you," she said to the waiter and paused to sip the tea just placed in front of her before turning back to Jabe.

"But I confess I didn't expect such beauty in the city. Zylla was right when she said that the building is a perfect blend of high culture and utility."

Maddie inhaled deeply, closing her eyes for a brief moment. "It's amazing, really, that there's so much light and air in a city building." Her eyes blinked open and a smile spread on her face. "I feel as though I'm at an English country estate rather than in Boston."

Zylla and Jabe shared a quick smile. "That was pretty much the goal of the architect," Jabe informed Maddie. "A sort of autonomous commune. Or so Zylla tells me."

"Draped in elegance," Zylla added.

Maddie smiled behind her teacup. "That's an oxymoron—*autonomous commune*." She paused and scanned the room. "Do you think such a thing is possible in the city? In America?"

Jabe leaned back in his chair and thought before he answered. "No, not completely. It didn't really work for Putnam. The rich lived here and only the rich. And modern urban Americans are too self-involved, for the most part, to really make a go at communal living, to slow down and see the whole picture.

"But I think a lot of people in the city crave the ideal of the wholesome and neighborly while simultaneously disliking the repetition of the suburbs, and this place provides the former."

"Exactly," Zylla added. "But at the same time, families can't afford city living and are forced into the suburbs, so the Charlesgate will hopefully help a few of those families by providing luxurious, healthy homes with the benefits of a small community and lower rent.

"Tenants have all the amenities they might need right in the building, a library, doctor, food and laundry service, entertainment, but they also have the option of stepping out the front door and into the city," she finished.

"How many apartments in the building?" Maddie inquired.

"It depends."

Maddie raised a brow.

"The apartments expand and contract, depending on a tenant's needs," Jabe explained. "A single person may want less space or no kitchen. That would allow for another apartment."

Maddie poured another cup of tea. "Pardon me for asking, dear," she said to Jabe, "but surely you won't make a profit here?"

Jabe laughed, his green eyes alight. He admired her frankness.

"Nope. This was purely a labor of love. I won't have to put more money into her, she'll run herself, but I'll never regain the funds used for restoration."

He looked out the window to the Fens and Kenmore Square. "It was worth it, though." He turned his gaze to Zylla. "It was definitely worth it."

Twenty-five

After lunch, Jabe led them across the dining room and into a parlor that was part of the old Barnes mansion. The tiny room opened into a hallway of blue-veined marble and brilliant sunshine.

As they approached Italian-style double doors, Zylla swung around and walked backwards ahead of them, hands linked behind her back. She smiled at her aunt. "This is my absolute favorite room."

"This is part of your niece's new job, keeping the auditorium filled with musicians and plays, a poetry reading here and there..."

"And bringing back J.P. Putnam's Charlesgate Lecture Series," Zylla added with a nod.

Maddie's face brightened. "Ah, I remember you telling me about the political lectures that were held here. What I would give to have heard some of the speeches on women's suffrage! As well as—oh!"

Maddie stepped into the mansion's former music room and twirled slowly. The opaque dome that capped the auditorium allowed light to bounce off the teal walls and stained glass windows of knights and their ladies. Intricately carved cherubs and vines bordered the curved white ceiling and snaked along the balustrade of the orchestra balcony above them and, across the room, a stage set into the wall patiently waited for Shakespeare to bring the room to life.

Maddie inhaled. "It smells like paint and sunshine in here."

"Just finished yesterday," Jabe supplied. "All that's left is the basement," he added, indicating the padlocked door to the right of the stage.

Puzzlement creased Maddie's features. "I thought the basement had been converted into kitchens and laundry."

Zylla nodded. "On the Charlesgate side. But this was an addition to the original building—it's actually older than the Charlesgate."

"Only the heating system is down there, along with some rickety old stairs," Jabe said. "We're going to install an exercise area and spa after the wedding."

Jabe extended his left arm and pulled Zylla to his side as he flashed an irresistible grin. "Let's go. It's getting late and you girls have a bachelorette party to attend."

Zylla's mouth dropped open. "How did you know about that?"

"Oh, I have my ways." He winked.

The group wandered down the hall and left through the Barnes exit with its proper Bostonian edifice so different from the Romanesque entrance just one door down. Jabe locked the building and slid the keys into his pocket.

"And will you be attending a similar party this evening, Jabe?" Maddie asked innocently.

"Nope." He grinned, baring that dimple that Zylla loved. "I'm off to Vermont to pick up my mother. We'll be back tomorrow."

"You're picking up your mom on you bike?" Zylla quizzed.

He shook his head. "Rye gave me the van for the night."

They were halfway down Beacon Street when Maddie stopped short, her eyes wide. "I left my bag in the music room. I put it on the stage while we were talking."

Reaching into his khaki pocket, Jabe pulled out a set of keys. "Wrong ones," he muttered and used his other hand to awkwardly reach into the same pocket while already retracing his steps back to the Charlesgate.

"Here, give me the keys to the van and I'll bring it around," Zylla said.

Jabe tossed her the keys, fished out the Charlesgate set, and caught up with Maddie who was rushing down the sidewalk. Zylla shook her head at the pair—Jabe with his long, sure strides and Maddie with her quick, anxious steps.

~ * ~

Three and one-half hours later, Jabe stood at his mother's gas stove, lazily stirring the marinara sauce she had prepared for dinner while Jenny filled a stock-pot with water.

Sunset's ghost and the scent of fresh basil saturated the kitchen, enveloping Jabe in a blanket of memories from boyhood.

On days like this, just as the weather started to turn and autumn's magic seemed to shift underneath his feet, Jabe would enter his mother's kitchen after school saddened by the loss of the season. Then Jenny would rush smiling into the room to sit in the rocker by the fireplace and ask Jabe about his day. In no time, the smell of supper would waft past his nose as he completed his lessons at the kitchen table under warm lamplight, all well with the world again.

He looked at his mother now, blonde hair turned almost white, still pulled back in a low ponytail, and small, elegant lines etched at the corners of her eyes. Despite signs of years, she was still ageless in her denim jeans and plaid flannel.

"What?" Jenny demanded as she lifted the pot from the sink and handed it to her son.

He placed it on the burner and bent to light the flame. "I was just thinking how pretty you are."

She smiled and blushed, then stood on tiptoe to kiss her son. "I bet you say that to all the girls."

"Not anymore," he joked, grinning.

Jenny smiled in return. "I can't wait to meet your Zylla." She added linguine to the boiling water. "Kent and your niece are flying into Logan tomorrow night and little Jude's excited to finally have an aunt. No doubt she'll wear out poor Zylla before the wedding and she'll decide not to marry you after all."

During dinner, they discussed wedding plans and the Charlesgate restoration, and after eating, Jabe washed dishes while Jenny went upstairs to pack.

Lulled by the sudsy water and dying embers in the fire, he started to hum an old Cure song that Zylla constantly hummed. The tune had rattled in his head during the entire drive to Vermont and he crooned it now, hoping to exorcise the melody from his brain. Knowing that his mother liked a cup of tea before bed, he set the teakettle to boil and stoked the fire to full blaze while he sang.

Jenny appeared in the doorway wearing her wire-rimmed glasses and a flannel nightgown, sheepskin slippers on her feet, and watched her son toss another log on the fire. She cocked her head at the mournful tones of the song.

"What are you singing?" Jenny asked.

Jabe laughed self-consciously. "Oh, it's just an old song that's stuck in my head, driving me crazy."

"Ugh." Jenny laughed. "I hate when that happens. I always get Madonna songs stuck in my head. That *Like a Prayer* in particular."

Jabe grimaced. Somehow, his mother listening to Madonna was frightening. He had a sudden vision of Jenny dancing around in her underwear, and he shuddered. The kettle whistled, and Jabe turned to answer it.

"I know that song you're singing, though, and I can't think from where." Jenny walked to her rocker and sat, bafflement on her face. "Aha! I have it. Thank you, darling." She took the tea from Jabe. "Your brother used to play it over and over again when he was in his morose, dress-in-black stage." She shook her head. "That music drove me crazy. I did like that song, though. Very haunting. What's its name?"

"*Charlotte Sometimes*," Jabe answered as he sat at the table and studied the fire, the song still playing in his head. Really, the lyrics made no sense whatsoever. *Charlotte sometimes. Sometimes what? Sometimes Charlotte, sometimes someone else?*

With an imaginary hand, he swiped at the tune stuck inside his thoughts. Whatever. He just wanted it out of his mind before he went stark raving mad and started sewing people's lips together.

Jabe rubbed his temples and looked at his mother quietly reading. Suddenly, he felt blood drain from his face and he had to clutch the edge of the table to keep from crumbling.

Charlotte, sometimes. My God.

"Mom?"

Jenny peered at Jabe from over her glasses. "Why, you look like you've seen a ghost."

"Not exactly," he said dryly. "I wanted to ask you... did you ever believe in the Thayer curse? The one Dad used to talk about after his fifth Jim Beam."

Jenny scowled and her eyes turned hard. Then she softened, sighed, and tucked her feet beneath her. "No," she said. "I never believed it." She held out her mug to Jabe, and he rose to pour more water into it.

"Thank you, darling. No, I think the curse story was something Admiral Thayer made up because he couldn't live with the guilt of hanging the woman he had loved, despite her crimes." Jenny clucked her tongue and shook her head.

"Here you go, Mom," Jabe said, placing the mug on the table next to her.

"Thanks. I don't know what sort of man he was to hide behind duty and not have the guts to fight for the woman he supposedly loved."

"But, Mom, she was a criminal."

Jenny shrugged and looked at the fire. "Maybe. But he betrayed her. He betrayed love. I wouldn't blame her if she did curse him, but no, I don't believe it.

"Unfortunately," Jenny said, folding her hands in her lap, "too many Thayer men believed it, and blamed their own misbegotten choices on Lady Charlotte and her curse, even your father. Somebody should have burned old Admiral Thayer's letter with its warning a long time ago."

Jabe's voice was ragged when he spoke. "Why didn't you?"

"Oh..." Jenny sighed, "Because it's your history, yours and Kent's. I couldn't take that from you. All I could do was raise you not to put store in such superstitions."

She paused. "And I think that's why your dad married me," she continued thoughtfully. "He saw me as a fresh start, far away from his family that gossiped and gambled and hurt each other all in the name of petty superstition." Her voice was bitter.

"I'm sorry," he said gently, and Jenny looked up at him in surprise.

"Oh, I have no regrets. I have two beautiful sons and a granddaughter. Hopefully," she smiled wickedly, "there will be one with long blonde ringlets soon." She looked sternly at Jabe and wagged her finger at him. "But not too soon."

He smiled thinly. Jenny's frown deepened and she asked suspiciously, "Why did you ask about the curse? Are you having trouble of some sort?"

Jabe forced a laugh. "No, no reason, really. That song triggered the memory about Charlotte."

"Ah," Jenny said, her unspoken worry hanging in the air. "Good night then, son." She rose from the rocker, and Jabe bent to kiss her cheek. "It's late and we have an early day tomorrow."

"I love you, Mom."

"I love you, too, darling."

Jabe had known that Jenny had never believed in any curse, and his attempt to find a moment's solace in his mother's words could not hide the truth he had been ignoring for too long, the truth Lydia had been so desperately trying to show him. Truth had finally been revealed in a song—Charlotte, sometimes.

There were two ghosts in the Charlsegate. Sometimes, it was Lydia, the ghost who belonged there, who had followed the Berrys since her murder in the eighteen-hundreds, and revealed herself through wafts of lavender and peace. Sometimes it was Charlotte de Berry.

"She's stalking Zylla just like she once followed Lydia," Jabe whispered, and buried his head in his arms as he guessed what was happening. Charlotte was haunting Zylla through torturous visions and splitting headaches as she had with Lydia, biding her time until Zylla made that one fatal error—marriage. Only this time, their marriage had the power to banish Charlotte forever.

She was real. And now she was at the Charlesgate. The signs had always been there: the accidents, Frank's possession, the rank ocean smell, the same odor that Zylla had described to be in her visions, and the fact that she had visions at all.

How could I have been so stupid? he thought. *How could I have been so damn stupid?*

The Charlesgate wasn't evil at all, as Rye had surmised. It was merely a backdrop where a war was being waged, and sometimes Lydia was the victor and sometimes, Charlotte.

Well, he would see to it that Lydia won the war. Since hiding the diary, Jabe's insides had been shredded with guilt, but now he felt only righteousness.

He and Zylla would marry, uniting the Thayers and Berrys in love, just as Lydia had wanted, and Jeremy's spell would be fulfilled. But he was resolved that Zylla should never know a moment of fear or doubt. The less she knew about her history, the better. After the wedding, when it was all over, he could give her the journal.

He waited for the fire to die and went to bed for an uneasy sleep.

Twenty-six

Zylla twisted the engagement ring on her finger and swore her fingers must have swollen from nerves over the wedding. Only two days! Any minute now and hives would surely bubble her skin. She paced the floor of Jabe's office.

This morning, while she was jogging with Anne, they had passed the crazy cow-god man. He had stared straight at her, pointed his bony finger, and bellowed, "Moo." Surely that was a bad sign.

These moments spent by herself were dangerous to her mental health. Near-brides should never be left alone two days before the wedding, she decided. Worlds could end at such moments. She sighed. She should have gone with Jabe, Jenny, and her aunt to lunch, but she needed to finish her work at the Charlesgate before the rehearsal tonight. She glanced at the mantel clock. Nearly two o'clock. They would return in an hour or so and her preoccupation would pass.

Zylla sank into a brown leather chair and rested her head against the back. Everything was set. She was all moved into the Charlesgate and Jabe would join her the day after the wedding. Anne, Billy, Mike, Uncle John and Aunt June, her cousins, and Jabe's family would all be there when Aunt Maddie gave her away.

She blinked back sudden tears. Sometimes, in moments when all her thoughts and lists and worries about the wedding stopped spinning for just a second, sadness that her parents weren't alive to see this day swooped underneath her to knock her off her feet.

When that happened, Zylla dammed the tears that scalded her eyes and throat and forced her mind to plan her pirate novel. This is what she did now and the trick worked—in seconds, a great plot epiphany popped into her head. She scrambled to her feet and ran to Jabe's huge carved oak desk that was covered in miles of paper.

"Figures," she muttered after rummaging through the sheets. "No blanks." Opening the top drawer of Jabe's desk, she spotted a pen, but glimpsed no paper or notebooks. She started to shut the drawer then yanked it open again when she glimpsed a ledger in the back.

"Aha! Gotta be some blank pages in there." The instant Zylla's skin touched the smooth leather binding of the book, she knew it was not Jabe's work ledger. It positively crackled. *It's his diary*, she thought, pursing her lips. *I need to put it back right now before I'm tempted*. But the musty smell grabbed her nose and the frayed yellow pages lured her eyes. It was too old to be Jabe's. *But it isn't yours*, a voice in her head chimed. Then again, if something smelled this ancient, the statute of limitations had to be up, right? She inhaled sharply and opened the cover...

And squealed in glee. She closed Lydia's diary and held it to her chest as she jumped up and down in a little circle. Not only was Jabe the most stunning man in the Creator's great watercolor of life, he was her knight in shining armor. He slew all her dragons and brought back treasures as well.

She rested against the side of Jabe's desk and slowly re-opened the diary then quickly snapped it shut. It was her wedding present, Zylla was certain. She scrunched her eyes tight and forced herself to imagine Jabe's disappointment if the surprise were ruined. When that didn't work, she scrunched harder, but her fingers tingled against the soft leather.

She felt like she was seven again, peeking under her aunt's bed for a glimpse of a Christmas present, knowing full well it wrong, but shamefully enjoying it anyway. *Just one entry*, she promised herself, and read five.

20 April 1893. It was nigh dusk as I made my way through the library doors and walked toward Beacon Street to catch the trolley back to the Charlesgate. The ride was quick—it seemed a mere moment before her splendor loomed above me. The entire Back Bay is a veritable army of gilded mansions and ostentatiously dressed matrons. At times, when the sun is bright, the sight is near blinding.

But the Charlesgate! Here is a creation of elegance. It is a stroke of good fortune that I reside here.

When Pickering (how he despises to be called by his middle name!) built it, all apartments were let immediately. Now the address rules the Social Register and women in feathered hats vie for a chance to win residence here, clawing at their husbands with vulture talons until they gain admittance. But Sarah, Pickering's sister, is my best friend besides Lily, and she quietly pulled us in. It is now I who makes a bower in what I call the Scheherazade Tower, my library in the sixth floor's turret room. From here, I overlook both the Charlesgate East and Beacon Street entrances to see who comes and goes and if I glance straight ahead, I spy the muddy Charles.

I can't imagine being anywhere else. I can spend hours tracing the tragic and charming animals, cherubs, and satyrs in the tiles that edge the ceiling of the halls. Pickering commissioned the popular artist Grueby to design them and only the smiling likeness of Sarah's niece, Elsa, belies the utter gothicness that the tiles add to the structure. The building seems to me a vortex of sorts where the chasms of the centuries are happily joined. Lily laughs at me, but at least she appreciates the great beauty of the place, unlike the upper-crust females that spend their days playing bridge in their apartments.

My, but I do run on. I best get to bed. Tomorrow is Sarah's birthday and I promised her a picnic in the Commons.

One entry turned into twenty. Zylla laughed aloud, eyes dancing merrily across the pages and sometimes she felt tears bubble in her eyes. Most often, she just nodded in agreement with Lydia's thoughts. When she caught herself in the midst of one of these actions, Zylla blushed, embarrassed by her emotion. At the same time, her soul was close to bursting at the thrilling discovery that Lydia was just like her. Why, she was a throwback to her great-great-great grandmother! With fevered hands, she turned the pages.

May 21, 1893. I awake once again to the remnants of a reoccurring dream: I can still smell the stench of the sea on my skin and feel the bite of a coarse cord at my throat.

Last night, I went to bed with another megrim, so weak and nauseous that Lily stayed by my side to rub my head and murmur soothing words, yet even she could not prevent the nightmare that has accompanied the pain since I was a wee girl.

The dream never varies. It begins with a beautiful woman standing on a scaffold, a proud glint in her violet eyes and the wind wild in her black hair. Then the scaffold cracks and the sea bleeds until she returns as a succubus, a living corpse, cackling and mad. Charlotte de Berry. I cannot fathom why she tortures me as I am not married nor even in love, although I want to be. Perhaps my imagination merely overworks and I am doomed to madness.

Zylla gnawed her bottom lip as she looked up from the page. She was surprised to read entry after entry about Lydia's debilitating migraines and visions, so like her own. Yet while her own nightmares consisted of swirling noises and colors around the scattered form of her mad pirate, Lydia's dreams about the same woman were vivid and narrative. She bent her head to the journal and continued to read.

> *July 8, 1893. I have found him at last! Can it be Heathcliff himself sprung from the pages of Brontë? He is divine and I am in love.*
>
> *Early this morning, I awoke from yet another nightmare sans megrim, thank the gods. My mind spinning, I donned my dressing gown and went downstairs. It is not seemly to be without my corset, but so many women are refusing to wear them now and the women of fashion who disapprove of such statements were in bed at that early morning hour.*
>
> *The grill elevator growled at the intrusion on its sleep but descended the six floors swiftly and opened his doors to the smiling face of Elsa in her tile and the rhythmic ticking of the grandfather clock in the hall. The dining rooms dark, a breeze stirred the white muslin barricade to the terrace and gardens behind the Charlesgate and for an instant, my heart dropped. I thought that I had seen a spirit!*
>
> *I caught my breath and made my path through the dark toward the library's burning lights, and the smell of cigars and the crack of a billiard ball meeting its mates revealed that the gentlemen were awake sipping whisky and discussing politics. Luckily, a fire burned in the great marble fireplace in the drawing room. Although there are fireplaces in every room, I prefer this one for the mere fact that the Putnam family crest, a wolf's head, hangs above the mantel.*
>
> *As I curled my legs under me on the settee, I caught a man staring at me from the library. My heart lodged in my throat for a solid five minutes—he was that handsome. His wavy dark hair barely brushed the wide black lapels of his smoking jacket. His eyes, lonely and wild and mirthful blue doorways to other worlds offset*

by thick, dark brows. He is a wolf, or a vampire, surely dangerous. Yet there is sadness about him. I'm certain he needs me.

He winked at me, and I smiled back. Certainly, losing one's corset causes some loss of sense. With a smirk and a raise of a brow, he turned back to his game. I was giddy with excitement and let a giggle escape.

"And what is so humorous, may I inquire?"

I jumped at the appearance of a head from behind a high-backed chair across from me.

"Sarah Putnam! You scared me nearly to death." I laughed as she turned her chair to face mine. "Oh Sarah, wouldn't it be heavenly to be able to play billiards and smoke cigars to the wee hours of the morning. It is so tedious being a woman!"

"For shame, Lydia! There is plenty of reason to be happy to be a woman nowadays." (Here, I rolled my eyes and prepared myself for one of Sarah's lectures about women's rights.) "If you'd only join us in my brother's apartment! He and Grace host the most wonderful conversations, sometimes all night. We talk of literature and life and politics, why, even Mark Twain participated one evening."

"Then, my dear," I said, "why do you sit so morose in front of the fire mooning at the gentlemen in the library?" I glanced again into that room in hopes of seeing my rogue, but he was gone. "Are there not any world problems to be solved this morning?"

Sarah's countenance was distressed as she poured a cup of chocolate for me. "Look at that." She nodded her head at the table between us. I looked over and picked up yesterday's edition of The Boston Daily Herald. *"Another Meeting at Faneuil Hall Brews Trouble."*

The headline was no news to me. Countless gatherings at Faneuil occur more and more frequently as the unemployed become disenchanted. The economy is horrid and the men talk of nothing but depression while the women fret about the inability to find good help. Even Kate was unusually surly as she served a gaudily dressed pair of cackling females last night at dinner, not that I find fault with her.

"I am scared, Lydia, that we will soon have no peace in Boston's streets. I fear that another revolution is on the rise. If only the work of my brother and the others could progress. If only those poor people..."

"Sarah," I interrupted, "you talk and talk of helping the working class, but that's all it is! Your brother's Charlesgate has rents that start at eight-hundred a year. And look at the people that live here with their baubles and five outfits a day! All they care about is their own wealth, and Pickering is catering to that for all his talk of nationalism."

"Not all rich are bad, Lyddie," she chided. "You know that. Some of us realize our responsibility to those less blessed, and nationalism is on the rise. You must start with what you know, as Miss Alcott told you, remember?"

I nodded. Miss Alcott once told me, when as a young girl I met her, to leave off my fantastical writing as it offers no substance to society and I could do more good writing about what was around me if I just opened my eyes. Yet Miss Alcott could never understand that I have opened my eyes, and all I see is Charlotte de Berry.

"The Charlesgate is John's example of what life could be," Sarah continued. "He is wealthy, so he must start with his peers, and the only means he has of showing them what's right is to show them through what he knows."

"Architecture," I replied.

"Yes, Lyddie. He wants to bring people together in one apartment house so they must learn to share, to care for others. The rich don't need this communal house: they can afford to buy their own palaces, but look! This is the most popular address in the city.

"It is true that the rich inhabit it, but think. No more tenement houses that cram people in with no air, no light to grow! John has ended this here. We all have warmth, we have air and sun, we have a park, and the efficiency of such a building: one building rather than ten on one block allows expense for better plumbing."

"And electricity," I laughed. "Now that's a gift from above."

Sarah chortled. "John wants to do this all over the city. Imagine! Charlesgate Hotels everywhere: beautiful buildings and parks. Surely, that's what Winthrop planned when he imagined a City on a Hill. Surely, with such beauty, the quality of life will rise. The suffering of the poor will be alleviated by the means of the rich."

"Sarah, human nature won't allow it. People are too greedy. There will always be a separation of the classes."

"It is so, Lydia, and perhaps it is rightly so, but must the separation be so drastic? Must the working class be without a healthy home and food because of poor city planning? I am not suggesting that the rich must give their wealth away, only that they pay attention. There can be improvement to make everyone happy. John already plans to build a magnificent apartment building called the Commonwealth. It will have everything the Charlesgate has and more, perhaps a skating rink! And the working class will be able to afford it.

"We must start small, Lydia. The only thing I fear is that starting small takes too long to grow and we don't have the patience."

I admire Sarah's optimism and passion, but I blush to admit that my only passion lies in books and, perhaps, my new friend in the library.

July 9, 1893. His name is Caval. How mysterious.

The next entry was dated over two years later.

September 30, 1895. I am in pain nearly each day. It sits in my eye like a heavy fog and is unbearable, yet I bear it. I cannot sleep but fitfully and can no longer discern reality from dreams. She is always near, angry and formless, hating and loving with equal passion. When I close my eyes, I see a beautiful monster, and I am in constant fear.

What is real?

Caval worries and tries to be strong, but I can see the stress in the hard planes of his face. Lily is increasingly frustrated and tells me that the pain and nightmares are my imagination. Do I lose my mind? I must be well for the sake of the child that grows within me.

October 2, 1895. Another nightmare. It was my witch ancestor again, and her lips were sewn together in tight, black stitches, her eternal punishment for her cruelties in life.

I woke to Lily's hand grasping my own and all is well. Still, I know the truth. The curse has control of me now. Charlotte is my puppeteer, and soon she will close the curtain on my life as she has with countless other Berry women. I must write what I know before I die, I must prevent Charlotte from striking again.

October 25, 1895. Papa had liked to tell the story of our family curse on winter evenings when the wind threatened to shatter the windows of our Dorchester home...

...All my life, I've dreamed of pirate ships rolling in bloody seas and with my headaches, she comes with her wretched stink of the decaying sea and stitched lips, to moan her threats.

Since marrying my beloved Caval, my blue-eyed gypsy, she has been uneasy, following me with her red eyes. My headaches are worse, and even the lavender I carry with me cannot ease the pain. She grows stronger, and soon I will be dead.

I only desire to remain in the peaceful splendor of the Charlesgate and raise my family, but Charlotte wants my destruction, and she shall have it. I cannot fight fate.

But when she visits to wail her story of murder and revenge, she leaves unsaid one small part of the tale.

The curse can end.

For Papa's winter tale isn't finished, and Charlotte's specter knows and fears it.

While Charlotte was dying in the noonday sun, young Jeremy, stricken by his mother's words, recovered enough to amend her curse. He clipped a tress of black hair from his mother and a blond tendril from Jabez. As he braided the two together, he vowed, "May a descendant of Thayer and a child of Berry meet again. If they have the courage to hold love above all else, then my mother's reign will end, and all the souls she intended to destroy will be at peace."

And to this, I add my own charge.

May I remain on this earth to ensure the success of Jeremy's promise. May I have the strength to fight Charlotte when the two lines meet again. Left alone,

Charlotte will never allow this event to occur, and she must not prevail.

The Berrys are my own as well as hers. She will not destroy my family.

The curse can end. Papa knew what Charlotte wouldn't tell me, and I shall name my new son after Charlotte's son to remind the Berrys of this hope.

Zylla devoured the tale of Lydia's ancestor, and her own, she realized with a grimace, and knew innately that the curse was true. Despair stifled her and her blood chilled.

She turned the page. The last entry was written in a different hand, stained with what looked like tears, and she squinted to discern the hurried scrawl.

October 27, 1895. My sister passed early this morning, murdered by angry workers. Caval died on the street. He fought to protect his wife and received a slashed throat for his efforts. I am empty inside. I will myself to cry, but the tears will not form.

They brought her bleeding into her room, barely conscious, her pallor sickly. My beautiful Lyddie! Toward the end, she regained lucidity and begged me to care for little Jemmy. Poor child!

I write in her journal because I cannot cease thinking about her ravings while she was unconscious and the event that took place soon after her death. While the doctor worked on her, Lydia babbled about the pirate's curse, how we women must never marry because Charlotte would kill us.

I ignored most of her fevered murmuring until she grasped my hand tight and her eyes flew open to stare past me. "It is she," she said before turning to me. Clearly, she was in earnest. "She killed us, Lily. I saw her face."

The words chilled me, but I quickly forgot them until after her passing. I let go of her hand, still warm with life, and went to her basin to splash cool water on my face. For a second, as I glanced into the mirror, I saw a figure—a face with red-rimmed eyes and stitched lips, wild black hair hanging from her head. I screamed and turned, but no one was there. I noticed that the room filled suddenly with a horrid odor, the reek of low tide, which even Lyddie's lavender could not mask.

Writing this renders the scene foolish. Surely, my grief, exhaustion and Lydia's ravings combined to conjure the image, yet it is necessary for me to record this last entry in Lyddie's beloved book.

I will bury this book, now, in the room where my sister died. Grandmama once said that murdered souls do not rest and while I don't believe in such folly, Lyddie did, and she may have need of her little journal should she come back.

I love you, dear sister, and I will raise your son to be a man of honor, like his father, and gentle and loving, like his mother.

~ * ~

"...and the light from the dome just gives the music room such a lovely blue glow. Just perfect for a wedding. Let's hope that Saturday is sunny."

Jabe, busy fiddling with the pepper-shaker, barely heard Maddie.

"Jabe! Maddie is talking to you," Jenny reprimanded. "Whatever is the matter with you?"

Maddie smiled gently and said, "I imagine it's just wedding jitters."

Jabe looked up into Maddie's warm eyes, leaned back in his chair, let out a breath and confessed, "Actually, it's Zylla and something I've decided to do that may affect her."

He told Maddie and his mother about Lydia's journal, Zylla's nightmares and pirate novel, and enlisted his mother's help to explain his own family history to Maddie.

Maddie's complexion paled and when she reached for her wine glass. Her hand trembled. Concerned, Jabe grasped her other hand and asked softly, "What is it?"

Maddie hesitated. "I—I don't know. The other day, when I left my purse in the Barnes Room, I saw... well, I don't know that I saw anything." She sighed and looked away, pulling her hand away from Jabe to clutch her napkin. Jabe noticed that her knuckles were white.

She bit her lip. "But I did smell something rank and sickening by the basement door, which means nothing, certainly. It is a basement after all, right?" Maddie gave him a wan smile and glanced uncertainly at an unreadable Jenny. She closed her eyes briefly before continuing.

"But that odor! It reminded me of so many horrible events. I've smelled it near the lake on the day my sister died and later when Zylla's grandmother died." Maddie paused. "Sophie had been petrified. She grabbed her throat and her eyes and—"

Maddie's face crumbled before she gulped back her fear. Jabe and Jenny lurched forward at the same time to support her, but she waved them off and lifted her chin. "Please..."

She straightened. "I'm fine, really. It seems like I'm tear-bound this month." Maddie gave a little laugh and turned wide eyes to Jabe and Jenny, serious again. "I watched Sophie die, you know. The doctors had said it was a stroke, but, I don't know... *that stench.*

"I never smelled it again until the other day." Maddie shuddered and gripped Jabe's hand until he feared the bones would break. "You cannot take the chance that the curse is over now that the lines have found each other again. Zylla is overly romantic, and the less she knows, the better, at least until it's all over. Hide the journal. You're absolutely right."

During the conversation, neither had noticed Jenny's darkening face or the tight line her mouth had become. When they finally spotted the furious darts that sprang from her eyes, both Jabe and Maddie felt the urge to hide under their seats.

"I don't doubt your belief in this curse," Jenny said, her gentle tone belying her flashing eyes. She then leaned forward, interlocking her hands on the table in front of her, her knuckles taut and white.

"I'm a practical woman, sensible enough, in fact, that I can't deny the existence of a so-called curse. Neither can I confirm it. This journal, as I see it, offers no proof to anything: it's the viewpoint of a self-admitted fanciful woman."

Jabe opened his mouth to speak, but Jenny held up her hand. "And if it is true, if such an evil exists, I am sensible enough to understand that goodness and love can overcome it. This is what I believe." She took a breath. "This is what I know."

Another flicker of anger passed across Jenny's eyes and her words were clipped. "But what I cannot condone is your action, Jabe! I understand your reaction, but to purposely conceal something from your fiancée because of that reaction is wrong. It is not love that is guiding you. It's fear."

In quieter tones, she continued, "I trust that you'll make the right decision, son." Jenny leveled her gaze at her future in-law, then at her son before smiling. "Now, let's order some dessert, shall we?"

~ * ~

After confessing his deception to Maddie and his mother, Jabe's burden had lessened. He had sought to substantiate his action of hiding the journal by creating a bond with Zylla's aunt. He had done so to convince himself that his decision was in Zylla's best interest and believed that his action had nothing to do with alleviating his own fear. Allied with Maddie, Jenny's admonishment didn't rattle him until they reached the Charlesgate and he suddenly knew just how wrong he had been.

He held the door for his mother and Maddie. The two were giggling like old chums and seemed to forget that he was there. *Girls*, he thought with a shake of his head, and reminded himself to tell Zylla about their teenage behavior, but as he thought of Zylla, a great pang sickened him as he realized the disservice he had done her.

Coward, he thought and said aloud, "I'll give her Lydia's journal tonight, after the rehearsal dinner."

But Jenny and Maddie hadn't heard him and his intentions were carried away on a puff of lavender-scented air.

Twenty-seven

Zylla jumped at the sound of feminine laughter and Jabe's deep voice. His tall, muscular form filled the doorway, and the smaller figures of the two women crowded behind him. Shame clouded her features as Jabe's laughter ceased abruptly and his gaze riveted on the open journal in her hands.

Heat flushed her cheeks and she opened her mouth to explain when she noticed that Jabe's face had gone stark white.

"Zyll, I—I'm sorry. I know I shouldn't have kept it from you. I meant to—"

"Huh?" Zylla interrupted, confused. *She* owed the apology, not Jabe. Zylla's gaze darted to her aunt and Jenny to see the former's eyes lower and Jenny cringe. Zylla understood then and anger fused into her very bones. It wasn't her wedding present, after all. *He had intended to keep this from her. Why?*

"Why?" she demanded.

In the ensuing silence, Zylla saw him wince, witnessed the flicker of pain in his eyes, and felt her heart lurch for him, but then fury, swift and consuming, overcame her. Her gaze raked over him in disgust.

"I was going to give it to you..." he explained. Saying the words aloud made his fears seem foolish and he held out his hand, palm upturned. "I'm sorry," he finished lamely.

Tears scalded her eyes and she swallowed hard to stem the hurt—and failed. Bright red indignation spewed from her pores as she accurately assessed Jabe's reason for his deceit. Righteousness made her stand straighter.

"Zyll, I'm sorry," Jabe started again. "Please..."

"No!" she spat. "I don't know you at all. I thought you were noble. I thought you understood me. You lied to me. You knew how much this would mean to me," she continued, indicating the journal. "My history. *My* history. What right do you have to hide it from me? You *lied* to me. You, you... *turd!*"

Jabe would have laughed at her choice of expletive if her hatred toward him was less formidable, but he saw that her scorn was again disintegrating into lashing ire built to conceal her hurt, the hurt that he had caused, and he did not smile.

"I thought we were partners. I thought you loved me." She sobbed. "But you don't even trust me. That's why you hid this, isn't it? Isn't it! That I'd let some stupid curse come between us?"

Jabe's expression incredulous, he asked, "You don't believe it?"

"Of course I do," Zylla snapped. "But I'm not going to put my life on hold because some demented pirate ghost wants to come between us. Didn't you read this?"

Jabe opened his mouth, but she kept going. "All we had to do is put love before all else, but you put your own damn fear before your love for me."

"No." Jabe's voice boomed. "I did it *because* I love you, Zylla. I thought it would protect you. I was wrong, but I didn't mean to hurt you."

"If that were true, then you would have given this to me and trusted our *love*," she mocked, "to see us through."

Jabe didn't answer and tension mounted in the long, silent moment. Zylla couldn't focus anymore. Unshed tears and her throbbing head only allowed her to see betrayal.

"How can we get married without trust? Or did you think I needed your bloody protection from my own truth? My own ancestry? Well, I don't. I don't need you or anyone else," she finished in an anguished whisper.

Her fury left her in a long hiss only to be replaced by sorrow and the tingle of a migraine hovering near her left eye. The tears threatened to flow now and her pride rebelled against letting that happen here. She hated them all. She hated her aunt for not realizing that her silence had been just as superstitious as her grandmother's evil eye. She hated Jenny for her face full of compassion. And most of all, she hated Jabe for breaking her heart.

She would not do them the honor of breaking down in sobs and proving to them that she did need them after all. She would not. With a show of cool disdain, she placed the journal onto Jabe's desk. She turned around, chin lifted, and walked to the door, shaking as she passed Jabe.

She had just reached the doorway when two strong hands gripped her arms. She stiffened. "Let me go," she hissed through gritted teeth.

"Zyll," he pleaded.

She swiveled in his grasp and faced him, willing her eyes to be hard.

"Jabe, let her go."

It was Jenny that spoke and although gratefulness sparked in Zylla, she did not look at Jenny, or any of them when she turned and left. Her engagement ring twinkled atop Lydia's journal.

~ * ~

Torrents of tears streamed down Zylla's face as soon as she fled the building. Where to go? She had to escape. But the pain! A wave of nausea overcame her. Damn migraine. A spoon digging out her eyeball could only feel better. She didn't have time for this now. She needed to find someplace to rest but couldn't go to her new home, nor could she go to Anne. They'd find her in both places and she didn't want to be found.

She couldn't think and she had to think. Zylla stumbled past the recessed Charlesgate East entrance, past the windows of the new restaurant. A couple paused as they passed her, the man shaking his head and the woman scowling at her as if she were a bug, but they didn't offer her help. This was the city after all and she was just another freak on the street, another crazy person.

She continued down Charlesgate East, past the iron-gated door to the Barnes addition, then stopped and backed up. The door was ajar and she quickly slipped inside, carefully closing it tight after her. As so many times before, the Charlesgate saved her one more time. Another rush of tears burst from her eyes, causing the pain in her eye to triple. She had to calm down. She had to rest.

Zylla wandered down the hall to the music room. One of the double doors stood open and she saw the room where she would have been married on Saturday. The wall sconces were lit and cast a warm light over blue velvet squabbed pews all ready for a ceremony that would never take place.

The scene should have disturbed her but instead the cool blue of the room seemed to be the most soothing place in the world. She entered, calm for the first time, all thoughts gone, and closed the door behind her. She inhaled deeply. Only the head pain remained and she felt at peace even with that. Experience taught her that once she reached acceptance, she would be able to relax and the migraine would soon disappear.

She lay down on her side in the first pew and closed her eyes, instantly succumbing to a state of sleep and drifting thoughts. The blue aura of the room swirled about her and she could smell lavender, strong for the first time in a couple of months. *At least*, she thought, *Lydia hasn't left me.* Then self-pity overcame her, squeezing tears from between her closed eyelids.

She must have fallen asleep because she jumped with a frightened gasp and couldn't remember where she was at first. Insidiuos laughter had jerked her from slumber, yet when she scanned the room, she found it empty.

Her eyes felt swollen and Zylla remembered the migraine, now thankfully gone, and the horrible event that had preceded the onset of pain. The room was so quiet that the lights in the wall sconces seemed to whisper. She was very thirsty, but otherwise felt numb and bewildered, all anger gone.

Why did Jabe hide the journal from her? The thought popped into her head and despair stabbed her. Aunt Maddie may have kept silent because of a need to protect her, Zylla admitted begrudgingly, but she couldn't fathom Jabe's actions. She again saw the pain in his eyes when she had realized that he never intended the journal as a wedding gift. Zylla pushed the image away, but it stubbornly returned. She sat up and curled her legs under her. There was fear in his pain, she realized. He was afraid of something besides her anger.

Was he afraid of Charlotte? Zylla shook her head. She believed it, of course. Every word. Reading that journal had connected the puzzle of her life in a snap. It had bridged the gap between dreams and reality, science and myth. Curse or no curse, she had found peace. Her gene map was part of a woman who died so many years ago. Zylla actually smiled. The expression 'blood is thicker than water' finally made some sense to her. She fully belonged to the world.

Surely Jabe saw that as well. He knew her enough to understand that. Didn't he? Anger surged through Zylla again. But even if he didn't, he should have trusted her! He had lied to her. How long had he been lying? Did he have the journal when he proposed? That night, once magical and pure, was tainted now. He didn't trust her and he didn't trust their love. Anger knotted in her stomach. Well, it was all over now.

He would never lie to her again.

As the thought sputtered in her mind, Zylla heard Jabe's deep laugh, saw the terrible beauty of his face, felt the calming, burning touch of his hands and she felt a horrible emptiness.

And there was her answer. Jabe did know her. He had been wrong to lie, but she realized now that his reasons were not born from mistrust. Not really. He loved her, he feared for her and he sought to protect her, all because she never gave him evidence to do otherwise.

He had known that if he had given her that journal, she would have gobbled up Lydia's story and made it a part of her belief system. Jabe knew that she was too much of a romantic to avoid marriage because of some curse, but he also had realized that she was enough of a romantic to get married in spite of the curse, damning herself to an untimely end simply because it *was* romantic. She would have put more faith in the curse, because it was a romantic story, than in their love. Jabe knew this.

"What a little hypocrite I am," she spat. "Jabe knows me better than I know myself."

Zylla's fingers crept up to fondle the blue glass eye that hung from her neck. This pendant was a perfect example that she had always put faith in something other than herself. All this time, since Mike's marriage, she had thought she was living life. Instead, she had let fate decide.

Fate had decided whether or not she would have Mike. His marriage had forced her to face her discontent. She had always loved research and writing, but she took the first job offered to her after college and had remained in that position until fate intervened and nearly gave her a nervous breakdown.

Zylla groaned in self-disgust. She had only made two decisions of her own. One was to search her ancestry against the fate Maddie had planned for her. The other was to believe in Jabe after he hurt her terribly. If left to fate, she would now have regrets and a broken heart and Jabe would be on to another woman by now.

Yet here she was again, willfully handing the reins over to fate by letting her anger and pride keep her from happiness. What a fool she had been! Did she never think for herself?

Above it all was this damn blue eye, a trinket that prevented her from facing life full in the face. She lifted the pendant to eye level and studied it. The only protection she needed was from her weak self. In one rip, she made her choice. The silver chain broke, and the eye bounced to the floor once, twice, then rolled toward the stage and stopped.

Nothing happened. Zylla looked around expectantly, but no great catastrophe befell her. No earthquakes, no lightning bolts, no axe murderer. No mad pirate with crazy black hair and mad eyes. She laughed aloud, long and heartily. "Some curse, huh, Lydia?"

Zylla wiped her eyes and shrugged. No matter. Her only concern, which grew increasingly frantic by the moment, was to reach Jabe. She didn't know what time it was or where he would be, but she had to find him—tonight.

She reached the door and clicked off the light. As she turned to leave, she glimpsed a shimmer of purple between the stage and basement door. Chills scurried down her spine as she peered into the dark and in the purple glow saw the shape of a woman.

"Lydia," she whispered. Mesmerized, she slowly walked toward the form, blinking often to be sure it was real. She felt no fear. As she grew close enough to touch, she had to squint against the bright light that rendered the woman's figure insubstantial. The shimmering mass retreated and Zylla followed, but as she reached forward with her hand, the figure and light disappeared and too late Zylla realized she was on the precipice of the basement's dark staircase.

She grabbed the doorjambs, rotten and soft, with each hand and managed to balance herself. She breathed a sigh of relief and wondered why Jabe's workers had left the basement door open and why Lydia would lead her into such a dangerous situation.

Her heart slowed its frantic pace and she took a step backward, away from the dark hole, only to be enveloped in an oppressive cloud. The fetid scent of the air caused Zylla to retch, and all she heard was a roaring in her ears and the menacing cackle of her dream pirate—Charlotte de Berry.

"Oh, God, no," she choked, but the cackle grew louder and Zylla felt a burning pressure on her back, pushing her toward the gaping blackness of the basement.

She opened her mouth to scream, but the sound rushed back into her throat as she fell and rolled down the rotted stairs. Pain ripped through Zylla's body when she came to a final rest at the bottom. Thick wetness tickled her temple and her head spun as a sickening veil of senselessness fell around her. The last thing she heard before she lost consciousness was the maniacal laughter of her pirate queen.

Twenty-eight

When Zylla fled the room, the void in Jabe's belly nauseated him, froze him to one spot, and he was unable to go after her. His sense of Zylla's hurt and the warning pasted on Maddie's face had told him chasing her would be of no use anyway.

Maddie placed a hand on his forearm in a gesture of apology—he took it and squeezed to let her know she wasn't to blame. Her niece's pain was on his shoulders and he had raised his eyes to his mother, expecting to see anger in her face, surprised to find only pity.

Now it seemed that Zylla just disappeared. Jabe closed his eyes, fighting the fear that bubbled to the back of his throat. Maddie had just informed him that she hadn't gone upstairs to their apartment, then she and Jenny had retreated upstairs, sensing they could be of no help to his present anguish.

"Where is she? Where would she go?"

The phone receiver stuck to his cold hand while his fingers dialed Zylla's old number. "Shit," Jabe swore at the sixth ring and was about to hang up when Anne said hello.

"Anne."

"Hey Jabe. All set for the rehearsal?"

"Yes. No... Anne, is Zylla with you?"

"Nope." He heard silence on the other end before Anne asked, "What's wrong?"

Damn. She wasn't with Anne. He took a breath and confessed, "I screwed up."

"I see," Anne replied coldly. He heard the seething condemnation in her voice and guessed what she had concluded.

"No, not that," he insisted. "Although Zylla probably feels just as betrayed. Please, she just ran off, and I don't know where to look. Will you help?"

Anne was quiet for a few seconds then said, "You know, the only place she ever went to when she was upset was the Charlesgate."

"Not tonight," he sighed and fidgeted with the phone cord. "I'm going home. Call me there or on my cell if you hear from her, just let me know if she's all right, even if she doesn't want to see me. I'm worried as hell."

"Ditto for me, both about being worried and calling if you hear from her."

"I will," he promised. "G'night, Anne."

Jabe reluctantly placed the phone on its hook and scooped his keys from his pocket. They felt too heavy in his hand. The very air seemed to want to smash him to the ground.

As he went to shut the office door, a white sparkle pierced his vision and he remembered the diamond on top of the now hated journal. He clutched the ring in his hand and squeezed his eyes shut for a second of silent prayer before dropping the ring into the pocket of his jeans and leaving the room.

He grasped the doorknob for a minute longer, reluctant to start for home. It seemed so far away from Zylla. He sensed that if she decided to look for him, she'd come back here but his mind quickly dismissed that hunch. Zylla wouldn't be back.

Outside, he squared his shoulders in defiance to the cold November moon, as if that mercurial sphere was the cause of his present sorrow. He continued to walk down Charlesgate East and was already at Commonwealth Avenue when he remembered that he had taken the Indian into town that morning and had parked it on Marlborough Street, thus the keys in his hand. He shook his head and retraced his path.

Jabe turned onto Marlborough and crossed the street to his bike. Turning back to the Charlesgate, he glimpsed the pale light through the stained glass window of the Barnes music room.

"Crap," he muttered as he walked around the corner to the entrance. One of the carpenters must have left the lights on after installing the benches that day. He fished the building's keys out of his pocket, unlocked the door, and walked down the dark hall to the music room.

Almost immediately, he saw the gaping hole to the basement. Work wasn't supposed to be done on the basement until after the wedding, but his crew apparently started and foolishly left the door open. He paled at the thought of an unsuspecting wedding guest attempting to explore the basement by means of those rotten stairs.

Irritation at his crew momentarily pushed Zylla from his mind as he crossed the floor, but even that fled when he heard a crunch underneath his boot. As he bent to investigate, his nostrils flared at the familiar rank odor described by Lydia to come from Charlotte's spectre.

He picked up the object and felt his stomach roll when he recognized the blue eye beneath the cracked glass. Panic burst inside him, rendering him immobile, but somehow he forced his feet to move and rush down the rotten steps, miraculously avoiding the weakened spots.

"*No*. Zyll!" he cried as he crouched next to her still form. His eyes adjusted to the darkness and he saw the white face, the wide staring eyes, and dribble of dried blood from her temple.

She was dead.

Charlotte's stench surrounded him, but a pleasant trickle of lavender wafted from Zylla. *This is what Lydia smelled like when she died*. The notion popped into his head unbidden. *She's with Lydia now*, he thought madly, Wild and desperate, he searched the darkness for some ethereal sign of her. He willed himself to cry but grief remained inside, churning and scratching at his mind.

"Zyllie," he whispered brokenly.

He heard the low whimper and glanced about the room before realizing that Zylla had made the noise. When he looked down at her face, he saw that her eyes were now closed and that her head lolled toward him. His right hand was instantly in his jacket, grabbing his phone and dialing 911, while the tears finally rolled unbidden down his cheeks and a great hope burst in his chest. He grabbed her hand, his head close to hers so that he could hear her breath, afraid to touch her for fear of causing damage.

"Zyllie," he coaxed. "Zyllie, wake up, darlin'. Wake up and I'll make you the biggest fried egg and bacon breakfast this side of the Mason-Dixon."

She didn't stir and fear rose again in him, creeping over the hope that still sighed in his chest, smothering it with its furry black claws. Jabe realized she might never wake.

~ * ~

"Zylla. Zylla, my darling, wake up."

The sweet voice lured her from the black pit she rested in, and Zylla focused on the tiny pinprick of plum light before her. The light spread and she inhaled a burst of lavender before seeing Lydia's smiling face above her. Her head was pillowed in softness and she realized that it rested in Lydia's lap.

"Am I dead, Lydia?" she whispered.

"No, dearest, merely unconscious, although if you hadn't taken off that amulet so that I could enter your body, you would be dead."

"Where am I?"

Lydia smoothed her hand over Zylla's brow before answering. "You are still in the Charlesgate basement, unconscious. Charlotte lured you to the door—it wasn't me, dear—and you fell down the stairs as she intended. She is clever, you see, and knew that you would equate the color purple to my lavender oil. Thank the gods, the fall did not kill you, and I managed to slip into your body before she finished her intent."

"But, I don't understand. If I had not taken the eye off, she couldn't have touched me."

"No, Zyllie." Lydia smiled sadly. "I'm afraid that your grandmother was mistaken, although I fear my own attempts to save Berry women have failed. Your amulet was never strong enough to repel Charlotte, but it did possess the strength to banish me. I had been trying to warn your mother about Charlotte, then I tried to protect you, but your grandmother mistook me for the malevolent spirit. Too late, she realized her mistake. You see, Charlotte killed her, too."

"Then you are the family ghost *and* the Charlesgate ghost. But how...?"

Lydia nodded and reached for Zylla's hand. "How is it that I was able to be near you despite your amulet?"

Zylla tried to nod but couldn't move her head.

"Ah, well, this is my home and I reign here. Charlotte has caused some mischief, but I've been fighting her, and that is why her realm is limited to this basement, although her power seeps elsewhere when I need to rest, such as on the night of the fire. You see, dear, you and Jabe had become a little too close for comfort, and the fire was her attempt to successfully part you. She counted on Jabe's wariness of relationships to overcome his desire for you, and it worked, but she underestimated his love for you.

"In the Charlesgate, however, I am as strong as she, and nearly as strong as your amulet. It is only natural that you love the Charlesgate as much as I—you and I are much alike, my Zylla, but I used all my power to lure you here... and to Jabe."

"The visions that I used to have, in the beginning?"

"*Mmmhmm* and the lavender. That's all the eye would allow or I would have appeared to you a long time ago to tell you all. You were the only Berry baby to notice me."

She smiled and squeezed Zylla's hand. "But I managed to unbury my journal and Jabe found it, as I intended. Unfortunately, he panicked, but you know the truth, now.

"But, come, there is much work to do."

"What do you mean? Shouldn't the curse be broken? I realized that Jabe didn't put fear over his trust in me—he lied to protect me. And I..."

"Yes, dearest, you were very brave to remove your eye. And no, Jabe *was* wrong. He did let fear conquer love, but he made it right, in the end. He openly declared to his mother and your aunt that he would give you my diary before the wedding. I heard him say so. You found it first, but I suspect you had a lesson to learn.

"The curse is not ended. You are safe so long as I am within you, but your young man is not."

"Jabe?"

"Yes, he's right here, holding your other hand. He's found you, but Charlotte will kill him now that she can't have you. He is just as dangerous to her—he's a Thayer and you are a Berry. You have both learned to put love for each other above all else, but you must put love before all else, even Jabe, something Charlotte could not do. Do you understand?"

"No, no I don't," Zylla whispered frantically. "Please, please don't let her hurt Jabe."

"That is for you to do, darling. I can only hold her off for so long, but my power is waning, and I need to show you some of your history before it is too late."

"No, Lydia, please, you must save Jabe."

"Hush, now. You must see Charlotte's hanging first hand, and you need to witness her crimes against those she took from you. Be silent, my love."

Zylla moaned as the world went black again, and she no longer saw Lydia, although she could feel her presence as images began flashing across her mind.

The first image that Lydia showed her was of a woman, ocean and sky around her. She was the demonic pirate in Zylla's nightmares, only in this vision, she was just a woman, beautiful and strong, but mortal. Charlotte de Berry.

It was as if she were watching a really good movie, the sort where the viewer ceases viewing and instead becomes part of the story, laughing and crying right along with the actress. In this strange movie, Zylla had become Charlotte at the scene of her hanging.

The crowd roared and launched rotten fruit and vegetables at the beautiful but filthy woman who stepped out of the rowboat onto the small island of Nix's Mate, where all good pirates met their end. Her hands tied behind her, Charlotte shook her captor's hands from her as he tried to help her out of the boat. She raised her chin and walked straight through the jeering crowd, her eyes never leaving the scaffold that loomed before her, never once glancing at the man who walked beside her, the man who had dared say he loved her.

Nor did she glance at her young son, whose bottom lip trembled as he forced back tears and tugged at his mother's sleeve. She ignored him for if she looked at him with all the love she felt, her battered heart would bring her to her knees.

Her lover had done this to her, her 'noble' Jabez.

The crowd became more unruly as she stepped up to the scaffold, but Charlotte blocked out most of what they said and did not feel the pain and humiliation when a tomato thumped against her body, did not flinch when a rotting fish slapped her face. Her eyes remained cold and empty while anger, pride, and ignored sorrow raged inside her.

A rotund man in a gray powdered wig spoke above the crowd. His skin was oily and beads of sweat trickled under his collar as a result from the hot sun and humidity.

"... and for all your crimes thou shall suffer death by hanging, and as thou choose no repentance, as your corpse rots in the sun, so shall your soul burn in hell's fire." His beady eyes narrowed at the woman who gave no indication of hearing what he said, and he continued, "Will thou repent, Charlotte de Berry?"

"Lady Charlotte!" Someone in the mob jeered, causing the cacophony to start all over again. But Charlotte ignored her tormentors as her eyes searched out and condemned the man who stood at attention in the uniform of the British Royal Navy, his gray-green eyes begging something of her.

All the anger and scorn inside her swirled and gathered force, squelching the love she still felt for him. "I do not," she said, and a hush fell over the crowd.

"Jabez Thayer." Charlotte's voice was monotone and precise and very unlike the cultured voice of the highborn lady she had feigned for so long. "A curse I lay on the Berrys and Thayers.

"Jabez, ye'll live out the rest of yer pitiful life in fear. Yer beloved King William may fawn over his loyal subject and bestow my gain in gold upon ye, but ye'll never be happy, nor any of yer kin."

She turned her rage on the young man. "My son," she spat, and for the first time pain cracked her voice. "Take care of yer heart. Guard it well and follow my example. I will not see my granddaughters suffer the pitiful agonies of love. Love means no more than death and if ye do not take pains to warn them, be assured I will."

Then Jeremy's lip quivered again, but his gaze upon his mother did not waver. Charlotte fell silent and fastened her eyes on a spot above the blue water, over the heads of the people below her, and waited to hang.

The crowd remained silent even after the give of the scaffold cracked the humid air. Slowly, they turned with slumped shoulders and downcast eyes and returned to their boats that tossed and bumped on the shore with the sole cry of a gull and the rhythmic creak of the taut rope to accompany their travel.

Only two figures remained on Nix's Mate long after the sun descended.

Zylla became detached from Charlotte again and watched the image that Lydia showed her. She observed the shape of a broad-shouldered man, his hand resting on the thinner shoulder of a boy. Although she could not see details, she knew that their backs were to her, just as she knew that the darker shadow that occasionally swayed and spun in front of them was dead.

Twenty-nine

Jabe let out a long breath to calm himself. The paramedics would be here soon. They knew to enter by the Barnes entrance, and he thanked God that he had left the door unlocked. He did not want to have to leave Zylla, not with Charlotte's hovering menace still about.

He could still smell lavender, but it was fainter now, and he guessed that Lydia had been protecting Zylla since her fall. Jabe didn't want to know how much longer that protection would last. He wished that he wore a crucifix but then laughed aloud, which caused Charlotte's stench to quiver and become more oppressive.

"Crosses only work on vampires, huh, Charlotte?"

He looked down at Zylla with her pale, pale face and ragged breathing. At least her eyes were closed now. She looked ill, but alive. "C'mon, Zillie, you've been unconscious too long. Wake up, darlin'. Where are you?"

~ * ~

"Zylla, darling, I'm here."

"She loved him so much, Lydia, and he did that to her. How could he?"

"He placed his duty to the king above love. He suffered for it, believe me, as all Thayers have, unjustly so. Remember your pity, my dear, I have worse to show you."

"Lydia, Jabe is...?"

"Still there. He's just called the physicians. We haven't much time. She will strike before they arrive. Come..."

"I feel like I'm in a Dickens novel and you are all three Christmas ghosts combined," Zylla said wryly. Lydia's tinkling laugh faded and more images wove into her mind.

These images caused her to feel as if she were being stalked, as if she were caught in a nightmare where something evil was chasing her and in seconds she would be captured and devoured.

Lydia showed her a sequence of violent images, all of Charlotte's revenge on Zylla's ancestors. She watched as Jeremy crumbled before a mound of fresh earth where his last daughter, dead of smallpox, was buried next to her sisters and mother. He raised his fist and muttered a soundless oath to the shadows of the pines where a woman with matted black hair and lips sewn shut danced in mirth.

Images flashed forward to the French and Indian War and she watched as a violet-eyed native raped and scalped Olivia Berry. When Olivia gulped her last breath of air, Charlotte's form fled the native's body and disappeared.

Shock ripped through Zylla. How could one woman do this to another because of some long ago slight? Her own family! She couldn't fathom Charlotte's evil and willed the scenes away, but Lydia showed her the next one. This time, she watched as Lydia and Mike...was that Mike in a top hat? How could that be?

Lydia sighed. "Caval, dear. Your Michael Sullivan is Caval's great-great-great grandson. Before Caval met me, he was quite the rake, you see, and had a daughter by a French prostitute. Michael is the image of Caval. You do have my taste, dearest."

"But..."

"Hush! This is my death scene. Pay attention."

She witnessed Lydia and Caval as they laughed and cavorted under the gaslights next to the Charlesgate. Suddenly, Caval pushed Lydia behind him as a man with a knife rushed upon them. Caval fought hard, but was stabbed in the back by a second man. Lydia screamed, her tears blinding her, and she collapsed on top of her husband.

Caval's dying eyes widened in warning and Lydia turned too late. The murderer loomed above her, and before the knife plunged into her chest, Charlotte's face imposed upon that of her murderer.

The vision of Lydia's blond hair, now dripping red with her own blood, became the red-blond hair of Anna Berry, Zylla's grandmother. Once a beautiful woman, Anna Berry sat in her sunlit garden, ravaged by madness. She talked to a woman named Lady Charlotte as she carved pumpkin after pumpkin.

Lady Charlotte must have said something to incense Anna because she jumped up and waved the knife at the invisible specter. Zylla glimpsed the shade of Lydia behind Anna. Lydia wrung her hands, worry etched on her face, and she cried when Anna turned the knife on herself, surprise still in her eyes as she died.

Shock fled and was replaced by deep grief as Lydia next brought Zylla to the lake house. Her mother, Cindy, waded waist-high in the water and waved at her husband and her sister, who sat on the blanket with her as a baby.

She watched as Charlotte's hands grasped her mother's ankles and pulled her under the water's surface. She heard Maddie scream and helplessly watched her father, John, splash into the water to grab Cindy, only to have his own legs tied tight with seaweed from Charlotte's belt. Mercifully, bubbles obscured the rest of the scene from unfolding.

The last image that Lydia revealed was of Zylla's grandmother Sophie, her father's mother, not a Berry but a victim of Charlotte's selfish anger against the Berrys simply because Yia-Yia tried to stop her. Maddie had just finished brushing Sophie's long sable hair, still without gray despite her age. Maddie turned and Charlotte appeared to Sophie as a bloody, decaying corpse.

"It's that smell again!" Maddie exclaimed as she spun around to see Sophie's stricken face and the remnants of Charlotte's image. Zylla watched as Maddie tried to revive Sophie and failed.

Zylla couldn't sob, although she wanted to. Grief and horror at her ancestor's sick cruelty festered inside her, and spread through Zylla's still form until a deep hatred killed all fear of the self-called Lady Charlotte.

Charlotte would not take another. She would not touch Jabe. Zylla's hatred finally exploded in volcanic anger that had nowhere to go so she opened her mouth and screamed. She was still screaming when her eyes flew open. The sound trailed off as she recognized Jabe's worried face above her and felt his warm hand around her cold fingers.

"Oh, thank God," he said. A great tear plopped onto Zylla's cheek, and she reached with a shaking hand to brush the wetness from Jabe's eyes.

Zylla caught the stench before she saw the hands creep around Jabe's neck. Ignoring the pain in her head, she jumped up, swayed on her feet, and started forward, seeing nothing but anger and Charlotte's ragged lips.

Jabe reached for her leg. "Stay down, Zylla! You don't—"

His words strangled as Charlotte's frigid hands choked him and lifted him from the ground. Zylla growled and rushed at Charlotte to grab a handful of her snarled black hair. Instead, her hand went through Charlotte's seemingly solid form and smacked Jabe on the back of the head, which earned a high-pitched chortle from the demon.

For a millisecond, Zylla stood stunned, then frustration fueled her ire once more. "No wonder your Admiral hung you, you goddamn bitch! Let him go! If you want to take someone on, take me! I hate you as much as you hate me, you good for nothing slut. You'll have a fair fight for once in your demented existence."

Charlotte crowed maniacally, tearing the stitches from her sewn lips. She dropped Jabe with a thud and turned to Zylla.

Jabe, through his desperate gasps for air, clutched at his throat and shook his head at Zylla. She ignored him and, vibrating with hatred, took a step toward Charlotte, who continued cackling.

A burst of lavender hit Zylla in the face and she spotted Lydia behind Jabe out of the corner of her eye. "You cannot fight her, Zylla. Not like that. Remember what I showed you."

"I am remembering," Zylla bit back, still staring at Charlotte. "That's why I'm going to kill her. Again," she added.

"Please, Zylla," Lydia pleaded, and Zylla had the sense that she was wringing her hands. "Remember your pity."

A coughing Jabe cast a startled glance in Lydia's direction and blinked in surprise at the ghost before throwing her a half smile and turning his attention back to Zylla.

"Zyll," he said, his broken voice rough and strained. "Do you forgive me?"

Zylla tossed a confused glance at Jabe and faced Charlotte again. "Of course I do," she replied.

"I did wrong, and I wouldn't blame you if you hated me, but you don't and now I can be *at peace*." He stressed the last two words as much as his wounded voice would let him.

"What?" Zylla felt flustered, her anger melting a little into fear as Charlotte approached closer. The stench was choking and Zylla took a step back. Panic unsettled her shield of anger and she forced herself to stand tall and face Charlotte.

She looked into Charlotte's red-rimmed violet eyes and saw the madness and cruelty there. She saw the woman that killed and mutilated all those Berrys. Her family. *Their family*. But then she saw something else. She saw pain, deep and unhealed. She saw grief, and a little bit beyond that, hope.

Suddenly, Zylla was on the scaffold again, as Charlotte, shivering in fear while Bostonians jeered at her, as her son, Jeremy, gazed at her with love and disappointment, and as her Jabez, the man who had taught her to trust in love, took that love and twisted it around her neck.

And Zylla remembered her pity.

With a trembling hand, she reached out to Charlotte and stroked her face. To her surprise, she felt skin. Charlotte flung Zylla's hand away and snarled.

"Charlotte, I was wrong about what I said. Jabez betrayed you—he should not have put his King before your love. He was wrong to hang you. I'm so sorry for your pain, but Charlotte, not all men are like your Admiral. Jabe is not like his ancestor.

"Your son was a good man, beloved by all, and you destroyed his family. All those women and Lydia..." She gestured toward Lydia's silent form. "Did you even give Caval a chance to betray Lydia before taking your revenge on them?"

Zylla reached out again toward Charlotte. She smoothed her wild black hair, and this time, Charlotte growled but did not move.

"Lydia did not deserve your hatred, your cruelty. You killed her for your own selfish reasons. You drove my grandmother insane because she tried to avoid the curse by not marrying the man she loved. You punished her for following your rules, and you scared my other grandmother to death."

Zylla choked back a sob and struggled to keep her hand still on Charlotte's head, tried with all her might not to scratch those eyes out. "And my parents. They loved each other—my father died trying to save my mother's life. You left Maddie and me all alone, Charlotte!

"In your warped mind, you tried to protect me, but instead you took away my family, and now I know why Aunt Maddie never married. She couldn't, because you would kill her, too, and she didn't want to leave me alone."

She removed her hand from Charlotte and angrily brushed away her tears. "Aunt Maddie watched her mother go insane and die, she never knew her father, and in one year, you took her sister, brother in-law, and Sophie away from her. Look what you've done to your family, Charlotte!"

Zylla's lower lip trembled, tears erupted from her eyes, and she covered her face as she crouched on the basement floor, sobbing. She cried long and loud, and when she stopped, she looked up to see Jabe watching Charlotte warily. Lydia stood beside him, her hand on his shoulder.

She felt Charlotte kneel beside her and put a slender arm around her. She tensed, expecting death, but Charlotte simply drew her close, and she realized that she no longer reeked of death and rot. Instead, she smelled of the sun and sea and Zylla felt a peculiar wetness drop on top of her head.

She peered up at Charlotte's face. She looked different. Zylla tilted her head and frowned. Her hair... It seemed smoother, no less wild, but beautiful, and her tortured eyes were no longer red-rimmed, although tears fell unbidden from them. Her mouth was no longer bloody, the stitches had disappeared, and soft, gentle lips trembled.

"I am so very sorry, my daughter." Charlotte bowed her head, and Zylla sat speechless. She glanced at Jabe and Lydia, and Lydia nodded once.

"Charlotte," she whispered as she lifted Charlotte's chin with her fingers. "You are forgiven. I forgive you. You are family, and I... I love you."

Charlotte smiled, uncertainly at first, then wide and beautiful, her violet eyes alight with peace and contrition. Lydia held out her hand, and Charlotte rose to walk to Lydia and take her hand.

"Goodbye, Zylla, my darling. Take care of her, Jabe. I'm finally going home to my Caval, and Charlotte will never know misery again. There is someone waiting for her as well."

Sirens blared from the street above and moments later, the paramedics appeared at the basement door. Before they could descend, Charlotte bent down and kissed Jabe's cheek.

"I will tell Jabez that he has a handsome namesake," she said and laughed, her voice full of star twinkles, and the two ghosts faded into a lilac light before disappearing completely.

Thirty

Jabe held Zylla's hand in both of his as she sat up in the hospital bed.

"Lay down," he commanded.

"I'm bored, Jabe," she complained. "If I get any more rest I'll go insane, I swear. And it won't be pretty." Her russet eyes looked mournful. "Can't we go home now?"

He let go of her hand to gently stroke her wounded head, but she shrank from his caress. The cut from the fall was tiny and hidden beneath her hair, but it had bled profusely and the doctors were concerned about a concussion. Truth be told, it gave her the willies.

"Does it hurt?"

She shrugged. "Nothing that pistachio ice cream won't fix. So let's go get some!"

Jabe folded his arms and shook his head. "No way. Not until the doc says it's okay."

She sighed.

"How about we pass the time with a story?" he suggested.

"That sounds good. Go ahead, I'm listening." She rested her head against the pillow and sculpted an expectant look on her face.

"Nuh-uh," Jabe said, shaking his head again. "How about you tell me what happened while you were unconscious."

Zylla rolled her eyes. "How am I supposed to know? I was unconscious."

Jabe raised a brow.

"Okay. There was darkness, then there was light."

His brow lowered so that he could better glower at her.

Exasperated, she sighed and said, "You wouldn't believe it."

"I saw them, too, Zyllie," he said quietly. "Hell, one of them kissed me!"

She lowered her eyes, and she felt Jabe lean forward to capture her hand again. "Tell me," he said, giving her hand a brief squeeze of encouragement.

For the next thirty minutes, she related everything that had happened to her from the point of waking up in the Barnes music room to her fall down the stairs and finally, her visit with Lydia and the images of the past.

"So, Lydia was giving the ultimate test," Jabe commented. "Showing you the massacre of your family then asking you to forgive Charlotte. That's pretty intense."

He glanced down at their joined hands then back at her face. "Good thing you passed, huh?"

She laughed. "I couldn't have done it without you," she said. "I was so furious. All I wanted to do was rip her hair out and choke her with it, then you asked if I'd forgiven you. I caught on then." She batted her eyelashes and moaned, "My hero."

Jabe grunted.

"Ooo! I forgot to tell you one part. Mike was there—well, I thought it was Mike. It was really Caval. Get this..." Zylla grinned. "Mike is Caval's great-great... something grandson. Isn't that wild? I can't wait to tell him."

"So you and Mike are related."

She nodded and pursed her lips. "Yup. It literally explains why kissing him felt as if I was kissing my brother."

Jabe laughed, but his face changed as he registered what she had said. She felt her skin burn as a storm cloud passed over his features.

"Wait a minute," he snarled. "You said Mike had never touched you."

Zylla felt herself turn maroon. "Yeah, well, that was before he did."

"When...?"

"Um, remember that night you ran into us at the Charlesgate?"

Jabe nodded, his brows lowered over stormy eyes.

"Well, just before that, we kissed. Anyway," she blurted, "Lydia said that Mike was the spitting image of Caval."

"Lydia can have Mike," he rumbled and to Zylla, he looked like a hurt little boy. She giggled. "He's coming to our wedding so you'd better restrain your jealousy."

His expression softened. "So..." He cleared his throat. "There's still going to be a wedding?"

"Damn straight there is." She grinned. "I'm not letting you off the hook that easy."

His eyes grew solemn. "I was wrong, Zyll, and I know you won't believe me, but I had made up my mind to give you the diary that night, only..."

"Only I snooped where I shouldn't have been snooping?"

He sighed in relief and flashed her a grateful smile.

"Now," she said. "Where's my ring?"

Jabe barked out a laugh as he reached into his pocket.

~ * ~

Falling leaves swirled in a maelstrom of vivid hues and hopped along Boston sidewalks in the chilly breezes of late November. Wood-burning stoves already scented the air with promises of snug winter evenings spent with family and friends, and neighborhood pubs suddenly seemed all the friendlier. The sun, though bright as always, allowed its embrace around New England to loosen and cast a dusky pink-orange glow over the city.

Inside the Barnes music room, the late afternoon sunlight pierced the stained glass topped dome to transform the space between the teal walls into a sacred realm.

Maddie peeked into the room from where she stood sentry by the doorway and sighed dreamily. She turned to Anne and Zylla and smiled, her eyes reflecting the beauty of the scene in the music room. Zylla hopped forward to steal a glance, but Anne grabbed her arm and Maddie laughed as she blocked her path.

Zylla pouted and demanded, "It's my wedding, isn't it?"

"Yes, dear, but later, you'll thank us for this restraint. You'll want your first glimpse to be perfect." Maddie adjusted her niece's antique lace mantilla and Zylla moved forward to kiss her cheek. She studied Maddie's happy face.

"You look beautiful, Aunt Maddie." In her sapphire velvet gown with low-cut square neckline and fitted sleeves, her hair swept in a casual chignon, Maddie did indeed appear majestic.

Maddie's eyes filled with tears and she visibly struggled to blink them back. "Now look what you've done. Ungrateful brat."

From inside the music room, the mandolinist strummed the first chords of a medieval tune.

"That's me!" Anne jumped and breathed deep. She stepped onto the petal-strewn aisle, a vision in russet velvet, her gold hair plaited and adorned with a simple wreath of berries. Zylla didn't see her wink at Billy and smirk at Jabe who broke his stoic expression to grin back at her.

A great burst of bagpipes heralded the entrance of a piper in full dress, and Zylla and Maddie followed. He moved to the side of the entrance to reveal the candlelit room to Zylla.

Although the guest list was intimate, her stomach fluttered as she felt all eyes on her, and she was grateful for the veil that separated her from her small world.

In her anxiety, she was aware only that Jabe was at the other end of the long hall and she must hurry to get to him. She started, pulling Maddie with her, but her aunt stood firm and tugged Zylla's arm, which was linked through hers.

"No," Maddie whispered. "This is no time for nerves. Take a deep breath and look around. This is the most wonderful moment of your life. Enjoy it."

Zylla inhaled and forced herself to really see her surroundings. She saw the flurry of colors from all the flowers in the hall illuminated by warm flutters of candlelight. She saw that all the people staring at her were smiling in happy reassurance and that Uncle John wiped his eyes with a torn hanky that didn't detract from the elegance of his tux. She saw the last sparkle of sun glint through the stained glass and reflect off the balding head of the kindly eyed pastor. She spotted Anne's jaunty grin and realized that she was proud and grateful to have such a friend.

Then she saw Jabe. He stood tall and proud, his hands folded patiently as he waited for her. The features of his rugged face were stern and for a second, she was afraid of this formidable stranger, but then her eyes snapped to his, and even from afar she saw the depths of his pride and love.

She smiled, a great joyous grin that lit her eyes and suddenly, she didn't want that veil to stand between them. As Maddie stepped forward, it was Zylla's turn to tug and make her aunt wait while she raised the soft lace above and behind her head.

"Good girl," Maddie whispered and led her niece on her journey to Jabe's waiting arms.

~ * ~

The reception was held in the Charlesgate restaurant, which was closed to the public for the event, although all the tenants were invited. The bagpiper led the procession into the candle-and fire-lit room where all Jabe and Zylla's tenants waited expectantly, all smiles and applause when the couple took their seats at the head table.

Anne, Billy, Jenny, and Maddie had decorated the room in a bounty of autumn flowers and pumpkins, and Jabe had hired the bluegrass band Tin Roof to play for the evening. The guests feasted on wine-soaked chicken and rice, artichokes, and a score of delicacies and desserts, and Zylla insisted on a rich chocolate cake smothered in mounds of homemade whipped cream for a wedding cake.

The evening passed quickly and the usually reticent Zylla was surprised to find that she truly enjoyed attending to her guests. She made the mistake of introducing Uncle John to Dean Pendergast and cringed when an hour later, she noted that they were still in the corner, drinking tequila and arguing, undoubtedly about politics.

Scanning the room, she was pleased to see that her guests were all enjoying the night. Mike, still stunned that they were actually distantly related, stared at her with the proud glint of an older brother in his melting blue eyes. Pete flitted around the room searching for damsels in distress.

She barely spent time with Jabe, so consumed were they with their guests, but every so often, their eyes would meet and burn in such longing that Zylla's very hair quivered. But then, Rye or Mike or that charming friend of Jabe's, Emmett, would twirl her into a dizzying two-step and the next time she and Jabe met, the peat fire had gasped its last breath and the guests' eyes were heavy with drink and sleep.

Rye led her in what must have been her fiftieth dance of the evening, and she had just twirled under his arm when she was halted mid-spin. She looked up in surprise to see Jabe's amused grin. Her husband. "Hello."

Jabe lifted an eyebrow at his best friend and said threateningly, "Haven't you danced with my wife long enough this evening?"

Straight-faced, Rye replied, "I don't think so, Jabe." He shrugged and pulled Zylla into his arms, turning his back on Jabe. "If the lady wishes, however, you may have the next dance," he called out over his shoulder.

In the next beat, Rye turned Zylla so that they danced a few steps then twirled and the two promenaded smack into Jabe. Feigned menace schooled his features. Rye released her and backed away, hands raised.

"I see that your mother is in desperate need of a partner."

A dimple appeared in Jabe's cheek.

"It's my duty as a bachelor," Rye explained to her.

"Hello, lass," Jabe said in a low brogue as his arms crept to her sides. He held her loosely, but his craving for her was a magnet between them. The desire that Zylla ignored for so long slammed into her, causing her insides to liquefy and somehow become Jabe's essence, and she tilted her head up and parted her fevered lips.

At her expression, Jabe stopped dancing and pulled her against him, lowering his mouth until her breath tickled his lips. His ears buzzed and all he could feel was the hunger of wanting her. He slid his hand up her back to grip her neck and brushed his lips against hers, mouth already opening to take the kiss deeper. Then he sighed and leaned his head back, suddenly aware of his guests and Uncle John's disapproving visage.

Zylla opened her eyes, bereft at the shift in Jabe's attention. The corner of his lips curled up to reveal his dimple.

"What?" she asked

"I think we're being observed."

"Lydia?" Zylla asked with such hope that Jabe laughed and shook his head. She glanced about the room and saw the amused faces of Mike, Rye, Billy, and Anne. She blushed and buried her face in Jabe's chest. He cupped her chin and raised Zylla's head.

"You know," he said, eyebrow raised, "I really don't think either one of the ghosts will be at peace until we make this union complete."

Zylla's face clearly revealed that his meaning was completely lost on her.

"If you come upstairs with me," he whispered, "I'll show you what I mean."

Understanding dawned and crimson still stained her face while they bid goodbye to their guests, causing many a joke.

She swore under her breath. "This is humiliating," she muttered. "Remind me never to get married again."

"No fear of that," Jabe averred as his hand at her waist tightened. "You won't have the opportunity."

~ * ~

Anne had lit candles around their room and had turned the velvet patchwork quilt down to reveal fine silk sheets, but Zylla and Jabe hardly noticed Anne's efforts. Their eyes locked only on each other as Jabe carried Zylla across the threshold of their bedroom and stopped at the end of the bed.

His mouth slanted onto hers and moved hungrily, all heat and hardness, drowning thought from her brain. She could taste his fever and moaned into his mouth, straining to get closer to him.

Jabe gently released his hold on her and she slid down the length of his body while his mouth nibbled the skin of her neck, burning molten patches where he traveled. She massaged his back with frantic hands and struggled to pull him closer, to somehow release the pressure building low inside her. He stopped kissing her and gently held her away from him, the rustle of her gown and the fire crackle the only sounds in the room.

The intensity of his gaze unnerved Zylla and she looked away for a second, but could not stop drinking him in. The rugged planes of his face in combination with the smooth lines of the tuxedo jacket that defined his broad shoulders triggered a primal need in her, causing her blood to pulse and tingle low in her belly. He seemed to possess the ability to protect and devour a woman at once, and he was finally hers.

With a small cry, she threw her arms around him and in an instant was tearing at his mouth with hers, one hand clutching the back of his head, the other pulling at his shirt. He groaned and pulled her tight against him so that she could feel his length against her stomach, while the fingers of his other hand worked at the buttons on the back of her dress.

She gasped when her bare breasts finally met the crisp hairs on his chest and nearly knocked him off balance when his callused palm lifted the heavy weight of her breast while his thumb sought and found her swollen nipple. He reached behind her and lifted her out of her gown. Instinctively, she wrapped her stocking-clad legs around him, kicking off her heels as he turned and fell with her onto the velvet and drew her arms up above her head, his eyes glinting wickedly in the firelight.

His lips and tongue licked and sucked the cream of her skin, nibbled and bit as if she were a ripe nectarine, ripping her stockings in all the right places, all the while securing her straining hands until she writhed against him.

Her fingers scraped down his back when he finally released her. His face hovered above her, eyes watching, and she lifted her head slightly to capture Jabe's fevered lips again. She could taste her own sweat on him and she moaned into his mouth, her fingers working at the zipper of his trousers.

Jabe helped her remove the remainder of his clothes and rested his full weight against her so that his fiery skin branded her.

"Jabe," she whispered into his ear. A damp tendril of his hair clung to her cheek. "I want..."

He ravaged her neck to silence her and pulled her leg up to lick the inside of her thigh. "Shhh," he said against her skin. "Not yet, darlin'."

He continued to lap her tender skin in slow, small circles, which only brewed frustration inside Zylla instead of the erotic effect he intended. She sat up abruptly, startling Jabe, and wrapped her arms around his back, melding her breasts into his chest, biting his neck as she flipped him over onto his back.

Clumsily positioning herself so that his length slid against the moistness between her legs, she straddled him. He moved an inch to the side and the tip prodded her damp, swollen sex. She gasped and sank down, taking him in, a low keen rising in her throat.

Zylla flailed at Jabe's restraining hands on her waist and when he released her, she plunged down. Her eyes watered and she chewed her lip, avoiding the furrow of concern on Jabe's face until the pain faded and tingles of pleasure built again.

She rose in quest of the delicious feeling, but Jabe's fingers dug into her hips once more, holding her fast. The strain of passion darkened his face and the struggle in his half-closed eyes made her tilt her head to the side in wonder.

She, Zylla, had caused this tightening of his muscles, this lack of control in him, and she reveled in her glory, tossing her hair back to let it tickle the flesh of his thighs.

He gasped. She smiled. She began to move in slow, dripping rhythms until the smile on her face was gone and she could only will his name to her lips, which Jabe answered with ragged breaths. Their coupling had all the manic fury of a tornado and it coiled and tightened until it culminated in searing funnels, then unwound into a soothing breeze.

She collapsed on top of Jabe, her sweat-slick skin melting into his. He wrapped his arms around her and rolled her onto her back, covering her mouth in endless kisses while his hand sought hers, intertwining their fingers. With one more kiss, he smiled down at her face.

"Hello, wife," he said quietly, love warming his eyes.

Zylla giggled, suddenly unable to bear the sweet turn the night had taken. She wanted to laugh and dance and yowl and drink Guinness and shoot pool. She suddenly imagined herself running down the halls of the Charlesgate, stark naked, wailing like a banshee, and the thought amused her so much that she had to bite her lip to prevent laughter from erupting.

Jabe stiffened and frowned at her face, contorted in its struggle to contain her mirth. "May I ask," he ventured dryly. "What is so amusing?"

At his droll tone and wary glint in his eye, Zylla did howl. Tears streamed down her face as she covered her mouth with her hand. Jabe propped his head on his hand, mock tolerance on his face.

"I don't think it's the champagne," he intoned, lips twitching, "since the effect has surely worn off. And as we've only been married a few hours, dear wife, I hope your goal isn't to emasculate me by laughing at my performance."

Her eyes widened in disbelief at that and a fresh spurt of laughter welled in her throat. With a great gulp, she managed to restrain her hysterics and wipe the moisture from her eyes. She grinned impishly at her husband.

"Yes," she said in mock solemnity. "You see, I've just discovered that you are not man enough for me and we shall have to get a divorce." She ran a long finger down his muscled arm and smirked. "Unless, of course, you can make me think otherwise."

A half-hour later, she was again pitched into carnal fire until shards of light flooded her mind and she sank into a lovely void of nothingness. Being with Jabe was as clean and light as a sun shaft and at the same time as lonely and wild as the moaning pines. This, then, was heaven on earth. Content, she snuggled against Jabe's body, his arms wrapped around her, his breath light in her ear.

"Nope," she sighed before drifting to dreamless sleep. "I'm never getting married again."

Thirty-one

Christmas came without snow for the third year of their marriage. A stark gray cloak swallowed the sun and rendered the earth a frozen palette of grays and browns. Boston was rubbed raw and its citizens, already weary of winter, longed for the touch of the sun's fingers.

The warmth of summer, though faded, remained inside the walls of the Charlesgate and lifted the spirits of its tenants and patrons. The restaurant remained packed every night, and Chef Anton kept his guests satiated with hearty stews and sumptuous winter meals.

A giant Christmas tree with tiny white lights presided over the restaurant from its throne near the French doors, and the pianist cheered his subjects with joyful renditions of holiday music. Holly boughs with ivy sprigs and plump red berries decorated the hearth and each table.

Every night, Zylla arranged a concert or lecture in the music room and on Saturdays, Dickens's *A Christmas Carol* was performed, free to the general public. Guests streamed in from all over the city, rubbing their hands together as they sipped homemade cocoa with mounds of fresh whipped cream sprinkled with cinnamon.

The tranquil mood was reflected upstairs in Jabe and Zylla's home. Billy and Anne had just arrived from New York to spend Christmas with them, and Maddie and Jenny had arrived a few days earlier to spend time with their new granddaughter.

Lydia Charlotte Thayer was born at the Charlesgate on the thirteenth of April before Zylla even had a chance to get to the hospital. She had arrived with fists clenched, bright violet eyes, and a deafening scream, and Jabe shook his head as he complained that it was his lot in life to be surrounded by Aries women. His grin was wide as he said it.

The group spent a quiet evening talking and eating, then settled near the warm glow of the Christmas tree and crackling fire to laugh over the video of Billy and Anne's wedding. Rye stopped by to play a few carols on his banjo, which prompted great squalls from little Lyddie, and nobody could decide whether she was trying to sing along with the bluegrass tunes or if she simply hated them.

Zylla retired early to give Lydia a bath and feeding before placing her daughter in her crib. She caressed Lydia's cheek and sighed. Sometimes, in the cool silence of the baby's room, Zylla would stand for hours and watch her daughter sleep. Tonight was no different, but Zylla had a goal to meet. She had vowed to herself that she would finish her second book before Christmas and she only had until midnight to complete it.

Her first book, a biography of Charlotte de Berry, had done quite well on the market, and Zylla was just as determined that her new fiction novel perform equally well, if not better.

She glanced one more time at Lydia, sighed again, and went downstairs to the Spring Room to her laptop.

~ * ~

Jabe lay on his back under the blankets, hands behind his head, and gazed at the embers in the fireplace across the room. A slight smile played on his lips.

After bidding his guests good night, he had crept into Lydia's room and was disappointed to find her sleeping. He stroked her plump cheek and when that hadn't wakened her, he had cleared his throat. She slept on, and Jabe wisely decided to leave her alone. Waking the baby meant waking Zylla, and he wanted his wife to open sleep-filled eyes for another reason this evening. Except when he had reached their room, she hadn't been there.

Since Maddie and Jenny shared the small study next to Zylla's writing room, Jabe had stolen down the spiral staircase installed from their bedroom to the Spring Room. She worked with her back to him, but he had glimpsed the ivory skin of her cheek and temple, the curve of her bottom lip, and a flutter of lashes. Zylla had been wearing the pale green silk robe he had bought her for her birthday, 'strictly for writing purposes', and a pair of wire-rimmed glasses. Her thick hair had been pulled back in a low ponytail, but one reckless lock refused to be captured and he longed to push it out of her face.

He had taken one more step down when he had heard the machine-gun tapping of her fingers on the keyboard and had nearly been able to smell her concentration, so he sighed quietly and slowly retraced his steps to the bedroom where he climbed into bed.

A log fell in the fireplace, breaking Jabe's reverie, and he reached over to snap off the bedside lamp. Maybe the Charlesgate and Lydia had been the means of bringing them together, he thought, but he suspected that he and Zylla would have found each other, and this bliss, eventually.

Their life at the Charlesgate was more than content. Zylla no longer suffered migraines or any nightmarish episodes, and Lydia's diary was a treasured keepsake on their bookshelf.

Although grateful that Lydia and Charlotte had found peace, both missed the lavender, and Zylla compensated by arranging fresh sprigs in their rooms and also in all the public areas. She merely smiled when their tenants joked that after Zylla died, she would surely come back to haunt the place with the scent of lavender.

"What are you smiling at?" Zylla placed her glasses on the dresser and pulled the elastic band from her hair. In the dimly lit room, her silk robe shimmered.

"I'm smiling at my beautiful wife."

"Uh-huh," she murmured suspiciously.

He chuckled. "Did you finish?"

"I did." She wandered to the window and held back the burgundy velvet drapes to gaze out the window. Jagged edges of frost made a crystalline mosaic on the windows and breathed chilly air on her skin.

He raised eyebrow. "And? Did Lydia meet an untimely end?"

"Of course not," she replied stubbornly. "She got the ending she deserved."

"You're rewriting history, Zylla," Jabe teased. "What will Aunt-Maddie-the-High-School-History-Teacher say to that?"

Jabe could hear the trepidation in her reply. "I'm more worried about what she'll say after she reads the sex scenes."

"Hmmmmm," Jabe murmured, a sly grin on his face. "I'm certain that they are not good enough. You haven't had nearly enough experience for it to reflect in your writing."

"Really, now? Is that a challenge?"

"Come here, my wife."

Zylla shuddered at the heat in his voice and when she looked across the room, the fire's embers illuminated that desire in his half-closed eyes. She glanced through the window one more time before allowing the drape to sever the stark winter scene and climbed into bed to willingly burn in Jabe's arms of summer.

Author's Note

Charlotte de Berry was a seventeenth-century female pirate who dressed as a man to follow her husband into the English Navy. Her adventures led to her capture by the crew of a ship bound for Africa. She joined a mutiny, murdered the captain, and became a pirate. Not much else is known about her, and I've taken quite a few liberties with her character, but she did indeed sew men's lips together as a form of punishment.

The Charlesgate Hotel is an actual building located in Boston's Back Bay. Built in 1891 by John Pickering Putnam, its three street addresses—Four Charlesgate East, 535 Beacon Street, and Ten Charlesgate East became known as a premiere location during the city's Gilded Age.

A theory exists that Putnam's design of the Charlesgate was heavily influenced by his interest in Nationalism, a movement that, in part, strove to solve the country's social ills, but the Charlesgate was a hotspot for the wealthy until 1920 when it became a female seminary. During the 1950's through the 1970's, Boston University transformed it into a dormitory and later, Emerson College used it for student housing as well.

In the 1970's, the Charlesgate began to acquire a reputation of disrepute. Rumors that the residence had become a drug den, a bordello, a mafia headquarters, and an illegal rooming house were rampant in the city, and tales of ghosts, originally told by college students, persisted. The Charlesgate was also a creative haven for artists and musicians, immigrants, and those down on their luck—communities that otherwise could not afford to live in the Back Bay.

By early 1990, the building had been abandoned and had fallen into disrepair until renovations began in the 1900's. Currently, condominiums are available in the Charlesgate.

John Pickering Putnam's goals for the Charlesgate Hotel and future buildings as models of national reform were unrealized: he died before he could make his dream come true. *Charlesgate* seeks to remedy that.

As for Zylla and Jabe, Lydia and Caval, well, who's to say that they don't exist?

I wish to thank Alex Steele for taking me through the Charlesgate while it was still a ruin and my brother, John, for getting me in when it was not. Thanks also to the Emerson College Library Archives for supplying the facts and theories behind the rumor and dilapidation.

I can't write without music and special thanks is due to Jabe Beyer and Bow Thayer for their friendship, talent, musical brilliance, and the loan of their names.

I am indebted to several people for their unswerving support, advice, and friendship through the writing of this book, especially Kristen Stevens, John Keratsis, Roberta Vise, Ryan Asmussen, Tia Dalelio, Kathryn Bloom, Michael and Lori Gilman, Jill Myers, Gina Mammone Deibel, Janelle Browning, Suzy Cope, Kathy Black, Gunther and Maria Winkler and most of all, Mom and Dad and my family.

Thanks to my editor, Elizabeth Struble, and Wings ePress for taking a chance on me.

And to Keith Harris—to steal shamelessly from E.M. Forster, thank you for reconciling my deities.

Sources

Damrell, Charles S. (1895) *A Half-Century of Boston's Buildings.*

Excerpts from the *Diary of Sarah Goell Putnam.* Massachusetts Historical Society.

Johnson, Cathy. (2000) *Pyrates in Petticoats: A Fanciful & Factual History of the Legends, Tales & Exploits Of the Most Notorious Female Pirates.* Graphics/Fine Arts Press.

Lupo & Rezendes. (1981) "The Charlesgate Chronicles: Portrait of a Landmark." *The Boston Phoenix*, February 3.

Southworth, Susan & Michael. (1992) *Guide to Boston.* Globe Pequot Press.

Shand-Tucci. (1978) *Built in Boston: City & Suburb 1800-1950.* University of Massachusetts Press.

Turner, Florence. (1987) *At the Chelsea.* Harcourt.

Zurier, Rebecca. "Visionary in Boston: The Charlesgate as Housing in a Nationalist Utopia." On file in Emerson College's Archives.

Meet Dina Keratsis

Dina Keratsis graduated from Wheaton College with a bachelor's degree in English Literature and earned her EdM at Boston University. She is a member of RWA and lives in Boston with her husband and two dogs. Dina is currently at work on her third novel.